FELLOW TRAVELERS

THOMAS MALLON

FELLOW TRAVELERS

PANTHEON BOOKS, NEW YORK

*This is a work of fiction. Names, characters, places, and incidents either
are the product of the author's imagination or are used fictitiously.
Any resemblance to actual persons, living or dead, events,
or locales is entirely coincidental.*

All rights reserved. Published in the United States by Pantheon Books,
a division of Random House, Inc., New York, and in Canada by Random House
of Canada Limited, Toronto.

Pantheon Books and colophon are registered trademarks of Random House, Inc.

Grateful acknowledgment is made to the following for permission to reprint
previously published material: Alfred Publishing Co., Inc.: Excerpt from
"Monotonous," lyrics by June Carroll, music by Arthur Siegel. Copyright
© 1952 (Renewed) by Chappell & Co., Inc.; excerpt from "No Love,
No Nothin,' " lyrics by Leo Robin, music by Harry Warren. Copyright © 1943
(Renewed) WB Music Corp. All rights reserved. Reprinted by permission of
Alfred Publishing Co., Inc. · Random House, Inc., and Faber and Faber Ltd.:
Excerpt from "The More Loving One," from *Collected Poems* by W. H. Auden.
Copyright © 1957 by W .H. Auden. Reprinted by permission of Random House,
Inc., and Faber and Faber Ltd.

Library of Congress Cataloging-in-Publication Data

Mallon, Thomas, [1951–   ]
Fellow travelers / Thomas Mallon.
p.   cm.
ISBN: 978-0-375-42348-2
1. Nineteen fifties—Fiction.   2. Washington (D.C.)—Fiction.   3. United
States—Politics and government—1953–1961—Fiction.   I. Title.
PS3563.A43157F45 2007   813'.54—dc22   2006024586

www.pantheonbooks.com

Printed in the United States of America
First Edition
2   4   6   8   9   7   5   3   1

FOR JOSEPH GRAMLEY

FELLOW TRAVELERS

October 15, 1991

U.S. Embassy, Tallinn, Estonia

"Very snazzy, Mr. Fuller."

"Very retro," replied the deputy chief of mission. "Not my tie," he added, giving both ends of the black bow a last adjustment. "Your 'snazzy.' " He turned around to face Ms. Boyle. "It's a long time since I've heard that one."

"I suppose I could say you look 'baaad.' "

Ms. Boyle, Hawkins Fuller imagined, was just on the sunny side of forty, old enough to know "snazzy" and young enough to know "baaad," though for that matter, even he, at sixty-six, knew that "baaad" meant "good."

She lingered a moment, the way women still did in the presence of Hawkins Fuller, imagining when the full head of silvery hair had been black, the way the eyebrows still were, in Gregory Peck–style contrast. But Mr. Fuller was better-looking than Gregory Peck.

He, too, lingered for a moment, prolonging the familiar comfort of admiration. "These," he finally said, pointing to the stack of badly printed telexes near the edge of his desk: "*Very* bad. Not 'baaad.' Just lousy."

"I know," sighed Ms. Boyle, who doubted that the embassy, still being flung together, would be getting even internal e-mail anytime soon. "But that guy's been working miracles with the phones. They're twenty times better than last week. The ambassador talked to Brussels and Washington twice today. Clear as a bell both times. And here," she said, darting back out to her desk and returning with some regular mail from the pouch. "A primitive but reliable means of communication." She could see that the envelopes were personal, so she set them down unopened and left with a friendly marching order: "Don't dawdle. Lucy will be downstairs in five minutes."

He wondered how many years ago Ms. Boyle would still have been saying "Mrs. Fuller" instead of "Lucy."

"All right," he replied. "And if I do dawdle"—he always did; the shambling and the daydreaming made his good looks even more appealing— "just buzz me, Miss Blue."

Ms. Boyle looked puzzled.

"Ah," said Fuller. "That one you *are* too young for."

She left, smiling as she closed the door, leaving Fuller to pick up the two bright-orange envelopes atop the pile of mail she'd just placed on his desk: Halloween cards, a little early, from the grandchildren in Potomac. Farther down the stack, a letter from Lucy's Realtor in D.C., about that house in Chevy Chase she was determined to buy.

They'd be home for good in another year, and he'd finally take up the half-time job being held for him at the Carnegie Endowment. Odd to find himself here, in the meantime, helping out with the New World Order. He was supposed to have wound up his career last spring, after the six years in Bulgaria. It had never been that *much* of a career, and he'd never much minded that, but as he looked out on the darkening Gulf of Finland, he seemed compelled to make a fast review of it, as if it were one of the checking-for-Alzheimer's exercises that Lucy wanted to add to their breakfast regimen of bran muffins and Centrum Silver tablets.

All right: the six years in Bulgaria; the four before that in D.C.; the four years prior to those at the U.S. mission to the UN. Which put you back in the mid- and late seventies—some luck for *that* to be the era when they finally got posted to New York! And yet, for all the fiscal calamity and crime (that awful broad-daylight hour when Lucy came home with a bruised cheek and no purse), he'd ridden the handbasket through some interesting stops on its way to hell. At fifty, he'd been too old, really, for the underground pleasures that were suddenly so unpoliced. But his looks had granted him an extension, allowed him occasional, plausible entry to the throbbing middle-of-the-night world west of West Street. It *had* been some luck, a portion of his lifetime's worth, to have made it home from those forays without so much as a hangover, let alone the time-released fate that would now be necessitating one of those humiliating obits with their mention of a "long illness" or "pneumonia" that even Lucy, behind her newspaper and bran muffin, could manage to decode.

But I digress, he thought, resuming the fast, reassuring rewind. He reached the six years in Austria (Nixon mostly); then the four in Sweden, where the draft dodgers had more social status than the embassy people, who ran down LBJ as much as they decently could while shaking their heads and nibbling the host's gravlax. And before that? The fourteen years, 1952 to '66, right in Foggy Bottom in the State Department's Bureau of Congressional Relations, where he would have been happy to stay forever, until Lucy decided that he should use his small accumulations of clout and connectedness to effect a shift, at the age of forty, from the civil to the foreign service. It was time for them to see the world, she had decreed.

And that was it, a life span so well recollected, he decided, there was no need to do the date ranges for the early sojourns in Oslo and Paraguay, let alone Harvard and the navy and St. Paul's. Nope, no Alzheimer's for Mrs. Fuller's little boy. Tomorrow morning he'd tell Lucy to skip the muffins and to scramble some eggs in an aluminum skillet.

He wondered: When they got home, would there be bus service from Maryland down to the Carnegie on Massachusetts Avenue? During his last period at State—'81 to '85, Reagan I, thank you very much—he had never gotten the hang of the new Metro, whose underground rumblings had, in any case, never been permitted to disturb Georgetown. He was wishing that Lucy would just let them go back *there*, and forget about this pile in Chevy Chase, when he noticed the small white envelope addressed in a feminine hand with the neatness of his wife's generation.

One of her Wellesley pals? Maybe, though he couldn't recall any Russell in Scottsdale, Arizona. Only after another few seconds did he see that the letter was for himself and not his wife. So he slit it open—and soon heard himself saying *Christ Almighty.*

Dear Fuller,

Tim Laughlin died September 1 in a Catholic hospital in Providence, Rhode Island. He was 59 and had been sick for some time. I heard from him often—almost never saw him, but counted him a good friend.

I don't know whether you pray (I myself don't), but if you do, I know that, even now, he would appreciate your prayers.

Whatever the case, I thought you should know.

Yours sincerely,

Mary (Johnson) Russell

It had been more than thirty years since he'd talked to either one of them, and it was easier, now, to think of her first.

She had never called him Hawkins. She'd thought it a preposterous first name and told him so, said "the last shall be first" and that he would be "Fuller" with her, under any and all circumstances. He'd replied that she didn't know the half, that "Hawkins" was really his middle name, "Zechariah" being the first. And they'd laughed, she with the sharp glint in her eye that sometimes made him call her *La Pasionaria,* not because the glint was passionate but because it declared, so plainly, that you, Z. Hawkins Fuller, shall not pass. It wasn't the castle of sex from which Mary Johnson had barred him during their long non-affair; that had never really been at issue. It was any sort of confidence she had barred him from. It was her trust.

He put her letter back in its envelope, and the envelope into a drawer, a different drawer from the one into which he'd put the grandchildren's cards and the Realtor's letter.

Poor, sad, merry little Tim, he thought, looking at the clock. AIDS, of course.

He stood up and walked into the outer office.

"You beat my summons by ten seconds," said Ms. Boyle. "She's downstairs."

And so she was. Almost as slim as she'd been at Wellesley; her hair, now a silvery gold, in the same thick little pageboy she'd always worn; her outfit the one she'd explained to him at breakfast. A robin's-egg-blue jacket over a white blouse above a black skirt: add it up and you had the Estonians' new, which was to say old, tricolor flag. No one would expect the number-two man's wife to go to this sort of trouble, and no one would fail to notice how much prettier she was than the number-one man's wife.

"So," said Lucy, smiling brightly as she brushed down a couple of unruly stalks in her husband's eyebrow, "Ms. Boyle tells me the mails are coming through."

"Yes," said her husband. "Neither rain, nor sleet, nor geopolitical convulsion . . ."

Lucy continued to smile, brushing Hawkins' lapels and enjoying the way two or three of the Estonian wives here in the reception hall were noticing her spousal attentions. Perhaps they were deciding she and Hawkins looked like that older couple in the Ralph Lauren ads. Hadn't a Polo shop opened up in Tallinn? Almost everything else already seemed to have arrived.

"Your Realtor wants us to go a little higher," said Fuller.

"*Our* Realtor, dearest." She performed one last primp, pulling down Hawkins' right cuff. He, too, knew that she was showing off their extended youth and vigor, as if freedom were a good brand of moisturizer they had wisely chosen long ago. *This is what you've been missing for fifty years,* she seemed to be saying to the Estonians, less from patriotism than personal pride.

Fifty years? thought Fuller. More like all but twenty of the last five hundred. Who *hadn't* rolled over this place? First the Swedes; later the Germans; only after that the Russians.

Having at last let go of her husband, Lucy now clasped both hands of the foreign minister's wife, exclaiming over her like a sorority sister who'd finally made it back for a reunion. Fuller took a glass of champagne from one of the waiters and moved away from the center of the room.

Though guests were still arriving, the American ambassador had already begun his toast to the embassy's reopening, and all at once Fuller thought he could recall a party he'd gone to maybe thirty-five years ago, at the Estonians' "embassy" in Washington, a sad little outpost shared by one of the other two captive Baltic nations. A handful of unlucky young fellows from State had been sent into a room full of smoked fish and stained suits to keep company with the exiles, to smile at them as if they were a girl with polio that everyone pretended would one day, somehow, get up out of that chair and walk again. Was it possible he'd brought Mary Johnson that night? Then taken her home in a cab and kissed her, on the cheek, before ten p.m.?

The ambassador was speaking of the long, unbroken "legal continuity" of U.S.-Estonian relations, as if the crippled girl had in some manner gone on dancing all along. But now they could all welcome her "peaceful return to the family of nations that are free in *fact*." Applause, while Fuller mused upon how this return had very nearly not been peaceful at all. The Lithuanians, the first to flex their muscles after the wall came down, had driven Gorby into a real Stalinist snit, and Tallinn was lucky to have escaped the nasty thrashing, however futile, he'd dished out to Vilnius.

Now the ambassador tried a bit of wordplay, sparsely appreciated, about the speed with which Estonia had gone from being a "captive" nation to a "most-favored" one. He went on to recount the astonishing events of the past two months: the failed coup in Moscow; the U.S.S.R.'s panicked recognition of the Baltic nations' independence; the UN's offer of seats to the three of them. The ambassador continued on, even as a murmur of bored chatter began to rise on the periphery of his audience. Fuller felt a tug at his elbow, from a young man eager to introduce him to a "formerly persecuted intellectual" who was now helping to draft the constitution. And once the ambassador officially subsided, this same avid introducer told Fuller it was "a great imperative" that he should meet the grizzled old man now being pulled toward him.

"Yes, of course," said Fuller, smiling and shaking the old man's hand. He understood that here was one of the "forest brotherhood" who after the war had refused to come in from the cold and accept the Soviets' dominion, preferring instead to remain hidden in the woods. Not guerrillas, exactly; more, Fuller thought, like those Japanese soldiers who would turn up on a Pacific island, decades after the war, still hanging on to the fresh shirt they were convinced they'd wear on the day the emperor took the Americans' surrender. Of course, these forest brothers had *known* the war was over, and still they'd stayed out there eating bark and twigs— a mystery to Fuller, who was pleased when the old man, looking hungry even now, relaxed his grip.

The guest list sent over by the Estonians had been overwhelmingly indigenous, whereas State, good sports as always, had made sure to add a dozen or so of the old occupying Russians, like the one Fuller was being introduced to now, a florid, white-haired man who'd spent the last thirty years running a phosphate mine—and five hundred people's lives—in the northeastern part of the country. Fuller heard "phosphate" and made a joke about the fizz in his second glass of champagne; the Russian smiled uncomprehendingly, until a young man from the Foreign Ministry who'd just joined them translated the English remark—into Russian. Fuller realized that after three decades here, this amiable backpedaler, who had raised his glass higher than anyone else to the ambassador's toast, knew fewer words of Estonian than Lucy had made it her business to acquire on the plane to Tallinn.

"Mr. Deputy Chief," said the young Foreign Ministry man, "my pleasure it is to present Mr. Lennart Meri."

Fuller had been briefed on this polymath: a writer, a film director, and now the foreign minister himself. Meri was, Fuller now assured him, handsome enough to be in front of the camera as well as behind.

"And look who is talking!" replied the minister. In another minute the two of them were arranging to have lunch—"anything but you Americans with your *breakfasts!*"—at the Stikliai Hotel.

A man who'd been with the more conservative wing of the Popular Front interrupted them. An advocate, until recently, of "autonomy" rather than full-blown independence, he was in as much of a rush as the Russian phosphate boss to ingratiate himself with the new reality. Fuller, displaying the same wide, whitened smile he did for everyone else, welcomed the gentleman into the circle that was forming around him.

"You see, Mr. Vice Ambassador," said the Popular Front man, more for the foreign minister's ears than Fuller's, "it was what you would call a 'neat trick' for us to declare independence once the Soviet parliament finally pronounced the Molotov-Ribbentrop pact and the 1940 annexation to have been illegal all along."

"Explain that to me," said Fuller, in the same bright tone Lucy was using to ask the phosphate boss's wife how she managed to keep up with her grandchildren in Moscow.

"It was easier for them to admit that we had never been part of the U.S.S.R. than to let us secede," said the man from the Popular Front, making sure his explanation registered with the foreign minister. "*That,*" he elaborated, "would have created a bad precedent. One that many other of the Soviet republics might still be wanting to use."

"Nothing succeeds like secession," said Fuller.

The foreign minister smiled, but the Popular Front man, not getting the jest, began to fret that he had scored no points after all. Fuller gave him a friendly tap on the arm and thought: *The Jesuits.* That's what Tim would be saying, with his strong, high laugh about the logic that had just been offered. *The Jesuits would love that, Hawk!*

To Fuller's relief, the musical program was about to begin, peppy alternations of Cole Porter and Baltic folk songs that Ms. Boyle had helped to pull together. She was at it even now, setting out the enameled-eagle party favors they'd been unable to find all afternoon.

After twenty minutes and a fast vodka tonic, and while the Russian phosphate boss applauded the conclusion of "Friendship"—*just a perfect blendship!*—Fuller left the room. He knew that Lucy would cover for him.

In half a minute he was out on the cobblestones, stepping off into the night, happy with the autonomy—if not exactly independence—that he'd always taken as his right. Lucy might make him drive her to see the sights in Narva next week, and come June she'd have a houseful of dull friends over from the States to see the White Nights; but however late he came home tonight, it would be all right. She lived, he knew, in a perpetual White Night of her own, pushing the clock back to whatever hour she decided he had come in at after all.

It was really too cold to be out, and Fuller was still wary of walking here at all. Hard to imagine there were no longer Soviet troops on patrol. Actually, there *were* still some, not due to leave for a year or two more, by which time the Estonians would also have gotten rid of the rubles they were using even now. Awfully good-looking, some of those Russian boys he'd seen. Sweet faces, trying to look so hard under their stiff caps. Alas, how quickly those faces aged and sagged, the way it was with every good-looking Jewish boy he'd ever had back home.

Fuller looked up toward a small, pearl-onioned dome, not far from a stone staircase connecting the city's old and upper towns. A strong wind was blowing across the gulf, maybe all the way from Finland, that country so like himself, for so long half free and quite comfortable, somehow exempt from the fuss of near-apocalypse.

A young man was passing in the opposite direction. A student, Fuller supposed: slightly built, hands in big overcoat pockets, puffing a cigarette. Suggestive of another era; one imagined a book of censored poems inside the overcoat. Fuller looked back over his shoulder and, sure enough, found the young man doing the same. But Fuller's smile unnerved the boy, who soon continued on, eyes front, toward his destination.

Fuller was drunk enough that he might have nodded, tried his luck. But he'd realized, even before the young man averted his gaze, that all he himself wanted right now was to look at the small receding silhouette and imagine that it belonged to someone else, another boy, whose memory was proving persistent tonight, like that last Porter tune, which even here, in the darkness, he couldn't quite dislodge from his head.

He wondered what time it was in Scottsdale, and whether the embassy's new phones were as good as Ms. Boyle said.

PART ONE

SEPTEMBER–DECEMBER 1953

In the era of security clearances to be an Irish Catholic
became prima facie evidence of loyalty. Harvard men were
to be checked; Fordham men would do the checking.

—DANIEL PATRICK MOYNIHAN

CHAPTER ONE

September 28, 1953

Tim counted four big fans whirring atop their stanchions in the news-room. Every window here on the seventh floor was open, and summer had officially departed six days ago, but that was Washington for you. When air-conditioning might come to the *Star* seemed to be a perennial matter of sad-sack speculation among the staff: "When hell freezes over," went one answer Tim had heard in his three months here. "Because then we won't need it."

Miss McGrory, one of the paper's book reviewers, arrived with a bottle of whiskey, which she set down next to the punch bowl and cake, whose single chocolate layer and frosted inscription, "Happy Trails, Sheriff," would soon be cut into by the retirement party's guest of honor, Mr. Yost, a pressman who'd been at the *Star* since 1912 and took his nickname from a weekend job he had as a constable over in Berwyn Heights.

More people drifted in. "We could use a piano," opined Miss Evers-man, the music critic. She'd covered Liberace's concert two nights ago at Constitution Hall and was telling a police reporter that the pianist's mother had been in the president's box with one of Liberace's brothers, Rudy, who'd served in Korea.

"So she's got one boy who's a soldier?" asked the reporter. "Maybe she's got hope of grandchildren after all."

Miss Eversman laughed.

"Forget Liberace," said Mr. Yost, who'd started to reminisce about his first years here at the paper. "I remember seeing Wilson himself—that's *Woodrow* Wilson, not Charlie, to you youngsters—up in *his* box at Keith's Theatre. You wouldn't have figured it from an egghead like him, but did that man ever love his vaudeville. You could sell him any player-piano roll the minute it came out."

"We really *do* need a piano," Miss Eversman sighed, as the national and managing editors walked in. Mr. Corn and Mr. Noyes took up positions off to the side of things and remarked to each other, a bit shamefacedly, on the smallness of the spread.

"Well," said Mr. Corn, quoting the late Senator Taft's famously impolitic advice about higher food prices: "Eat less."

The party was making Tim feel nostalgic, and thus a bit foolish, since he'd been, after all, only a summer hire allowed to stay on through September—or, more exactly, this coming Friday afternoon. They'd put him in the city room, even though he'd never been to Washington before June and knew nothing about the District as a place where many citizens lived life quite oblivious to the federal government. His placement, he'd come to understand, was typical of the *Star*, a paper both venerable and feckless, produced each evening by an eccentric, occasionally brilliant staff. He had liked it here and would miss the place, but given the shortness of his tenure he wasn't sure he should even take a piece of the cake once it got cut.

A small stack of the paper's early edition lay atop an open drawer of the file cabinet he was leaning against. Ambassador Bohlen was flying home from Moscow to talk with Secretary Dulles, and this morning Louis Budenz, a Fordham professor and former red, had testified to the McCarthy committee that, in his "humble opinion," parts of an Army-commissioned pamphlet about Siberia—something put together to educate the Far Eastern Command—contained large chunks of Soviet-sympathizing stuff that had been taken, without footnotes or refutation, from Communist writers.

Cecil Holland, the reporter who'd written the Budenz story, now saw Tim reading it and asked, "Laughlin, you just graduated from Fordham, didn't you? Ever study with this guy who says the army's been indoctrinating itself?"

Tim smiled. "I had somebody else for Economics, Mr. Holland." He grimaced. "I think I got a C-plus." Holland laughed and walked over to claim a piece of the cake that had finally been sliced.

At Fordham, Tim had mostly studied American history and English literature, and his plan in coming to Washington remained, even now, to combine his major and minor into a job writing for a politician, though throughout the city's hot, depopulated summer he'd made little headway finding anything on Capitol Hill. Well, he'd have plenty of time and motivation come Friday afternoon!

The party conversation had turned to Senator McCarthy's imminent wedding. "What kind of guy picks lunch hour on Tuesday to get married in a church?" asked the financial-page editor.

"A guy who's busy taking over the world," answered Cecil Holland.

"That's why he's marrying a girl on his staff," added the police reporter. "Maximum efficiency. She'll be able to crank out the press release for Joe's firstborn as soon as she's cranked out the baby."

"Well, from what I hear," said Miss Eversman, "McCarthy's mother might be more surprised by all this than Liberace's." Everyone had heard the rumors.

Would the president show up for the wedding? People began to take bets. Ike's contempt for McCarthy was by now well developed, but it would be hard, some argued, for him not to put in an appearance, now that he was back from vacation, and with St. Matthew's being only a few blocks from the White House.

Miss McGrory, who appeared to regard this talk of McCarthy on the order of a frog in the punch bowl, returned to an earlier subject and insisted that they didn't *need* a piano. She patted Mr. Yost's arm and dared him to get everybody started singing "Oh, You Beautiful Doll"—Woodrow Wilson's absolute all-time favorite, the retiring pressman had reminded them.

Tim, who had been to all the West Side weddings of his uncountable cousins, right away felt Irish instinct trump shyness. He joined in as soon as Mr. Yost and Miss McGrory got things going, and within a moment, even as he remained alone with his thoughts, was singing the same words as everyone else:

> Let me put my arms about you,
> I don't want to live without you.

His job at the *Star* had come through the nephew of an old pal of his dad's from Manhattan Criminal Court, where Paul Laughlin had worked during what everyone in the family now called the old days—the ones before Mr. Laughlin, nearing forty, put himself through LaSalle, by correspondence and then at night, completing his transformation from process server into accountant, making possible his family's move from Hell's Kitchen to the unimaginably big and bright new rooms of Stuyvesant Town. Those rooms seemed even larger now that Tim's older sister, Frances, the Laughlins' only other child, had gone off to Staten Island to live with her husband.

> *If you ever leave me, how my heart would ache,*
> *I want to hug you but I fear you'd break—*

While singing these lines, Tim realized that most of the partygoers' eyes were on him. His pleasing tenor voice—a surprise to those who'd heard only his soft, polite speech with its occasional stammer—had risen above everyone else's in volume, though to anybody paying attention to the lyric, it seemed far more likely that any hugging to involve this five-foot-seven, 130-pound young man would result in *his* breakage, not the girl's. Realizing what had provoked the attention and smiles, Tim blushed and lowered his voice, while everybody else raised theirs for the song's big finish:

> *Oh, oh, oh, oh,*
> *Oh, you beautiful doll!*

Mr. Yost led the revelers' applause for themselves, and when it subsided, Mr. Brogan, Tim's boss on the city desk, announced: "It's clear to me that we kept too much of Laughlin's light under a bushel this summer. I wish we'd had more for you to do, Timmy."

Tim smiled and thanked him. Since June he'd mostly typed and done rewrites, bringing the perfect grammar of the nuns to the fitfully produced copy of the oldest city reporters, who teased him about being a college man, and about a pretty girl named Helen, another summer hire who answered a phone in Classifieds and sometimes stopped to chat at his desk.

They might have kept on teasing him now, but they didn't really know enough about this conscientious, if cheerful, boy, and so the spotlight soon moved elsewhere. Tim shrank back into himself as Cecil Holland redirected the conversation to—what else?—the senator from Wisconsin.

What would McCarthy do next? people wanted to know. Holland advised them to watch what was going on up in New York: Cohn had been running subcommittee meetings there, taking testimony in closed sessions when he wasn't snooping around Fort Monmouth over in Jersey. You watch: McCarthy would soon be taking shots at the army for whatever security breaches he could discover or invent.

"I'm gonna love you, like nobody's loved you, come Cohn or come Schine," crooned the police reporter, reprising a song spoof from last spring, when McCarthy staffers Roy Cohn and David Schine, colleagues and pals (some people said more), had gone on their tour of USIA libraries in Europe, ridding the shelves of anti-American books by American authors.

No one ever talked half so much about Eisenhower as they did about McCarthy, Tim reflected; the senator was as constantly on people's lips as FDR had been when he was a boy, even if the only other thing Roosevelt and McCarthy might have in common was the admiration of Tim's father. Paul Laughlin still revered FDR (Mrs. R was now another story), as he had since the First Hundred Days. Before the arrival of the New Deal, already the father of two babies, Mr. Laughlin had spent plenty of afternoons playing stickball on the pavements of the West Fifties, unable to scare up any work pushing dress racks or plastering or even delivering groceries to widows in their Ninth Avenue walkups. But by the end of '33, Paul Laughlin had become, according to the family joke, "the oldest man in the CCC," upstate for weeks at a time, cutting down trees or planting new ones for what was at least half a living wage. Some kindhearted supervisor took notice of his hard work and referred him to a pal in the courts, where he worked his way up toward something like security and, at last, the cessation of sleepless nights.

Nothing—not even Grandma Gaffney's cutlery-tapping recaps of every Father Coughlin broadcast—had ever put Mr. Laughlin off Roosevelt. He remained true to the president's memory even when the war ended and the accounting money started coming in and he began bringing the *Journal-American* instead of the *Post* home to Stuy Town, which he eventually took to reminding them had been built by a private insurance company, not as a government project. By the time Tim was finishing high school, he'd gotten used to hearing his father say that Bishop Sheen—fine anti-red that he might be—nonetheless had a foolish sympathy for some of the labor unions. And a couple of years after that, once the television came into the living room, Dean Acheson could not come on it without Mr. Laughlin announcing, in sarcastic imitation: "I will not turn my back on Alger Hiss." The line always made Tim and Frances laugh, as if Acheson were not a person but a corporation with a trademark pledge, like "Lucky Strike Means Fine Tobacco."

But for all that, Tim saw no reason why his father—the mildest of Cold Warriors, really, looking eastward not so much for invading Soviets as for the house he now hoped to buy in Nassau County—wasn't right about the fundamentals of politics.

Mr. Brogan, Tim now noticed, had been buttonholed by Betty Beale, one of the society reporters.

"Miss Canby isn't pulling her weight?" asked Brogan, laughing. "You *shock* me, Miss Beale."

"Joke if you want," said the reporter, to whom the women's-page editor was a constant thorn in the side. Miss Beale took her own work seriously and made a point of actually *going* to the events she covered, not just relying on a phone call to the hostess to ask what cabinet wife had "poured" for which white-gloved ladies in attendance. "I cannot do this wedding alone," she now told Mr. Brogan. "We need more than one piece out of it—something for tomorrow's edition, something for the next day, and something for my weekend column. You know, Mr. Brogan, tonight McCarthy and his fiancée are having a buffet supper at some friend's farm out in Maryland, and thanks to Miss Canby there will be no one present from the *Star*."

The city editor continued listening as Miss Beale thrust home. "It's *McCarthy*, Mr. Brogan. It may be just a wedding, but surely this spills into your bailiwick—and even Mr. Corn's. May I *please* get a little help?"

Brogan looked around thoughtfully, until he spotted Tim, still standing against the filing cabinet. "How about making use of this fine fellow, Miss Beale? He can spell, he's got a few Hibernian freckles, and he can even sing. Surely he can get the goods on an Irish wedding."

"How about it, cookie?" Miss Beale asked Tim. "Do you think you can get the names of the people in as many pews as possible? And get as many quotes as they're willing to sling along with the rice? The reception's at the Washington Club right afterward. You can go to that, too."

Tim moved away from the filing cabinet and said sure. It was the only word he'd ever spoken to the still youthful but formidable Miss Beale.

"Good, then," said Brogan, having settled the matter.

"Better than good," said Cecil Holland, who'd overheard the exchange. "If Laughlin ever gets hauled in and investigated for anything, he can always say, 'But, Joe, I was at your *wedding,* for God's sake!' "

The bottle Miss McGrory had brought in was by now pretty well drained, and a sizable body of those in attendance were thinking about adjourning to the Old Ebbitt Grill over on F Street. Tim's momentary celebrity earned him an invitation to join the group, but he decided he'd be better off boning up for this opportunity he'd just been given, however late in the game it had come. And so within ten minutes he was on his way home with someone's copy of the *Congressional Directory,* the deluxe edition with photographs. He could study the pictures tonight and increase the percentage of guests he'd recognize.

Passing the Old Post Office on the other side of Pennsylvania Avenue, he was reminded that he'd yet to mail home the letter he'd been carrying around for the past two days. In it he made his job prospects sound a lot rosier than they actually were—but then again, who knew? Maybe this assignment was a portent of better things that might be coming once he left the paper and got back to passing out his résumé, this time in earnest, on Capitol Hill.

Should he go up to Hecht's and get a new white shirt? The collar was frayed on the only laundered one he had left. No, too expensive, he decided; he would settle for getting his shoes shined at Union Station tonight. Walking along Fifth Street, above Indiana and D, he continued on his career-conscious train of thought, contemplating the signs for lawyers and bondsmen, knowing that the former profession was still too much to aspire to, even if the latter one, like process-serving, now resided in a realm his father had lifted the Laughlins permanently above.

He bought a pint of milk and a sandwich before reaching his room on the Hill, in the two-hundred block of Pennsylvania, one flight above a hardware store. His occupancy was illegal, the lower floors of the building being zoned only for offices, but a landlady with no vacancies a couple of blocks away had tipped him off to the nice Italian owner here, who told him he could have the room cheap and not to worry. It came with a hot plate and tiny icebox, and a hall shower one flight up, where apartments were legal.

Tim always made sure to keep the radio low; he clicked it on now and waited for the tubes to warm up while he poured his glass of milk. A promo for *One Man's Family* became audible as he sat down and began to drink.

The job ads from Sunday's paper were on the table, and for a few minutes he gave them a second, mostly hopeless, look. The "Situations Wanted" had a hierarchy as discernible as the legal pecking order on Fifth Street.

YOUNG MAN, COLORED, desires evening or night work of any kind. Phone LI 8-5198.

After three months down here, the "colored" had ceased to shock; it was the "work of any kind" that now arrested his attention and made him wonder how many weeks might be left before he'd have to consider putting that phrase into an ad of his own.

YOUNG MAN, college education, desires a responsible position. Call WO 6-8202.

Pretty vague, to say the least, but except for the telephone, which he didn't have, it pretty much matched his own circumstances. He certainly couldn't compete with the ad just above it:

YOUNG MAN, 27, B.A., Yale, 3 years experience legislative research. 3 yrs. formal legal training, desires position with trade assoc. or law office. Box 61-V. Star.

He wondered if Helen had taken any of these down over the phone.

Setting the paper aside in favor of the *Congressional Directory*, he decided to put a ruler over the names beneath the pictures. He would see if he could correctly distinguish, say, Prescott Bush (R-Connecticut) from Bourke Hickenlooper (R-Iowa). At least he was familiar with his assignment's location, having gone to St. Matthew's last month on the Feast of the Assumption.

He wished he'd done more sightseeing this summer, or just spent a little less time in this room. He *had* gone to wait outside St. John's Church one Sunday morning in June, hoping to catch a glimpse of Eisenhower, but a disappointed tourist had told him that Ike was out of town. Everyone waiting by the church had had to settle for watching a small group demonstrate against the Rosenbergs' execution. There had also been an evening, back in July, when the second-string theater critic had comped him to a production of *Major Barbara*. They'd gone to see it together, and afterward the man had bought him a drink at the Hotel Washington's rooftop bar, then walked him all the way home and given him a funny little hug, which he somehow hadn't minded, even though the man was old enough to be his father and didn't really live, as he'd claimed, on Capitol Hill.

Excited about tomorrow, but a little restless after half an hour with the *Directory*, Tim thought he'd like to go out to a movie, but he'd been to see *The Robe* just last night, a quasi-religious act he'd used, pretty Jesuitically, as an excuse not to go to church this morning. He realized now that Miss Beale hadn't told him whether Senator McCarthy's wedding would be just a short ceremony or a whole Mass. If it was the latter, he'd have a legitimate excuse to sleep a little later tomorrow instead of starting his day at the seven o'clock inside St. Peter's on Second Street. Actually, he'd better go to St. Pete's either way. Even if it did turn out to be a Mass at St. Matthew's, he'd be too busy taking notes to line up for the Communion rail.

CHAPTER TWO

September 28, 1953

"Ready?" asked Hawkins Fuller, as soon as Mary Johnson entered his office.

"Ready," she replied, noting the gray-striped pants as he swung his feet off his desk. "But aren't you overdoing things?" Sporting a version of the foreign service's traditional trousers seemed ridiculous here in the State Department's boxy modern building in Foggy Bottom.

Fuller was unpersuaded. "It's true that we're civil servants, Miss Johnson, but our FSOs are supposed to wear gray-striped trousers for daylight calls. The reception to which we're heading constitutes a diplomatic assignment. It is now six-twenty; the reception begins at six-thirty; and sunset is not until six-fifty-five." He flashed his smile, put on his hat, and offered her his arm. "Just paying tribute to custom."

Out on Twenty-first Street, while they waited for a taxi, Mary reflected that on an actual foreign service officer the overcorrect pants would appear a clumsy attempt to get ahead. On Fuller they provided an opportunity to slow his own advance, to stay where he was through the prankish means of going by somebody else's book. A man in the Bureau of Far Eastern Affairs who'd known him when they were boys at St. Paul's had told Mary the other day: "Hawk could have been a real track star, but for the small matter that he could never see the point in outrunning anybody. Pretty odd for a sixteen-year-old."

Fuller held the cab door while she scooped up the edge of the skirt she'd shortened on her Singer last night.

"That new?" he asked.

"It's so old it was once New Look, which in case you didn't know is as dead as the New Deal. I miss both."

"Really?" was all Fuller replied.

Mary knew that she wouldn't have to elaborate on her feelings about FDR. She had never met a man, here at the job or elsewhere, more indifferent to politics than Hawkins Fuller. As for the New Look, she wasn't going to tell him she missed its long skirts because her legs were too skinny.

The driver, looking toward the orange glow over the Potomac, had begun to thrum his fingers on the steering wheel. "Where exactly are we going?" asked Fuller.

"Twenty-six twenty-two Sixteenth Street," said Mary, giving the address of the Lithuanian legation.

"I don't suppose it has a sign," said Fuller.

"I'm not even sure it has a telephone."

The driver pulled away.

"Well," said Fuller, "you're a sport to be my girl for the night. I'll take you to dinner after we sample whatever funny food they're serving."

Poor plump Miss Lightfoot, who had the desk next to Mary's, had been mad with envy when she'd heard about the invitation. Women in the building, including the married ones, generally went straight to the department's *Biographic Register* after their first sight of Hawkins Fuller. She'd done it herself, finding out that he'd been born in '25 to a businessman father (also St. Paul's); had performed some minor naval heroics at the end of the war; then finished Harvard in '50, just after his twenty-fifth birthday. Before coming to the department he'd spent one year working for a branch of his father's firm in Asunción and another on a Fulbright in Oslo.

Now he served with Mary in the department's Bureau of Congressional Relations. Their boss, Thruston Morton, an internationally minded Republican who'd once been in Congress himself, wanted Fuller at tonight's reception to help convince a particular congressman on HUAC that State really was serious about the captive Baltic republics and that a more aggressive approach could be expected from the still-new administration.

Mary liked Fuller, but experience and instinct left her immune to the swoonings of Miss Lightfoot and the rest of the distaff staff. Growing up in New Orleans, she'd seen any number of men, a few almost as handsome as he, making their solitary excursions into special precincts of the Quarter. She couldn't say she'd been surprised to learn from the *Bio-*

graphic Register that Fuller had arrived in Washington without a Norwegian wife.

She felt pretty sure he had done some checking on her, too. Fuller probably knew that she had, more or less, a boyfriend, and that this romance of hers with a doctor at Columbia Women's was, for Fuller's own purposes, at just the right state of intensity: not so hot that Mary couldn't accept someone else's invitation; not so cold that she'd be expecting a second date with Hawkins Fuller.

"Nice-enough house," he said, as the taxi reached the legation. "But not exactly the Pan-American Union building." Tomorrow night Secretary Dulles would be giving a dinner there for the Panamanian president—a tougher ticket than one to this party being held by the Estonian government-in-exile, an institution so small it had had to borrow the Lithuanian exiles' premises.

Mr. Johannes Kaiv, consul general at the outpost the Estonians *were* able to maintain in Rockefeller Center, greeted Mary and Fuller at the door. An assistant named Miss Horm ushered them into a parlor, pointing, as she led the Americans through a hallway, to the portrait of "our President Rei," presumably hung this afternoon and on its way back to Rockefeller Center tomorrow morning. "He was first elected to that office in 1928," Miss Horm told the guests, with a bittersweet smile. Fuller interrupted her recitation of all the posts Rei had held before and since to ask, "Is he here?"

"Oh, no," answered Miss Horm. "He is in Sweden."

"A disappointment," said Fuller.

"Do not believe the reports of his death," said Miss Horm, in a lower voice. "These rumors are spread all the time."

"I'm confused," Fuller whispered to Mary, once Miss Horm took leave of them. "Didn't the Swedes once conquer the Estonians? Are they now buddies?"

"Sorry, I never took the foreign service exam, either. In three years I've gone from being a secretary in the Passport Office to being more or less a secretary to the assistant to the Assistant Secretary for Congressional Relations." She had been in this new post, a few feet from Fuller's own office, for three weeks. "It hasn't been a meteoric rise."

Fuller looked to see if the complaint was serious, and her smile told him that it wasn't. Mary had come to Washington once she graduated from Sophie Newcomb and her daddy, an honest lawyer on Poydras Street who'd kept his head down during all of Huey Long, got a congressman friend to get her the job. With her striking thinness and very black hair she still looked more like the sort of coed who went to Paris than the kind who became a government girl.

The little cocktail crowd surrounding her and Fuller consisted, she soon understood, of a few exiles and a good many more high-achieving Estonian-Americans. The department, for all she knew, had an acronym for the latter, HAEAs. A series of quick introductions revealed the ones here to include a Maryland state legislator and a national officer of the VFW.

Fuller had found a seat on a couch and was now tugging at her navy-blue skirt, urging her to join him.

"We're supposed to circulate," she replied.

"Take a load off, Miss Johnson." He tugged a little harder, until she sat down. He was already bored, she could see, but confident—as he had no doubt been his whole life—that people would be coming to *him*, wherever he sat. Yes, the reluctant track star: Why run the race when you've already won it?

And come people did, like the wife of a Standard Oil man, who told Fuller and Mary that the plundered oil shale of Estonia was now helping to run the Soviet army occupying that little country. The woman was glad to be here, "showing the flag" with her husband, who believed in "keeping his hand in." However unlikely the Baltics' liberation might be, "you have to have faith," she told Fuller.

"There's an optimist," he said to Mary, once the woman was gone. "I'm guessing there's more Esso than Estonian in the husband's veins."

"Well, it *is* faith of a kind," Mary countered, less inspired by the woman's display of it than she was wearied by Fuller's insouciance. "Would you be as mocking if the faith at issue were the religious kind? The kind Dulles worries we're losing?"

"I would never mock John Foster Dulles," said Fuller. "My father's colleague on the board of the American Bank Note Company?"

Mary sighed. He hadn't, of course, answered the question, which had been about the secretary's sense that faith was losing its power to motivate America in the world. Declining to press the point, she settled for saying: "I miss Acheson."

"Are you always so awash in nostalgia, Miss Johnson? The New Deal? Long skirts? Retired cabinet secretaries?"

"I've got nothing much against the current one. But I do sometimes feel like part of the typing pool inside a big Presbyterian parsonage. With Acheson you knew you were working for a *diplomat*." On his last day, eight months ago, she had joined the long line of employees walking through the chief's office to shake his courtly hand: *Thank you for your good wishes, my dear young lady*.

"Never met the man," said Fuller. "When do you think we'll get a boss *without* a mustache?" Acheson's had been a bit reddish; Dulles's was snow-white. "I can't imagine growing one myself," Fuller continued. "Or would you like me to, Miss Johnson? Do you desire *my* advancement?"

"No," Mary answered. "All I want is that you save me from this." A burly man of about forty, carrying two fish-topped crackers, was moving toward her at considerable speed. An honest-to-God Estonian, she surmised. Before Fuller could act, however, the gentleman introduced himself as Fred Bell, born on the Lower East Side to immigrant parents, but completely American himself, down to his changed name. A veteran of D-Day who now owned three shoe factories in Massachusetts. Even so, he was part of an exiles' committee, and nothing in the world could have made him miss the opportunity to come down here and say something about the situation.

"Miss Horm back there told me you were with the State Department, ma'am. *Fifty thousand deportations* since the takeover. Including my cousin, just a peasant, who these days has to work on a Russian collective. My other cousin over there's a musician. The oboe. He gets to stay in Tallinn and play bad music."

"Why did they deport the peasant?" Mary asked, feeling foolish using the word.

"Because the peasants resist collectivization. Estonians are natural businessmen, ma'am. Very independent. You know, my relatives used to *vote*. Now they're impoverished and relocated, or just *gone*." In his anxiety to make the most of the few moments he imagined he was having in the presence of officialdom, Mr. Bell ate both of the hors d'oeuvres he had carried across the room. His eyes, Mary noticed, were watering. "We're a *colony*. Stripped of our machinery, forced to feed *them* with *our* crops.

Did you know you used to be able to get eggs from Estonia in *New York City*? So good they were exported all that way! What we need is a general strike, something that with a little encouragement from abroad might spread to the railway workers in Russia. If *they* went out, there's no telling how soon the whole system might collapse!"

Mary looked at him, apologetically. Despite the supposedly tough new policy that had dispatched her and Fuller to this party, they were still required, she knew, to speak the department's soothing Esperanto of noncommittal clucks and nods. She found herself urging Mr. Bell to contact the Office of Eastern European Affairs with his views—but then she couldn't remember the name of the Assistant Secretary for that particular bureau.

She turned to her companion, who'd been busy talking to a retired languages professor. Fuller saw, and misinterpreted, her desire for assistance.

"You're right," he said, rising. "We've got to go. Don't know how I lost track of the time. *Tere!*" he said to Mr. Bell, giving him his card and propelling Mary toward the door.

"See what I learned?" he asked. "It means 'Pleased to meet you.' "

"Actually, what I wanted—"

"I suppose 'Next year in Tallinn' would have been better, but for just a few minutes' work with the languages prof, '*tere*' isn't so bad."

Mary turned around and saw Mr. Bell, half ancient mariner and half modern PR man, already importuning someone else.

"Let's get out of here," said Fuller. "There's no sign of Congressman HUAC, in any case."

"We can't decently leave yet."

But Mary saw that they couldn't accomplish anything, either. A few minutes later—so soon after sunset that Fuller's trousers remained almost appropriate—the two of them were back out on Sixteenth Street. He put his arm around her waist as they began walking south. "What are you in the mood for?"

"Scrambled eggs, by my lonesome, at home." Mary could only imagine what Miss Lightfoot would say to her turning down dinner with Hawkins Fuller.

"Well, there's something to be said for an early night," he observed.

"Do you have them?" she asked. "Early nights?"

"Tonight I will," he answered. "I'm having lunch tomorrow at the Sulgrave with my mother's childless brother. Have to look sharp. I need to stay in his good graces."

Mary looked at him, but for a moment said nothing further.

"The pants are one thing," he declared. "But you don't think I bought these shoes on my salary, do you? Or that I want his winter place in New Mexico to go to one of my *sisters*?"

"How about other nights? Early or late?"

Fuller just smiled, and clasped her waist a little tighter. "What do you put on your eggs, Miss Johnson? Ketchup?"

He was not, she knew, doubling back to attempt a forward pass; he had no intention of pursuing an invitation to her place, though she now recalled the almost pro forma advance he'd made in the cafeteria two weeks ago, on her third day in Congressional Relations. He'd been pleased, she thought, when it was blocked. Had she said yes, he would probably have followed through, happily enough—all the way from third base to home if she'd let him—but she had allowed him, she felt sure, to return to more ardent matters elsewhere.

"Cayenne pepper" was all she replied.

Fuller pretended to wince. "Ah, of course. New Orleans. All right, spitfire. Let me find you a taxi." Cabs would be thin on the ground until they reached New Hampshire Avenue. "Too bad we can't share," said Fuller. "But not all of us can live on the Georgetown reaches of P Street. What are you, maybe two blocks from your old friend Acheson?"

Mary, who still probably received more money from her father than Fuller got from his uncle, said, "So I'm not the only one who reads the *Biographic Register*."

"Knowledge is power," said Fuller. "Then you know I have a modest one-bedroom on I Street. Just blocks from the office, really. Makes the boss think I can't bear being too far away from my work."

And makes it easier, thought Mary, for you to arrive, after a late night, in a rumpled rush—as you often do, putting Miss Lightfoot into an even deeper swoon. She felt her attitude toward Fuller becoming, for a moment, almost sisterly. "Do you know," she asked, as they kept searching for a cab, "that McLeod is supposed to start doing interviews in our own little precinct before New Year's?" Scott McLeod, the new administration's security man, with his "Miscellaneous M Unit," was hunting through the ranks for moral turpitude of any kind, but one kind in particular, the kind that still got the men of the foreign service mocked as "cookie-pushers" whose striped pants might as well be aprons.

She had tried to ask the question as if it were merely a piece of office gossip, some water-cooler topic on the order of McCarthy's wedding.

"I came *in* as a certified paragon, Miss Johnson. Letters of recommendation from Cordell Hull and both Dulleses. Never let it be said that the Fuller family doesn't touch all bases."

She should respond, of course, that she hadn't been talking about *him*, only the morale of the division; but before she could get that falsehood out, he had flagged down a cab. "You take it," he said with a grin. "I'll get the next one." He opened the door and made sure her skirt didn't get caught. "There. Much easier, I'm sure, than when you were taking the New Look to such lengths. I'll see you tomorrow, Miss Johnson."

She waved, and watched him pass up another available cab. He continued along Sixteenth Street, toward downtown, instead of turning onto New Hampshire, which would have taken him to his apartment.

CHAPTER THREE

September 29, 1953

"Our Holy Father cordially imparts to Joseph R. McCarthy and Jean Kerr on the occasion of their marriage his paternal apostolic blessing."

When the priest finished reading the pope's official good wishes to Senator McCarthy and his bride—a pièce de résistance with which to end the ceremony—the crowd's appreciative murmur turned into applause. A second later, the organist struck the first note of the recessional and the congregation snapped to its feet for the newly married couple's walk back up the aisle.

Joe and Jean—as even Timothy Laughlin couldn't help but think of them at this moment—turned from facing the huge mosaics behind the altar and began their march to the cathedral's doors. Standing near the back of the church, Tim would have to settle for imagining the McCarthys' smiles until they were much farther along in their exit. In the meantime he gazed at the huge red-and-white marble pillars that seemed to be running with blood, and put a quarter into the poorbox: he'd taken the extra coin from his dresser when he left this morning, forgetting that, even if there *was* a full Mass with the wedding, there wouldn't be a collection.

He had just counted the twenty-four windows in the cathedral's dome, recording the figure in his Palmer-method hand on a page of his steno pad that included the following notes:

Mrs. Nixon next to Dulles (Allen, CIA not State)
Jack Dempsey! (TELL DAD)

Wilbur Johnson—family friend (Kerrs), brought bride to church
Roy Cohen—McC committee counsel, one of ushers

As soon as the bride and groom were out the door, Tim managed to leave the cathedral by a side exit, ahead of most of the crowd. On the church steps he was supposed to pass his notes to Miss Beale's assistant. The wedding itself would make it into this afternoon's paper, but coverage of the reception would have to wait until tomorrow's. He wouldn't need to deliver his notes on that part of things until the end of work today.

Finding a place on the steps behind several reporters, Tim tried on the feeling of being one of them. It was a bad fit, several sizes too big. All the newsmen seemed full of knowingness, and none of them was giving his dislike of McCarthy a day off. Eisenhower's absence—the president had claimed a conflict with the Panamanian leader's visit—was the subject of a few satisfied jokes before the reporters quieted down to get a quote from Nixon, who was pausing briefly during his descent of the church steps.

"A beautiful ceremony," said the vice president, slowly enough for any pencils still competing with microphones. "The bride was lovely, but then I've never met a bride who wasn't!" He snapped off a grin and quickly escorted Mrs. Nixon to the car.

"Did he just insult Joe's wife?" wondered a man from the Baltimore *Sun*. There *was*, Tim thought, something a little off about Nixon's effortful remark, part of the awkwardness you could feel all over the cathedral steps. "Kiss her, Joe!" the folks on the sidewalk kept shouting. But the senator wouldn't comply, and his expression continued to undergo the oddest alternations. For ten seconds at a time he'd look like one of Tim's Irish uncles, the smile ready to issue a song, but then some saturnine cloud would scud across the eyes and mouth, turning McCarthy into a baleful, preoccupied spectator at his own nuptials.

"He looks like he's ready to push some cookies himself," said one of the reporters, pointing to the gray-striped pants beneath McCarthy's morning coat.

"Did you know that Torquemada got her to *convert* for this?" his colleague asked. "The girl was a Presbyterian."

Tim scanned the faces in the crowd filling up a whole block of Rhode Island Avenue. Most of them were women, and the mood was cheerful, but here and there he could spot someone glaring up at the groom, displaying a resentment either abstract or deeply particular. These angry exceptions only added to the off-kilter feel of the whole event.

Once he'd handed off his notes, Tim hotfooted it two blocks to the Washington Club in Dupont Circle, where guests waiting to be let into the reception were sweltering alongside another crowd of gawkers. Twenty minutes passed before he could get inside this grand old building to make notes on the white chrysanthemums and blocks of orange ice in the bowl of nonalcoholic punch. He got as close as he could to the receiving line. If he were more aggressive, let alone taller, he might have secured a better vantage point, but even at some distance he could pick up most of what the politicians were saying in their overloud voices. Senator Hickenlooper *was* there—he recognized him from the *Congressional Directory*—along with Teddy Roosevelt's daughter, Mrs. Longworth, and a Congressman Bentley from Michigan, identified with the help of a *Detroit News* reporter. Between jottings Tim got further glimpses of McCarthy himself, who he suspected (from long observation of his male relatives) had just managed to get hold of something more fortifying than the punch. But the drink had not resolved the alternations in his facial expression; it was speeding them up.

"Had to settle for wearing this!" cried Joseph P. Kennedy, tugging at the lapels of his dark business suit. "My own cutaway's not back from the cleaners." This was understood, to general laughter, as a reference to his son Jack's wedding, less than three weeks ago, to Miss Bouvier, the *Times-Herald*'s inquiring photographer. There might be no sign of Senator Kennedy here this morning, but three of his brothers and sisters were right behind the old ambassador.

Tim kept at it until 2:05, through the bride's vigorous toss of her bouquet—"That gal can play on my team anytime!" someone roared—and the newlyweds' departure in a black limousine, not the red Cadillac rumored to be a wedding present from some of the senator's Texas supporters. Back out in Dupont Circle Tim soon felt himself sweating through his blue suit. His steno pad was already soaked from his own palm; thank God, at least, for ballpoint pens. Looking at the top page of his notes, he realized he would soon be mystified by his own abbreviations unless he made a fair copy, with amplifications, right away. So once he'd bought a half-pint of milk at the big Peoples drugstore, he sat down amidst the late lunchers and sun-catchers on a bench near the Circle's western rim. Across the expanse of grass he could hear the last of the wedding guests laughing through their departures.

He had just finished transcribing the first page on the pad when he noticed a shadow approaching: someone also wanting to sit down. As quickly as he could, he cleared off his milk carton, napkin, and two loose steno pages from the rest of the bench. "Sorry," he said, before he'd even had a chance to look up.

"For what?"

For *everything*, thought Tim, once he raised his head and saw the spectacular young man standing over him. Taking in the suit jacket slung over the man's broad shoulders and the faint glistening of sweat in the hollow of his neck where he'd loosened his tie, Tim wanted to say: *For being nothing like you. For being all you'll have for company on this bench.*

"May I?" said the man.

"Of course," Tim finally answered.

"Don't they give you an office?"

Tim laughed. "They're not even giving me a job past Friday." And then it all came out in a nervous, mortifying rush: his graduation from Fordham; his arrival here in June; his summer of rewrites on the *Star*'s city desk; his hope for a job on Capitol Hill; the chance to cover McCarthy's wedding.

Realizing that the man's suit was as fine as his physique, Tim asked: "You weren't a guest there, were you?"

It was the most foolish question he could have posed; if this man had been inside the Washington Club, or even the cathedral, Tim would certainly have noticed.

"No," said the man, pointing in the direction of Massachusetts Avenue. "I was having lunch with my uncle at the Sulgrave Club."

Tim nodded.

"So who was there from the State Department?" the man asked. "Come on: name names, as the groom might say."

Tim flipped through the pages of his pad, as cooperatively as if he'd actually been asked to do this in the witness chair. Searching for a relevant name, he mocked his own parochial-school penmanship, feeling certain his companion must have an altogether more manly scrawl. " 'The neat handwriting of the illiterate,' " he said, nervously quoting *1984*. "Here we go. Mrs. Dulles. And Mrs. Walter Bedell Smith, the undersecretary's wife. The Spanish ambassador? That doesn't count. Harold Stassen? Foreign operations administrator for the president? Not actually the State Department, I guess. Is that where you work?"

"Yes. The job also brings me to the Hill every week or two. But I'm not due there today until three-thirty. By the way," he said, taking Tim's pad and flipping back to something he'd noticed on the first page, "there's no 'e' in Roy Cohn."

"Live and learn," said Tim, who obediently made a correction. "Thanks."

"Come on. We can walk a bit and pick up the streetcar on Pennsylvania. It'll get us both where we're going."

Tim started gathering his things so quickly that the young man had to tell him, "Finish your milk. We've got time."

Taking two last pulls on his paper straw, Tim looked at the paragon beside him and hoped he wouldn't now tighten his tie.

"Okay, we're off," said the man, once Tim had trotted the waxed milk container to a trash basket. Only when he fell into step with the handsome stranger did he notice that the bench to the right of the one they'd shared had been empty all along.

Walking across the Circle to Connecticut Avenue, no more than ten minutes into their acquaintance, the much taller man said: "And to think you used to be so talkative."

Thrilled at being teased, Tim replied, laughing: "I do talk too much."

"No, you don't," said the young man, giving Tim's neck a momentary, affectionate squeeze. The touch rendered him mute, perhaps the only person in the United States who couldn't find one more thing to say about Joe McCarthy.

The man walking beside him broke the silence: "May I ask you a personal question?"

"Sure."

"Is this milk-drinking a habit of yours?"

"Sort of. I think they were always hoping it would make me taller. I didn't rise to the full five-feet-seven you see before you until I was seventeen. I guess I developed a taste for it."

The man nodded. "Glasses?"

"Two or three a day. Small ones."

"No, idiot. How long ago did you get *those*?" He tapped the right arm of the boy's spectacles.

"Oh!" said Tim. "Had 'em since time immemorial. I must have been eight. Farsighted. I can read a street sign a block away, but I've got a problem with print or even faces close up." With his eyeglasses in place, he could see the man's expression quite clearly, but couldn't be sure what it indicated. A trace of pity? A flicker of real interest in what he'd been telling him? Anxious when his companion said nothing more, he went nattering on. "They're not so bad, really. I used to have those old steelwire frames. Got these tortoiseshells going into my junior year of college. Pretty snazzy, no?" Looking up into the man's blue-gray eyes, Tim felt sure that they had never worn corrective lenses. His own glasses suddenly felt like an artificial limb.

They reached the corner with the streetcar stop.

The man tenderly removed Tim's eyeglasses. "How many fingers?" he asked, holding up three just an inch from Tim's eyes.

"Three," said Tim, just able to make them out.

"There. You're healed," said the man, folding the eyeglasses and slipping them into the handkerchief pocket of Tim's jacket.

"You're a riot," said Tim, smiling as his heart pounded. He retrieved the glasses and put them back on and saw that the man was looking at him with a gaze that could only be called appraising. He wanted to give this god a playful shove, and thought he could probably get away with making it look like only that, rather than his desperate desire to touch this person whose name he didn't even know.

The streetcar stopped in front of them.

"I'm Timothy Laughlin, by the way."

"I'm pleased to meet you, Timothy Laughlin."

Tim had time enough to see that the man *was* pleased, but then the doors of the streetcar opened and the most terrible thing imaginable happened. As the two of them boarded, three other people, two women and a child, got between them. Standing in the aisle of the crowded car as it went down Pennsylvania, struggling to see past those three other souls, Tim only briefly recaptured his acquaintance's attention. The young man gave him a helpless shrug and a relaxed smile that seemed to say: Oh well, sorry about this little turn of fate.

Tim got off—there was nothing else to do—when the car stopped in front of the *Star*. He waved goodbye from the sidewalk, unsure whether the man could even see him. Standing in the doorway of the newspaper's office, he watched the streetcar continue on its eastward way, and he knew that if he lived to be a hundred, he would never be more in love than he was now.

CHAPTER FOUR

October 6, 1953

The handful of observers at the back of Room 357 could see the shoulders of the witness stiffen. Mr. Edward J. Lyons, Jr., representing the Judge Advocate General, gamely proceeded to describe the frequency with which United Nations prisoners had been "discovered with their hands tied behind their backs and their eyes gouged out. They'd been used for bayonet practice and the like."

While still in charge in Korea, General MacArthur had been determined to do things differently from the way they'd been done during World War II. Rather than waiting for victory—or, as it appeared to be turning out this time, negotiated stalemate—he'd begun investigating North Korean atrocities as soon as anyone got wind of them. The evidence of torture and brainwashing was plentiful and compelling, and Senator Charles Potter (R-Michigan) appeared to relish running this hearing that had been convened to discuss it.

McCarthy had not finished honeymooning down in Nassau, but the atrocities task force of the Permanent Subcommittee on Investigations was Potter's responsibility, and he seemed determined to make the most of it. There were no cameras or reporters here at this closed executive session in the Senate Office Building, and public hearings on the subject wouldn't come until December, but even so, Potter remained energetic— no matter that the Democrats, who'd months ago quit the committee in protest of McCarthy's tactics, refused to come back even for this; no matter, in fact, that Potter was the *only* senator, amidst several staff members, to have shown up this morning. He still looked bent on getting to the bottom of something awful.

For most of the grim testimony it was hard to remember that this was the McCarthy committee. But there came a point, in the midst of eliciting information from Lieutenant Colonel J. W. Whitehorne III, when Potter made the mistake of thinking out loud: "I am curious about the twenty-three Americans who are still over there, whom apparently Communist propaganda got the best of. Or maybe they went into the service as pro-Communists. Is there any check being made as to the background of the men still there?"

Once Colonel Whitehorne declared that information on the defectors was indeed available, Roy Cohn, as if hearing a whistle, sprang from a midmorning slumber: "What was the answer on that? Did any of those people have Communist backgrounds?"

"Some of them had leftist leanings," said Colonel Whitehorne.

"Would we be able to get some documentation?" asked Cohn, more in the imperative than the interrogative. All at once he was in possession of the hearing, which now seemed, more familiarly, to be concerning itself with domestic subversion.

Tim Laughlin had a much better view of Cohn than he had had at McCarthy's wedding last week. He wasn't sure whether to take him for a mobster or a boy wearing his first suit. The dark, hooded eyes; the scar down the nose; the slicked-down hair—all these features fought against the committee counsel's improbable, extreme youth. Twenty-six, Cecil Holland, back at the *Star*, had said.

Tim could see the concern that Cohn's line of questioning had provoked on the high, creased forehead of the army's new counsel, John Adams. But Tim was looking more closely at Potter, to whom he might actually be talking once the hearing reached its conclusion. Yesterday afternoon he'd called the senator's office to confirm his appointment and been told by the secretary that he might like to get a glimpse of Potter in action before coming in for an interview.

With his horn-rim glasses and balding brow, he reminded Tim of the lay teachers in math and science at St. Agnes' Boys' High. He would have been surprised by Potter's own youth if he hadn't looked him up in the *Congressional Directory* during his last afternoon at the *Star*. Only thirty-six, and already in the upper body after three terms in the House! In addition to his regular committee assignments, the senator served on the Battle Monuments Commission, a fact that somehow appealed to

Tim, who last night had imagined getting the job and making phone calls that would spruce up the cannon at Bull Run or the statue of Father Duffy in Times Square.

But the crisp zeal Potter was again showing, now that Cohn had subsided, had to do with far-more-distant battlefields that had barely cooled. None of the POWs who'd been rescued or exchanged—in a mental condition more frightening than their physical one—was seated here this morning. Only the brass were at the witness table, and it was painful enough hearing the descriptions of torture filtered through them. Tim could only guess what the impact would be when the victims themselves testified in a couple of months. Cecil Holland had told him how McCarthy liked to perform a sleight of hand between the committee's executive and public sessions. When pink witnesses who'd been subpoenaed to reveal their former Communist ties showed any instinct to fight back during the closed session, they most likely wouldn't get called for the open hearing, where McCarthy preferred to display the timid and guilty-looking. Things would operate with a strange similarity in this case, Tim imagined. The more shaky the repatriated prisoners, the more powerful Senator Potter's point would be.

All this activity felt reassuring to Tim. Whatever the committee's reported excesses, surely not even Miss McGrory, back at the *Star*, could object to this particular inquiry. Only three days ago the pope himself had called for new international laws against war crimes, and two years before that, Tim had heard Father Beane, the visiting priest from the Chinese missions, tell about what he and his brothers had suffered at the hands of Mao's advancing armies. Even now he remembered the friar's cadences and fervor, and how he himself had sat in the Church of the Epiphany, between Frances and his mother, thinking: Some "soldier of God" *I* am! That was, after all, what he was supposed to have become on the spring Sunday in 1944 when Bishop O'Neill confirmed him with a symbolic toughening slap to the face.

But maybe here, in the smallest of ways, he could be helpful in the fight against godlessness and cruelty. If he went to work for Potter, he would not just be keeping Father Duffy laureled; he'd be affording protection to Father Beane as well. It might be the only soldiering he ever did. He'd never been able to think through what he'd do when the draft board got around to calling him up. *Do you have homosexual tenden-*

cies? Check yes or no. When he'd registered, almost four years ago in that little office up at Fordham, he'd realized he was damned either way he answered: he could be an outcast or a liar. He'd chosen to lie, rationalizing that "tendencies" could be proved only by experience, and he'd certainly had none of that. *Homosexual tendencies:* had Uncle Alan, his mother's never-married brother, kept them tucked away with his St. Christopher medal, inside the backpack he'd carried onto Corregidor? Tim had often wondered.

Potter was making ready to adjourn, telling the military men that he'd be out on the West Coast later this month, doing some more preliminary interviews. While he was away, he expected them to keep getting ready for the open hearings in December. "We're working toward the same purpose," he said, with midwestern nasality and a smile. His gavel came down at 11:45 a.m.

Everywhere in the city one could feel that autumn—the season not of death, Tim always thought, but of quickening—had finally arrived. What Drew Pearson still called the "Washington Merry-Go-Round" had, after a summer idling in the weeds, rattled to life, even without McCarthy in town to flip the switch. Yesterday Governor Warren had been sworn in as Chief Justice, while Nixon was embarking on a ten-week tour of Asia.

Potter stood up, with a wincing, unexpected slowness, and came out from behind the committee dais. How large his head seemed in proportion to the rest of his body, Tim thought, before noticing what was seriously wrong. An aide had handed the senator two canes. From the stiffness of his gait, Tim realized that the man was walking on artificial legs—not the sort of fact that went into the tabular pages of the *Congressional Directory.*

And yet, all at once this fact seemed more joking than somber. Each cane had a little electric flashlight near its top, and Potter was now playfully using one of them to signal a man three seats away from Tim.

That man—small and gray and grudgingly groomed, with a thin face somewhere between mottled and ravaged—returned Potter's smile. He then got up to leave the back row, nodding genially to Tim.

"Excuse me," said Tim, before the man could depart, "do you know where Room 80 is? I tried to locate it on my way here. I've got an appointment there in—"

"That's number 80 in the *Capitol,* son. Not here in the SOB. In fact,

Charlie's the only s.o.b. not housed with the other ninety-five s.o.b.s here in the SOB."

"I have a job interview with him. With Senator Potter, I mean."

"Well, come with me, young sir. I'm heading there now."

They trotted down the stairs to the subway that ran between the two buildings. The older man explained how the senator had his office in the Capitol to make his handicap less of an inconvenience. "Of course it's not so damned convenient when the committee meeting is *here* instead of there, but it helps more often than not."

Tim could smell a peppermint on the man's breath and wondered if it was there to mask a morning shot of Four Roses. He could easily imagine the two of them saying hello on Ninth Avenue, the older man having emerged from McNaughton's saloon to slap him on the back with best wishes "for that fine woman, your Grandma Gaffney," who would decline the wishes with a lace-curtain shudder once Timmy brought them to her kitchen.

The man ushered him to a wicker seat on the jammed little subway. Tim could see Potter in the car ahead as the two-car train started down the monorail. While it moved, the man continued talking in a rat-a-tat-tat like Winchell's. "It was a land mine that did it," he explained. "January 31, 1945, Battle of the Bulge, in the Colmar Pocket. No choice but to amputate both his pins. Spent a year in Walter Reed and had to learn to walk all over again. Fella who'd once been a high jumper!"

Tim nodded gravely in the darkness.

"The VA calls him 'permanently and totally disabled'!" cried the man, cackling over the clatter. "Well, it doesn't keep him from voting on their budget."

"What are the lights on the canes for?" asked Tim.

"Hailing cabs." The man paused for a moment. "Well, we'll soon see how 'abled' Charlie turns out to be among this crowd he's in with now." He pointed to one of the heads in the lead car. "See our boy Roy up there?"

"Yes," said Tim. They had reached the end of the Lilliputian tunnel, and he could make out the back of Cohn's freshly cropped skull.

"Don't use the men's toilet when he's around, if you catch my drift. Though he tends to be enchanted by fellows a little huskier than yourself." The man laughed as the train bucked to a stop.

"Are you on Senator Potter's staff?" asked Tim.

"No," the man answered, chuckling, as he and Tim made their way to the Capitol's first floor. "Let's just say I'm authorized to help him out a bit from time to time. Him and some of the other Michigan GOP men. My name's McIntyre, Thomas McIntyre. Call me Tommy. Was a newspaperman for several eternities, down here and up in Detroit."

Tim shook hands and introduced himself, trying to understand what this slight, fast-moving man meant by helping the senator out, and wondering who had authorized him to do it.

"Potter's a good-enough egg," said McIntyre, the heels of his unshined shoes beating a fast rhythm across the marble corridor. "He's managed to vote for foreign aid but not forget it's the automakers who sent him here. You know," he continued, almost reflective, "he *ought* to be an interesting fellow. He was actually a social worker before he went off to the war. But he's got one handicap worse than no legs."

"Really?" asked Tim, as McIntyre knocked on the door of Room 80.

"Yeah. A permanent charley horse between his ears!"

McIntyre was still laughing when the door to the senator's office was opened—by a man with one arm.

"His driver," whispered Tommy. "No foolin'!"

Miss Antoinette Cook, the woman Tim had spoken with on the phone, introduced him to Robert L. Jones, a still-young man who looked as if he might be Potter's executive assistant, and whose speech carried the salt of a Maine accent. "Oh, yes, Mr. Laughlin," he said, appearing less than pleased by Tim's arrival, let alone McIntyre's. "The fellow that Hawkins Fuller recommended when he was up here to defend State's latest excessive appropriation."

McIntyre looked at Tim with an encouraging smile, and then alarm. "Jesus, kid, your face has gone white. It's only a job interview. This ain't the Depression."

Hawkins Fuller.

Tim managed to nod and shake Mr. Jones's hand, while McIntyre cheerfully took charge of the situation. "Put him to work, Jones. See what he can do. Better yet, see if he can do the bit of work *I* was going to do for you today. Here, son, this is a copy of what Knowland's planning to say on the floor a couple of hours from now. I got it from his press man. It's no different from what he said at his press conference yesterday, but it's a couple of decibels higher, and it's going to make a splash. So why don't you sit down at one of the Underwoods here and write a couple of paragraphs that Charlie can say in support of it?"

Mr. Jones had already lost interest in Timothy Laughlin; he was on a phone behind Miss Cook, cupping his hand over the receiver.

"Go on, read it, read it," said Tommy McIntyre, as he wheeled a typist's chair into position behind Tim.

Senator Knowland, the majority leader, had come home from his world tour the other day and learned of Adlai Stevenson's call for a nonaggression pact with the Russians—a proposal that had irritated the California senator to an extreme degree. "Now watch the Koreans drag out the Panmunjom talks," he was warning. "This will be one more sign that we need to put our house in order and our rifles at the ready. Time is not on the side of the Free World, and we don't need Mr. Stevenson, after his massive repudiation at the polls, recommending that we play at useless diplomacy."

Tim had only a slight idea of how Potter spoke, but he was pretty sure the point of this writing assignment was to make him sound as implacable as Knowland. So he took up a yellow pad and made several notes for a few paragraphs of oratory. To begin with, Knowland must be extolled. To continue, Stevenson must be excoriated, for his attempt "not only to bend over backwards, but to roll out the red carpet for our adversaries of that same color." The prose began to flow almost automatically. The defeated Democrat was proposing "a nonaggression pact with a flagrant aggressor." To conclude, one needed to take a shot at India, a sentimental favorite of liberals, which Knowland had accused of backing the North Korean position before the peace talks had even gotten underway. "In my great automobile-making state," wrote Tim as Potter, "we're wary of any car or country that stays in 'neutral' for too long. 'Neutral' is what you're in when you roll downhill."

After penciling in a few revisions, Tim rolled a sheet of paper into the Underwood and typed up this stentorian boilerplate. Struck by his own speed, he realized how the words—for all that he believed them, and he more or less did—seemed to be coming from neither Potter's brain nor his own. He was speaking in another voice entirely—the way, as an altar boy during Mass, he would be saying his Latin part while still hearing the English words of whatever hymn had soared through the church a few minutes before. He proofread the little speech a second time, to make sure he hadn't typed the words "Hawkins Fuller" somewhere in the middle of one of its sentences. Then he handed the page to Mr. McIntyre.

"Fast fella, aren't you?" the lined little man said with a grin, before carrying the speech to the suite's innermost office. Before five minutes passed, he reemerged, in the company of Senator Potter and a third man. All of them, carrying their hats, headed toward Tim.

"Another Irish wordsmith!" enthused the senator, who put both his canes in his left hand, so that his right could extend itself to Tim. "Welcome to the staff, Mr. Laughlin."

Tim shook Potter's hand and realized with embarrassment that he had been looking down at the senator's feet.

Potter seemed pleased by the chance to alleviate an awkwardness he encountered daily.

"I was just telling Mr. Jeffreys, my Lansing constituent here, that I'm looking forward to some duck hunting on the Upper Peninsula this winter. These days I'm able to glide around in some paper-thin galoshes my wife gave me, while my pals have to clomp and sweat in boots that weigh a ton. 'Aren't your feet cold?' one of them asked me last year. 'Not exactly!' I told him. 'Unless they're feeling chilly wherever I left 'em in France!'" He paused to laugh. "Everything's got its advantages."

Tim smiled, more in awe than humor. Potter clapped him on the shoulder and continued on out with McIntyre and Mr. Jeffreys. Miss Cook then presented him with two forms to be filled out. "You can bring these back with you when you start Monday morning, Mr. Laughlin."

Tim thanked her and everybody else still in the office. A minute or so later, halfway down the Capitol's east steps, he paused to sit beside a huge stone pediment supporting an ornate lamppost. He closed his eyes and shook off the image of Potter's severed feet, lost somewhere in the soil of France. It wasn't hard to banish the picture; his mind had no room for it, or even for the fact that he could now pay the rent and write home with some good news. His mind was filled with the afternoon of McCarthy's wedding, exactly a week ago.

An hour after getting off the streetcar, he'd been summoned to a telephone on the other side of the city room. "A call from Capitol Hill," he'd been told. Through the receiver had come the voice he'd heard an hour before and never expected to hear again: "Send your résumé and a letter of application to the attention of Miss Antoinette Cook. The job is a junior assistant with writing duties."

Dumbfounded, Tim had written down the address and phone number for Potter's office. "Thank you," he'd managed to say.

"If you get the job, treat yourself to a glass of chocolate milk."

And with that the still-nameless voice had left the line.

Hawkins Fuller.

Now, a week later, Tim sat for another moment on the steps, before he opened his eyes to see a flag being run up one of the distant poles on the Capitol's roof. It was a familiar sight: he knew that this flag would wave for only a moment before being lowered and shipped to some elementary school in Cheyenne or Mill Valley, where the teachers could tell the students it had flown over the U.S. Capitol. But for the few seconds it was aloft, filled with what might be two new separate futures, Tim looked at it with his hand over his heart.

October 6, 1953

Dear Rep. Fish:

You may assure your Dutch-American constituent in Wappingers Falls that the Department of State views all recent violence in Indonesia with the greatest possible concern. As Secretary Dulles remarked on . . .

Mary Johnson proofread her letter to the New York congressman and sank into the feeling of futility that often overcame her by midafternoon. What could any of these well-meant epistolary stitchings and swabbings really do to treat the wounds of the tortured world? There was news this week that Lockheed had begun work on a nuclear-powered airplane; no doubt it would be carrying an atomic bomb as well.

Behind Mary, Miss Lightfoot was speaking to Beverly Phillips about the woman in the Office of Legal Advisors who'd just won a four-thousand-dollar car in WMAL's "Mystery Voice" contest.

"Well," said Mrs. Phillips, "*she* won't have any trouble making her Community Chest contribution."

Mary laughed. Underneath the correspondence piling up for the bureau chief's signature lay her copy of the memo from R. W. Scott McLeod, security officer to 1,142 employees, informing all of them that if they chose not to make a Community Chest contribution this year, they must report to his office for an interview. Secretary Dulles was chairman of the department's drive, and McLeod's zeal to show the boss what a little extra aggression could accomplish had sparked much grumbling about the "Conformity Chest."

"There's nothing wrong with what McLeod is doing," said Miss Lightfoot, in her near-chronic tone of irritation. "He's just trying for one-hundred-percent participation. He'll *lend* you a dollar if you can't contribute one on your own."

Mary turned her small swivel chair so that she and Beverly Phillips could each raise an eyebrow to the other. Miss Lightfoot also found nothing wrong with McLeod's unceasing security-risk investigations. Indeed, she seemed disappointed with the estimate that his review of things wouldn't reach Congressional Relations until December.

A young man carrying a book now came through the door, confusing Mary, who took him for the summer office boy from Eastern European Affairs. Hadn't he returned to school?

"Is Mr. Fuller in?" the boy asked. He stammered over the "F" in Fuller. "I couldn't find him on the wall directory, but the man at the front desk told me to come here."

Mary smiled. She realized that this wasn't the boy from EEA, though he did look a little like the lovesick Donald O'Connor in *Call Me Madam*, the only musical anyone would ever care to make about this place. And then it occurred to her. This skinny fellow *was* lovesick. She looked at him gently, filling up with annoyance toward Fuller as she did so. What new recklessness of his had made this boy venture here with a handful of pebbles to throw at Romeo's window?

"I'm afraid he left early. To go to the Georgetown library, I believe."

"The library at George Washington U.," Miss Lightfoot corrected.

"Thank you," said Mary. Her colleague, already matronly though no more than thirty-five, certainly kept track of Fuller.

"Will he be back?" the young man asked.

"I doubt it," said Mary.

Managing not to stammer, the boy said, "I was bringing him this." He handed Mary a new biography of the elder Henry Cabot Lodge. A receipt from Trover's bookshop stuck out of it. An odd present to bring here, thought Mary, Lodge not exactly having been an internationalist. But it

was a big and serious book—impressive, the boy had probably reasoned—
and he had spent six dollars on it.

"You could leave it here," she said. "I'll see that Mr. Fuller gets it."

The boy still looked crestfallen.

"You can leave a note, too," Mary added. "So he'll be sure to know
who it's from."

"I'll write one inside the book," the young man declared, looking more
hopeful.

Mary pointed to the empty chair at the side of her desk and watched
him fumble for his ballpoint pen. His handwriting was so neat she could
read it upside down without the least effort.

> *With thanks to Hawkins Fuller*
> *(I got the job. You're wonderful.)*
> *Timothy Laughlin*

"Does he know where to reach you?" asked Mary, trying to sound
casual instead of confidential. "Is there a number you'd like to leave?"

"I'm not on the phone," said Timothy Laughlin. A cloud rushed over
the map of Ireland that was his face—mortification, Mary thought, at
having used such a tenement archaism. "But I'll put my address with it,"
he added, recovering enough equilibrium to accept the index card that
Mary gave him to write it on. He also removed the bookshop receipt, and
asked if she could direct him back to the Twenty-first Street entrance.

After he'd gone, she prepared the envelope for another soothing letter,
to Congressman Ikard of Texas. Adjusting her typewriter's left mar-
gin, she noticed Miss Lightfoot smoothing her strawberry-blond permanent wave, and realized what close attention the woman had paid to the
boy's visit.

CHAPTER FIVE

October 16, 1953

Senator Kennedy, the radio was saying, had today called for "the development of a strategic air force with sufficient retaliatory powers to threaten a potential aggressor with havoc and ruin." However strong his words, they could not compete with McCarthy's announcement, just made in New York—and deemed worthy of a bulletin—that one of his Fort Monmouth witnesses had broken down crying and admitted he'd been lying to the committee. According to the announcer, the senator had rushed out of the hearing in the Federal Building, spoken to reporters, and then rushed back in to get what the witness promised would now be the truth.

After a full week in Senator Potter's suite of offices, Tim had grown used to the radio's steady murmur. The Fort Monmouth hearings were making so much news—lab secrets said to be going to East Germany; the alleged spies' links to the now-dead Julius Rosenberg—that you would think they were open to the public, whereas in fact all the news they made came straight from McCarthy himself, whenever he decided to hit the microphones outside the committee room's closed door. The senator seemed determined to justify the urgency with which he'd interrupted his honeymoon last Sunday, even though he was right now the only senator up in New York at the executive sessions. Several staffers—including Mr. Jones, for Senator Potter—were up there, too.

Still not sure what Jones's exact position was, Tim felt it probably didn't matter much. In practical terms, the office's secretary, Miss Cook, a single woman who lived at the Hotel Continental, was the person who kept everyone, Potter included, hopping. She'd directed Tim to answer constituent mail this morning, and right now had him writing a speech on fishing-industry issues that the senator would deliver the next time he was home. Tim had just looked up "sea lamprey" in the encyclopedia.

The staff were encouraged to go into the galleries and listen to the floor debates as often as they liked. The Potter legend—what Tommy McIntyre called "the gimp log-cabin lore"—included the story of how, while learning to walk all over again at Walter Reed, Potter would ask to go to the House and Senate in order to observe the doings of those two august institutions in which he would later serve.

There was little enough action on the floor this week; debate had been replaced by high-pressure caucusing behind the scenes. Since the Democratic mayor of Cleveland had been named to fill the late Senator Taft's seat, it wasn't entirely clear which party controlled the show. At this moment there were forty-eight Democrats and forty-seven Republicans, but between Senator Morse (an Independent pledged to organize with the GOP) and Vice President Nixon, who could break a tie, Ike's party might be able to hang on, just barely, to its committee chairmanships and agenda. "Our fellas better get some exercise and lay off the spuds," Tommy had declared while breezing through the office a couple of days ago. "One bad heart attack and we'll all be ordering new stationery."

Tim now took care not to let any crumbs from Mrs. Potter's sugar cookies fall onto the draft of the speech. Everyone agreed that the senator's wife, who often baked for the staff in the kitchen of the Potters' ninety-dollar-a-month Arlington apartment, was a warmhearted, if flighty, woman. Lorraine Potter's particular part in the legend of limblessness involved her supposedly having sprung bolt upright in bed, back in Cheboygan in '45, at the exact moment Potter stepped on the land mine in France. Her own legs, she swore, had gone numb for several minutes.

So far nothing Tim had worked on came close in importance to the paragraph of remarks he'd auditioned with, and which, so far as he could tell, Potter had never actually delivered. The little speech now sat in a file with Stevenson's original call for a nonaggression pact, along with Knowland's subsequent attack and reactions from several other figures. Winston Churchill himself had announced that he saw nothing terribly wrong with the idea—perhaps, Tim thought, a backhanded way of suggesting its irrelevance.

"The scourge of Adlai!" cried Tommy McIntyre, suddenly passing through the room with a cackle and a snort. The interruption made Tim happy. He hadn't talked to anyone for an hour and a half.

"I bring you tidings from the New York Federal Building," Tommy said.

"You mean the witness who broke down crying?"

"No," said Tommy, smiling even wider. "Somewhat older tidings," he said, slapping an inch-thick typescript onto Tim's desk. "Last Thursday's transcript. Turn to where it's dog-eared, Mr. Laughlin."

> MR. COHN: Have you been told about any of the charges against Mr. Yamins?
>
> MR. CORWIN (witness): No, sir, I haven't.
>
> MR. COHN: Was he pretty friendly with Mr. Coleman?
>
> MR. CORWIN (witness): Well, I would say they were friendly. I don't think they had much social contact.
>
> MR. JONES: Friendly in what respect, then?
>
> MR. CORWIN (witness): Well, they worked together, and it was a companionship.
>
> MR. JONES: Scientific companionship more than a social companionship?
>
> MR. CORWIN (witness): I would say so, yes, sir.
>
> MR. SCHINE: Mr. Corwin, you lived with Mr. Coleman, didn't you?

Tim looked up, worried where this transcribed colloquy ("it was a companionship") might be headed. But Tommy, who seemed to have something different on his mind, just roared with delight and derision: "Jones and Cohn and Schine. Like three kids playing gumshoe up in their tree house! Our boy Roy even calls Schine 'Mr. Chairman' from time to time! Dontcha think a little adult supervision might be in order? There ain't a single solon in the room. And look at this," Tommy added, flipping to the title page of the binder, where he'd circled "Robert Jones, administrative assistant to Senator Potter."

For his look of perplexity, Tim earned a playful swat with the transcript. " 'Administrative assistant' my Aunt Fanny," declared Tommy. "He's a goddamn researcher, almost as low on this totem pole as *you* are, if you'll forgive me, Mr. Timothy."

"Is he in trouble?" Tim asked. "Mr. Jones, I mean."

"All in good time, all in good time. Why don't you take this document and put it on his desk, sport? And keep it open to the dog-eared page."

McIntyre then quickly left, no doubt headed back to the cloakroom machinations over the Republicans' new minority majority.

Tim walked into the next room and put the transcript on Mr. Jones's desk. He could see from some notes on the blotter that Jones, too, was trawling after statistics on the sea lamprey. But that was hardly all. The desk, even with no one in the chair behind it, appeared to be a very busy place. Even more prominent on the blotter was a cutting from last Wednesday's *Star*, a small, discreet story about a twenty-five-year-old theological student's conviction for soliciting an undercover police officer in Lafayette Square. The item wouldn't have made the paper at all were the student not the son of Senator Lester Hunt, a Democrat from Wyoming.

The clipping made Tim burn with a terrible feeling of foolishness. He could see himself as the hapless theological student and Hawkins Fuller as Officer John A. Constanzo of the District Police. For days now he had been imagining the contempt Fuller must be feeling for him, ever since the sentimental gesture of the book, with its unguarded inscription, had revealed Timothy Laughlin to be someone who'd gotten completely the wrong idea about a friendly chat in Dupont Circle, and completely the wrong idea about Hawkins Fuller, a normal man whose fraternal, collegial favor—a simple job-hunting tip—had been twisted by the recipient into a distasteful opportunity to seek another sort of favor entirely.

For each of the last several nights, Tim had been unable to banish his longing for Fuller, or the stupid, unextinguished hope that the older man might yet send him a kind note, maybe when he had finished the Lodge biography. Nor could he cease dwelling on the ugly probability that the book had been thrown away, along with whatever few seconds of infinitesimal regard Fuller had had for that skinny little queer on the park bench.

It was 4:35 p.m. Tim fought the temptation to picture, for the hundredth time, what Hawkins Fuller must look like sitting at his desk in the clean aquamarine precincts of the State Department. Instead, he took one last look at the desktop in front of him and could not resist picking up the topmost letter on yet another stack of Jones's pending concerns.

It was typed with a lack of accuracy that seemed more heartfelt than sloppy:

> the Chinese doctor threatened to take me to to the hospital, on account of my frostbitten feet. My two big toe bones were sticking out, and the area around them looked real decayed. I knew that 90 or 95 percent of the men who went to the hospital never came out of it, so when the doctor left the room for five minutes, I took a fingernail (all our fingernails were real long and dirty) and punched it around the bones and broke off both of my big toes. I threw them across the floor so they'd be out of sight. The Chinese doctor came back in and he said "you go to hospital" and I said "nothing doing, my feet are okay," and he said "let me look." And he took a look and I had the bones broke off, and the feet now didn't look so decayed and he said "okay" and went outside the door and never bothered me again. I knew if I'd gone to the hospital I'd have never got out of it.

This letter from Sergeant Wendell Treffery, recently repatriated from Korea to the army hospital at Walton, Massachusetts, must be part of the preparations for Potter's atrocity hearings.

A second letter in the pile came from Sergeant First Class George J. Matta, who described the shallow graves he'd seen dug for American POWs in Korea:

> we would come the next time and the rain would have washed the dirt away and there would be nothing there but bones. We went back and we got on to them about it, about the people digging up the graves and taking the clothes. They tried to tell us it was the dogs that did it, that did the digging. (They must have had pretty smart dogs that could dig the graves and take the clothes off the men.) I suppose you could call that "brainwashing," but you'll excuse me if I tell you I think it was just typical b.s. from these monsters.

This, Tim told himself, was why he was here. Communism—and whatever could be done about it—was more important than Jones's grandstanding, or even McCarthy's, more important than his own being in love with some handsome phantom who must now despise him.

He lingered at Jones's desk, reading letter after letter from hospital after hospital. He thought of Father Beane and the missionaries, and he wondered, guiltily, why his own feet should not be freezing and bleeding in the Asian snow.

———

"Can't say much for the hat," Beverly Phillips declared. "It looks like an upside-down lightbulb, don't you think? The suit's pretty, though."

Mary looked hard at the hemline. "That's *still* shorter than what I've got, I'm pretty sure. I raised the last of my old skirts a couple of weeks ago, and I'm not about to drag out the machine again."

"Ah," said Beverly. "Your evening with Fuller, right?" She mocked herself with a sigh: "*Some* of us are just barnacles on his dreamboat."

Mary laughed. "Oh, Jesus, Beverly."

"I'm sorry. I sound like Miss Lightfoot, God forbid. It's none of my business, honey. I also apologize for dragging you here." This morning Beverly had asked Mary if she'd like the second of two complimentary tickets she had for this late-afternoon fashion show at the Mayflower Hotel. During the past hour the women had finished off a plate of sandwiches and two cocktails apiece.

"Anything that's gratis," said Beverly. "I'm still 'Helen Holden, Government Girl.' " When Mary's expression showed no recognition of the old radio serial and its plucky, thrifty heroine, Beverly sighed. "You're too young to remember. And I'm too old for the part." Nearing forty and divorced for several years, Beverly Phillips was raising two sons, who would soon be waiting for their dinner, up in Friendship Heights.

The last pair of new outfits started down the makeshift runway. "Did you see Perle Mesta's article this morning?" asked Mary. The city's best-known hostess was over in Russia, filing pieces with the *Washington Post* on the subject of Soviet women.

"About all those butch gals wearing construction helmets and rebuilding Stalingrad?" Beverly asked.

"She says even the expensive dresses look like junk compared to what you can get over here for five dollars at Woodie's."

"Well, the one that came past me a minute ago cost forty-five bucks, and I'm not a big enough capitalist for that."

"Are you sure you won't join us?" asked Mary. After agreeing to go to the fashion show, she had phoned her date and told him to meet her here at the Mayflower.

"Don't be silly," said Beverly. "I never mind being a fifth wheel, but if I don't get going soon the boys are likely to burn down the house. So where's he taking you?"

"We'll probably wind up having dinner here. Maybe the movies afterward, though I think the poster for *From Here to Eternity* scares him a little."

"The shy type? I like that. In fact, I'd rather have that than Burt Lancaster. Who is this non-beast?"

"His name's Paul Hildebrand. His family owns one of the breweries along the river."

"What happened to young Dr. Malone?"

"He's been operating a little slowly for my taste."

"So how'd you meet the brewer?"

"It's embarrassing. Millie Brisson, the secretary to the congressman who got me my first job—that friend of my father's—fixed it up. The poor woman must feel I've got her on a lifetime retainer."

Beverly reached for her gloves. "Mary, you're a catch. And I, personally, would kill to be—what are you, twenty-eight? Anyway, are things with this guy promising?"

"I've got no idea. It's only a second date."

"Okay," said Beverly, a strong believer in realism in these matters, "when and where was the first date?"

"About ten days ago. The last of those outdoor Watergate concerts, on the river. He's been traveling since then."

"See?" said Mrs. Phillips. "You're keeping track. You *are* interested."

"He hates politics," Mary added.

"Grab him," said Mrs. Phillips.

The temperature was supposed to drop into the forties tonight, so Tim opened up the window to coax in whatever cool breeze might be on its way. After work he had stopped into church, and back here he'd fallen asleep on the couch. He had awakened only a few minutes ago and changed into a T-shirt and dungarees. Keeping the radio low, he now listened to *Mr. Keen, Tracer of Lost Persons*, as he opened up a can of soup. With most of his old programs turning into television shows or disappearing altogether, it was nice to know that this one could still be found on the air at eight o'clock on Friday nights.

He added water to the pot and decided that once he got past a couple of paydays, he would call Bobby Garahan and agree to that dinner at Duke Zeibert's. His old Fordham friend was now working for an insurance company down here and thought the two of them ought to go out one night and act like big knife-and-fork men to celebrate being grown-up wage earners who lived away from home. Bobby was sort of dull, but it might be some time before Tim made friends at work, given how the location of Senator Potter's office put him so far from all the other Hill rats over in the SOB. Maybe when the subcommittee got back from New York, he'd get to spend more time over there.

Mr. Keen's voice was giving way to the announcer's pitch for tooth powder when Tim heard a knock on the door. He turned off the radio. Could there really have been a complaint from someone? He was wearing socks, after all, and had hardly stepped off the thick braided rug. He moved quietly toward the door, which had no peephole—another sign of the apartment's illegality—and cautiously opened it up.

"You're not 'on the phone,' " said Hawkins Fuller, who placed his hands high on each side of the doorframe. A head taller than Tim, he smiled down as if from a crucifix.

"I'm not even on the lease." Tim could feel his face getting very red. He imagined he was smiling, but wasn't sure.

"Ah," said Fuller, "a desperado." He took his hands from the doorframe and put them on Tim's shoulders, moving the smaller man aside so that he himself could enter the room. He sat down on the desktop and motioned for Tim to take the chair next to the hot plate.

"Hey," said Tim, laughing. "Whose place is this, anyway?"

"Not yours, apparently."

"You're right. But as long as I lie low, and don't have any *visitors* . . ."

On the desk beside one of Fuller's flanneled thighs, Tim noticed the *Star*'s radio listings. Why couldn't it be the serious novel that was open but unnoticeable at the foot of the neatly made bed?

"What's in there?" asked Fuller, pointing toward the hot plate.

"Chicken noodle soup." Grateful for something to do besides stare, Tim went over to stir the pot. "There's probably enough for two."

He saw Fuller look at the Campbell's can and make a face. "Why don't you let me buy you supper someplace? You brought me a book, remember?"

"But that was to thank *you*. Besides," said Tim, swallowing the last inch of a glass of milk he had on the counter, "it's a sin to waste food."

"Mortal or venial?" asked Fuller.

Tim looked into the pot as he resumed stirring. "In this case, I'd have to say venial."

"What if you were to let me kiss you, Laughlin? Would that be mortal or venial?"

It was as if Father O'Connell, made somehow young and beautiful, had appeared in a dream to examine him for Confirmation.

"Mortal, I'm pretty sure." He felt the beating of his heart. "How come a Protestant like you knows stuff like that?"

Further resembling Father O'Connell, Fuller refused to countenance any wriggling out of the matter at hand. "Would you *like* me to kiss you?"

Tim stopped stirring and looked down into the bubbles that began to hiss around the wooden spoon. "No, Mr. Fuller," he made himself say.

"Well, that one's got to be mortal."

Tim shut off the hot plate but didn't turn around. "What do you mean?"

"If the *size* of the lie figures in, that one can't possibly be a venial sin."

Fuller got up from the desk. He took down two bowls from the open shelf. "Spoons?"

"Who is that awful woman?" asked Paul Hildebrand.

"May Craig," Mary told him.

"Some sort of news-hen?"

"Yes," said Mary, who had to laugh. How could a native Washingtonian not know of this character who wrote for a handful of newspapers up in Maine but managed to attract the continual notice of presidents? Miss Craig had swept into the Mayflower's dining room a few moments ago, around nine-thirty, having just come from New York and, before that, Morocco, where she'd spent a couple of weeks in the U.S. Air Force hospi-

tal with a touch—"a *big* touch," she now squawked—of food poison-
ing. She continued in a near-shout: "I thought Senator You-Know-Who
would still be cuddling his bride down in Nassau when I docked. But
there he was, right in Foley Square!"

Somebody at the table next to Miss Craig's asked if she'd been outside
the room for "Mr. Lied-and-Cried" this afternoon.

"No," she admitted, "but that'd be a good headline for tomorrow's
Daily News!"

Paul Hildebrand swallowed half a chicken croquette and a gulp of
Cutty Sark. "God," he said softly. "I wish she'd shut up."

Mary looked across the table and considered her date. It pained him
to make such a remark about a woman, she realized. Yes, he was old-
fashioned, as was the style of his pleasant looks: the three-quarter part in
the curly dark-blond hair, the slightly reddish complexion. Was there,
beneath, she wondered, more of a spark than resided in her doctor?

"They were even talking about 'Mr. Lied-and-Cried' at the fashion
show," she finally said.

"That's only because we're *here*," he replied. "In Washington, I mean.
They wouldn't have been talking about it in Omaha." He mentioned the
city without a trace of condescension.

"I doubt the dresses would have been as pretty there."

"Probably not. Another?" he asked, holding up her own empty glass
of Cutty Sark.

"Yes."

As he signaled for the waiter, Mary said, "Well, I'm just praying that
he flames out soon."

Even Paul Hildebrand didn't need to be told who "he" was, but he
responded with a question: "Know what I'm praying for? *Rain*. The
drought in the Midwest is driving the price of hops sky-high. You think
the country's really waiting around and wondering if Ike's going to start
fighting McCarthy? Mary, most of it just wants him to fire Ezra Taft
Benson and get a new Agriculture secretary. You know, my brother and I
are going to have to dump the brewery into the Potomac if things don't
get better soon."

"Are you looking for a new line of work?" asked Mary.

"Not yet," he replied. "First I'm looking for a girl to marry me."

Fuller grabbed one of Tim's wrists, lifted the boy's arm, and pinned it to the pillow. Tim surmised the shift in position to be for the greater comfort of the older man in the narrow bed, until he felt Fuller kiss his armpit. He froze for a moment, but with the increasing pressure and sweep of the other man's mouth, he felt Fuller's avidity and abandon transferring themselves to him. He realized he was no longer caressing Fuller's thick black hair; he was pulling it, forcefully.

The act seemed to agitate Fuller—to excite or anger him, Tim couldn't tell for sure. But the older man, fully aroused, began to press his body more and more forcefully against him. Tim could see the damp beginnings of sweat on Fuller's face and in the hollow of his neck, where he'd seen it two weeks ago and had thought about its being every day since. He felt an ardor in his own helplessness, recognized that what he right now most desired was to have no say in this, no word about it but yes.

By the time he was in Fuller's mouth, and digging his clean, bitten nails into the other man's shoulders, he could feel the tears on his own face. He became afraid of losing all physical control, of ejaculating before he was supposed to. But when, and where, *was* he supposed to? Would Fuller tell him? The older man seemed to sense the approaching climax and relented in his attentions; his face rose back up and smiled wordlessly into Tim's.

And then, at Fuller's unspoken but insistent direction, each of them was lying on his side, facing the same wall. Fuller grasped him from behind and held him close, kissing his neck and asking, "Are you my brave boy?" As Tim nodded yes, Fuller caressed one side of his face; the other side brushed the sheet. Fuller's aroma overpowered the smell of Clorox on the linen, banishing the more familiar fragrance, the one redolent of a thousand Monday nights when Tim had fallen asleep on the results of his mother's wash day.

He turned his head far enough to plunge his face into the muscular flesh of Fuller's chest and shoulder. In response, Fuller tousled and petted his hair, but the next words he said were inflamed, not soothing. "Who owns you?" Fuller whispered, sharply, into his ear.

It sounded like some early piece of the catechism, a cosmically important question-and-answer he had somehow missed, on the order of *Who made us? God made us.* But Tim's confusion, and the desire to respond with the right answer, were lost in his own arousal. He whispered, "Hawkins Fuller," not as an answer to the question, but simply an amazed statement of the other man's actuality. "Hawkins Fuller," he said, repeating this name for a discovery he felt the need to radio from one world to another, this name for a new Eden, whose recently glimpsed existence had now been fully confirmed.

CHAPTER SIX

October 17, 1953

Mary Johnson was awakened in Georgetown by a phone call from Beverly Phillips. At the first ring, she imagined she was back in her old place, a block away, which she'd shared with three other girls. There the phone had always rung early Saturday morning with someone's request for a postmortem of someone else's Friday-night date.

"You want details," Mary said, once Beverly had identified herself. "There aren't any." Which was true. It had been a pleasant but early night whose conversation had turned only moderately flirtatious, even though she and Paul had been drinking more as if he were heir to a distillery than a beer business.

"Well," said Beverly. "As long as there are no *gruesome* details, that qualifies as a good second date. I'm afraid I've got some gruesome details on this end."

"Did the boys burn down the house?"

"No, but Scott McLeod's set fire to Jerry Baumeister. Canned him."

Rubbing her eyes, Mary tried to think. Jerry Baumeister. Office of Educational Exchange? Yes: early thirties; bow tie; made courtly little jokes. "I hardly know him," she told Beverly.

"Neither do I. But he's here, and he's coming apart."

"At your house? At seven-thirty in the morning?"

"He practically arrived with the milkman. I think he'd been wandering around all night. Honest, I barely know him, either, Mary. A couple of lunches in the cafeteria. We've got divorce in common; he's got two well-behaved daughters instead of what I've got. Hang on a second. *Boys*, pipe *down*! I *told* you to go to the *playground*! Sorry, Mary. Anyway, Jerry's girls live with him. The ex-wife drinks and long ago went home to mother. Now he's wondering how he'll feed himself, let alone the daughters."

"What's he done to inflame McLeod? He's a little young to have been in the Party, isn't he?"

"It's more personal than that."

Mary paused for a moment, no more able than Beverly to use the real name for what she now realized they were talking about. "Even with two children?" She knew it was a foolish question.

"Maybe that's why the wife drank. I don't know. I also don't know what to do. He's in the next room. I've given him three cups of coffee and two plates of eggs. The man is *sobbing*, Mary. He thinks he's going to be arrested, for God's sake."

"What can I do?"

"I've no idea. But you actually *know* a couple of these congressmen I've been typing memos to for six years. Isn't there one of them who might apply a little humane pressure?"

"You imagine McLeod will respond to pressure? Let alone the humane kind?"

"I know, I know. There's another half dozen they've just let go besides Jerry, and God knows he's not the prepossessing type anybody's going to make a federal case over. Mary, I'm sorry, I don't know *why* I called. His panic's getting to me. God, maybe *I* should marry him. He'd probably still be a better husband than what I was used to."

"What exactly do they have on him?"

"Just some odds and ends. Rumors. A sighting of him in a bar he shouldn't have been in. Plus things they won't say. He's never been convicted of anything. But he failed their lie-detector test."

Mary looked at the thermometer outside her window and said nothing for a minute. "Beverly, give me your number and let me call you back in a little while."

She dressed for work, agitated by Beverly's news and almost wistful for the cacophony of those Saturday mornings with the roommates on Q Street, when she'd be hacking through the nylon kudzu dangling from the shower-curtain rod and discovering that one of the girls had walked off with her umbrella.

Once out of the house, she moved on foot through Georgetown, passing the antiques shops and little restaurants. She supposed she could understand why the neighborhood drew scorn for being home to the city's "rich, red, and queer," even though right now half its dowagers and old New Dealers were still just heedlessly sleeping. Soon they would awake to shop for groceries or take a stroll along the canal with the same fitful anxiety about the Bomb, no more and no less, as anyone else.

Her mind returned to Scott McLeod and the mystery of why, if the State Department was so ineffectual, everyone worried about it so. If the men only pushed cookies, what should be the harm of their doing it with limp wrists? And why must half the organization have to put in overtime to *help* them do it? The government's Saturday-morning workday had been disappearing before the war; been reinstated for the duration; and then dispensed with once again. And now it was back, at least here and there, thanks to zealousness about the deficit. Mr. Morton, that bright spot of internationalism, didn't come in himself, but the rest of the Congressional Relations staff were expected to put in an appearance, however loosely policed by the weekend time clock. With any luck, poor Beverly could keep attending to Jerry Baumeister and not be missed.

Coming into Foggy Bottom, Mary walked past the chipped Watergate bandshell and the Negroes' gingerbread shanties, which some of State's employees had begun to buy up and make charming. She continued past the warehouses and the gasworks, down toward the old Observatory with its shuttered dome, and, finally, on into State's big box. The building had been put up a decade ago for the War Department, which had outgrown it before ever moving in. From its new Pentagon across the river, the Department of Defense, euphemized and elephantine, was happy to let State have the place.

Three cabinet secretaries had since made the best of it, but that didn't mean she, Mary Johnson, would stay indefinitely in these waxed corridors, down which her low heels now clicked on their way to CR. She removed her scarf as she crossed the threshhold into the bureau's outer office and heard, from farther in, a strong baritone at work on "Surrey with the Fringe on Top." Fuller, who sometimes couldn't make himself stay through a Thursday afternoon, was here bright and early on a Saturday morning.

Mary put a piece of paper into the typewriter and then stared at it, before hearing Miss Lightfoot join Fuller, coquettishly, in song. That thick-skulled cow who so loved to proclaim herself "nobody's fool." She must live at the Y, thought Mary, or in some ancient boardinghouse. Surely no roommates would put up with the array of resentments she so enjoyed displaying here at work, as if they were a tray of jewelry. The woman seemed to imagine that she glowed with wit and good sense whenever she decried the uselessness of Mary's college degree or the "terrible unfairness" of Beverly Phillips' having put her husband through law school only to "wind up" as she had.

But Mary was resentful, too, more than ever—of Fuller. Did he know about Jerry Baumeister? He was perfectly capable of singing even if he did.

"Would you like this to go to *both* Pennsylvania senators?" trilled Miss Lightfoot, whose hat was visible in Fuller's doorway. Mary guessed that the two of them were working on another appeal for votes against the Bricker Amendment, which would radically limit the president's ability to make treaties with foreign powers. Love must trump politics, thought Mary; she could not imagine that Miss Lightfoot wasn't personally in favor of the amendment, a pet conservative proposal.

"Oh, yes," said Fuller. "The more the merrier, Miss Lightfoot. I'll be back in a flash."

He emerged from his office, startled to see Mary, who continued to peer at her typewriter carriage.

"Do you enjoy her company?" she whispered, almost in a hiss.

Fuller sat down on the edge of her desk. "What do *you* think?" his expression seemed to say. Mary remained silent.

"We *are* likely to set an office productivity record for a Saturday morning," he cheerfully declared. "Except for you. What's this blank page supposed to be?" He tapped the typewriter.

"My letter of resignation." Visibly upset, Mary rose from her chair. Fuller followed her into the corridor. "You're carrying this nostalgia for Acheson a bit far," he said.

"Stop playing the handsome idiot." She paused long enough to make him certain that he was being insulted, not flirted with. "It just occurred to me," she then added, "you're pretty much my boss. Fire me, and I'll get whatever unemployed GS-4's get."

Fuller said nothing.

"Do you know they've fired Jerry Baumeister?"

"I don't even know who he is."

"He is, or was," Mary explained, "in the office of Educational Exchange."

"What's his problem? Pink or lavender?"

For a moment she would gladly have thrown Fuller himself to McLeod's wolves.

"Lavender," she forced herself to reply.

Again, he said nothing. He seemed to be searching his memory, trying perhaps to recall whether Jerry Baumeister had been one of the department's "summer bachelors," the type known to make a pass at another man while his own wife was up in Maine.

"Fuller," she said, as evenly as she could, "this is not right."

"Would your resigning be?"

"It would give me the pleasure of making a gesture."

She saw that he would not be drawn in, and she knew that she should walk away. But she was too angry for that. "I don't see any bags under your eyes," she told him. "I guess you didn't have one of your late nights *last* night."

Fuller shrugged. "A moderately late one."

"Oh? When did you fall asleep?"

"When Irish eyes were smiling," he answered. And then he disappeared down the hall.

Maybe he *would* fire her. Once he was out of sight, Mary composed herself and returned to her desk. Miss Lightfoot was singing "People Will Say We're in Love."

"We are all back here on Saturday because an urgent situation has arisen," Roy Cohn informed everyone in Room 29 of the Federal Building in New York. "There is a direct conflict in testimony which we have to resolve."

The urgency of determining whether or not Mr. Joseph Levitsky had actually said, upon the arrest of Julius Rosenberg in 1950, "But for the grace of God there go I," was, to Levitsky's lawyer, Leonard Boudin, debatable at best. Boudin announced that he was instructing his client, who a decade before had been with the Army Signal Corps at Fort Monmouth, to plead the Fifth Amendment to all questions involving Rosenberg and Mr. Carl Greenblum, the man who had lied and cried in front of the committee yesterday afternoon.

When Senator McCarthy, "in fairness to the witness," now informed Levitsky that he would be cited for contempt, Boudin asked if any members of the committee other than the chairman were present in the hearing room.

"No," McCarthy explained. "There is the administrative assistant to Senator Dirksen, Mr. Rainville, and the assistant to Senator Potter, Robert Jones."

For the rest of the morning, Jones himself remained pleased at the thought of his name being read into the record by the chairman himself. Otherwise he was principally aware of a new tenseness between Cohn and John Adams, the army counsel who was here in the service's interest to observe the proceedings. Adams had so far been stressing the absence of any problem between the Pentagon and McCarthy, but now, as today's hearing was recessed until Monday, Jones noted the cool glances exchanged by the army's lawyer and McCarthy's. The chairman tended to ignore Adams, but McCarthy seemed inexplicably deferential toward Cohn, even scared. Before questioning Levitsky himself, the senator had almost sought the young counsel's permission.

There was no time to puzzle out the incongruity, because to Jones's astonishment, McCarthy was now walking toward him. "Bill!" called the chairman, clapping his shoulder. "Why don't you come out to lunch with all of us at Gasner's? After all, we don't know how much longer Dave will be around." The induction into the army of committee consultant G. David Schine was said to be imminent.

Jones's pleasure at being invited trumped any disappointment over the chairman's forgetting that he was Bob, not Bill. There might be an opportunity to straighten that out over lunch, a prospect that looked even brighter once he got a seat next to McCarthy, with Adams across from him and Schine and Cohn at the other end of the table.

"Senator," Jones asked, while the waiter set down some glasses, "did you hear what Eleanor said up in Connecticut last night? She told the League of Women Voters that Roy and Dave are a bigger threat to the country than Hiss ever was."

McCarthy, chuckling, seemed pleased. Jones looked down the table and saw that Cohn, busy regarding Schine, had not overheard.

"You know," said McCarthy, grabbing a Manhattan off the waiter's tray, "the Pentagon could use some guys like you, Bill." The senator added, with a certain embarrassment, to avoid offending Adams: "I don't mean you're not all right, John."

Adams, efficiently ordering from the menu, gave a thin smile to indicate that no offense had been taken. But then he looked away, toward Cohn and Schine, and it was McCarthy who seemed a little hurt.

"So," Cohn called out, once he'd caught the army counsel's eye, "am I going to be allowed in on Tuesday?" The committee had told Secretary of the Army Robert Stevens, Adams' boss, that it was planning a field trip to the radar operation at Fort Monmouth.

"It's uncertain," said Adams. "In Stevens' view, it's up to the commanding officer."

"Communists can get in!" cried Cohn, throwing his napkin onto his plate. "Whole carpools of them can go to work there for years at a time! But not me!"

"Roy," McCarthy said, evenly, "hold on."

"I will not hold on! We're getting nothing but excuses and obstruction. We were promised cooperation."

Adams crumbled some crackers into his soup. "We have been very accommodating and will continue to be—"

"Horseshit, John," said Cohn, who then looked at Schine and recalled that the hotel-chain heir's family did not like swearing. "Baloney! What I want to know most is, what's going to happen when Dave's inducted in two weeks."

Adams ate a spoonful of clam chowder. "Mr. Stevens will try to find him something worthy of his talents."

Schine, handsome and blond, seemed moderately intrigued by how little it took to get Roy all excited.

"Dave is essential to the operation of this commitee," insisted Cohn. "His expertise—"

Knowing that Schine's expertise had been demonstrated mostly by his authorship of a pamphlet about communism's historical perfidy—an error-filled monograph that had gone into his family's hotel rooms like the Gideon Bible—Adams quietly repeated to Cohn that Secretary Stevens would see what he could do.

"That's your answer for everything—from clearances to Communists to KP! Which Dave is not going to be wasted doing with some bunch of goddamned hillbillies in a barracks!"

Schine put his hand on Cohn's arm. "Roy, enough. It's okay."

"No, it's not okay." Sotto voce, he reminded Schine of all the favors his family had done for Adams during the last couple of weeks up here in New York—the free hotel rooms, the comped theater tickets. Then, back to fortissimo, he barked out, for the whole table's benefit, statistics on security risks and Communist sympathizers at Fort Monmouth.

McCarthy grinned nervously at Jones, as if trying to pretend to a guest that there was nothing seriously wrong with the child at the end of the table. "Tell me about yourself," he said to the research assistant. The chairman indicated to Adams, still methodically finishing his soup, that it was okay for him to join this precinct of the conversation instead of Roy's.

In the course of giving an abbreviated life story—from his birth in Biddeford, Maine, to his days at Bates College and in the army during the war—Jones gently clarified the fact that he was a Bob, not a Bill. Reaching the recent past, he told the chairman: "Before Potter, I worked for Senator Brewster."

McCarthy nodded, recalling his retired Republican colleague from Maine. "Better than that old bag they've got in now."

It was Jones's turn to laugh, at McCarthy's scornful reference to Senator Margaret Chase Smith and her now-famous "declaration of conscience" against the chairman. "Sir, she couldn't find her bloomers, let alone her conscience. Or a Communist."

McCarthy slapped the tablecloth in appreciation, then signaled for another Manhattan. He'd decided to skip any food. "So what's it like working for Charlie?" he asked Jones.

After a moment's hesitation, the research assistant answered, "Oh, he's a fine guy." But realizing he had nothing more to say, Jones boldly changed the subject. "Sir, can you tell me how you plan to handle Levitsky in open session?"

McCarthy, who proceeded by more or less constant improvisation, had clearly not given the matter any thought. "Got any ideas?" he asked Jones.

"Yes, I do," said the research assistant, seizing his chance. "You need to leak what he said about Rosenberg to the press. That piece of testimony where he directly lies."

"Actually," said Adams, cutting into his fish, "Levitsky didn't say that himself."

McCarthy invited Jones to respond, which the younger man did almost immediately. "Does it matter? Greenblum *says* he said it. And at this point his word is better than some Fifth-Amendment Communist's. If we want to sustain public interest in this, let people think Rosenberg is still influencing things from beyond the grave. That'll scare them a lot more than one more fag at the State Department. Or at the head of the Democratic ticket."

McCarthy waved an empty fork to get the interest of the other end of the table, as if here at last were a topic around which he could unite the whole family. "Roy," he called, "you think there are any reporters still around the Fed building?"

Jones's mind was moving fast. If he could make himself useful here, he'd be able to get that drunken leprechaun McIntyre off his back. Maybe even get himself out of Potter's office and into the chairman's own.

Tim sat in a pew at the front of St. Peter's fifteen minutes before Saturday afternoon confessions were to begin. Nearby he could see two women who had arrived early for the sacrament: an elderly lady, perhaps eager to begin the only conversation she would have all week, and a pretty girl his own age, probably hoping to finish here in plenty of time to get ready for a date.

From the moment he'd reached the corner of Second and C streets and stood before the church doors, Tim had known that he would not be entering the confessional this afternoon. The church's yellow brick tower and parapets had seemed like a papier-mâché stage set for one of Shakespeare's sunniest Italian comedies, just as here inside, the red-and-green pattern repeating itself from one stained-glass window to the next resembled Christmas wrapping paper, the kind whose expense always provoked disapproving clucks from Grandma Gaffney before she slid her own annual gifts, unwrapped cartons of cigarettes, across the dining room table to her daughters and son. Even the plain Ionic columns here inside St. Peter's, so different from the blood-streaked marble at St. Matthew's, seemed ready to invite Kilroy's signature or the crayon drawings of children.

Tim would pray, but he would not confess. He was here to make a separate peace, the way the Russians had—he'd seen it referenced in the Lodge biography—during the First World War. Rising from the pew, he headed to the little chapel, just off the altar, dedicated to the Blessed Virgin Mary. He had been hiding behind her skirts his whole life, and as he knelt before the chapel's rack of tall blue candles, he felt certain she would understand his predicament. She might not be part of the Trinity, but her ex officio position, as the intercessor who had God's ear, had always made her something like Mrs. Roosevelt, the person to go to first.

In the *Baltimore Catechism*, the source of all Tim's knowledge of the world above this one, the Trinity had been depicted as a shamrock—the visual analogy closest to hand for the Irish clergyman who'd written the text. But what if one added another leaf, the way one used to, with an artful graft, after hunting in vain for four-leaf clovers on the small patch of grass in the playground near Holy Cross? Tim did not plan to worship Hawkins Fuller, but why couldn't his love for him be attached to the love he already felt for the actual Trinity? Had he not, in fact, always been in love, physically and particularly, with Christ, whose dark, haloed image on every calendar and classroom wall glowed more handsomely than any man walking His Earth? Had not Father McGuire, in the first pages of the catechism, promised a kind of divine romance? *God has been very, very good to you. He thinks more of you than He does of anything else in this world. To you alone He has given an invitation to live with Him in heaven forever.*

When Hawkins had removed Tim's shirt and seen the scapular beneath it, the older man had not seemed surprised, and he had made no joke. He had hung it, without comment, over one of the bedposts at the headboard, where, whenever Tim glimpsed it during the night, it seemed no more out of place—and no less protective—than it did when draped over his own narrow chest and back.

How many mortal sins had he committed last night? Did each separate act he and Hawkins performed constitute an individual transgression, or was their entire three hours together—until Hawkins left, after some chatter and a tousle of his hair but no actual goodbye kiss—a single offense? It didn't matter, because either way, he, Timothy Patrick Laughlin, was dead. Mortal sin, said the catechism, *kills the life of grace in our souls. That is why the sacrament of penance is called a sacrament of the dead.* And one could not perform penance without making a confession, any more than one could make a confession without perfect contrition—which he did not feel. To his astonishment, he did not *want* to feel it, however well he had once mastered Father McGuire's illustration of these matters. *Elizabeth says: "Anyone who commits even one mortal sin does more harm than hundreds and hundreds of earthquakes ever could do." She is right.* As the words came back to Tim now, he pictured the ground below the 38th Parallel opening up and swallowing a thousand American soldiers.

Bless me, Father, for I have sinned.... Because he could not say these words this afternoon, his heart would pound with fear tonight. *If I should die before I wake ...* Could he live, for even a little while, without grace—drained of it, like the empty black milk bottle the catechism drew for a soul with mortal or Original Sin? No. And he could not take Saint Augustine's approach, asking to be made pure but just now, because the truth—and God loves the truth—was that Timothy Laughlin had never felt so pure as he had last night.

CHAPTER SEVEN

November 10, 1953

None of the twelve televisions on display at Hecht's had its sound up. Eleven of them, this Tuesday night, were tuned to Milton Berle, cavorting in women's clothes and silence, while the twelfth showed Bishop Sheen returning from a commercial break to find that his blackboard had been erased, as always, by Skippy, the unseen angel he liked to claim was a member of the cherubim's Local 20. The clean slate waited, in the silence, for a word, the name of the last theme Sheen would take up before the program ended at eight-thirty. RECONCILIATION, it turned out to be, and as soon as he'd written it, Sheen turned his elegant figure and blazing eyes to the camera.

Tim was almost able to read the bishop's lips, which he knew would soon speak the broadcast's weekly envoi, *God love you*, that comforting wish caught somewhere between the subjunctive and imperative.

Tim figured he could spend another half hour browsing the book department until the store closed at nine. And then, knowing that Hawkins didn't like him showing up till past ten, he would kill another ninety minutes out on the street. In the past few weeks he'd been to the apartment on I Street four times, and before each visit, including tonight's, he had called hours ahead from a pay phone near his own room to make sure he'd be welcome.

Exiting the store under a cloudy night sky, Tim wandered through what was left of Lincoln's Washington: east on F Street past the Patent Office and old marble Tariff Building, then all the way down into China-town toward Mrs. Surratt's boardinghouse. Turning south, he made his way to Pennsylvania Avenue, where he began to walk in the opposite direction from the one he'd traveled on the streetcar six weeks ago with the then anonymous Hawkins Fuller. Passing the White House and looking at the lights in the residence, Tim wondered if Eisenhower would be up late deciding whether to support or criticize HUAC's subpoena of Harry Truman. All these years later, Attorney General Brownell was now insisting that the ex-president had knowingly promoted a Communist at Treasury named Harry Dexter White.

The snow from Friday's freak blizzard was already gone. Tim now recalled setting out for Hawkins' apartment that night, after it had started coming down. Although he'd been greeted with the gentle ministrations of a terry-cloth towel, he had even then not been asked to stay the night. Around two a.m. Hawkins had drawn attention to a lull in the storm and matter-of-factly discovered an extra pair of galoshes that would just about fit Tim.

Who, he'd wondered, had been their previous owner? But he had not asked. After all, nearly a month since their first hours in his own bed on Capitol Hill, he and Fuller had yet to take a walk together or share a meal. Hawkins *had* once shown up, unannounced, at the room above the hardware store, bearing a quart of milk (a joke) and a candy bar. They had eaten the candy bar in bed, but that hardly ranked with going out to a restaurant or making supper together.

Were he and Hawkins having an "affair"? Actually, Tim couldn't see that the word, with its implications of brevity and furtiveness, did the situation justice. Devoid of any previous romantic experience, he had lived these three weeks as an eternity of happiness. This wasn't, he told himself, even technically like *Back Street*, since Hawkins, thank God, had not turned out to be married. That possibility, the ne plus ultra of Tim's imaginings about the worldly and perverse, had been lifted from his mind the first night he had walked into Fuller's almost comically authentic bachelor apartment on the fifth floor of 2124 I.

Reentering the pale brick building tonight, Tim decided to take the stairs instead of the elevator to number 5B, partly to experience a pleasant envy of the career girls and med students who got to live in such proximity to Hawkins—but mostly to kill a last minute of time, enough to put him past ten-thirty on his graduation wristwatch.

"It's open," said Hawkins, above the clatter of kitchen cleanup.

In Tim went, but only past the threshhold. From that spot he stared into Hawkins' bedroom through its half-open door. He could see the Norwegian flag, half curled up like the tin of a sardine can, a souvenir of the Fulbright year. On the floor were sneakers and a T-shirt—used, Tim supposed, late this afternoon in the twice-a-week handball game Hawkins played at the GWU gym. Tim felt an even stronger desire to take hold of the shirt, to put his face against it, than he did to rush into the kitchen and touch Hawkins himself—as if the saint's relics would provide an equally keen, but less risky, jolt than the saint. He forced his eyes away from the shirt and sneakers, and away from the framed photograph of Hawkins' parents, who surely couldn't, any more than his own, imagine or tolerate what would happen tonight in this bedroom.

And then, there, all at once, wearing dark suit trousers and a white shirt, the sleeves rolled up and his arms still wet—stood Hawkins himself.

"Hi, buddy." Hawkins' arm fell across his shoulder, helping to lead him to the living-room couch, where, until he was encircled by both arms, there would be several minutes of conversation, during which he would probably learn another few facts of Hawkins' life story: the name of a sister or childhood pet, the location of his boat on the day Japan surrendered. While scavenging these bits of knowledge, Tim would feign casualness, like an undercover agent in East Berlin. Desperate to avoid expulsion, he would never try the patience of his quarry by asking one question too many.

Hawkins poured them both an inch of rye whiskey from the bottle on the coffee table—a real drink, not the *dulce de leche* (another milk joke, out of *Guys and Dolls*) that he'd been offered his first time here. Tim hardly needed the alcohol to be unlocked like Sister Sarah, but he knew a shot of it would complete his abandonment, would make him crave and even ask for whatever piece of action or technique Hawkins had last time had to coax him toward with a soothing interrogative or sharp, warning whisper.

Tim looked past the coffee table at *See It Now*. The television was barely louder than the ones in Hecht's, and Hawkins now made it clear he hadn't actually been waiting for Edward R. Murrow to come on with the latest about Trieste and Harry Dexter White. "The thing's been running since *Pantomime Quiz*," Hawkins informed him, as if the television were just some curiously animate table on which he'd rested two Lena Horne records and his hat. Tim nodded, his eyes leaving Murrow in order to proceed with his usual inventory: the extra alarm clock; the Harvard diploma; the necktie from Saltz Brothers draped over the diploma's frame.

"I'm sure you can read more of it than I can," said Hawkins, pointing to the diploma's Latin text.

Tim smiled. "Do you really think there's not a *single* Communist on their faculty?" Harvard's new president had declared exactly that, yesterday, in response to McCarthy.

"Harvard doesn't *need* Communists," said Fuller. "The Ivy League undergraduate mentality is already more collective than anything you'd find on a Soviet wheat farm." He made some robotic rowing movements that had Tim laughing just before the telephone rang.

The caller was somewhere so noisy that Fuller tried covering his free ear to hear him better. "You sound like you're down at the Jewel Box," he shouted over the apparent din on the other end. "You *are*?" he asked, laughing, his voice higher than usual. "Well, let me get back to you tomorrow." A second call, almost immediately after the first, was from Fuller's mother; he told her, too, that he would ring back the next day.

"Mother is bored with Father," said Hawkins, returning to the couch and once more putting his arm around Tim. "She needs a new cause. Getting Eisenhower nominated wasn't much of one, and it's been made obsolete by its own success."

"I did my own small bit for that," said Tim, knowing he was setting himself up to be teased. He told Hawkins of how, while at Fordham, he had worked part-time, mostly running errands, for Tex McCrary's public relations firm. "You weren't aware of my proximity to the famous, were you?" he asked, hoping to provoke some laughter and roughhousing. "I had to pass out leaflets at the big Draft Ike rally in Madison Square Garden. My father wanted Taft, and he was *not* pleased."

"Neither was mine," said Hawkins. "I was at the rally, too."

"You're kidding," said Tim, almost wheeling out of his embrace.

"Accompanying my mother. And thereby annoying my father, who reminded me that a State Department employee shouldn't be at such a gathering."

Tim's mind was far away from politics and the Hatch Act. He had soared into the realm of romance and fate, and before he could stop himself, he asked: "I wonder what would have happened if we'd met there, that day, instead of in Dupont Circle." He winced as soon as the words—too presumptuous—were out of his mouth.

Hawkins grinned from his well-defended battlement. "You'd have been sorely disappointed."

"How so?" said Tim, the whiskey putting him in for a penny, in for a pound.

"Because I had an assignation that night with a musician. Who," Hawkins said, pulling Tim close enough for whispering, "does things you haven't even dreamed of." He pulled back in time to catch the blush he knew this would raise. "A clarinet player in Hell's Kitchen."

"I'd have walked you to his apartment," said Tim, after only a few seconds' hesitation. "On the way I'd have shown you where I used to go to school and church."

The scenario was ridiculous, and yet so likely that both men laughed. Even so, Tim was soon feeling bad about himself: pride might be a sin, but self-mortification, detached from penance, could be one, too. He reached for the tumbler of rye, his arm knocking into Fuller's, which he realized had raised itself, tenderly, in order to caress his face. There was a softness, a sense of pathos and protection in Hawkins' expression, that he had never seen. But the collision of their two arms caused Hawkins to withdraw the gesture and replace the look on his face with one of relief—the look of a man who was, upon further reflection, pleased not to have given away something he didn't need to.

Swallowing more whiskey, Tim asked: "Does your mother ever fix you up with girls?" His own parents, curiously tactful, never seemed to try. Hawkins said nothing. Tim bit down on an ice cube and tried to blunt the query with playfulness: "She's probably too busy beating them away from the door."

Hawkins unbuttoned his own shirt. "She does do a little matchmaking for yours truly. And of course she'll succeed at it one of these days."

Tim tried to hide the revulsion and fear coming over him by pressing his face against Hawkins' now bare chest.

"But that doesn't amount to a terribly compelling crusade," said Hawkins, as he removed Tim's eyeglasses. "What she should really carry the banner for is religion. You know, she's more than a little attracted to *your* people. I think she imagines herself as Loretta Young or Mrs. Luce, converting herself at the feet of Fulton J. Sheen."

"I was watching him tonight, on a TV at Hecht's." Tim was relieved to think they might be finding their way back to the more usual precincts of raillery.

"Well, Mother was no doubt watching it up on Seventy-fourth and Park. I've seen it with her several times myself. I'm sure what she really wishes is that we still had an Irish maid she could Lady-Bountifully invite to join her on the sofa."

"You're talking about your *mother*," said Tim, poking Hawkins' thigh.

"No, we're talking about you," said Fuller, drawing Tim up so that their two faces were only inches apart. "Tell me, Skippy, how'd *you* escape Local 20 of the cherubim? Why didn't they make you into a priest?"

For the same reason you should never be a husband, he wanted to say.

"Maybe because I like doing *this* too much instead," he settled for answering. He kissed Hawkins' neck, receiving in return only a familiar, opaque smile, as if "this," and all it signified, did not even register. Was Hawkins ever really conscious, Tim wondered, of their doing anything at all? Or had he somehow made "this" into an automatic, harmlessly recurring condition, like sleepwalking?

Hawkins lifted him from the couch, and turned off the television. Once they were in the bedroom and he was removing the last of his clothes, the older man finally said, "Of course, there's my father's great dilemma to consider, too."

Tim propped himself up on the pillow, surprised at what seemed to be a waiver of the rules. He prepared for the imparting of real, personal information, unprompted by any risky question of his own.

Hawkins flopped onto the bed, holding a shiny brochure. "The old man is deciding whether he can permit himself to drive an automatic transmission—or whether that's something that was never meant to be, like filter tips." He climbed on top of Tim and, between kisses, began a comic recitation of the advertisement. " 'Now your hand, foot, and mind are completely free from all gear-shifting work,' " he whispered. Tim remembered to laugh, but this transposition of the brochure's promises, accompanied by Hawkins' insistent touch, was ludicrously thrilling, a smoothly narrated trip into the helplessness he sought. " 'Masters the steepest grades without asking a thing of you,' " said Hawkins, who shut the light and placed one hand under the small of his back. " 'Instant response to throttle.' "

When they were through, Tim held on to Hawkins in the dark for as long as he could, knowing he would soon hear the serious joke about this being a school night, and how he ought to get home so that come morning he would be fresh for "Citizen Canes," as Hawkins liked to call Potter. But for the moment he could feel the beating of their hearts, at different rates, and recognize in Hawkins' touch a fondness, an attachment, that was sanctioned only by the dark.

At that same hour, a mile or so away, Mary Johnson was sitting down to a late supper with Jerry Baumeister at the Occidental. She'd already had an early one with Paul Hildebrand, whom she was now seeing happily enough almost every other night, but Jerry's invitation had been urgent. His thin, ordinarily pleasant face seemed pallid. He had picked, she noted, the most brightly lit corner of the most respectable place imaginable, close by the Willard Hotel and White House.

His girls were with his mother, who lived over in Arlington, not far from his own place. "She thinks I've been 'laid off,' " he explained. "By the way, she also thinks I have a date. And she highly approved of your vital statistics, which I provided to satisfy her curiosity."

"Well," said Mary, "as far as dates go, I could do worse."

"No, you couldn't," said Jerry. He paused for a moment, as if taken aback by his new self-loathing. "And I suppose the dear old thing has a point about my being 'laid off.' " He joked that the federal government's dismissal of fourteen hundred security risks was assisting the attrition through which it was supposed to shed itself of fifty thousand civilian employees by next June. "Our—your, I should say—department is certainly doing its bit. State's getting rid of two people a week." He had almost, Mary noted, said "perverts" instead of "people," seeming to decide before the word's first syllable was fully out that this was more than he could bear.

"I honestly don't think all this would have happened under Adlai," said Mary, sipping a Dubonnet and knowing that, in fact, she wouldn't be the least surprised if Stevenson had felt compelled to expand the government's security program in just the way Eisenhower had done, putting everyone's personal quirks on the same level of importance as their loyalty.

"I voted for him, you know," said Jerry. "Eisenhower." He slugged back the last of a double. "Not that that matters. What matters is that I'm supposed to be 'blackmailable.' And ergo, I must go. You know, from my standpoint, blackmail would be better than what the past month's been like. It would certainly be cheaper. Presumably I'd get to keep *part* of my paycheck."

"Jerry, I can pay—"

Realizing the false signal he'd given, he raced to restore male-female economics. "Oh, Jesus, Mary, I didn't mean *that*. I asked *you*—as soon as Beverly called me up to say that you'd done something 'really extraordinary.' Those were her words, though she thought the details should be left for you to explain."

"I didn't really do—"

He waved a hand in protest, cutting her off, as if to prolong the anticipation of good news, to keep the wonder of its existence from being disproved. "You know, I still don't know what the 'M' in 'Miscellaneous M Unit' stands for," he said. "Maybe just McLeod himself, though he wasn't there for my questioning. I guess there are so many cases that he has to save himself for the big ones—Yale men, I suppose, instead of guys like me from Case Western. I wonder, though, if he knew he was getting a Lutheran with me. I suspect he thought from my name that I was just one more Jew to bother. Maybe he would have shown up if he'd realized."

Mary wished Jerry would stop. He reminded her of a Tulane boy who'd once cried on her sorority-house porch halfway through a confession of some hazing humiliation. She feared that Jerry, already moving fast through a second double, was about to shed tears himself.

"Almost nobody actually 'confesses,' " he continued, sounding more composed, taking on the manner of someone explaining a little-known principle of chess or bookbinding. "Though I've heard of one guy who, after he spilled everything, actually sent them a thank-you note." There was a pause, which Mary took as Jerry's invitation either to laugh or cry, before he resumed in a straightforward, insistent tone. "That I *did not do*."

He said it with actual pride, as if by not expressing gratitude to McLeod he had managed to salvage something from the situation.

"I don't know who that guy was," Jerry continued, now a bit sarcastically. "You know, 'we' don't all *know* one another."

"I understand, Jerry."

"I'm sorry. I don't mean to sound however I sounded. The sad truth is, Mary, if I'd known the name of one homosexual in the department— I mean knew it for sure—I'd have given it to them."

She would have preferred the earlier look of pathetic pride to the expression of shame now sweeping his face.

"I've seen Senator Fulbright," she at last interrupted. "He and my daddy were Rhodes scholars together. I talked to him about my troubled feelings. I didn't mention you specifically." Sitting across from Jerry was worse than it had been sitting across from Fulbright, who'd seemed appalled that a well-brought-up Southern girl should be aware of such things, let alone bothering him with them.

Jerry said nothing. He appeared to be waiting for the story's climax, the miraculous news whose pleasure he had deferred. And she had nothing like that to give him.

"He really just pursed his senatorial lips, Jerry. He said he might call Mr. Morton, my boss in CR, to ask one or two 'concerned questions' of a general nature."

She feared that Jerry would be crushed to realize the paltriness of her "extraordinary" action, but he now looked at her with an enormous smile—at which she felt obligated to throw cold water. "Jerry, he's never going to make that call."

"Oh, I know that," he replied, his smile undiminished. "But you were swell to do what you did. When Beverly said you'd done something great, I never figured it was *this* great. It's the first fine thing I've heard since I started looking for work. Which, by the way, I've found. At a hardware store in Falls Church. The job pays two dollars an hour. Think I'll get to use that master's degree in French?"

The smile was coming, Mary realized, not only from sincere gratitude, but also from his now being drunk. He put his glass down a little harder than was necessary and, with a glazed look that could almost have been construed as romantic, asked her: "Do you know what they do with guys like me in Russia?"

CHAPTER EIGHT

November 26, 1953

At seventy-seven, Grandma Gaffney remained drier and tougher than her Thanksgiving turkey. The bird's insides were just as bad: none of the widow's offspring could ever detect a single ingredient to her stuffing besides water, flour, and thyme. And yet no one was willing to suggest that she cede control of the dinner's preparation and location. Even in these spacious Stuyvesant Town days, the family continued to gather in Grandma Gaffney's Ninth Avenue railroad apartment, only a block from where the old woman had lived through the Blizzard of '88 as a twelve-year-old girl. Her oft-told tale of sliding down the drifts that had reached the second-floor window carried no wistfulness; she'd needed to get out of the tenement any way she could, she'd explained to Timmy the first time she told him the story. She was already *working*, dressing the hair of those snotty boarding-school girls, Protestants every one, over on the East Side.

Eight other people had squeezed around her dining room table this afternoon: two daughters and two sons-in-law; her unmarried son, Alan; her grandchildren Tim and Frances; and Frances's husband, Tom Hanrahan. Nine people if you counted the baby Frances was carrying. The child's annunciation had been the chief news and only source of real merriment around the table, whose centerpiece consisted, as always, of a dozen celery stalks, leafy ends up, in a cut-glass vase. The windows remained covered not with lace curtains but paper shades that appeared, like so many of Grandma Gaffney's possessions, oddly defiant.

Uncle Frank, whose three grown sons were off with their wives' families, had made a joke about Timmy's "falling behind" in the grandchild-producing department, which occasioned laughter from everyone but Uncle Alan, who, Tim had to concede, didn't laugh much over anything. Frances had led the saying of grace, including in it an expression of thanksgiving for the cease-fire in Korea. Since this political development had made a call-up of Tom's reserve unit less likely, Grandma Gaffney had allowed the prayer to proceed without any overt disapproval, though she was known to regard grace as "something the Protestants say," and during the canned fruit–cocktail course had tried to imagine what Father Coughlin—if the Jews hadn't forced him off the radio—would think about allowing the Communists to keep half the Korean peninsula.

Tim now busied himself washing the dishes. He normally did them with Frances but had today insisted she stay off her feet, even if she was less than two months along. His gesture allowed her to join the crush in front of the television in the small parlor. Paul and Rosemary Laughlin had a year or so ago purchased the TV for Grandma Gaffney, who had pronounced a favorite cryptic anathema on the givers—"Buy another and then stop"—before becoming intensely devoted to this latest modern wonder. Frances, arriving midmorning to face certain rejection of her offer to help with the cooking, had later sworn to Tim that Grandma'd kept the television on for the half-hour broadcast of the Gimbel's parade from Philadelphia, and then promptly switched it off when coverage shifted to Macy's own parade right here in New York—a demonstration of lingering resentment over a tablecloth the store had refused to take back in 1934.

Tim had grown up in an apartment almost identical to this one, but the Gorgon-like presence of his grandmother (who adored him and disliked Frances, for reasons unclear to both grandchildren) had rendered this place a sort of enchanted cave. Its heat still came from a coal furnace in the basement tended by an Italian super who had always let Tim play down there. Once he reappeared inside the apartment's little vestibule, Grandma Gaffney would brush the dust from his hair and face and tell him he looked like Little Black Sambo.

As he scrubbed the cutlery, Tim went from remembering the coal dust to recalling the condensation on his eyeglasses that Hawk had wiped off with his handkerchief yesterday at lunchtime. There'd been a call for Tim at the office, asking that he be at the Capitol Hill apartment at twelve-fifteen. He'd raced over and found Hawk already there, inside the foyer near the radiator, standing in his Harris tweed topcoat and flipping through *Newsweek;* his car was parked out front. He would be driving to New York, he said, as soon as the two of them finished "visiting." They had laughed at the word while racing up the stairs.

Hawk had never asked about his own Thanksgiving plans, but Tim had made haste to say that he needed to work through the afternoon and couldn't depart D.C. until six o'clock, when he'd be getting a bus. Failure to acknowledge this impediment would have made him available to ride to New York with Hawk—an invitation he feared might not be forthcoming.

As it happened, he did have to work, making long-distance calls to two of the POWs set to testify next week. Neither turned out to be much older than himself, and each had called him "sir." Now, a day later, plunging his hands back into the hot dishwater, he recalled the tales of horrific cold that he'd heard from one of them, whose frostbitten feet, like Senator Potter's, had been left behind a world away.

By the time Tim joined everyone in the parlor, the television was flickering with images of the Salvation Army dinner for bums on the Bowery. Political discussion overrode the TV's picture and sound. Ethel Rosenberg's brother had just yesterday given the committee a written statement about how spying might *still* be going on at Fort Monmouth, a speculation to which Uncle Frank now gave loud assent. Tim worried that this mention of the Rosenbergs would soon have Grandma Gaffney unleashing a fusillade of complaints against the "sheenies," the most arcane of her many terms for the Jews. When he had been a little boy, and the TV-star bishop just another voice on the radio, Tim had surmised the word to be a name for the followers of Fulton J. Sheen. If Grandma Gaffney came out with it now, Uncle Frank would be sure to laugh, while Paul and Rosemary Laughlin would remain silently disapproving—not from any real moral opprobrium they attached to the word, but only a sense of its being a crude immigrant relic, like the coal pile in the basement or Grandma Gaffney's bad teeth, something with which their newly middle-class children shouldn't be saddled.

"So, Timmy," Uncle Frank fairly shouted, "did you have a hand in that speech the other night?" He meant McCarthy's eleven-p.m. radio-and-TV address. It had been billed as an equal-time rebuttal to Truman's broadcast on the Harry Dexter White case, though in the event, McCarthy had spent more time attacking the current president than the former one, with a claim that Ike was "batting zero" against Communists in government.

Tim politely shook his head. "Uncle Frank, except for his wedding, I've never even *seen* McCarthy. He's mostly been up here in New York." The committee, Tim explained, had the other week done a little investigation of General Electric, before returning its attention to Fort Monmouth. But such details didn't matter to Uncle Frank: Tim's work for Charles Potter gave him in the eyes of everyone here, even Frances, an admirable proximity to the senator from Wisconsin. However much Tim tried to correct them, his family regarded him as a lucky oblate to an all-powerful monsignor.

The White case—with the once-more-front-page Truman calling the attorney general a liar, and J. Edgar Hoover branding Truman a liar in return—had all the elements to sustain long discussion, save one. "Where's McCarthy in all of this?" Uncle Alan asked Tim, at a decibel level low enough to indicate actual curiosity. "I mean aside from that speech."

"It's really HUAC's show," explained Tim, who realized with a touch of shame that he was tossing off such lingo to convey the very insiderliness he'd been trying to disclaim at dinner. But he *had* heard Tommy McIntyre remark that the White story was "making old Joe emerald with envy" each day it gobbled up the lion's share of column inches in the papers.

Political news soon gave way to neighborhood reminiscence. Talk of the Donahues, who'd recently moved from Fiftieth Street to Mineola, ushered the family toward a collective sleepiness. The television was at last turned off, and Tim began to hear the tick of the clock near the old radio cabinet, a kind of telegraph tapping out the unvaried existence of Uncle Alan and Grandma Gaffney, who sometimes seemed more married than his own parents. He noticed the thickness of the paint—another layer added by the landlord every five years—on the square strip of molding that ornamented the room's plaster walls. And he also regarded the telephone, which had come into the apartment only a few years before the TV. *I'm not on the phone.*

With the same finger he'd yesterday used to trace circles on Hawkins' bare chest, he could right now, if he chose, dial the Charles Fuller family, who were in the Manhattan book. What might be going on in those rooms at Seventy-fourth and Park, high above the doorman and flower-filled lobby that Tim could picture? Behavior there could scarcely be more specified or formal than here. Even now, Tim and his father and uncles had yet to loosen their ties, pride in their white collars supplementing a deference both to the day and to the family matriarch.

As conversation grew more intermittent, Tim's discomfort increased, as if, without much else on their minds and tongues, his parents and uncles and aunts would somehow be able to see images, like stigmata beginning to bleed, of his naked hour with Hawkins Fuller.

"Grandma," he said, too nervous to sit still any longer, "I'm going to wrap up some of the leftovers and take them to the church. The icebox won't hold everything."

"All right, Timmy," she replied, all but adding "if you must." She tended to view charity not as a corporal work of mercy but a species of busybodiedness, and yet, as a "nice boy"—her designation, seeming to signify a handicap that made certain actions unavoidable—Timmy "did such things."

Out on the street, carrying a bag of waxed-papered turkey and asparagus spears, Tim drew a great cleansing breath of the city's dirty air. He passed the corner of Forty-third Street and looked down to the old building where he knew Hawkins' clarinet player—the one from the day of the Draft Ike rally—must still have his apartment. Closing his eyes, he thought of yesterday, when Hawk had been inside him, and he wondered if he weren't now really more closely connected to this musician—at just one physical remove—than to everyone still sitting back in the parlor.

He found himself saying aloud a couple of lines from Dylan Thomas, the ones Tommy McIntyre had come into the office reciting the other day:

> Time held me green and dying
> Though I sang in my chains like the sea.

The Welsh poet had died in mid-bender here in New York only a couple of weeks ago. "Ah," Tommy had said with Irish reverence and envy, "he should have been one of ours, Mr. Tim. He should have been one of ours."

The lines of verse vanished onto the breeze racing down Ninth Avenue ahead of Tim, just as yesterday, in the apartment on Capitol Hill, his own whispering of the words "I love you," barely but deliberately audible, had disappeared into the pillow and walls, unanswered except for two gentle pats on the back of his head.

CHAPTER NINE

December 2, 1953

"Our orders was to hold at all costs," said Sergeant Weinel, "and that is what we was doing. We was holding at all costs."

Even so, the sergeant's unit had at last been overrun, on August 30, 1950, by the village of Chinju near the Naktong River, and that's why he was here today, three years later, in the Caucus Room of the Senate Office Building. After the unit's forced march from Chinju to Taejon, Sergeant Weinel testified, he and his sixty buddies had been beaten, indoctrinated, denied medical care, and put on display in North Korean villages; and then—with the exception of the sergeant himself—they had been massacred by their captors.

He explained his own survival to Senator Potter and the Permanent Subcommittee on Investigations: "Yes, sir; they covered me over with dirt, too. It was just loose dirt, with enough to cover my head up. I laid there and after they got through I could breathe through that loose dirt."

As if fearing that heroism might be ascribed to him, Sergeant Weinel quickly shifted the committee's attention from his success at playing possum to the last efforts of those actually dead. "Out of the whole bunch that was shot there, I never heard one man ask for mercy; none of them did. In fact, there was one of the boys that wasn't hit good, and he even asked them to give him another. Out of that many men, nobody cracked."

With this recollection Sergeant Weinel choked up, and appeared to be on the verge of sobs, which he managed to restrain when Senator Potter, rising to his artificial feet, leaned across the committee table to pass him a cigarette.

Watching from a seat behind his boss's chair, Tim felt his own hand trembling from some internal tumult of anger and fear, all of it overlaid and trumped by shame. Had he been in Sergeant Weinel's company, he *would* have cracked, and long before they reached Taejon. He would have begged for mercy and been killed by the enemy in full view of his own contemptuous comrades.

Sergeant Weinel quickly regained his composure, nodding while Potter explained how the evidence they were gathering suggested that the North Koreans had begun a coordinated effort to kill POWs, in numerous locations, on the day the sergeant's group was slaughtered. "It had to be a command order rather than a prison order," the senator reasoned. He was especially interested in the timing of a visit to the prison by a North Korean higher-up, a propaganda speaker, shortly before the massacre.

One could argue that a cover-up of the atrocities extended all the way to the Soviet Union—and beyond. Just yesterday, Vishinsky, the Russians' UN ambassador, had declared with a theatrical yawn, and considerable support, that the United States' heavily documented report on war crimes was just fantasy. But, Potter insisted, the particulars with which Sergeant Weinel and the other men were now harrowing the Senate proved otherwise. "When a Red Chinese nurse cuts off the toes of a GI with a pair of garden shears, without benefit of anesthesia, and wraps the wounds in a newspaper, this makes a liar out of Vishinsky."

In the row of chairs behind the committee, Tommy McIntyre leaned over to Tim and whispered, "Charlie sounds half like a senator today. Too bad his *luck's* not a little dumber." He pointed to the dearth of press at the back of the room. No television cameras, and only half as many reporters as would be there ordinarily: a strike by photo engravers had shut down the New York papers. McCarthy, Tommy had explained, was relieved that a break in the Fort Monmouth hearings should be occurring while there were no headlines to be had in Manhattan. The chairman, present here today and all modesty, had told newsmen, "It's Charlie's hearing," when he entered the Caucus Room this morning. "He's been a one-man task force on this important issue."

Seeing him now in half profile, Tim could sense McCarthy's boredom with the whole undertaking, this bit of pro bono work where the witnesses were praised instead of pilloried. As a display of his supposed confidence in the Michigan senator, McCarthy had told the reporters that Potter was free to disagree with his own approach to the POW issue, which involved getting tough on any country still trading with Red China, including Britain. "I myself believe it's time to stop sending perfumed notes to our supposed allies," he'd said, repeating a choice image from his pre-Thanksgiving speech.

Tim had hoped to see Cecil Holland from the *Star* here this morning, but the day's real action was over at the White House, where at a news conference Ike would—or would not—back up Dulles's own rebuttal of McCarthy's speech. There was also, here in the Caucus Room, no sign of Roy Cohn, who doubtless thought the hearings a digression beneath his notice. Even Robert Jones, Potter's own staffer, had gone to get a haircut in the Senate barbershop. Well, Tim would at least be able to tell Uncle Frank that he'd once more seen McCarthy, albeit the back of his head.

After a Pfc's testimony about a chaplain who'd been shot in the back while giving the last rites, the hearing was recessed for lunch. Tim had to do without eating, since he'd been assigned to prepare the witnesses' travel vouchers in the committee's office space down the hall. He'd hand them out once the men had had their meal and turned in their receipts. But before he left the Caucus Room he walked up to Sergeant Weinel to shake his hand and say thank you—not just for his testimony, he hoped the man would understand, but for what he'd endured in Korea. As Weinel mumbled, "You're welcome," Tim noted a smirk on the face of a reporter witnessing the exchange, and he wondered if he'd violated some protocol. When the newsman began to shake his head in what looked like knowing disgust, Tim felt something angry flare up inside himself. "What did I do wrong?" he asked the reporter, trying to make it sound like a genuine request for information. But his emotions were running high, and he found it hard to keep the edge out of his voice. "I'm Timothy Laughlin," he added, extending his hand without a smile.

"Kenneth Woodforde, *The Nation*," responded the reporter, whose facial expression, beneath a lot of curly auburn hair, had turned almost pitying. "Tell me, fella, don't you think these guys are just as much on display here as they were in those Korean villages?"

Tim looked at him blankly. "No, of course I don't."

"Well, guess again, buddy boy. They're trotting out these fresh-faced farm kids—victims of big bad communism—to inflame support for the committee's real work."

"Which is?"

"A gigantic domestic purge."

"You don't think these soldiers suffered?" asked Tim. At the start of the hearing, General Ridgway himself had testified that there was no precedent for the kind of atrocities being described.

"War is hell," said Woodforde, with even more sarcasm than before. "Bad things happen. So do exaggerations and outright lies."

"You sound like Vishinsky," said Tim, who immediately wondered if the insult wasn't beyond the pale.

"Well, I'd rather have worked for *his* Joe than for *your* Joe."

Tim was about to say "I work for Senator Potter," but Woodforde had already walked away. So he stood for a moment by himself, in silence, outraged over the idea that he should be ashamed to serve McCarthy, however indirectly.

He looked at Sergeant Weinel, now near the exit, and thought of him trying to breathe through the dirt and the corpses while pretending to be one of them.

Down the corridor, inside the committee's workroom, Tim found that Robert Jones, freshly shorn, had taken a seat next to Roy Cohn, who was now delivering an agitated monologue into a telephone.

"Laughlin!" called out Jones. "Which one of those fellows who testified is from Maine?"

Tim consulted his clipboard and found the name of the private from Augusta whose pus-filled arm had been slammed with a North Korean's rifle butt on the march to Taejon.

"Do *not*," said Jones, "repeat—do *not*—allow Margaret Chase Smith to get her picture taken with him. This afternoon, if the kid gets called to her office, I don't care what you do—take him to look at the Declaration of Independence or the White House Christmas tree—but do *not* let her pose near him."

Tim nodded, but this whole tough-guy marching order sounded so much like an imitation of Cohn imitating McCarthy that he had trouble believing Jones could be fully serious.

Cohn himself continued shouting into the phone: "Listen, Adams. You're double-crossing me for the last time! You told me that Dave would be assigned back to Manhattan after he'd finished his eight weeks of basic. Yes, you did, goddammit! And now you go back on your word and try to make him eat shit!" Pointlessly cupping the receiver's mouthpiece against his ever-rising volume, the committee's chief counsel declared: "If you don't get Stevens to straighten this out, Joe and I are going to wreck the goddamn army! Yes, that's exactly what I said, and it's a promise!"

Further upset, Tim went over to the table with the travel vouchers, amazed at the way Cohn and Jones seemed to think they could treat the army, as if it were some crooked dry cleaner down the street. After all, it was the army, with its million Private Garritys from Augusta, that was actually killing Communists and being killed by them. Still, Tim's anger toward the two staffers couldn't approach what he was even now feeling for smirking Kenneth Woodforde, who didn't seem to think the reds ever killed anyone at all.

Tommy McIntyre approached Tim's table in a grand mood. "It seems that for all the ordure Private Schine's been ingesting, he's so far had four weekend and five weeknight passes. Good thing he wears a uniform. Otherwise he might not know he was in the army at all."

Tim was too agitated to remember who Private Schine even was. Half the time he didn't grasp what Tommy was saying, let alone who really employed him and to what end. He didn't know why Woodforde should be one of the anti-anticommunists, as they were now called, and he couldn't be sure McCarthy, Cohn, and Jones wouldn't end up creating more of them. And he still could not understand why, even with the New York strike, there hadn't been more press in the Caucus Room this morning. There was a war on, for God's sake, between good and evil, regardless of whether Woodforde thought so, or even if he believed that each of those values had been ascribed to the wrong side.

"*Oh, god-fucking-dammit!*" Tim heard his own voice flying out of him when the heavy-duty stapler caught the tip of his thumb.

McIntyre and Mrs. Watt, the committee's chief clerk, began to laugh, mistaking his uncharcteristic profanity for exasperation over some clerical error. Cohn, ranting through another phone call, didn't even turn his head. Dizzy with pain, Tim held his tongue against further outburst; he wanted only for Hawkins to be here and to take hold of him, the way he had when Tim had stubbed his toe one night in the apartment on I Street.

"Jaysus," said Tommy, realizing the actual situation. "You're bleeding, kid."

"I'm okay." But he wasn't. He was a fool. Cowardly, and clumsy to boot. *I never heard one man ask for mercy. Out of that many men, nobody cracked.*

Mrs. Watt, also apologetic, now hovered over him.

"I'll get him patched up," said Tommy.

On their way to the nurse, his thumb wrapped in Tommy's handkerchief, Tim recognized Senator Hunt, the Wyoming Democrat whose son had been convicted of sexual solicitation. Tommy remained unusually quiet until the man passed and the two of them reached the elevators. "Timothy," he then asked, "have you got a girlfriend?"

Annoyed by the pain in his hand, and now by this question, Tim answered without suppressing the edge in his voice: "No, Mr. McIntyre, I don't."

Tommy threw an arm over his shoulder. "Before the coming shitstorm's over, you may want to get yourself one."

CHAPTER TEN

December 19, 1953

Thruston Morton wished Jerry Baumeister a Merry Christmas. He shook his hand while propelling his own six-foot-two frame and pretty wife, Belle, a few inches farther into Mary Johnson's apartment. He also patted the heads of Jerry's two girls, who stood politely in red velvet holiday skirts that their mother had made for them.

Watching from her kitchen, Mary took his skillful progress as confirmation of the rumors that Mr. Morton did indeed want to get back into elective politics with a Senate run from Kentucky in 1956. The bureau chief did not look like a man who had lately received any troubling phone calls, from Senator Fulbright or anybody else. He certainly didn't appear to know that the man he was greeting had recently been discharged from his own department.

About thirty of the people Mary had invited were already here, and it was warm enough for her to open the window. The place was beginning to smell a little like the Maine Avenue wharf where she'd gotten the crabs and cherrystone clams that Paul had helped her to steam all afternoon—work he'd enjoyed much more than sitting with her through the Mannes Trio at the Coolidge Auditorium Thursday night.

What was it she'd come in here for? Napkins, that's right. Okay, now she had them and could rejoin both Paul and Beverly Phillips, who'd arrived with some nice widower from the Social Security Administration.

"He said he wanted to take me to the Shubert!" crowed Beverly, who was in a fine mood. "I told him, 'Hey, what do you take me for!'"

"I had to tell her they haven't done burlesque in five years," the nice widower explained to Paul Hildebrand.

"See how far behind you get living out in the suburbs!" exclaimed Beverly. "Gosh, Mary, this place is cute. And jammed!"

"Everyone who's ever filled out a Form 57," observed Paul.

"How does this poor man know about that!" cried Beverly. "Oh, God, Mary, he's not going to make you *leave,* is he?" Paul Hildebrand's dislike of politics and government had become a matter of teasing and speculation among those who knew the progress of Mary's romance, and two bourbons had made Beverly even more direct than usual.

"No," said Mary. "I think Form 57 was mentioned in the monologue Paul got a little while ago from that girl in International Materials." She pointed out a young lady across the room. "She was telling him how well she hears women are doing at the FBI. Getting to be everything but agents."

Beverly's widower seemed interested in pursuing the subject, but it would have to be without Mary, who had just decided that she and Paul, as if they really *were* married, should be circulating separately through the party. Departing the conversation, she introduced one of her old Q Street roommates to the little circle Paul would now be in charge of. Betty Bowron, conspicuously tanned, had just been to Miami with her boss for a Commerce Department conference, and she seemed eager to talk about it.

Mary edged into another conversation. Her old friend Millie Brisson, the congressman's secretary, was talking about the suicide of a young guard at the Tomb of the Unknown Soldier.

"Mysterious, no?" said Millie.

"Redundant, I'd say," offered the young man Millie was talking to, a Lousiana acquaintance of Mary's who was up here trying to write a kind of national version of *All the King's Men.*

Mary checked the phonograph: the Christmasy Corelli concerto had another two inches to go before she'd need to change the record. But one of Jerry's daughters, she now noticed, was struggling with a hem that had fallen. Maybe the hard-drinking mother had dropped a few stitches. "Honey," called Mary, coming to the rescue, "let me get you a little old safety pin."

Inside her bedroom, while she rummaged the sewing box, Mary's glance was drawn through the window, to a scene made visible by the streetlamp two houses down P Street. Hawkins Fuller, dressed for her party and holding a small brown bag, stood talking to a smaller man in a woollen cap and zippered jacket. She now recognized him—the tortoiseshell glasses—as the boy who'd come to the office with the book a couple of months back. He and Fuller appeared to be saying goodbye. After giving Fuller a sweet, casual punch on the arm, the boy smiled and walked away. At which point her colleague turned around and started toward her apartment.

Mary wondered: Had that lovelorn little dogsbody leapt at the mere chance to walk Fuller to a party the older man wouldn't even let him enter?

What exactly should she be feeling? Disgust? Sympathy? She blocked the questions from her mind, and decided to use a needle and thread, instead of a pin, on the Baumeister girl's skirt. Picking out a spool of bright red, she heard Corelli give way, abruptly, to Eartha Kitt: *Santa baby, hurry down the chimney to me . . .*

Looking out into the living room, she saw Fuller at the turntable and realized that he'd had a phonograph record inside the little brown bag. People were beginning to cluster around him, just as they would have had he only blown some dust off the needle and dropped it back onto Corelli. An older man from European Affairs was asking in a loud voice if he didn't "think it terrible what had happened to poor George Marshall over in Oslo. You were over there once, weren't you, young fellow? The poor general, heckled by those Communists while picking up his Peace Prize!" Fuller agreed that it was a shame, and moreover an embarrassment to old Haakon VII, "a fine chap and top-drawer king." Even as his always-adaptable speech found him communicating in the EA man's idiom, Fuller began letting his own shoulders sway in a manner both slinky and manly, one that belonged to nobody else at the party. *Santa baby, forgot to mention one little thing, a ring . . .*

Mary watched him and nodded but didn't smile. She proceeded to Jerry's daughter with her needle and thread.

Ten minutes passed before she again needed to be in the kitchen, where she found Miss Lightfoot, middling drunk on Harvey's Bristol Cream and wearing a hideous hat. Mary had had to invite her, and poor Mr. Church, an old friend from the Passport Office, was having to listen to her.

"What do you mean by 'this'?" asked Miss Lightfoot, who knew perfectly well that Mr. Church had meant the sway of Senator McCarthy when he told her that "this could all end if Senator Morse just voted with the Democrats." Should Oregon's independent—formerly a Republican—throw in with the other side when it came time to organize the congressional session, then the chairmanship of McCarthy's committee, and much of his power, would pass to the opposition.

"Well, Morse won't vote with the Democrats. He's already said so," Miss Lightfoot informed Mr. Church, whose more serious error had been to assume, from the general tenor of those at Mary's party, that Miss Lightfoot, too, wanted all "this" to end. She did not. Nor, actually, did the Democrats, she now argued. "They don't *want* to take over. They'd rather carp. Which is why they left the committee in the first place."

Mr. Church was shaking his head with forbearance, allowing Miss Lightfoot to overprove her point, when Hawkins Fuller brushed past them both. Leaning against the sink, Fuller took note of Mary's sleeveless black dress and declared: "That appears to be a *very* cold shoulder."

Miss Lightfoot, already keenly stimulated, and wishing for a sprig of mistletoe under which to capture Fuller, tried to annex him to her own conversation. "Mr. Fuller, tell Mr. Church here how *you've* got to deal with the Democrats on Capitol Hill. Tell him how—"

Fuller ignored her ardent grasp of his forearm. He was interested only in the lady of the house, who he realized had already had enough to drink herself.

"You came alone?" Mary finally asked him.

"More or less," he replied.

"How is a *person* 'more or less'?" asked Mary. "Did you make that poor creature I saw from the window walk all the way back home by themselves?" Lit as she was, she took care to keep the pronouns neutral, even at the expense of grammar, since she and Fuller now had Miss Lightfoot's complete attention, Mr. Church having beaten a gentlemanly retreat once the handsome guest began having words with the hostess. Fresh from political triumph, but still smarting from Fuller's rebuff, Miss Lightfoot now appeared determined at least to savor victory over whatever hapless female Fuller had apparently declined to bring up to the party.

Mary attempted to move out of the kitchen, but Fuller blocked her, trying to smooth things over with a laugh. "If I'd brought him up, he would only have asked you for a glass of milk. And you don't seem to be serving any."

By now furious at being ignored, Miss Lightfoot could feel her over-powdered jaw suddenly slacken. *Him? He?* A small cascade of pennies started dropping in her head. After all her flirtation! She'd even *sung* with this man! Without hesitation, she began a loud, seething recitation of the words she'd seen that *boy*, that milk-drinking *nancy*, write in the Lodge biography: " 'With thanks to Hawkins Fuller. I got the job. You're *wonderful.*' " She made the inscription sound as if it were a cable from Moscow that had been discovered in Fuller's shoe.

Mary, still unable to get away, could picture the book lying on Fuller's filing cabinet. He'd never even taken the gift home—a bit of callousness that still appalled her, even as she wanted to defend Fuller from this harridan to whom he'd so foolishly exposed himself. Pushing Miss Lightfoot aside, she at last returned to the living room.

Fuller lifted the bottle of Harvey's Bristol Cream from the kitchen counter. He topped up Miss Lightfoot's drink and poured one for himself. He clinked her glass and said, "Miss Lightfoot, I *am* wonderful." And then, before walking away, he leaned over and whispered in her ear: "So why don't you just *suffer.*"

CHAPTER ELEVEN

December 23, 1953

At 6:05 a.m., the radio was saying that Cardinal Spellman, Catholic vicar of the armed forces, had departed for Korea to say Christmas Mass for the troops. On the Formica table near Tim's bowl of cereal lay the current issue of *The Nation*, which he'd been making himself read last night. Kenneth Woodforde's short sarcastic article on the Potter hearings argued that the Hollywood Ten might now be making a fine sentimental film about the forced march to Taejon if they hadn't been blacklisted from practicing their profession.

Since the atrocities testimony, Tim had more strongly than ever felt himself part of a great moral battle, and more and more he wondered how Hawkins, stationed at its international center, could exempt himself from the fray with the handful of liberal nostrums and jokes he uttered whenever Tim tried to draw him out on the subject. An attempt to discuss his encounter with Woodforde, for example, had resulted in Hawk's telling him only to "stay away from reporters. They dress worse than McCarthy."

Tim opened a box containing the cheap necktie, monogrammed with a huge, loud "F," that he'd bought the other night on Fourteenth Street. He would tell Hawk that the "F" stood for "Farouk," not "Fuller." The deposed Egyptian king was back in the papers now that his gaudy possessions were about to be auctioned off to help pay for the Aswan Dam, and a sketch that Tim had gotten up early to finish—of Hawk as a sultan surrounded by prostrate secretaries and ambassadors, each peeling him a grape or fanning him with palms—would go into the box with the tie. Tim drew well enough to have once thought about going to art school, and he'd felt a wonderful contentment while illustrating Hawk late last night, even if he'd had to work from memory. (Would he ever possess a photograph?)

He planned to deliver the tie before Hawk left for work. He knew he would be taking a risk by coming unannounced, and was certain there would be no present for him in return. But he could not face the trip home for Christmas without seeing Hawk once more.

There had been no question of buying a real gift. Any present that seemed to express deep feelings instead of high spirits might invite Hawk's disapproval. As it was, once Tim boarded the bus to Foggy Bottom, he worried about even this silly tie.

Traveling across the city, whose early commuter traffic was moving mostly in the opposite direction, he calculated how much time he had left to get to Hawkins' apartment, give him the gift, and then make it back to his own office on Capitol Hill. The time was tighter than he would like, but even so, he got off the bus in Farragut Square, in front of the Army and Navy Club, a few blocks from his destination. He liked to approach the apartment on foot, to walk down I Street savoring his own apprehension along with new details of his beloved's neighborhood. All too soon, he was there, at the front door of the building, able to avoid the downstairs buzzer by slipping in behind a meter man.

He had hoped to surprise Hawkins while he was still in bed, to find him wearing striped pajama bottoms and no top. But instead he was up, already in a shirt and tie. He'd been reading the paper at the kitchen table and seemed neither angry nor startled to find company at the door. Was there a chance he was pleased? He motioned Tim in, pointing to a story in the paper. "Have you sent a Christmas card home, Skippy? Even Guy Burgess has written his mother. From where is unclear, but he's let old Mum know he's still alive."

"I'll be seeing mine when I get back to New York tomorrow."

"I go up to Bar Harbor tonight. Not a *safe* harbor, either, with such a large gathering of the paternal clan in the offing. Before New Year's everyone will be wishing they'd spent the week somewhere warmer and with somebody else." He pressed the trash container's little foot pedal and scraped the remains of his plate into the can. "I should have arranged to go to Bermuda, with you."

Tim was thrilled beyond measure. Anyone would have told him this was only a pleasantry. *But it's the thought that counts,* he heard himself thinking.

Hawkins poured him some orange juice while glancing back at the story on Burgess, the British spy.

Say you'll miss me, thought Tim. *All* his thoughts were racing; all of them were upping the ante. Finally, he leaned over and kissed him. "Merry Christmas, Hawk. Here." He handed him the gift.

Hawkins smiled at the box's shape. "You may have noticed I already have one of these on." He sat down at the table. "Should I open it now?"

"Later's okay." Tim suddenly didn't care about the dangers of rejection, about all the unspoken protocols and endless calculations of risk. He climbed onto Hawk's lap and began kissing his face and neck with the desperate greed he always imagined the darkness hid.

"Hey, hey," whispered Hawkins, making a token effort to push him away. "My own juvenile delinquent. Careful you don't wind up in *that* Senate investigation."

"That's me," said Tim, kissing him some more and loosening the necktie that must have cost twenty times more than the one in the box. "I'm your hoodlum, your little j.d."

"Complete with switchblade," said Hawkins, feeling Tim's hard-on through his Sanforized trousers.

In another minute they were on the bed, shirts off, pants open. Tim forced himself to keep one eye on the clock, though his frantic ardor ensured that things would be over quickly. His tongue was soon moving along the thin line of hair that ran down Hawk's stomach to the waistband of his jockey shorts. As Tim sucked him, Hawkins tousled his hair and softly moaned, not for the first time, "You're the best," a phrase that always excited Tim, even if the competition it implied was more disquieting than complimentary.

He wanted Hawk to climax in his mouth, but soon found himself being lifted up, brought face-to-face with the man he loved, a man who wanted to kiss him—as if aware that this was what he truly needed to be soothed. With their tongues pressed together, he came all over Hawkins' stomach and chest.

The next kiss he received—for all the devastating tenderness of the one before—could not have been more perfunctory. "Time and tide," said

Hawkins, cheerfully, looking down at his own torso, from which he'd gently displaced Tim. "And I do mean tide." He got up to get a towel.

Tim lay in the bed, scarcely daring to breathe. This last kiss had put him back in his place, turned the ecstasy stale, and plunged him into a welter of self-loathing. He watched Hawk towel off and rebutton his shirt in front of the bathroom mirror. Knowing he'd soon be crying, unless he held in the tears by force of will, he grabbed for something on the night table. He wanted anything small that he could squeeze in his hand to distract himself, the way one forgets a pain in one place by introducing another somewhere else. He realized what object he'd picked up—a pair of cuff links, hooked together—only after he'd finished squeezing the metal as hard as he could and opened his hand to have a look.

Hawkins returned to sit on the edge of the bed. "Put your shirt back on," he said.

Tim obeyed, while Hawkins went and got a pair of scissors that he used to cut off the white buttons at Tim's wrists. After making two small slits to match the buttonholes, he proceeded to refasten the sleeves with the cuff links he'd seen Tim squeezing.

The silence and the gestures seemed ritualistic. Were the cuff links meant to be a return present, Hawk's way of saying "I didn't have time to shop"? Should he be insulted? Either way, he *wanted* them. They were proof, testimony to their union, a more elegant exhibition of it than the bottle of milk Hawk had brought with him that night to Capitol Hill, and which he'd never thrown away.

And yet—a horrible thought—what if the cuff links were someone else's? Left behind like that pair of galoshes? Tim could almost hear the stranger and Hawk laughing, as the jewelry clinked onto the night table just before some drunken dawn.

But then he saw the initials cut into the silver: HF.

Hawkins let go of his wrists and looked into his eyes. And then Tim understood: these were his reward for not crying, for not making the scene he'd been on the verge of making. He touched the cuff links, trying to enjoy the feeling that he was branded, owned; trying to appreciate the small bit of recklessness required of Hawk to give them. Wearing them would entail a measure of daring, too: what would he say if someone read the initials? His mind proceeded to construct the sort of fast little lie that people like himself learned to construct a dozen times a day. *They're not real silver. A Maryknoll nun gave them to me when I made a donation. The "HF" stands for "have faith."*

"I'm going to be late, Skippy." Hawkins got up and walked to the door, leaving him to show himself out.

Within fifteen minutes, Fuller was at the department. Inside Congressional Relations, a bottle of Kentucky bourbon—a gift of the bureau chief—sat atop each desk. On Mary Johnson's blotter there was also a tiny box, no bigger than two inches wide and high. A ring from the brewer, Fuller supposed, as soon as he saw it.

"He snuck in here around eight-fifteen," said Beverly Phillips. "An odd way to propose, no? Maybe he wants us to be cheering her on, telling her to accept."

"And we'll do just that," said Fuller. "Won't we, Miss Lightfoot? Marriage being such a grand institution? Something everybody ought to enjoy?"

Miss Lightfoot looked up from what she was typing to give him a thin, defiant smile, as if signaling that she would have to bear his presence here only a little while longer. Victory would be hers.

Fuller saw Mary enter the office, and he managed to halt her near the front door. Walking her back out to the hall, he said: "You've got a present on your desk from Mr. Right."

"I've been expecting it," she replied. She seemed calm, neither displeased nor especially happy.

"You're not going to let him take you away from all this, are you?"

She looked straight at Fuller. "Are we on speaking terms yet?" They had exchanged hardly a word since the party on Saturday.

"You can decide that within the next hour," said Fuller. "I'll be out of the office on a *date* with Mr. Right."

Mary looked puzzled.

"McLeod. The *real* Mr. Right."

"Oh, Fuller."

He saw her sudden look of concern. Clearly they *were* speaking. "The summons arrived yesterday," he explained.

Revulsion crossed her face. "Miss Lightfoot?"

He nodded. "I'm due in Room M304. I'm sure your friend Baumeister is familiar with it."

"Does Mr. Morton know?" she asked.

"The boss is always the *last* to know. I don't believe they tell him until after they've told the wife. Their idea of fair play."

An elevator ride and several hundred feet of waxed corridor brought him to M304, the Bureau of Security and Consular Affairs, whose name always sounded to Fuller like a CIA front: the little publishing house in Vienna, the art dealer in Rome. The office he entered had walls similar in color to those in his own, but there were no partitions and, it appeared, no secretary. On a small table between two chairs rested the department's *Investigative Manual* and several mimeographed copies of Scott McLeod's August 8 speech to the American Legion in Topeka: "I have attempted very frankly and honestly to face the issue of sexual perversion—the practice of sodomy—in the State Department," he had assured his audience, promising the Legionnaires that in trying to replace those discharged from federal service, he would be looking for men "well-grounded in the moral principles which have made our democratic republic a model form of government."

"Mr. Fuller," said a voice emerging from the wall intercom. "I'm Fred Traband. Please step into Room M305. And please leave your coat out there."

Fuller entered the inner office and shook hands with Mr. Traband, who immediately made it clear that there was nothing miscellaneous about the Miscellaneous M Unit. "I'm the special agent in charge of sexual-deviation investigations," he said, as matter-of-factly as if he were introducing himself as a budget analyst. "We believe we have reason to ask you a series of questions," he continued, without actually giving the reason. Miss Lightfoot's privacy, it seemed, must be protected.

"Sit down, Mr. Fuller, and let me be frank. Eighty percent of these sessions end with the admission of at least one proscribed behavior by the interviewee."

Fuller said nothing. He succeeded, without much effort, in looking courteous, as if he were listening to a purser explain the exchange rates for the next port of call.

"Security," said Mr. Traband, "is endangered by more than covert disloyalty, Mr. Fuller. The moral perversion and emotional immaturity inherent in homosexual behavior make those who engage in it targets of blackmail by anyone seeking to undermine the government of the United States. Moreover, that same perversion and immaturity are a danger to the homosexual's fellow employees. As I suspect you know, the Hoey Committee, whose investigation of sodomy within the State Department led to the reconstitution of this bureau, concluded that 'one homosexual can pollute an entire government office.' "

Fuller neither nodded nor shook his head, though Mr. Traband looked as if he expected a flood of personal confession. When none occurred, he made a request: "Mr. Fuller, please get up and walk across the room."

Fuller obliged and then returned to his seat.

"Again," said Traband.

When Fuller had finished his second walk, Traband gave him a newspaper and asked him to read a small story that he'd seemed to pick at random.

Fuller recited: " 'President Eisenhower revealed in his State of the Union message last January that he favors some form of home rule for the District. The pres—' "

"Thank you, Mr. Fuller, that's enough." Traband passed an open book across the desk. "This paragraph, please. The second-to-last one on the page."

Fuller picked up the book and looked at the spine—*Of Human Bondage*—before he commenced reading aloud: " 'Philip opened a large cupboard filled with dresses and, stepping in, took as many of them as he could in his arms and buried his face in them. They smelt of the scent his mother used. Then he pulled open the drawers, filled with his mother's things, and looked at them: there were lavender bags among the linen, and their scent was fresh and pleasant. The strangeness of—' "

"Enough," said Traband, almost as if he could no longer bear the voluptuous nonsense being inflicted on him.

Somerset Maugham? Fuller wondered. Was the interrogator expected to detect a tribal affinity between author and reader? Was it to be discerned in too much mimicry, a slightly excessive archness or lyricism in the tone of the recitation? Just as, presumably, too light a step in crossing the room might be added to his own too-expensive clothes in the bill of fairy particulars being drawn up against him?

"Mr. Fuller, I'm going to ask you to take a lie-detector test."

Fuller looked around but saw no machine. There was also no door leading to any Room M306. There was, however, the kind of curtained screen one found in a doctor's office, and it turned out that Traband's assistant had been sitting behind it, beside an apparatus, all along.

Fuller was instructed to open his shirt and roll up his right sleeve. Once he did, the sensors were applied.

"Mr. Fuller," asked Traband, "have you ever given or received presents of a romantic nature to or from another man?"

With thanks to Hawkins Fuller. (I got the job. You're wonderful.) "No."

"Have you ever frequented a Washington, D.C., establishment called the Jewel Box, at the corner of Sixteenth and L streets?"

The tufted purple walls. The bartender who looks a little like Alan Ladd. "No."

"Have you ever been present at a Washington, D.C., establishment called the Sand Bar, in Thomas Circle?"

The old redheaded queen leaning on the big plastic anchor at two a.m., shouting to no one in particular. The piano player hammering out "Some Enchanted Evening" for the third time in two hours. "No."

Fuller looked at the blank far wall. Silently, he sang to himself: *You're calmer than the seals in the Arctic Ocean. At least they flap their fins to express emotion.*

"Mr. Fuller, who was the president of the United States when you were born?"

A "baseline" question. "Calvin Coolidge," Fuller answered.

"Have you ever had inappropriate physical contact with a male foreign national either in the United States or while abroad?"

Behind the bicycle shop in Oslo. Lars? Who had no undershirt beneath his heavy fisherman's sweater. "No."

"Have you ever engaged in sodomy or oral-genital contact with another male?"

He sometimes counted them like sheep. *What was the name of that Italian boy in San Diego? The night before we both shipped out. The one who rubbed his feet together, fast, like a puppy having a dream, when he came. And that same week, the one who claimed to have gone to Annapolis, and tried—*

"Mr. Fuller, answer the question."

"No."

"Have you ever considered yourself to be in love with another male?"

Here, Fuller thought, was the first interesting query of the morning. He pondered it, sincerely, dropping his gaze from the wall to his lap and then his forearm, where, beneath the cuff of the machine's main sensor he noticed a golden-colored fleck of something dried onto his skin: the tiniest bit of exuberant Tim, he realized, missed by the towel. *That's me. I'm your hoodlum, your little j.d.* He filled up with a tender feeling, which he expelled, immediately, like a breath. "No," he answered.

Traband nodded to the machine operator, who tore off and labeled a long piece of paper. "Mr. Fuller," said the interrogator, "as soon as the technician removes the sensors, you may return to your office until you hear from us."

Outside in Room M304, Fuller was confronted with the sight of Scott McLeod himself, talking to whatever subordinate he'd brought along. Picking up his suit jacket, Fuller wondered if he himself might not be a bigger fish than he'd imagined. He nodded to the security chief, whose plump pink complexion and translucent eyeglass frames nodded back, before McLeod hastened himself and his underling into the room Fuller had just exited.

McLeod's chief patron, Senator Styles Bridges of New Hampshire, had once, around 1940, during Fuller's time at St. Paul's, given a speech to the students. Buttoning his jacket, Fuller could now recall its title, printed on the program passed out in the chapel: "How to Be a Man."

Alone in Room M304, he took his time, combing his hair and shooting his cuffs. He thought of Tim clutching the pair of links an hour or so ago—and then he heard conversation begin to filter through the cheap wartime-construction door separating Room M304 from Room M305. He walked back and put his ear to it.

"Clean?" asked an agitated voice he realized must be McLeod's.

"As a whistle," answered Traband.

PART TWO

FEBRUARY–NOVEMBER 1954

I am a strong believer in Purgatory.

—FLANNERY O'CONNOR

CHAPTER TWELVE

February 22, 1954

On George Washington's Birthday the upper body's only piece of business—now being performed by Senator Hunt before a handful of colleagues and a full gallery of holiday tourists—was a recitation of the first president's Farewell Address. Representative Metcalf of Montana was doing the honors in the House. According to Tommy McIntyre, the old-timers there could still remember the February tributes to Lincoln being conducted by Henry Rathbone, Republican of Illinois, son of the unfortunate fellow who'd been beside the president and knifed by Booth in the box at Ford's.

Tim couldn't imagine ever being an old-timer on the Hill, but after four months he no longer needed the *Congressional Directory* to recognize who came and went on the floor. He'd been able to pick out Hubert Humphrey, plump and happy and fast, as well as Senator Green of Rhode Island, frail and dusted with dandruff and said to be, like Speaker Rayburn and Senator Russell, "a lifelong bachelor."

Senator Hunt was doing his best, but very laboriously, with Washington's 150-year-old oratory. It was hard for Tim to believe, even as he tried peeling away the decades with his imagination, that this rumpled and tired-looking man, stolidly fixed to the carpet, had once played semipro baseball. Kenneth Woodforde could probably make some clever irony out of the way Hunt had spent much of his adult life, after baseball and before politics, as a dentist. It was, after all, another dentist bringing the Capitol to a boil right now. The building was ready to blow over the way General Ralph Zwicker had been questioned by the McCarthy committee in New York last Thursday about the promotion of Major Irving Peress, D.D.S. and onetime Communist.

It seemed obvious to everybody including Tim that Peress had gotten an extra stripe merely through the routine, unstoppable flow of army paper, with whoever had been in charge no more likely to notice the major's politics than to spot a pebble inside a glacier. And yet, for being in command at Camp Kilmer when the promotion occurred, General Zwicker had received an absolutely livid thrashing from McCarthy. The record of the hearing had been leaked in several places on the Hill and would no doubt be in the papers tomorrow.

It was hard concentrating on George Washington's rhetorical ghost while holding this incendiary onionskin transcript that Tommy had asked him to read. It had been typed over the weekend by Miss Cook, who'd called everybody in to the office this morning. (Tim could now get telephone messages through the hardware store below his apartment.) He'd intended to spend lunchtime on the banks of the Potomac, where, to mark the holiday, contestants in a model-plane competition would be flying tiny craft weighted with silver dollars across the river; but by 8:45 Tommy had been greeting him at the door to Room 80, informing him that they'd have to spend the day "telling Charlie what to think of all this business with the brass."

SEN. MCCARTHY: Don't be coy with me, General.
GENERAL ZWICKER: I am not being coy, sir.

Each translucent page was more startling than the one before. Lest Tim miss anything, Tommy had circled the worst bits with a laundry marker:

GENERAL ZWICKER: I don't like to have anyone impugn my honesty, which you just about did.
SEN. MCCARTHY: Either your honesty or your intelligence; I can't help impugning one or the other . . .

SEN. MCCARTHY: I mean exactly what I asked you, General, nothing else. And anyone with the brains of a five-year-old child can understand that question.

SEN. MCCARTHY: Any man who has been given the honor of being promoted to general and who says, "I will protect another general who protected Communists," is not fit to wear that uniform, General. I think it is a tremendous disgrace to the Army to have this sort of thing given to the public. I intend to give it to them.

On Friday afternoon, Zwicker, who'd stormed Omaha Beach on D-Day, had told reporters that McCarthy had treated him worse than he'd treated the actual Communist who'd been in the witness chair a few minutes earlier. Secretary of the Army Stevens, upon learning of the chairman's tirades, had told the general not to show up for the public testimony he was supposed to give tomorrow in Washington. Stevens would come to the Capitol and answer McCarthy himself.

The army and the subcommittee were now, indisputably, at war.

Roy Cohn had returned Stevens' fire, pronouncing "the army's attempt to coddle and promote Communists" too important for good manners from the subcommittee. His own part in the assault on Zwicker could also be found in the transcript, where Tim spotted Jones, too, charging in like a battle-crazed bugle boy. For the past couple of months there had been amused talk in the office about how the ambitious research assistant was beginning to acquire McCarthy's oral cadences and repetitions, those reiterated opening phrases that turned the senator's questions into little battering rams of sound.

" 'The nation which indulges toward another an habitual hatred or an habitual fondness is in some degree a slave,' " Senator Hunt continued, to the gallery's ever-decreasing attention. What might Woodforde make of that? Tim wondered. The Zwicker transcript was starting to upset him as much as Woodforde and Cohn had after the atrocities hearing. But even so, the larger, implacable fact remained: we *ought* to hate Russia, where people *were* slaves. China, too: the House had just gotten intelligence estimates that Mao Tse-tung had murdered more than fifteen million people. How differently, knowing of such mass slaughters, might George Washington be speaking today?

The conflict between sordid means and great ends had been gnawing at Tim—it was a kind of religious mystery beyond his powers of reckoning—and when it came to Hawkins Fuller, the last two months had been grindingly devotional. Tim realized he was practicing a kind of Trappist discipline that left him alternately exalted and exhausted. At Grandma Gaffney's on Christmas Day he'd felt the same isolation he'd experienced at Thanksgiving—only it had been twice as strong, a physical ache that stole his appetite and left him unable to concentrate on anything but endless, repetitive thoughts of his beloved. He had kept himself from sending a postcard to the Fullers' address in Maine, mailing one instead, pointlessly, to the empty apartment on I Street, which he'd walked past three times after returning to Washington early. He had tried to content himself with the awareness that this small, falsely cheerful expression of himself was sleeping in the mailbox of #5B, beside some unopened bills awaiting the still-absent tenant. He had finally gone to dinner at Duke Zeibert's with Bobby Garahan, his Fordham pal—*God, Laughlin, it's steak; how come you're just picking at it?*—but he'd returned home early to read a library copy of the Lodge biography. He still wondered where Fuller's inscribed one resided. At the office? In some jumbled corner of the apartment he'd never caught sight of?

Once Hawk finally came back to town, all had gone as it had in the fall, with a sort of unnerving joy, the possibility of banishment hovering over everything, more like a rival than a fate, a presence that seemed to listen in on the telephone and slip into bed between the two of them. Now, three weeks into February, Hawk had suddenly gotten busy at work. His preoccupation there was actually proving a relief to Tim: if Hawk had less time for him, there had to be less for any others as well.

A vote on the Bricker Amendment was fast approaching, with Hawk actually due to call on Potter later this week to explain the administration's opposition. "I'll make myself scarce when you get to the office," Tim had assured him. Hawk, seeing the embarrassment Tim was anticipating, had only laughed. "Skippy," he'd replied, squeezing the back of Tim's neck, "don't ever play poker." More seriously, he'd added: "Make yourself stick around when I arrive. It's good training."

"For what?" Tim had asked.

"For the life you'll be leading."

A life together? He had, for a moment, allowed himself to believe that that was what Hawk meant, though he soon realized that he meant the life Tim would be living once he'd been sent, schooled in doubleness, on his way.

All at once, Tommy McIntyre was in the galley, standing over Tim. The gleam in his eye would have made anyone guess he'd gone back to drinking—"the affliction of our people," he often told Tim in alluding to the problems of his past. But, along with a clipboard, Tommy's right hand held only an unopened bottle of 7Up.

"You're needed," he said. "Badly."

"I'm sorry," Tim replied, quickly gathering up the loose sheets of transcript.

Tommy flung his arm over Tim's shoulder. "There's *nothing* to be sorry about today, Mr. Laughlin." The gleam in the eye, Tim could see, bespoke an almost martial excitement. Tommy whistled while the two of them marched back to Room 80, which bustled with enterprise. Even Mrs. Potter was on hand, oblivious to the real drama and driving Miss Cook crazy with a display of the floral hat she'd bought to wear at Thursday's congressional wives' luncheon for Mamie Eisenhower and Mrs. Nixon. Everyone else in the office had already been made to inspect the hat; Senator Potter looked relieved to see McIntyre and Laughlin reappear.

"Here's the drill," said Tommy to the senator and Tim, as if both occupied the same rung on the staff. "The hearing with Stevens has been postponed until Thursday. And our Democratic friends have decided to come back to the committee." Potter seemed as much taken aback by this as Tim, who was now told why he'd been fetched. "All right, my boy," said Tommy. "Sit yourself down and compose a nice noble statement for our friends in the press about why we've just fired your colleague Mr. Jones."

Tim turned quickly to Senator Potter, who looked down, abashed, at his own artificially filled shoes. "I'm afraid," the lawmaker said, "that on Friday, without any authorization, Bob put out a statement in my name. It was just like Cohn's, all about how the treatment of General Zwicker was justified by the gravity of the matter under investigation. Apparently a couple of papers up in Maine, Bob's home state, went and ran it. I just can't have that."

"Nor," said Tommy, "can the senator have Mr. Jones engaging in impersonation at the hearings themselves. I've just shown him a couple of transcripts from last fall."

"I wish I'd known before," said Potter, who still seemed more perplexed than outraged.

"Well, Senator, better late than never. Don't you agree, Timothy?"

Earlier, thought Tim, would surely have been better still. Why, he wondered, had Tommy months ago shown him, but not Potter, the transcripts that had Jones playing senator along with Cohn and Schine?

"Bring the statement 'round to me at the Press Club an hour from now," instructed Tommy.

And why, Tim wondered, wasn't Tommy himself handling this crucial and clearly relished piece of business? Only, it seemed, because he had too much to do. From the way he proceeded to direct the senator back to his own desk, it appeared evident that Thomas McIntyre—this Johnny-on-the-spot, this come-and-go fixer—was now everybody's boss, Potter's included.

Fuller, too, had been called into the office this morning, no matter the holiday. Dulles, just back from Berlin, had scheduled a conference for congressional leaders. It was going on right now, and its participants included South Dakota's Senator Mundt, second to McCarthy on the subcommittee, who in the course of a lobbying session against the Bricker bill just the other day had demonstrated no real interest in talking to Fuller about the legislation.

"He preferred to squawk about all the commotion Marilyn Monroe's been allowed to cause in front of our boys in Korea," Fuller now explained to Mary. "It seems the army is in hot water it doesn't even know about."

"Diamonds should be *this* girl's best friend," said Mary, still cross about having had to come in today.

"You've *got* a diamond." Fuller pointed to the modest ring from Paul Hildebrand, whose stone Mary now twisted around to the hidden side of her finger.

"Is that or is it not an engagement ring?" asked Fuller.

Both realized that he had just fallen into mimicry of the Christmas-week interrogration they'd never talked about once it was over.

"The rumor is you passed their lie-detector test," said Mary.

"Yes, and I haven't yet had my raise."

"How's your French, Fuller?"

"Not as good as it would be if I'd had nuns teaching it to me in New Orleans."

"Do you know the difference between *sang-froid* and recklessness?"

"Yeah, that I grasp."

"No, you don't. *Sang-froid* is what you must have shown in front of the machine. In here you've just been reckless."

Fuller leaned back in his chair, daring her to elaborate.

"The ever-more-frequent personal phone calls. The louder laughter whenever you take them. The ever-shorter hours. It all adds up to a certain triumphalism. Dangerous, I'd say."

"Is she not gone from our midst?" asked Fuller, palms upward.

"Yes, she is." Another rumor had it that, before her disappearance into the Operations office, Miss Lightfoot had tried and failed to get herself transferred to McLeod's domain. But the handing over of Fuller had proved a poor audition for any job in the Miscellaneous M Unit.

"Well, there you go," said Fuller.

"Our real triumph is supposed to be over Senator Bricker," said Mary, as politely as she could. "I'm not sure that Mr. Morton's patience will last forever."

"I guarantee you that I'll fail upward. Even if every now and then I have to hide behind your old New Look skirts."

"So it's mothering you want from me?" She was embarrassed once she asked the question—it sounded as if she were fishing for some surprise romantic answer—and she did her best to withdraw it. "You still have a mother. Which is more than I can say for myself."

"I have a father, too."

"Are they happy together? Mother and father."

"You've got to be kidding," said Fuller.

"Why shouldn't they be? Mine were."

"The corridors at Park and Seventy-fourth are just as quiet, and nearly as long, as the ones we have here. Mother was more or less within shouting distance of my room, to the north. Father was around the corner and far to the south."

"A *sister*," said Mary, trying for lightness. "That's what you need."

"I have two of them. A surfeit, Miss Johnson."

"I'm making you angry. I should go."

"You're making me angry. *I* should go."

"I shouldn't pry."

"As if *that* were the reason you anger me!" said Fuller, with a laugh.

She suspected the real cause of his anger was his not wanting her to be a mother *or* a sister. A part of him—the part that hated what he was; even *he* couldn't be without that—must also hate her, for the way she got under his skin, ever so slightly, while remaining, finally, irrelevant. He wasn't angry because she knew his secrets; he was angry because she couldn't be the way out of them. Hadn't he looked at her, now and then, with a moment's real interest? An interest that quickly curdled into something like contempt—for himself, for her, for his inability to follow through? She doubted she would ever tell him her own secrets, not when some part of him might take an oblique pleasure in betraying them.

He got up from his chair, a folder in hand, and began to exit the office.

"Are you mad at me now?" she asked.

"Now and forever," he replied, with a tenderness that made the answer no less true.

Not a good day for the mimeograph machine to be on the fritz! But it was, and so once Tim cut the stencil announcing Jones's termination, he had to trot it over to the office of Senator Goldwater, another GOP freshman and World War II veteran, whose secretary would be happy to run it off. Eager for some air, he took the outdoor route, and on the sidewalk in front of the SOB came upon a cluster of photographers. They were shouting like the crowd he remembered outside McCarthy's wedding.

"How about giving her a kiss, Joe?" "How about signing the cast?"

"I've already signed it," said McCarthy, who grinned as he pointed to the plaster enclosing one of Jean McCarthy's shapely legs. She'd broken it in a taxi accident in New York, the night before the Zwicker hearing. Joe hadn't been injured, but his wife had spent a couple of nights by her lonesome in Flower Hill Hospital. McCarthy had just gone to Union Station to meet the train bearing his injured bride from New York. If ever there was a day when he could use a picture full of pulchritude and warmth, this was it. Jean flashed her beauty-queen smile and the cameras went in for tight shots that cut out the plainclothes policemen whose sidearms bulged beneath their coats.

Amidst this Hollywood clamor, Tim suddenly locked eyes with Robert Jones, who looked like a man just given his dream job, not one who'd just been fired. Jones smiled broadly at the lensmen, hoping to interest one of the cameras in himself. Tim made his way into the building without their exchanging even a nod.

A half-hour later he was down on Fourteenth Street, entering the Press Club with a hundred copies of the firing announcement under his arm. The first one went to Tommy, eating peanuts at the bar, and the second to May Craig, who sat beside him. Each already had another press release—not as neatly typed as Tim's—resting on the bar beside their drinks. Tommy picked up that sheet, damp with ginger ale, and gave it to Tim to read.

JONES DECLARES SENATE CANDIDACY

Robert L. Jones of Biddeford, Maine, former legislative assistant to Sen. Charles Potter (R-Mich.), announced this afternoon that he would challenge Maine senator Margaret Chase Smith in this June's Republican primary. Citing Sen. Smith's "shameful reluctance to face the Communist menace for what it is . . ."

"Running for office!" cried Tim. "Where will he get the money for that?" He recalled the peanut-butter-and-jelly sandwiches that Jones's wife sent him to work with.

"Wait till you see what Joe McCarthy's Texas supporters pony up!" cawed Miss Craig. "Jones'll be riding around Bangor in a red Cadillac all his own! Even so, it's only because the liar got canned. So in the meantime," she said, lifting her glass in a toast to McIntyre: "To the man who chopped down that miserable little cherry tree!"

"I cannot tell a lie," said Tommy. " 'Twas I." The gleam in his eye thanked Miss Craig, but behind its excitement, much farther back, Tim thought he could see the look of a man who knew he had entered a dark and perilous grove.

CHAPTER THIRTEEN

March 3, 1954

"Ah, seems Skippy fell into the coalpile in Grandma Gaffney's basement."

Tim stood, puzzled, at the doorway to the Bureau of Congressional Relations. His Ash Wednesday had begun so early, near the crack of dawn at St. Peter's on Second Street, that he'd forgotten the priest's black thumbprint on his forehead. Now he remembered.

"And to dust I shall return," he told Fuller.

"Come inside," said the older man, guiding him between the desks. "Meet our ambassadresses to that foreign country where you reside. I refer, of course, to Capitol Hill. Timothy Laughlin, this is Mrs. Phillips, my right arm, and here is Miss Johnson, increasingly our left wing." Fuller completed the roster with a reference to their Kentucky boss: "The colonel, I'm afraid, is nowhere to be found."

"Well," said Beverly Phillips, "I've got to go find him. Excuse me, all." On her way out, she smiled at Tim, whose October visit to the office she did not recall.

He knew that even mild political joking was proscribed at State, but Hawk had told him how the atmosphere in the office had become much merrier since a woman named Miss Lightfoot had gotten herself transferred to the Operations office. In fact, as he went to take a phone call, Hawk told him to sit at the desk that was still awaiting her replacement. Before disappearing, he took from Tim the manila envelope that was the reason for this visit.

"It's nice to see you again," said Mary. "You're the young man who brought Mr. Fuller a book sometime back."

Tim nodded, nervousness subsumed into pleasure over how this memory of hers certified that he had a *history* with Hawkins, that he was situated within his life. There was also something thrilling about the term "Mr. Fuller."

"Right," said Tim. "Yesterday he left some papers at—on the Hill."

Within the limits of the adjusted preposition, this was not a lie. Fuller had forgotten the envelope in Tim's apartment early last evening, when he'd come around after some late appointments in the House Office Building. Tim had meant to return the papers tonight, but Fuller had called Senator Potter's office an hour ago to say he needed them now.

"Did you at least manage a Mardi Gras celebration last night?" Mary pointed to the ashes on his forehead. "I should explain I'm from New Orleans."

"Oh, I know," said Tim, who feared, as soon as he said it, that he'd said too much. But Miss Johnson was smiling at him, and he felt suffused with a sense of safety. He forgot about his desire to see around the doorway and into Hawkins' office, where he'd worried about finding the Lodge biography, uncherished, lying atop a filing cabinet or beside a dying plant.

"We're usually a bit more busy here," said Mary. The defeat of the Bricker Amendment the other day—owed in part to the theatrics of Lyndon Johnson, who'd brought Senator Kilgore in on a stretcher to cast the deciding vote—had been a rare piece of good news. And it had been followed by another, when Secretary Dulles unexpectedly relieved Scott McLeod of his personnel duties, confining him henceforth to security matters—an amazing, tacit declaration that the two operations were not locked together in eternal emergency. McCarthy had complained about McLeod's diminution, but he had too many other fish frying—everyone could see something big coming—to say very much.

"It's nice," said Tim. "The calm, I mean. It's anything *but* calm where I am."

"He's right," said Fuller, emerging from his office. "These days poor Mr. Laughlin is even dodging bullets."

"You weren't near the shootings, were you?" asked Mary.

"No," said Tim. "I'm on the Senate side. But I was at the hospital this morning. My boss, Senator Potter, went to see Congressman Bentley. They're both from Michigan, and I came along for the ride."

It had been an odd delegation that went to Walter Reed to see Bentley, who'd been wounded by the Puerto Rican nationalists firing from the

House gallery. Tim had shared the car with Potter and his one-armed driver and Tommy McIntyre, whose eyes had remained, for the past ten days, continually ablaze. As near as Tim could tell, he'd been asked along because Tommy liked having an audience for all sorts of indiscreet chatter about the committee's impending showdown with the army. The confrontation would either break McCarthy—as Tommy tended to believe one day—or render him omnipotent, as he generally feared the next. Either way, for as long as it went on, Tommy insisted, Potter would have to be manipulated into doing the right, maybe even pivotal, thing. Robert Jones's campaign against Margaret Chase Smith—a small, distant theater of a much bigger war—was already another arena for Tommy's attempts at subversion. Cash was being mailed, phone calls getting made.

These were the sorts of things Tim told Hawkins on nights they were together, eliciting laughter at naïve points in the telling.

"Has McCarthy still got his guards?" Mary asked Tim.

"Plainclothes, I think. You wouldn't believe some of the mail Senator Potter gets, just from sitting at the same *table* with McCarthy. Which isn't really fair," he said, lowering his eyes toward Miss Lightfoot's old blotter, not truly confident of what he was saying. "The Communists are the real issue, and—"

Fuller cut him off: "I wouldn't open any packages that arrive, even after all this is over."

Tim, not sure if he was being teased or protected, said nothing, while Mary Johnson pictured this boy opening a parcel with his small scrubbed fingers and getting blown to bits. His destruction was, she thought, going to occur in any case. She watched him watching Fuller, his face like a paper target on a firing range.

"The rumor," said Tim, "is that John Adams, the army's lawyer, has a diary that lists all the pressures McCarthy and Cohn applied to get special treatment for David Schine. People also say McCarthy's own staff has been coming back to the office late at night to cook up documents that will refute the diary."

He spoke the last sentence as if refusing to believe it.

"My boss," Tim continued, meaning McIntyre, "had me go over there the other night and look around." He blushed at the admission. "I didn't really see much through the frosted glass of the door."

"All right, Mr. Laughlin." Fuller rose from the edge of the desktop.

"We can't waste the taxpayers' money by keeping you here any longer."
The dismissal was performed as a burlesque of impatience, but Tim knew
he was indeed meant to go, as if the two of them really were Mr. Fuller
and Mr. Laughlin, strangers. The touch of Hawkins' hand to his shoulder,
for the briefest moment as they reached the door, did little to erase the
impression.

"He's a nice boy," said Mary Johnson, once he was gone.

"Skippy?" asked Fuller. "Practically an angel."

She resumed typing thank-you letters to opponents of the Bricker
Amendment.

"You don't approve," said Fuller, not quite ready to reenter his own
office.

"Of what?" asked Mary.

The ensuing silence convinced her he didn't really mean to discuss it.
"Fuller," she finally said—a last effort—"I'm not Miss Lightfoot."

"I'll tell the brewer. He'll be relieved."

"But no," said Mary. "I suppose I *don't* approve. I doubt any woman
really does. And you can't expect me to: I was still getting ashes on my
own head three years ago. But there are things I approve of less."

"Of our boy Skippy railing against the reds?"

"No. Of your breaking his heart."

Fuller paused before saying, grandly, "I lack all such intention."

"But not all such power."

They were both still afraid of this conversation, and knowing that
Fuller could outlast her in any duel of silences, Mary got up to file a
handful of Bricker clippings from the European press.

"I suppose," she said at last, "Tim was imagining how he'd like to sit at
that desk every day, be at your beck and call." She nodded to Miss Lightfoot's empty station.

"He'd be excellent," replied Fuller. "Works very hard, and has his
race's gift of gab when he's working on paper. The stammer disappears
then, just as it does when he's drunk or—I'm sure—angry, though that
I've never seen. His handwriting is even neater than Miss Lightfoot's."

"Oh, you'd see him angry if he worked at that desk." Mary kept filing
as she spoke. "How do you think he'd feel taking your calls, and hearing
your conversations?"

Fuller said nothing, but still would not go back inside his office. Mary knew that he wanted to make her work even harder at this, force her to stick the knife farther in, get her—where McLeod had failed—to make the needle jump.

"Wouldn't sooner rather than later hurt him less?" she asked. "Couldn't you let him down easily? Give him up for Lent?"

Fuller pushed his hair above his forehead, making his ashless, marble brow fully visible. He returned to his office, declaring curtly, "I'm not Catholic, Miss Johnson."

CHAPTER FOURTEEN

March 10, 1954

"You're not coming in?" Senator Potter asked Tommy McIntyre at the threshold to McCarthy's inner office in the SOB.

"No," said Tommy. "I'll let Mr. Laughlin go in with you to make a record."

Surprised as he was by Tommy's directive, Tim was soon even more startled to feel the hard, friendly clap of Joe McCarthy's hand on his shoulder. The chairman didn't seem to mind his presence, taking him, perhaps, for an unpaid gopher, maybe even a page. There was nothing to do but go in and, after taking charge of Potter's canes, sit down on a beat-up horsehair sofa, a few deferential feet from the two senators.

"Now, Charlie," said the chairman. "I hope you haven't let Egghead R. Murrow scare you off from all the work we've still got to do together." McCarthy ran his tongue over his top front teeth, and smiled as he awaited a reply.

"I didn't see the program," said Potter.

Tim had watched it on Hawkins' television. The half-hour episode of *See It Now* had been unrelenting, even brutal, but Hawk had fallen asleep before Murrow closed with an ominous quotation from *Julius Caesar.*

"I gather the fellow doesn't like me," said the chairman, flashing another smile and twirling his big horn-rimmed glasses above the blotter. McCarthy was nervous, Tim realized, though only for moments at a time. At the doorway, when he realized he'd hit Tim's shoulder far too hard, a look of tenderness had crossed his face and then instantly vanished, been left for dead in the space of a second.

"Well," said Potter, who sat in a chair beside the desk, "my old aide

Jones is throwing you plenty of bouquets up in Maine. 'A great American, a great patriot, doing a great job.' " He tried smiling, but couldn't manage it; there wasn't enough mischief in him.

McCarthy, however, roared with laughter. "You never should have let him go, Charlie! I'm not sure I could get even Roy to put it so well."

"Jones has also been saying some things, not so flattering, about Margaret Smith," added Potter, just above a mumble. " 'A nice lady but for her left-wing ideas.' Stuff like that."

McCarthy shrugged, but Potter managed to warm to the topic of Jones, even if it wasn't the subject he'd come in with. "In his speeches up there, Bob now talks about having been a 'member of the committee.' "

McCarthy again laughed things off. "*There's* a go-getter! You should have kept him and given him a raise!"

"He seems to be doing pretty well up there for a guy who's no longer pulling in the eighty-five hundred a year I used to pay him."

"He hasn't gotten a *dime* from me, Charlie."

The smile was gone, and the "m" in "dime" came out as a prolonged, electrical buzz, the way McCarthy would have sent it through a radio microphone.

"Joe, I got a report last night from across the river."

There was no need to explain further. Everyone had been hearing rumors of the "Adams chronology," a timeline prepared at the Pentagon by the army counsel, detailing all the pressures exerted on Schine's behalf by McCarthy and Cohn.

"That prick Nixon wouldn't be behind this, would he?" When it came to exposing Communists, McCarthy liked to call the veep a Johnny-leave-early, an ambitious young man who'd traded his once-raucous sound truck for the smooth sedan of Eisenhower moderation, a vehicle he now thought he could ride to 1600 Pennsylvania Avenue.

"No, Joe," continued Potter, as sternly as he could. "I got this report from Wilson. He sent it to me himself."

Surely, Tim thought, even Potter knew that the secretary of defense had not dispatched this dynamite without a direct order from the White House.

McCarthy tried to stare down his interlocutor, but Potter managed to continue: "I'm disturbed by what I see in it." He sounded like the social worker he'd once been, regretfully forced to confront a relief recipient with reports of misbehavior.

The senator from Wisconsin would have none of it: "Charlie, you and I and the rest of the committee need to get back to finding Communists. We should be getting Scott McLeod the rest of his job back." The "Ms" and the "Ns" were buzzing.

"Joe," said Potter, delivering the line he must have rehearsed the hardest, "Roy Cohn needs to be fired."

Tim recalled the look on Cohn's face when the committee counsel had been on the phone screaming to John Adams about Dave Schine's having to "eat shit" in basic training. Had that remark gotten typed into the "Adams chronology," which Potter was nervously rolling and unrolling in his hands? Tim had no more than a second to ponder the question; the room's sudden, inescapable drama was the hurricane sweeping McCarthy's face, stirring up the expression that must have greeted General Zwicker a few minutes into his testimony.

"Senator Potter, believe it or not, I have some *friends* among the press. Men like Winchell and George Sokolsky. *Jews.* Strong, right-thinking Jews who have a clear sense of what communism actually is. They're a minority among their own people, from whom they take considerable abuse. They won't be pleased to see you and your friends go after Roy, who's the youngest and the finest and the strongest of this minority within a minority. Winchell has a microphone, Senator. And Sokolsky has a thousand of Hearst's printing presses. Go after Roy Cohn and they'll go after you, Senator. In fact, I'll make sure they do."

Tim gripped both of Potter's canes as if they might actually be needed to beat McCarthy back. And yet he could hear that the secretary sitting outside next to Tommy had not so much as interrupted her typing in response to the boss's bellow. She seemed to realize that the fierce-sounding storm would actually be a quick shower, not worth opening an umbrella for.

But McCarthy was not quite through. "Everybody's money comes from someplace, Senator. Even yours. Everybody's *people* come from someplace." McCarthy indicated the outer office with a raise of his chin. Was Tommy, Tim suddenly wondered, a former Communist? He looked toward Potter for some confirmation of the possibility. The senator did not respond. His courage, Tim realized, was of a purely physical kind; when Potter looked into the boiling face of his colleague, he appeared calmer than when he merely glanced at the carpet.

Then the sun broke through. McCarthy relaxed his chin and smiled. He shook his head. "Oh, hell, Charlie. I don't give a damn about Schine. He's just a dumb, good-looking kid hoping to get laid even more than he already does. I think he figures coming home with a few scalps and a few headlines will accomplish whatever his face and his old man's money can't." Potter said nothing, not even when one last cloud scudded across the chairman's face. "But Roy worries about him," said McCarthy. "And I'm not going to get rid of Roy."

What, Tim wondered—trying to think like Tommy—did Cohn *have* on McCarthy? It couldn't just be, as McCarthy was now saying, that "the Communists would take more comfort from Roy's being fired than they have from anything since Roosevelt recognized Russia twenty years ago." Nobody, thought Tim, not even Cohn, could be that smart or indispensable. Everybody said Bob Kennedy would have done just as well, been just as ferocious, if McCarthy had given him the counsel's job. Joe Kennedy had wanted it for his son, but McCarthy, who'd even dated one of Kennedy's daughters, had feared being tainted with the old ambassador's anti-Semitism, something he couldn't afford when the committee was investigating so many Jews. And so the job had gone to Cohn.

"Have a drink, Charlie."

The chairman, smiling again, now appeared to take Potter's silence for consent. It was settled; Roy would stay. And since the bottles in the glass-doored bookcase were all the way across the room, McCarthy reached a few easy inches for his briefcase, unsnapping its metal tabs and taking out a fifth of Jim Beam. He looked at Tim and laughed: "Are you old enough, son?" The "n" didn't buzz. McCarthy may already have had a liquid lunch, but he was fully himself—playing to the room, not the radio. Tim smiled and shook his head, declining as politely as he could, while wondering if Tommy's hatred of McCarthy might not spring from this alone, the drinking, the loathing a reformed drunk has for an active one. No, Tim decided, it wasn't enough of an explanation, any more than Cohn's talent for fighting communism could explain McCarthy's determination to keep him around.

While the chairman, still smiling, took a drink by himself, the junior senator from Michigan sat in silence for a last few seconds. But then—perhaps only, Tim thought, because he feared Tommy's displeasure—Potter found his voice and seeded the clouds for McCarthy's next mood-storm: "We can get the army to fire John Adams, too, Joe. We can make it look like a trade, with fault on both sides. But unless Roy goes, this whole thing is going to have to be investigated, maybe even in front of television cameras."

McCarthy's smile disappeared, but no thunder issued from behind the new clouds on his visage. He seemed to be considering the possibility those cameras would present him, how they might be a risk worth taking if he could bend the hearings in his own direction, change their subject once the lights came up and the lenses opened. For the moment, however, it seemed he would err on the side of caution. "You tell your new friend Wilson to keep that report to himself from now on. We've got files of our own. We've got typewriters, too. You tell him that, Charlie."

The meeting was over, and by all appearances McCarthy, now on his feet, was judging it a success. He reached into the office refrigerator for three small wheels of Wisconsin cheese, one for Tim, one for Potter, and one for Tommy McIntyre. All of them, the chairman included, were soon exiting Room 428 and walking down the corridor.

"Did you hear Flanders on the floor yesterday?" asked McCarthy. "It was better than Murrow and all that *Julius Caesar* crap. Listen to this," he said, urging them to slow down while he pulled a newspaper clipping from his pocket. McCarthy began quoting the Vermont senator's remarks: " 'In this battle of the agelong war'—I guess he means against the Communists—'what is the part played by the junior senator from Wisconsin? He dons his war paint. He goes into his war dance. He emits his war whoops. He goes forth to battle and proudly returns with the scalp of a pink army dentist.' "

McCarthy's laughter bounced off the walls of the SOB. At the landing of the staircase, by the blue-and-white peppermint-stick columns, he said goodbye to his visitors with a high, enthusiastic wave that parted the halves of his unbuttoned jacket and revealed the holstered pistol beneath.

CHAPTER FIFTEEN

March 19, 1954

Whenever the radio played "Secret Love," Tim believed for a few moments that he had something in common with other Americans in the throes of romance. The song had been riding the airwaves for weeks, and it made him feel more normal than furtive, at least until Doris Day reached the tune's happy ending. Right now, late on a Friday night when he was home alone working, the song seemed more than he could stand, so he turned the dial and arrived, almost immediately, at the sound of Joe McCarthy, speaking live from Milwaukee about the Democratic party's "twenty years of treason, twenty years of betrayal." Along with roars of approval from a hotel banquet room, the microphones were picking up traces of a "Joe Must Go!" chant from the opposing rally outside.

"Tonight," McCarthy intoned, "I shall place before the greatest of all juries, the American people, an indictment of twenty counts, picked at random."

The "m" buzzed through the mesh of the Philco.

McCarthy's text and the protesting chant competed like the parallel columns Tim was constructing on a legal pad. The crux of the charges and countercharges already seemed pretty clear to the public: the army, through its secretary Robert Stevens and counsel John Adams, was claiming that all sorts of extravagant pressure had been brought to bear by Senator McCarthy and Roy Cohn to make Private David Schine's life in the service a kind of holiday; on the contrary, the senator and Cohn continued to assert that the army was holding Schine "hostage"— preventing him from continuing to assist the committee and threatening the young man with overseas duty as a means of getting McCarthy to call off his probe into the army's tolerance of subversives at Fort Monmouth.

But if the crux was clear, a farrago of detail still swirled underneath it. Tim looked at the columns he was composing for Tommy McIntyre and Senator Potter, and wondered if he'd ever master their contradictions:

ARMY CLAIMS (ADAMS CHRONOLOGY)	McCARTHY MEMORANDA
Dec. 9: Adams says he complained to Sen. McC about Roy C's behavior and threats re Schine.	Dec. 9: Confidential memo from Roy C to Sen. McC: "John Adams said today . . . that he had gotten specific information for us about an Air Force base where there were a large number of homosexuals. He said he would trade us that information if we would tell him what the next Army project was that we would investigate."
Jan. 11: Adams visits Cohn's office. Claims Cohn said Stevens is "through" as Army Sec'y if Schine gets sent overseas.	Jan. 14: Memo from Roy C to Sen. McC: "John Adams has been in the office again . . . said this was the last chance for me to arrange that law partnership in New York which he wanted. One would think he was kidding, but his persistence on this subject makes it clear he was serious. He said he had turned down a job in industry at $17,500 and needed a guarantee of $25,000 from a law firm."

Sitting amidst piles of newspapers from the past two weeks, Tim decided that the whole thing was impossible, like some assignment from the nuns requiring you to cross-connect the Seven Deadly Sins and the Four Cardinal Virtues. Was Cohn in love with Schine, or was Adams in love with money? A week ago, Tommy McIntyre had had Tim compose Senator Potter's statement demanding that everybody be put under oath to sort things out, and four days after that, meeting in executive session, the committee had agreed—beginning in a few weeks, in front of television cameras—to investigate itself.

Tim was growing accustomed to the circularity of all this, and to the possibility that truth might be reachable only by riding on wheels within wheels. Did McCarthy have something on Tommy McIntyre (*"Everybody's people come from someplace"*), and did Tommy also have something on Potter? Something to account for his ever-greater command of the senator's office? Since the afternoon when the three of them experienced McCarthy's wrath and bonhomie, Tommy had been so busy that Tim had had no chance to question the older man about his political past. When McIntyre slowed down enough for even a short snatch of conversation, he talked in riddles, *sententiae*, and snippets of poetry.

Closing his eyes and breathing in the woody aroma of the hardware store below, Tim tried to reestablish the concentration required for his parallel columns, but was stopped by the sound of footsteps on the stairs.

"You need a TV, Skippy."

As soon as he came in, Fuller pointed to the radio, from which McCarthy's consonants continued to buzz. Slightly and thrillingly drunk, he sat down on the edge of the desk and nodded toward an especially ugly picture of Cohn in the *Evening Star*. "Without a TV," said Fuller, "you missed him on *Meet the Press* last Sunday. Trust me: he's not as sweet as he looks."

He took off his suit jacket—all the warm, nearly spring night required—and extracted from it a white card, which he handed to Tim. "For your information," he said. "Forwarded from Bar Harbor by the paterfamilias." The card invited the holder to the Maine state Republican convention, set for the first and second of April. "According to Father," Fuller explained, "your Mr. Jones's supporters are urging that he be allowed to speak to the delegates along with 'Magrit.'" He pronounced Mrs. Smith's name with an old Mainer's accent.

Tim mentioned the latest that he'd heard in the office. "Jones is now giving speeches that refer to himself as a 'member of the committee'! He used to just say he 'sat in' once in a while."

Fuller flipped through the stack of newspapers on the desk until he found Monday's *Washington Post*. "Good boy," he said. "Glad to see you're sometimes trading up from the *Star*, if only a small bit." As Hawkins looked for the correct page, Tim considered the praise he'd just been given, which was really a piece of the tutelage that sometimes con-fused him—as when Hawkins suggested he get himself something better than the Van Heusen shirt he'd regarded as a splurge to begin with.

"Here it is," said Hawkins, pointing to a column by the Alsop brothers, Joseph and Stewart. " 'The uncensored Adams chronology is also under-stood to contain an indication that Cohn was receiving substantial finan-cial assistance from Schine, while he was threatening to "wreck the army" in order to make his rich friend's life more comfortable.' "

"That's not true," said Tim. "It's Adams who was interested in money. I think."

"Then what *is* the truth?" asked Fuller. "Where Cohn is concerned."

"Cohn is in love with Schine." Tim was struck by the difficulty of just saying it.

"Good," said Hawkins. "Our little boy is growing up. But read on." He pointed to the column's next sentence and handed the paper to Tim, who read from it aloud:

" 'This financial dependence would help to explain Cohn's feverish desire to be of service to Schine. It does not explain the strength of Cohn's apparent hold on McCarthy.' "

Tim looked up, confused. "It's true," he said, "that McCarthy doesn't speak very well of Schine unless Cohn is around."

"Think harder, Timothy."

Tim put down the newspaper. "It gives me a headache. I've been trying to figure out what McCarthy has on McIntyre and what McIntyre has on Potter." He walked over to Fuller and kissed him. "I know what they could all have on me."

Hawkins lightly kissed him back and let him sit on his lap. "I could tell you what I've got on Joe Alsop," he whispered, thinking of the spring day last year when the elder, unmarried brother of the columnist duo had first leered in his direction at the coat check of the Sulgrave Club. The card that came around the following morning had read more like a mash note than a luncheon invitation.

"You're as bad as Tommy McIntyre," said Tim, who believed Fuller was kidding. "The only thing I want to have on you are these." He pointed to his lips, before kissing Hawk's neck.

"Just remember, Skippy. The only thing that counts in all this is what anybody has on McCarthy. Got that?" He gently deposited him back in the desk chair, as if Tim, freshly instructed, could now return to work.

For the past week and a half, Tim had wanted to tell Hawkins about his ten minutes in McCarthy's office. But after the night of the Murrow program, when Hawkins seemed to keep him at arm's length, he had forced himself not to come around; he'd made himself wait for Hawkins' appearance here. He now wanted to say "I'm glad you came over," but it was too simple and direct, somehow even more honest than the kisses he'd planted.

"I need to believe," he explained instead, "that there's still at least a chance Adams and Stevens could be the worst ones in all this. Maybe they're *not* worthy of the soldiers they're in charge of. Maybe they *were* trying to stop the Fort Monmouth investigation—you know, because they're bureaucrats trying to protect themselves."

He knew, as he spoke, that his dread of McCarthy must be showing in his face, as it had started doing months ago in front of Kenneth Wood-forde. He further knew, as his eyes darted to the parallel lists, that the "McCarthy Memoranda," especially the communications from Cohn, had the too-good-to-be-true smoothness of forgery. *We've got type-writers, too.*

"Where have you been?" he asked Hawkins, willing to risk humiliation if it would extract him from the conundrum of McCarthy.

"Out with the dullest crowd imaginable."

"Was the brewer there?" He knew that Hawkins didn't think much of Mary Johnson's fiancé; he also knew Hawk wasn't about to answer for the whole last ten days.

Fuller shook his head. "No brewer. Two former classmates. Plus one wife, one girlfriend."

"How about you?" asked Tim. "Did you go with a girl?"

"Of course," said Fuller.

The girls never made Tim feel jealous; the ease with which they were pressed into service—like handkerchiefs taken from a drawer—only added to Hawkins' allure.

"Did you know Schine?" The question had only now occurred to Tim. "When you were at Harvard?"

"Ever so slightly. We overlapped—so not to speak—for a year or two. He would have fit right in with tonight's crowd."

"He's not your type, right?" said Tim, hoping his teasing would provoke a measure of the same.

"Nor is Cohn his. Private Schine likes the ladies. Your buddy Roy is going to wear out his lawyer's larynx barking up that particular tree."

"Yeah," said Tim, amorous once more. He got up from the desk in search of a kiss. "You like them shorter, skinnier. With a few freckles. A stammer." He buried his head against Hawkins' shoulder.

"Easy, Timmy, it's a school night."

He felt immediate despair: if Hawk really wanted to go to bed with him, there would be, he knew, no consideration less important than the clock.

"I hate working Saturdays," he managed to complain. "It's only those ancient bachelors like Senator Russell who enjoy them. They get so lonely in their hotel rooms they wish everyone would come in on *Sundays*." He paused, hoping that Hawk would reconsider, would sigh forbearingly, then laugh, then throw him down on the blue bedspread. But nothing. "Don't you have to work tomorrow, too?"

Hawkins shook his head. "Middle rank has its privileges." Since his triumph over McLeod, he'd come in fewer Saturday mornings than he'd missed. "In my case, the night is young."

"Take me out into it." Tim knew his smile must look as desperate as any flashed by a politician behind in the polls. "Make me the drunk version of your type. One spiked *dulce de leche* and the spectacles come flying off. The stammer disappears." *Be here with me at seven in the morning. Force me to stay in bed another hour. Keep me from going to Mass and being the only Catechumen there, the one who sits in the back no longer daring to take Communion.*

Fuller smiled but didn't move. After a long moment, he at last said: "All those things—skinny boy, freckles, specs, stammer—they're certainly a *part* of my type."

Tim warmed with encouragement. "I can supply the rest of it, too."

Hawk tugged on his ear. "Let's go *find* the rest of it."

Tim looked around, comically, to his left and then right and then behind, as if trying to spot the rest of himself.

"Let's go out and find it *together*," Hawkins said, his voice lower than before. He put his arm over Tim's shoulder. "Maybe the two of us can become the three of us."

Tim felt the back of his neck flush.

Hawkins tried for a lighter touch. "*You* know," he joked. "Like Joe and Roy and Dave. What do you say?"

Tim crossed the room and stood at the sink. "No, Mr. Fuller." They were the words he'd said at this same spot five months ago, but this time there was no chance of their being a sin, mortal or venial; they contained no lie.

What he said next might have been a line from a movie, except for the excruciating effort it took to summon the words: "Get out and don't come back."

Fuller straightened the papers he'd displaced in sitting down on the desk. Ten seconds later, the door had closed and Tim could hear the ex–track star's light, heedless descent of the stairs.

Out on the street, Fuller walked west, wondering where he could catch a cab on the deserted Hill. He passed a telephone booth and thought of calling Mary Johnson, who probably was out with the brewer, which was too bad, because he remained curious about something. He wanted to ask her what credit one got for giving something up when Lent was halfway through. Did you get more if the renunciation was meant to be for good, to go beyond Easter? *I did what you told me to,* he wanted to say. He'd devised the stratagem himself, but had carried it out for the reason she'd suggested. *Wouldn't sooner rather than later hurt him less?*

Now that he'd done his good deed, he was—what, precisely? Angry? Sad? He dismissed the questions and kept walking, not in the direction of a bar, but toward home, where tonight, for once, he'd intended going all along.

CHAPTER SIXTEEN

April 7, 1954

"Well," said Tommy McIntyre, "there's Jeannie, but where's Joe?"

McCarthy's young wife sat across the dining room of the Carroll Arms, lunching with George Sokolsky, the Hearst columnist who'd helped script her husband's televised rebuttal of Murrow last night. The senator's reply had come late and—even Joe's friends thought—fallen rather flat, consisting largely of references to Murrow's left-wing friends from the 1930s, most of them respectable not only now but then.

Tommy took scornful note of the wine bottle between Sokolsky and Jean McCarthy. "They'll probably keep at it straight until they pour themselves into a cab for dinner at the Colony."

Tim looked at Mrs. McCarthy, pretty as a Miss America, and wondered why she hadn't ended up with a man who looked like Hawkins Fuller instead of someone fifteen years older who was running to blotches and fat. The answer had to lie in the way she lit up, as if for a camera, each time she caught a senator or reporter, or even a staffer as junior as himself, turning an eye in her direction. Joe McCarthy was the source from which all that derived.

Sokolsky's speech had contained one peculiar patch, a piece of hit-and-run rhetoric in which McCarthy offered up the possibility that everyone hearing his voice might soon die, and the nation itself be destroyed, because of unnamed traitors who had slowed down production of the U.S. hydrogen bomb. And now, as Tim looked into his water glass, he felt himself wishing for the prophecy's fulfillment—a manmade Second Coming, all doom and no redemption.

Weeks without Hawkins had left him with circles under the eyes and even thinner. He now took a cigarette whenever Tommy offered an open pack, and after work crawled into the bed he'd left unmade that morning. Good Friday was nine days away and he would not be heading home to New York: longing for Hawkins had made Thanksgiving and Christmas hard enough; consciousness of banishment would be unbearable in Grandma Gaffney's parlor.

Once he failed to make his Easter duty at the Communion rail, his estrangement from the Body of Christ would become official and another mortal sin upon his soul. Several times during the last few weeks he had come close to entering the confessional, in search not of absolution but some temporary solace. Yet what could he possibly say in the darkened booth? *Bless me, Father, for I have been unable to sin; he won't see me.*

Should he have gone looking for the third man, then gone to bed with him and Hawk? Should he send Hawk a funny, forgiveness-seeking note that made a joke about the Holy Trinity? Or just offer an abject below-stairs apology, as even his implacable grandmother must once or twice have done to the snotty boarding-school girls, lest she lose the situation on which her life depended?

Would sleeping with two men have been doubly sinful, or just "immature"—as men like himself were judged to be by even sympathetic observers? Would it have been, perhaps, no worse than joining the jerkoff circles of other boys on the rooftop over Ninth Avenue, or by the lake up near Ellenville during one of the family's rare summer weeks outside the city? Maybe. But if he'd not been able to make himself enter those harmless groupings in the light of day, how could he now expect to lie in the dark while, with one hand, Hawk caressed him and, with the other, pleasured someone else?

Tommy hit his water glass with a knife. "Snap to it, Mr. Laughlin. There's work to be done."

Three other Senate aides—assistants to Mundt and Dworshak and McClellan—were at the table. All had extracted pads from briefcases, ready to focus on the ground rules for what people were already calling the Army–McCarthy hearings. Mr. O'Brien and Mr. Matthews, Mundt's man and McClellan's, laughed when each saw the other click open a PaperMate pen whose barrel bore the signature of Majority Leader Lyndon B. Johnson. "He must give out five hundred of those a day," said O'Brien.

Tommy began making energetic notes. "All right, gentlemen," he said, "let's remember the decision from the executive session: nothing procedural about these hearings will create a precedent for any other set."

"That's fine with my man," said O'Brien, whose boss, the unprepossessing Senator Mundt, would chair the sessions. "He sure isn't going to want to do *this* again."

Sandor Klein, assistant to Senator Dworshak, nervously sketched a little chart. His own boss's position was the most delicate of any of the panel's senators, McCarthy having handpicked the Idaho Republican to replace him as a voting member of the committee. McCarthy would still be allowed to cross-examine witnesses—when he wasn't being questioned himself. "Christ," said Klein, "how *could* this create a precedent? Joe is going to be plaintiff, prosecutor, and defendant—not to mention his own mouthpiece, when Cohn is otherwise occupied."

Matthews recalled the laughing plea that McCarthy had made to Senator McClellan, the committee's former chairman, when the majority shifted to the Republicans in '52: " 'But, Jack, you've *got* to stay on as ranking Democrat. Who the hell else is going to keep an eye on me?' "

Klein fretted: "I don't know how we're going to have enough people to handle the mail this is going to generate."

Tommy, beginning to relax a bit, smiled. "We're short one staffer ourselves. I refer of course to Mr. Jones." Tommy had helped to arrange a rude reception for Mrs. Smith's challenger at the state convention in Bangor; he'd also, he now informed the table, managed to spread across Maine the story that Jones had run over his own dog and taken its stillbreathing carcass to the town dump. This produced laughter all around, except from Tim, who felt ever more gray and stateless in a world of black and white. McCarthyite tactics were all right, it seemed, so long as they were applied against McCarthy.

Maybe in his despair (another mortal sin), he was taking too seriously what was just the ordinary stuff of politics. After all, Mr. O'Brien, aide to the McCarthy-supporting Mundt, was laughing louder than anyone.

A small commotion across the room caught everybody's attention. Two tables away from Jean McCarthy, Mrs. Watt, the committee's chief clerk and supposedly a fan of Joe's, was sharply dismissing someone who'd set down a piece of paper and a pen beside her buttered roll.

"Ruthie looks miffed," said Matthews.

"Timothy, go see what that's all about. Discreetly."

Obeying McIntyre, Tim rose from the table and got himself as close as he could to Mrs. Watt by pretending to straighten his tie in front of a mirror.

"I won't sign it!" she repeated, loud enough for half the dining room to hear. Unnoticed in the hubbub, Tim moved even nearer to her table, then returned to his own.

"It's a loyalty pledge," he listlessly reported, just as his sandwich arrived. "A messenger gave it to her waiter. The committee staff are being asked to guarantee their support for Senator McCarthy and Mr. Cohn."

"By whom?" asked Matthews.

"I couldn't tell," answered Tim.

"Well, what's it supposed to accomplish?" Matthews inquired.

"It's not what it will accomplish," said Tommy McIntyre, delighted. "It's what it signifies. A touch of desperation, I'd say. The two of them are soldering themselves a little closer together. Nice work, Timothy. We ought to reward you with another pair of those." He pointed to Tim's cuff links.

"FH," said Klein, noticing the initials but reading from the right wrist to the left. "What does that stand for?"

"Fordham History," said Tim, after taking a sip of water. "It's the department I majored in at school."

He could see that Tommy didn't believe the explanation. Fine, he thought. Now you've got something on *me*.

"With any luck," said O'Brien, "you can win a pair of links off Joe." He pointed with awe to Oklahoma's Senator Kerr, who'd just entered the dining room. The richest man in the upper body was also its best card player, never going anywhere with less than five thousand in his pocket. Once or twice at the poker table he'd taken almost that much off his colleague from Wisconsin.

Tim could see Jean McCarthy coming back from the powder room, waving to the waiter who'd done his duty with the loyalty letter, whatever its ultimate lack of success. He could also now see Senator Hunt waving a swollen right hand—there were rumors of kidney problems—to greet an elderly lady near the maître d's stand; she congratulated him on having the other day announced that he would run for another term after all.

Mr. Matthews, getting back to business with the others, elaborated upon the "musical chairs" rule that had been adopted to accommodate the cameramen who'd be televising the hearings: each day senators and lawyers around the giant table would move one seat to their right, so that the same players wouldn't fill the screen day after day.

"Well," said Senator Mundt's aide, "this will give Joe a bigger microphone than he's ever had before."

"And you think that'll be *good* for him?" snapped Tommy.

"McIntyre," asked Matthews, "where is *your* man in all of this?"

"I believe," said Tommy, "that he'd actually like to get at the truth. Poor bastard."

Tim suspected this was true, that he and Senator Potter were in the same forlorn position, hoping the army's executives might be lying a little more than McCarthy and Cohn. And if they weren't? Would that invalidate everything else the committee had tried to accomplish? Would it leave Father Beane and his exemplary kind any safer from the Communists' universal advance?

He closed his eyes and again, almost peacefully, imagined a Russian H-bomb flying toward Washington.

None of it mattered. He now knew that he himself would tell any lie, deny even Christ, for one more touch of Hawkins' hand. These past few weeks, in his own bed several blocks from here, he had found himself unable even to masturbate. He would try, thinking of all the two of them had done, of the smell of Hawk's hair and neck and armpit, where his own tongue had long since gotten used to going. He would manage to arouse himself, until some tender memory—*There. You're healed*—would invade his loins and he would climax, if at all, with a strange lack of sensation, like the absence of grace.

Are you my brave boy? No, I am not. I need you to rescue and redeem me.

"So Charlie Potter wants the truth," said Matthews. "Well, maybe he'll get it for us."

"Oh," replied Tommy to the rest of the table, "he's going to get us much more than that."

CHAPTER SEVENTEEN

April 30, 1954

"So, yesterday," asked Cecil Holland, "who was calling who queer?"

"Whom," said Miss McGrory in her softest voice. The *Evening Star* had freed her from the book page to write colorful sidebars for Holland's regular reports on the week-old Army–McCarthy hearings, and the two of them were waiting for the Friday afternoon session to start, recalling the previous day's exchange between McCarthy and Joseph Welch, the Boston lawyer for Secretary Stevens and John Adams. The winsome attorney had sarcastically wondered if McCarthy thought a "pixie" was responsible for cropping a photograph whose alteration McCarthy claimed to know nothing about. Pressed to define "pixie," a creature McCarthy suggested Welch "might be an expert on," the lawyer explained that a pixie "is a close relative to a 'fairy.' Shall I proceed, sir? Have I enlightened you?"

The press had given the round to Welch. Even though propriety kept them from noting his apparent, if oblique, reference to rumors of McCarthy's homosexuality, they regarded the attorney's innuendo as a fine achievement, whereas McCarthy's suggestion of the same about Welch was considered a smear. All of it, thought Tim—who was trying to take pleasure in the greetings he'd just gotten from Miss McGrory and Mr. Holland—felt much the same as Robert Jones's dead dog. Any rules of engagement, let alone any standards of personal conduct, were now laughably antique. Even the ferocious Roy Cohn, the lights in his glass house turned up high, had looked nervous during yesterday's duel between McCarthy and Welch.

Cohn looked a bit nervous now, too, waiting as they all were for the testimony of Private Schine. Secretary Stevens had been on the stand almost the whole week, and he'd be back after the break he was being granted today for exhaustion. In the meantime, soon, they would be hearing from the young man who, in immediate terms, this was all about: G. David Schine, either the object of Roy Cohn's obsession, or the "hostage" of an army fearing Cohn's scrutiny.

The atmosphere in the Caucus Room was eerie, that of an interminable midnight Mass. The bemedaled army brass that Welch each day brought to the front row of spectators' seats sat, brave and solid, like a mute choir in coats of different colors. To keep glare off the TV cameras, the room's thick curtains remained closed, a purple backdrop for the cigarette smoke rising up the chamber's great Corinthian columns. Against the front wall a large wooden bench with a high back panel made the committee table look even more like an altar, albeit one whose feet were beset with snakes from some netherworld: the television cables on the carpet.

Once the principals had reassembled, Senator Mundt gaveled the proceedings to order. He complimented the audience on its good behavior, the way he did at the beginning of every session, as if fearing a turn to the riotous at any moment. Tim brought a stack of papers to Senator Potter's place at the enormous table, atop which he could actually hear the slosh of McCarthy's bourbon bottle when somebody moved his briefcase. Although everyone continued to remark on television's influence over the proceedings, Tim had been more reminded of his old radio programs like *Mr. Keen*. Listening to the different speakers while his eyes concentrated on the notepads and transcript in his lap, he found himself following the alternations by changes in voice. He had learned to distinguish the loud Tennessee drawl of Ray Jenkins, the temporary counsel hired to question both sides, from the thick Arkansas locutions of Senator McClellan, whose bad mood never seemed to lift. The nasal, countrified tones of Mr. Welch, a sharpie masquerading as an innocent, actually sounded a lot like Fred Allen.

Tim now exchanged a nod with Kenneth Woodforde in the press section, though they'd never had another conversation since the atrocities hearings (long since forgotten and still lacking a final report) back in December.

Before Schine took the oath, the senators spent yet another several minutes on the "doctored" version of a picture taken during Secretary

Stevens' visit to Fort Dix last fall, when cooperation still reigned between the army and the committee. This particular print contained only Stevens and Schine, as opposed to the original, which had included a third man. When first contested three days ago, the photo had provoked the pounding of desks and McCarthy's barked order that handsome Senator Symington be quiet. This afternoon, however, the committee's disagreements seemed like a weary seminar in art appreciation, full of ineffable and arcane questions about the meaning of the picture and its provenance. As Tim saw it, Stevens *was* looking, affably, at Schine—and no one else—in both the larger and cropped versions, although the photograph was so innocuous that either way it made no difference. On this matter, surely, Roy Cohn was right. In fact, given that McCarthy and Cohn's "eleven memoranda" were looking more suspicious by the day, shrinking the picture seemed about the *least* underhanded thing the senator's office had recently done in this case. But the press kept awarding the army points over what Welch continued to call the "shamefully cut-down" photograph, making it sound like a farm boy whose arm had been sliced off by some shoddy piece of machinery.

At last Private G. David Schine raised his hand and swore to tell the truth. Blond, Jewish, and beautiful in a lazy way, he appeared to Tim like the corrupt young emperor from a biblical movie. When asked about the manner in which he'd delivered the vexing photograph, once it had been requested for the investigation, he said he'd brought it to George Anastos, a committee staffer, at the Colony restaurant:

MR. JENKINS: Do you remember what you ate there that night?
PVT. SCHINE: I had a butterscotch sundae.

The soldier was soon pouting and talking back to the committee: "Since I have been in the army, sir, I have been subjected to many pressures. I have been called upon to do many things." And yet, there were hints of enjoyment in his own performance. Tim had this morning heard Mrs. Watt complain to another secretary about Schine's asking if he could expense the calls he'd made alerting friends in California to the exact time of his appearance on television. Would the hotel-chain heir, unpaid during his days on the committee staff, take the $6-per-day witness fee? Tim wondered, as he watched Cohn study the disputed picture and then Schine himself. Was this the look of love? Or did the chief counsel's intense expression indicate only an attempt, telepathic and fervent, to will Schine into a higher articulacy than the private could accomplish on his own?

"I have no questions," said Senator Potter, once his turn came around. A moment later, when it came again, he declared, "I have no further questions." Maybe he *was* hopeless, thought Tim, who'd lately been hearing Tommy McIntyre refer to the senator as "our pottered plant." Even so, Tim could see no real look of displeasure on Tommy's face as their boss for a third time let the microphone pass. Perhaps McIntyre didn't want his plant, so carefully tended, to bloom too soon?

An hour would expire before McCarthy exploded with a defense of Schine that he'd kept bottled up during all the inquiries into the private's whereabouts, weekend passes, and butterscotch sundaes. His colleagues' questions were "ridiculous," the senator claimed; abusive even, if one considered how Stevens was being pampered with a day off. The photographers, as always, sprang into action at the first sign of Joe's agitation, and this time one of them even managed to knock over McClellan's water glass, earning a rebuke from Senator Jackson. Before long, Welch was suggesting it might be time for them all to adjourn—and for Schine to get himself a lawyer. With an excess of either nerve or stupidity—Schine often looked so impassive it was difficult to tell—the private asked the chairman: "Since I am in the army, sir, and since Mr. Welch is the counselor for the army, sir, doesn't that automatically make him one of my counselors?"

"I believe not," Senator Mundt replied.

Cohn, too, shook his head no, while allowing his gaze to linger on the handsome soldier. In the two of them Tim saw a crude Herblock cartoon of himself and Hawkins Fuller, though he felt sure nothing had ever been consummated between the lawyer and the private. And he wondered: Would he himself have been better off loving Hawkins without any physical return? Without the illusions of emotional requitement he sometimes allowed sex to impose? One heard that Schine actually *liked* Cohn; could anyone say that Hawkins Fuller liked Timothy Laughlin?

Tim would never learn whether he was ready to face this last question, because at the moment he posed it to himself, he heard Hawkins whisper: "I've decided to forgive you, Skippy."

Dumbstruck, he turned around to look. Hawk's hand was on his shoulder—a mirage brought forth by his own weeks of thirst and suffering?

"Go tell them you're sick and have to leave right now. Don't wait for the gavel. Meet me in ten minutes on the southwest corner."

He made it there in eight, after lying to Tommy McIntyre, racing back to Potter's office in the Capitol, shutting his desk lamp, and, once he saw Hawkins' big green Buick waiting for him outside the SOB, wondering if he'd left any lights burning at home. He realized now that they were going away. To Charlottesville, for the weekend, Hawk explained.

He sat in silence all the way over the Memorial Bridge and through the red-bricked garden apartments of Arlington, offering no argument or banter, nothing that began "You're forgiving me?" He said nothing at all, as if, unlike the doubtful Private Schine, he really were a hostage, one who at any moment might be thrown out upon the open road. Hawkins, too, all the way to Manassas with the radio off, said nothing.

But no, this could only be good, could only be another miracle on the order of Hawkins' telephone call to the Star last September.

"A hundred minutes ago," Tim finally said, as they passed the battle-field cemetery, "I'd have been wishing I were lying there."

"Having to look at Karl Mundt will do that, I'm sure," said Hawkins, never taking his eyes from the road.

Tim struggled to keep from fishing, from begging for reassurance: You know what I meant.

"A hundred years ago," said Hawkins, "you would have been here, freshly dead. While your Grandma Gaffney was out rioting against the draft that stole you for a drummer boy."

"Before I died I would have had a case on you, in your fancy uniform at the head of a Zouave regiment."

"No, you wouldn't have. You'd never have met me. I'd have bought my way out of conscription for three hundred dollars, so that I could still be eating oysters at Delmonico's while you were cracking your poor Irish teeth on hardtack."

Tim smiled and rested his head against the backseat. A minute later he fell asleep, exhausted with relief as they continued riding westward. He slept until the beginning of a bright orange sunset made itself felt through his closed eyelids and woke him to the sight of a hundred pink flowering trees, the smell of their blossoms rushing through the car's open windows like the surge of violins on one of his sister's Puccini records. He burst into sobs.

"I can't—" said Hawkins.

"I know," said Tim, recovering as quickly as he could. "I know. You can't have this."

In fact Fuller was thinking: *No, what I can't do is even tell you why I came across town—how it was the television picture I saw of you emptying Potter's ashtray, looking gaunt and desperate, the circles under your eyes as dark as the ones under McCarthy's. And because of the glimpse I caught of that cold-eyed prick Bob Kennedy, no different from the way he was at Harvard a half dozen years ago, glancing at you while you fussed over the ashtray, annoyed that this hardworking little fairy was cluttering up a piece of history in the making.*

That was what he wanted to say and couldn't. But, yes, he did want Tim to stop crying now, and he was wishing he'd resisted the impulse to drive across town and get him. He was wishing he were right now back with the uncomplicated cracker kid he'd had the other night, a rawboned boy who no more considered it sick to mess around with another man than it might be to eat a bowl of ice cream between two helpings of cotton candy.

He wished he weren't putting them both through this.

And yet, for all that, he wanted to hear Tim's chatter, wanted the intermittent pleasure of protecting him; and wanted to fuck him on the floor of the car once it was dark enough to pull over into the woods.

They stopped to buy him a toothbrush and underwear and a second shirt, and then had dinner on King Street before browsing the used bookstore a block away and walking along the colonnade of rooms on the university lawn, where they looked out of place with their un-crewcut hair and made jokes about the white-bucked college boys, even jokes about taking one of them back to the hotel.

When they checked into their room, Tim's tears came again, from some borderless place between anguish and joy, where he was struggling to believe that the two of them had actually been *visible together*, out in public, in a restaurant and a store. "Do you know what? It's the same question!" he cried, laughing and shaking. "The same question! The one I was asking myself when you wouldn't come back to me and the one I've been asking myself all night, when you've made me happier than I've ever been! *What did I do to deserve this?* The same question!"

During all the coltish kisses with which he always sought Hawkins' attentions, he had never asked for a specific pleasure or gratification, taking care always to follow Hawk's direction, maximizing his beloved's satisfaction and thus, he thought, his own. But tonight, physically spent before he had opened a single shirt button, he walked over to the wall, shut the light switch, and in the darkness, well above a whisper, said, "Hit me."

Hawkins looked at him for several seconds. And then, not for excitement, and not from vexation, but only because he thought he understood and had been asked for a tenderness he could actually express, he raised his open hand and struck Tim once across the face.

CHAPTER EIGHTEEN

May 12, 1954

"He sounds a little like Mr. Peepers," said Beverly Phillips. "You know, whatsisname, Wally Cox."

Listening to John Adams' clipped, nasal tones on a television set in the State Department cafeteria, Hawkins Fuller and Mary Johnson couldn't disagree with her. The two of them and Beverly were having a mid-afternoon cup of coffee amidst a few dozen other employees who were generally delighted by the embarrassment the hearings had caused State's senatorial nemesis, Joe McCarthy.

The committee's special counsel, Ray Jenkins, had become even more theatrical than Welch, thought Mary. He clearly relished what Senator Mundt called his "Dr. Jekyll and Mr. Hyde role" of conducting both the direct and cross-examinations of whoever might be in the witness chair. This afternoon it was Adams, the army counsel, who seemed exasperated by almost everything—especially, Mary thought, the way Jenkins kept calling Schine "this boy." Instead of helping to establish what Adams suggestively called Cohn's "extreme interest" in the private, its effect was to make Schine seem just another all-American draftee who couldn't possibly have stirred up such a fuss.

Adams was now trying to rebut Cohn's charge that back in December he had offered to trade some juicy leads about homosexual activity on several navy and air force bases—surely a good subject for the McCarthy committee to investigate—in exchange for Cohn's pledge to drop the Fort Monmouth inquiry.

"I never made such an offer," Adams now declared. "I never would make such an offer. I never had such information to offer."

Beverly and Mary avoided each other's glance. Fuller added another teaspoon of sugar to his coffee.

What, Adams said, he *had* mentioned to Cohn—without ever suggesting a "trade"—was an ongoing investigation of homosexuality, by Secretary Stevens' office, at a single *army* base, in the South. That was all.

MR. JENKINS: It wasn't in Tennessee, Mr. Adams, was it?

MR. ADAMS: No, sir; it wasn't.

SENATOR MCCLELLAN: A point of order. Let's exclude Arkansas.

MR. ADAMS: I can do that, sir.

SENATOR MUNDT: The Chair would like to raise a point of order in behalf of South Dakota, which might also be included in the South.

MR. ADAMS: I can include all of the states of the members of this committee.

The camera panned the room to show the loud, prolonged laughter that was filling it. Roy Cohn's participation in the merriment, visible for a second or two, was hearty enough that viewers might reasonably think he would now, at this moment of relaxed male fellowship, extend his hand across the table and ask Adams to bury the hatchet.

"*That,*" said Fuller, "would be a hearing worth hearing. Shining a light on Camp Pink Palmetto. I'd say this current show lacks the really dire elements of the committee's best work." He went on to tell the tale of how a witness in one of McCarthy's investigations, accidentally subpoenaed for 10:30 p.m. instead of a.m.—a clerk's typo—had shown up anyway, trembling before the night watchman.

Mary guessed he'd gotten this story from Tim. She and Fuller spoke of him infrequently, but enough for her to be aware of the Lenten attempt at renunciation and how temporary it had proved. She was surprised that the boy remained in the picture amidst the comings and goings of so many others, attributing his survival to what must be his own desperate persistence.

Adams now spoke of a visit he'd made to the McCarthys' apartment in mid-January, when things had begun to fray badly between the army and the committee. Jeannie McCarthy had sat at some distance from the two men and claimed to be writing thank-you cards; in fact, Adams felt sure she'd been taking notes on his conversation with her husband. The army lawyer was proud of how, during months of "being pounded and pounded and hounded and hounded about where Schine was going," he'd had the temerity to tell Cohn that the private, like ninety percent of all draftees, would likely be spending some time overseas.

As Adams went on about this and other matters, Mary noticed in the witness a hint of the same petulance she'd observed in Private Schine himself. "I never asked Dave Schine for a stick of gum," declared Adams, when questioned about the hotel heir's largesse with tickets to the theater and the fights; "I am not afraid of Mr. Cohn," he further insisted.

"I would be *very* afraid of Mr. Cohn," said Beverly.

The camera looked into the farthest reaches of the audience, catching Perle Mesta in its field of vision; the other day her spot had been filled by Mrs. Longworth in a wide-brimmed hat.

"That's Jack Kennedy's wife, isn't it?" asked Beverly. Mary said she wasn't certain.

"I'm sure it is," said Beverly, who noted the newlywed's cute gamine hairdo. "*He's* not on the committee, is he?"

"No," said Fuller, taking a good look at the young senatorial bride. "She's here to watch her brother-in-law. No one in the family seems able to afford a comb."

Jenkins' assistant began questioning Adams about "Senator Potter's persistent concern" over the army counsel's leaks of information to members of the press, particularly Joe Alsop.

"I thought Potter was supposed to be a cipher," said Mary, pointing to his image at the right of the screen.

"He's been getting some training," said Fuller. "Or perhaps I should say some marching orders."

"You seem well informed about what goes on in his office," she ventured.

Beverly interrupted their banter. "You're forgetting about your *own* office." She pointed to her watch, reminding them that Mr. Morton had called a staff meeting for four o'clock. "Maybe you want that new girl putting us all to shame."

Fuller nodded in the direction of the *former* girl, Miss Lightfoot, who sat close to the television, unhurriedly drinking her tea and taking notes on the proceedings. "It's just not the same without her, is it?" he asked, feigning a wistful sigh.

Miss Lightfoot's former colleagues, after hearing one more partial piece of the story from one side of the Caucus Room's tangled web, began strolling back to the Bureau of Congressional Relations. Fuller and Mary walked a step or two behind Beverly.

"Even the brewer's been watching," said Mary. She'd given up and begun referring to her fiancé by the only name for him that Fuller ever used.

"This is turning into a long engagement, isn't it?" he asked.

Mary pursed her lips.

Fuller pressed her. "Want to talk about it?"

"With you? Heavens, no."

"Yeah, you do," said Fuller. "Let me know when and I'll pencil you in. By the way," he added, pointing toward her open-toed footwear, "your feet are too cold for those shoes."

At eight minutes before five, just prior to adjournment, Jenkins' assistant was moved to ask Adams whether it wasn't true "that many of these remarks or abuses that you have detailed on the part of Mr. Cohn were actually made in a facetious or jovial vein?"

Quite the contrary, Adams replied. "On the subject of Schine, nothing was funny. Nothing was facetious. Nothing was jovial." Tim heard this last exchange on the radio in Potter's Capitol office. He was happy to be overworked, fielding calls while rewriting a speech and folding one stack of papers into another. The more he had to do, the less time there was for being lovesick, which he'd been more often than not since Charlottesville. In the hotel room there, after a ferocious storm of sex that had followed the slap to his face, he had for the first time been allowed to lie all night in Hawkins' arms. But when the two of them returned to Washington, things reverted to their regular pattern, making him miss the near-hysteria he'd felt during the unexpected travel idyll, and causing him to consider the possibility that there really was no such thing as happiness or unhappiness. Maybe there was only intensity—and then everything else.

He now heard Tommy McIntyre and Senator Potter, fresh from the Caucus Room, coming into the outer office. Tommy's sharp voice was telling the boss that he needed to get a friendly photograph taken with Welch's bemedaled brass in the front-row seats.

"Tomorrow, pull yourself out from behind the table the minute Mundt rings the lunch bell. Let the shutterbugs get a shot of *you* instead of Joe. If they see you leaning on your props—one of 'em maybe lit up by mistake—they'll come over and take a picture, believe me."

Potter said nothing, and Tommy filled the silence with congratulations for the way the senator had this afternoon "followed the script" in questioning Adams about leaks.

"I still don't understand," Potter wondered, "why you didn't want me going after Schine a couple of weeks ago."

"Because I don't want you tearing into a soldier, even that one. Anywho, Charlie, remember the picture when you're back in there tomorrow."

With this reminder, Tommy left the premises to head back to the SOB, where he'd get the latest on the Maine campaign from Mrs. Smith's assistant.

Tim had two letters for Senator Potter to sign. Once he heard him settled down at his desk, he knocked softly on the door of the inner office.

"Come in, son," said Potter, "though I'm afraid I don't have long." The senator explained he was expected at home in Arlington in half an hour.

"Say hi to Mrs. Potter for me," Tim requested.

The senator smiled. "Will do. What have you got there?"

"A couple of things for signatures. Plus some telegrams from Lansing, and two out-of-state interview requests, if you want to consider them now. The Boulder *Daily Camera* and the *San Francisco Examiner*."

Potter allowed himself an awed little whistle over the immense circulation of the latter publication. He dropped the slips of paper onto his blotter.

"So what do you make of it all, Tim?"

Surprised to be asked, Tim fought against his stammer to declare that things looked "pretty much as you said, sir. Somebody is not telling the truth."

"Yes," said Potter, "but who?"

"I hope it's the army, sir, but I guess that wouldn't be much to be happy about, either."

"No, it wouldn't be."

After a pause, Tim became bolder. "Mr. McIntyre thinks McCarthy and Cohn cooked up all the memoranda. He's sure Mr. Adams *is* telling the truth."

The senator gave a soft, nervous laugh. "Mr. McIntyre tends toward strong opinions about everything."

Tim laughed, too. "The other day he told me you're still trying to get used to him. Which I guess makes sense: he hasn't been in the office much longer than I have."

Potter's smile was suddenly thin and tired. He looked over toward the bookshelf, where a Detroit Tigers cap crowned a cigar humidor. "Oh," he said softly, "I've known Mr. McIntyre for years."

CHAPTER NINETEEN

June 2, 1954

"Sir, I probably don't have any wisdom on this subject at all."

Roy Cohn's testimony had drawn even longer lines than usual to the Caucus Room, but his affectations of modesty, however shrewd, were disappointing those who'd come to see fireworks. For weeks he'd been attracting notice for the mutterings and glares he would exchange with Bob Kennedy, who had encouraged ridicule of Dave Schine's record as anticommunist gumshoe and thinker. Spectators who came every day like courthouse inveterates were still hoping the two young committee counsels would get into a fistfight before things adjourned *sine die.*

But here was Cohn, at last before the footlights of television, expected to thrust and parry and soliloquize—and all he would do was "sir" the committee: "It is hard to answer that, sir." "Sir, that is a little high for me to pass on."

He even conceded the likelihood that President Eisenhower opposed communism as strongly as he did, an admission that came in response to a soft question from Senator Potter—a tricky change-up from the series of fastballs the lawmaker was throwing. Tim had seen Tommy McIntyre scripting the queries yesterday afternoon, and the soundness of the Irishman's approach now became evident: the simple questions seemed more damning than Cohn's answers seemed exculpatory.

SENATOR POTTER: Did you threaten to wreck the army?
MR. COHN: No, sir. Not only did I not threaten to wreck the army, but Mr. Adams never believed that for one minute.
SENATOR POTTER: Did you threaten to get Mr. Stevens' job?

MR. COHN: No, sir, and if I had done that, Mr. Adams would not have acted the way he did, I am sure.

What emerged, however filtered, was Cohn's sense that last winter Adams had been too dumb to respond sensibly to threats that had indeed been made.

"You can catch your breath, Charlie," offered Acting Chairman Mundt. Senators were wanted on the floor for two quick votes; the committee would take a ten-minute recess.

Tim used the time to annotate the previous day's transcript and comb through press requests, as well as to hold a place for Mrs. Potter in the spectators' front row.

"You got enough room there, son?"

"Yes, sir, thank you," said Tim to one of Welch's telegenic officers, a General Airlie, according to the nampelate beside his large fruit salad of decorations.

"What do you do here?" asked the general.

"I work for Senator Potter."

The officer nodded respectfully. "I had my picture taken with him the other day."

Tim might have mentioned how his real boss, Tommy, had last week scolded Potter for not yet "watching the birdie with the brass." But he looked for something else to kindle conversation and came up with the way Senator Potter planned "to propose a law that would ban Communists from joining the army."

General Airlie smiled. "Son, I can't say I've found them dying to get in."

Tim laughed.

"Have you been in the service yet?" asked Airlie.

"No, sir," said Tim, ashamed that the general would surmise how he'd chosen, like most of his friends and classmates, to wait for the draft instead of enlisting. He felt an absurd temptation to confide—as if it were a tale of heroism—the story of how he had at least kept himself vulnerable to call-up by not admitting to "homosexual tendencies" when given the chance.

"I'm guessing you're a college graduate," said General Airlie. "Well, you'll find we've still got plenty to offer fellows like yourself—whether you come to us or we come to you." He smiled gently.

Tim nearly saluted. The army itself—apart from its lawyers and political administrators, what it was when left to do its duty outside this room—sometimes seemed to him the way he imagined Father Beane's Chinese chapel: "a clean, well-lighted place," forthrightly positioned on good's salient against evil.

He nodded to the general and went back to annotating the transcript, which six weeks into the hearings confirmed the near impossibility that any definitive picture would emerge from them. During recent days McCarthy had been arguing the duty of federal employees to leak to him any information they had about ideologically suspect colleagues; he wanted everyone to know how much he missed doing the committee's real business of fighting "brutalitarian regimes." Even so, one could measure the embarrassment he had been suffering the past several weeks by a speech in which the vice president had gone out of his way to declare that the real exposure of Communists was being accomplished by J. Edgar Hoover and Attorney General Brownell. "I prefer professionals," said Nixon, "to amateurs on television."

No matter how murky the truth about Schine remained, the hearings were going the army's way. Twenty-four hours ago, Senator Flanders had taken the Senate floor to ridicule his colleague as an anti-Semitic and possibly homosexual version of "Dennis the Menace." In contrast to what might have happened even a month ago, there had been no outcry over the denunciation.

The president's decision to float above the battle, in a kind of military observation balloon, had been vindicated to his strategists. This afternoon, as Cohn retook the witness chair, Ike, the recipient of his Communist-hunting compliments, was at a Washington Senators game to benefit the Red Cross.

"I would like," said Senator Potter, who now resumed his questioning, "to have you comment on the extent of Communist influence in our government."

"Yes, sir," said the still-modest Cohn. "It can only, of course, be a comment, because I don't know all the facts."

"When did that ever stop him?" whispered Miss McGrory.

"During the 1930s and 1940s," said Cohn, "the Communist Party of the United States was, I would say, remarkably and unbelievably success-ful in placing Communists in a number of key spots in our government." But sheer numbers, he explained, weren't important. "One is too many. I think Stalin or Lenin, one of the top Communist theoreticians, once said something to the effect that it takes a thousand people to build a bridge; it takes one person to blow it up."

For a moment Tim thought he could feel the Caucus Room expand with history and purpose. Something *important* was being offered for discussion. But the senator and the witness soon returned to the question of whether, on or around December 9, Adams had offered to trade Cohn an air force scandal for the Fort Monmouth investigation.

"Somebody is not telling the truth," said Potter, reiterating what had become his catchphrase.

"Somebody is certainly mistaken, sir," responded Cohn. "It is cer-tainly not us, sir."

"So," said Potter, with the logic Tommy McIntyre had supplied him, "perjury has been committed."

"Well, sir," answered Cohn, "somebody is certainly mistaken, and, once again, sir, I am not."

Tim noticed that Cohn might be denying no more than stupidity; he had not denied lying—let alone denied that the eleven memoranda over his name had been typed on an office machine he was never even near.

When the session ended and the lights went down, the witness gath-ered his papers and stood up just two feet from Tim, who still occupied the seat Mrs. Potter had decided to pass up for an afternoon's shopping. Full of anger and a certain relief, as if he could now shed a cloak that had made him itch unbearably, Cohn stepped up to Tim's left ear and whis-pered: "If your soldier-boy boss isn't careful, he may find that his balls go the way of his legs." Not waiting for McCarthy, he exited the room.

Tim said nothing, just stood there breathing a little hard over the first words Cohn had ever spoken to him directly. When Tommy came to col-lect the transcript he'd been working on, Tim repeated Cohn's remark.

"That's nothing to worry about," Tommy reassured him. "Charlie's balls are safe. They're in my pocket."

Tim frowned, prompting Tommy to complain. "What are *you* stewing about? It was a good afternoon. For Charlie, for all of us."

"I'm fine," said Tim, who wanted to get out of the room as fast as Cohn had. In exiting, he allowed himself one glance in Potter's direction and realized that Tommy was right: the senator appeared perfectly content, pleased with the crispness of his own performance. He wore the look of serene dignity that he could maintain for hours at a time, the same expression he'd no doubt worn when reading one of Everett Dirksen's five unpublished novels, a task he'd undertaken, he explained to Tim, "because Senator Dirksen values my opinion."

"Come on," called someone from the crowded elevator car that was just about to close. "You're skinny enough to fit in!"

Tim emerged from his distraction to realize that the voice belonged to McCarthy, who was forgoing, as he often did, the Senators Only car. As Tim squeezed into place, he felt a gentle, almost fatherly, hand on his shoulder. "Pete over there better not complain," said the senator, indicating the elevator operator. "Not when he's owed me ten bucks since Thanksgiving!" The tightly packed car, its atmosphere perfumed with bourbon and a moment's unforced laughter, descended toward the street.

CHAPTER TWENTY

June 19, 1954

"Drink, Skippy."

Tim downed two inches of the highball.

"More," commanded Fuller.

"What's it that people say? 'It's a little early in the day for this'?" Tim pointed to the clock beside the radio.

"Eleven-forty-five a.m.," said Fuller. "You think so?"

Tim drank more while Jo Stafford sang "Let's Just Pretend." He looked away and said, softly, "You're nice to let me come over, Hawk."

He'd arrived five minutes ago, in a state. He was calmer now, but even so, Fuller decided to pull him a couple of inches lower onto the couch cushions. He stroked the hair at Tim's right temple with the side of his index finger, the way one would a cat's whiskers. Tim turned to bury his face in the hollow of Hawkins' neck, surprised by the comfort he could take in the smell—amazed, really, that something still so exotic and *sought* had also become familiar, longstanding.

"Start again from the beginning," Fuller said.

"I was at my desk by five after eight, I think—even though it's a Saturday."

"Ah, yes, a workday. I seem to have forgotten."

"I was working with the hearings transcript," Tim explained. "The part from Thursday, the very last day. The *thirty-sixth* day of all that. And you know what I was realizing?" He took another swallow of the highball. "How it's always easier to follow the printed words from the morning sessions. By the time things would get restarted in the afternoon, a lot of them had put away three drinks at lunch. The sentences would get longer and sloppier and angrier, even with Mrs. Watt cleaning up what the stenographers took down. Anyway, there I was a little while ago, typing out my boss's closing remarks for a couple of Sunday editors who are planning to run bits of what every senator said." Loosened by his own drink, he treated Fuller to some pompous mimicry of Potter: " 'I wish to assure the American people who are watching that this is not normal.' "

"Making fun of Citizen Canes!" said Fuller. "There's hope for you yet."

Tim sat up straight but still clutched one of the pillows on the couch. "And then of course there's the big bombshell statement that got him all the headlines. 'There is little doubt that the testimony on both sides was saturated with statements which were not truthful and which might constitute perjury in a legal sense. . . . The staff of the subcommittee will have to be overhauled.' God! It's been quoted so many times I've got it by heart! All the Sunday editors think it's in the transcript, but you won't find it there, Hawk. The 'perjury' and 'overhaul' stuff was in a statement Tommy McIntyre had me mimeograph an hour before the close of the hearings. He passed it out to the reporters without Potter ever having *seen* it, let alone composed it. McCarthy went white when he got a copy! It's what the Democrats were hoping for all along—a Republican saying out loud they've got to fire Cohn! Now there'll be a vote to do that, and Potter will join the Democrats and make it 4–3. He never would have said it on his own, and he said no such thing in the hearing itself. Tommy tricked him—but you know what? Potter kind of likes it. They're drawing him as a lion in the cartoons. He's a big hero of free speech and fair play now. And it's all *phony*." He shook his head and finished off the drink. "All *phony*. Potter was more surprised by what he said than McCarthy was. *All phony*."

"Steady there, Skippy." Hawkins took the empty glass and pulled Tim back down on the couch. "Tell me when you heard the rifle shot," he said. "And tell me how you knew what it was. From all those childhood moose-hunting trips up Ninth Avenue?"

"I *didn't* know what it was. Except that it was unbelievably loud. I checked the paper on the streetcar coming over here: the wind today is north-northeast—perfect for carrying the sound from the SOB to the Capitol. Honest, I thought the Bomb really *had* gone off." The week had begun with Operation Alert, a ten-minute civil-defense drill that halted traffic across the city and saw white-armbanded marshals herding pedestrians into the doorways of stores and office buildings.

"Senator Hunt got there at eight-thirty," Tim continued. "He brought the rifle from home, they're saying, even though he always had a few guns in his office. I got all this from Miss Cook, who went over there to help out. Afterward."

Tim's agitation and gestures had subsided, but noticing how pale he still looked, Fuller reached over to put the fan on a higher speed. Along with its dry run for the apocalypse, Monday had brought the beginning of an early, unbearable heat wave.

"Miss Cook says he moved some pictures of his daughter and son from a bookcase to his blotter. Maybe so they'd be the last thing he saw before he pulled the trigger. He did it sitting in his desk chair. Miss Cook also says he left notes to everyone in his family and to half the staff. And that just last week he sent his papers off to the University of Wyoming archives."

"The radio is saying it was his health. That he got bad news from Walter Reed a couple of weeks ago." Fuller spoke matter-of-factly, making a casual effort to control Tim's excitability—which, left to itself, veered ungovernably, they both knew, between something that charmed Fuller and repelled him. "Hunt did," he pointed out, "quit the race for a second time. The day after his physical, I think."

"*You* don't believe that, do you?" asked Tim.

"You mean me of all people?"

"Yeah, *you*, who's always knocking me off the turnip truck. An hour after it happened Hunt's office put it out on the wire that he was going to the hospital because of a 'heart attack'! *You* remember what happened with his son in Lafayette Park. How he got arrested for trying to pick up a cop? Well, Tommy says a week ago Senator Welker and Senator Bridges were letting Hunt know that if he didn't pull out of the reelection race his son's record would be an issue."

Hawkins, who had never told Tim about the lie-detector test ordered up by Bridges' protégé, Scott McLeod, pretended to laugh. " 'How to Be a Man,' " he said cryptically, getting up to make a second drink that he said they could split.

"You know what was the first thing I saw on my desk this morning?"

Tim asked. "A 'subpoena.' They made the invitation to the farewell party look like one. Everybody was going to celebrate the end of the hearings on Monday night, all together, Democrats and the press included. I'll bet Kenneth Woodforde would've been there, knocking one back with Cohn. Well, now maybe they'll be going to a funeral instead. These *stupid* hearings."

"They're over, Timothy." Hawkins returned to the couch with the second highball. "They ended with a whimper. *And* a bang."

"Yeah," said Tim, taking the first big sip. "They're over, and they were about *nothing*. Or, as Welch would say, they were all about 'the 'tis and the 'taint.' Which puts it better than 'Somebody is not telling the truth.' You know what? *Nobody's* been telling the truth, my boss included. And you know what else?" Tim asked, sitting up again to project a louder indignation. "You know what Jenkins said at the end?" He took a deep breath to begin a baritone imitation of the Tennessee counsel: " 'Is it askin' too much of inscrutable Fate to hope that the paths of all of us will sometime cross again?' Like he wants to have a *reunion*, or start an alumni association. What a *dick*."

Hawkins laughed as loudly as Tim had ever heard him. "Now you'll be getting amorous, Skippy, because you always do when you're angry. And I don't have a lot of time."

The circles that had been under Tim's eyes in April were gone, but Hawkins noticed that his pupils were dilated almost to the point of death. Even so, he could feel his belt being loosened. "Have you no decency?" he asked, quoting the words that had gotten Welch so many headlines and making them both laugh. "Have you at long last no decency, sir?" He caressed the back of Tim's head, which had already gone to work on him, but after a minute he quietly withdrew, pulling Tim up beside him. "Don't finish me off," he whispered. "We'll save things for another day."

The last two words struck Tim's ears like the gift he was never allowed to take for granted, never permitted to expect. With "another day" for once in the bank, he decided to borrow against it. "I came by looking for you last night," he admitted. "I know I'm not supposed to." He drank an inch of the second highball. "So where were you?" he persisted.

"Early or late?" asked Hawkins.

"Let's say early," Tim answered, picking what might be the easier answer to bear.

"At the Sulgrave Club. Near whose elevator, I may have told you, Joe McCarthy once kicked Drew Pearson in the balls."

"How did McCarthy even get in the door there?" Tim experienced a short surge of ethnic fellow feeling. "A place like that must make him feel like Martin Durkin." People still joked that Ike's Labor secretary, a union man, had made for a cabinet of "eight millionaires and one plumber."

Hawk leaned over and kissed him. "Ah, the pluck of the Irish."

"So who were you *with* there? Some Episcopal bishop?"

"Close. Joe Alsop."

"Pardon *me*."

Fuller turned serious, made his embrace more sheltering. "You say the hearings were about nothing. Do you want to know what they *were* about? I'll tell you."

Tim looked him in the eye. "Are you saying you know what Cohn has on McCarthy? Did Alsop tell you what he was hinting at in that column?"

"Cohn holds nothing over McCarthy," said Hawkins. "Even Alsop gets things wrong. But in the months since that column ran he's managed to get them half right."

"What is it, then?"

"It's what *Schine* has on McCarthy. Something a house detective in one of the Schine family hotels saw Joe doing. And apparently photographed."

"Doing *what*?" asked Tim.

"Can't tell you," said Hawkins. "Because I don't know, and neither does Alsop. But it happened last fall, during one of those committee trips to New York, when your Mr. Jones would play at being a senator, and when old Joe was getting tired of Schine's laziness, not to mention a little wary and weary of the whole Roy-and-Dave show and the rumors in the press. He was thinking about cutting Schine loose. And then suddenly Schine—what is it that people say?—'knew too much.' "

"Well," said Tim, "I guess the draft notice made everything moot."

"No, the induction made things worse. All at once Schine would be needing a slew of favors down at Fort Dix. And McCarthy was powerless to refuse. The most he could do, when Cohn kept pressing, was complain a little about Schine to Adams and some others. But he never complained about him in front of Roy."

"Because Roy would threaten him with what Schine had."

"No. Roy doesn't know that Schine has anything over Joe. He thinks Joe went through two months of nationally broadcast hearings because Joe sees Schine as the same paragon he sees. Love *is* blind."

"But as my grandmother still says, 'The neighbors ain't.' "

"Yes," said Hawkins, "though some of them are a little too fastidious to believe what they're seeing."

Tim was still struggling to work out the algebra of blackmail. "How does Joe Alsop know?"

"Some smart reporter who owes him a favor gave him this story that he'd half pieced together and couldn't write because the other half was missing."

"How do you know Alsop? I never asked you."

"People like us always know each other."

Tim knew that "people like us" meant wealthy Protestants and not secret homosexuals, but he still had to ask: "Is he in love with you?"

"Probably," said Fuller. "But only enough to bat his eyes at me from the other end of the chesterfield sofa. I'm given to understand that he likes things a little rougher back in the bunkhouse."

"What do *you* get out of it?"

"Excellent company," said Hawkins. "Interesting information."

"I guess you *do* have something on him," said Tim, whose memory of their conversation about Alsop's column, swallowed up by the rest of that catastrophic night in March, was now coming back.

"Plenty," said Hawkins, who rested Tim's head on his chest. He began rubbing the boy's back with long, insistent strokes that, for all their strength, didn't seem a prelude to anything.

"What are you doing?" Tim finally asked.

"Trying to stop your flesh from crawling."

The answer, Tim thought, contained every part of Hawk's feelings toward him: protectiveness, affection, distance, enforcement. "How to be a man," Tim felt inspired to say, though he still didn't know what Hawk had meant by the words a little while ago.

"Yes," said Hawkins. "A man of a certain kind."

Tim hated hearing him say this. Not because he disputed his own membership in the homosexual subspecies indicated by the phrase; only because he hated being forced to acknowledge that God had assigned Hawk to this same slum precinct in His creation.

"Well," said Tim, eager to return the conversation to McCarthy, "I guess I now know at least the half of it."

"Less than half," Hawkins replied. "You still don't know what McIntyre has on Citizen Canes."

"That's true."

"Find out."

"Why?"

"Despite whatever they taught you at St. Aloysius, knowledge isn't power. But it is insurance. Even Schine, who's dumb as a post, knows that much."

"Tommy was *in excelsis* when things ended Thursday. But he didn't slow down for a second. Not even this morning. It's the last weekend of the primary campaign, and he says he's going to keep what they're calling Jones's 'hidden vote' well hidden. He was on the phone even while the ambulance was leaving with Senator Hunt. They must have heard the siren up in Maine, through the line."

It was at this moment, when the half hour of Jo Stafford numbers had concluded, that the radio announced the death of Wyoming's senior senator. Tim said nothing, just picked up the second highball.

"Gulp it, Skippy. I've got a date."

Hawkins rose from the couch to put on a sport coat. After picking up his keys, he seemed to realize that this was maybe a bit much even for him. With a certain tenderness, he added: "It's nothing, Timothy. A friend I made during Monday's 'air raid.' We were escorted into the doorway of Quigley's drugstore by one of the white armbands."

"A wartime romance," said Tim, picking up his own jacket.

"There you go," said Hawkins.

CHAPTER TWENTY-ONE

June 24, 1954

"Jesus, I can almost see Ike and Mamie. Behind the pink curtains."

"No, that's Kay Summersby on her knees. Mamie's in the room next door."

"Walking into the walls."

"Mrs. Eisenhower does *not* drink. She has an 'inner-ear imbalance.' "

Tim stood at the railing of the Hotel Washington's rooftop terrace, listening to this exchange between two reporters. They were pretty plastered, and he was getting there, too. If not the life of this huge party high above Pennsylvania Avenue, he was as loose-limbed as he could reasonably be in the midst of his anxiety over whether Hawk would show up.

The night was warm but breezy; the terrace's awning flapped, and the party's din had banished most people's memory of the service conducted for Lester Hunt two days ago in the Senate chamber. Still, his position at the railing prompted Tim, amidst all the drink and shouting, to recall what he'd seen looking down from the gallery on Tuesday: the impassive, straight-ahead expressions of Styles Bridges and Herman Welker, not far from the white, papery face of Hunt's son.

The conversation in the gallery, like the whispers on the floor, had concerned not the corpse, but the count. Once Wyoming's Republican governor picked a replacement for Hunt, the GOP would, by a single seat, have a real majority. In politics, too, it seemed to Tim, there was only excitement—and then everything else. Even at the service, the Democrats had been thrilled by new peril; the Republicans had been electric with fresh ascendancy.

The hearings' farewell party had remained canceled, but the formidable, impromptu combination of May Craig and Perle Mesta had filled the void yesterday morning by announcing this party. The invitations to it had pictured a Maine lobster with the face of Margaret Chase Smith. Trapped in its claws was a tiny schoolboy figure meant to stand for Robert L. Jones, who had gotten his comeuppance on Tuesday night. Right now Tim could see the wide hat brims of both Miss Craig, the Maine newswoman, and Mrs. Mesta, the eternal arriviste and party-giver, clinking like martini glasses in a self-congratulatory toast, even if the guest of honor, Senator Smith, had demurely decided not to come.

Mrs. Mesta had provided her usual "mostes' ": the money and social brass that rendered political affiliation or listing in the city's *Green Book* irrelevant to her recipe for a blowout. She and Miss Craig might both be Democrats, but they were happy to be celebrating the triumph of at least this one Republican (albeit over another). Along with Estes Kefauver and Henry Jackson from the Democratic side of the aisle, Jerry Persons and Jim Hagerty were here from the White House, and everyone seemed equally pleased about the real conquest being commemorated— Joe McCarthy's recent self-decimation.

Red roses—Mrs. Smith's signature flower—bloomed atop each tablecloth and drinks trolley. Posters with her winning slogan ("Don't Change a Record for a Smear") depended from the flaps of the awning. Standing near one of them, Tim heard Mrs. Persons and Mrs. Hagerty loudly agreeing that Clare Boothe Luce, so refined—and a *genius*, really—was a *much* better choice of female ambassador than Mrs. Mesta had been. No wonder she'd been posted to a *real* country like Italy instead of that toy one Truman had sent Perle to. Liechtenstein? Luxembourg? Knock the Eisenhowers, if you wanted: yes, purple orchids at state dinners might be putting on the dog, but did people really wish to see Bess Truman back stuffing daisies into vases she'd brought to the White House from a Woolworth's in Kansas City?

Tim tried to lose himself in this Washington version of the conversations he remembered between the women of Ninth Avenue when they reeled in the washlines between one apartment and another. But he couldn't keep himself from looking, every minute or two, toward the entrance.

At one door to the terrace Tim could see only Bob Kennedy, who seemed obliged to look ashamed of himself for being here at all, while his wife, Ethel, loudly imitated the bark of Mrs. Mesta's poodle, Fifi. Kennedy began an attempt to reach the circle that had formed around one of the evening's great catches, Vermont's Senator Flanders, who'd continued in the past two weeks to up the ante against McCarthy. Before the hearings ended, he'd strode into the Caucus Room and, before the cameras, plunked down the text of a motion he was about to make on the floor—one that would strip McCarthy of his committee chairmanship. Flanders had explained that the warning was a courtesy; McCarthy pronounced it a combination of publicity-seeking and senility and urged that a net be dropped over the Vermonter. Senator Mundt had settled for asking Flanders to leave the room.

And yet, here he was, his nerve and his star still rising. People now expected him to drop his motion in favor of one by which the Senate would issue a blanket censure of McCarthy. Indeed, a feeling had taken hold that the hearings might turn out to have been no more than an exercise for actors who would soon be appearing in a much larger drama.

Lyndon Johnson's boys, Walter Jenkins and Bobby Baker, formed part of the cluster around Flanders, though Baker, about as young as Cohn, was really talking with Eddie Bennett Williams, another legal prodigy and a buddy of Scott McLeod who was thought to make a lot of money getting people security clearances. Williams was also a pal of George Sokolsky, McCarthy's Hearst columnist, and rumor had it that he'd already been asked to undertake Joe's defense again censure.

Bobby Baker wanted to know whether this rumor was true, but Williams' answer was drowned out by the sudden crowing of Mrs. Mesta—"You old rascal!"—her way of reminding the just-arrived Drew Pearson that she'd forgiven him for all the nasty things he used to write about Harry Truman. The ex-president and newspaperman were now frequently in touch, not so much to bury the hatchet as to plunge it jointly into McCarthy's back.

"And you, too!" cried Mrs. Mesta, this time to Senator Kerr.

"Honey," he replied, "you and Drew mighta been oil and water, but me and you have always been oil and oil!"

"Oklahoma crude!" she roared back, offering their shared geographical history as confirmation.

Senator Flanders now had competition no more than three feet away.

Joseph Welch had arrived and was talking to Miss McGrory, whose last dispatch from the Caucus Room, after the attorney's have-you-no-decency speech, had been a kind of public love letter.

"After all this, can you really go back to Boston?" she asked.

"My dear young lady, can you really go back to the book page?"

Tim knew that he, too, would never again be what he had been, and he knew it even more surely once he saw Hawk enter the room, smile at him, and mouth the word "Skippy." After smiling back, he turned and looked the other way, behind him, toward the rooftop's railing, telling himself that if he leapt over it now he would die happy, the mortal sin of suicide just a redundant count in God's indictment, earning him only a concurrent eternity in Hell.

Hawk approached with an improbable entourage: Mary Johnson and the man who must be her fiancé, along with Mrs. Phillips and a fellow Tim didn't recognize. They all took drinks from a tray, a waiter having glided instantly up to Hawk, just the way Tim remembered it had gone at the restaurant in Charlottesville. With one hand Hawkins selected a summery gin and tonic, and with the other he made a discreet wave to Joe Alsop, who, engaged in conversation with Ike's press secretary, gave a businesslike one in return.

"Here," said Hawk, presenting Tim to his companions, "is the real source of your invitations." In fact it had been a joyful, capering Tommy McIntyre who'd pressed a fistful of Mrs. Craig's invites upon Fuller when he'd visited the office yesterday morning to talk to Senator Potter about the St. Lawrence Seaway legislation.

"It's nice to see you again," said Mary Johnson, who reacquainted Tim and Beverly Phillips before introducing him to Paul Hildebrand and Jerry Baumeister.

"Mr. Fuller," she explained to Tim, "is making us as impolitic as he is." Their boss, Mr. Morton, could hardly be displeased with the results of the primary, but he would have discouraged their attendance here, lest it appear that employees of the Congressional Relations bureau had taken sides in a primary election.

Senator Gore's chief of staff came over to greet Hawk, displacing Tim from the circle of conversation. The new vantage allowed him to watch the almost formal way in which Hildebrand held Mary Johnson's hand—

a contrast to the easy exuberance of the arm Mr. Baumeister kept draped over Mrs. Phillips' shoulders.

"My mother," Baumeister was telling Miss Johnson with a loud laugh, "didn't feel completely keen on my going out with a divorced woman."

Mrs. Phillips laughed, too. "Jerry is an *excellent* companion. A lot more fun than the widower turned out to be."

"And I got her a free window sash from the hardware store!"

Hawkins pulled Tim back into the group and away from an oncoming conga line whose members were shouting the defeated candidate's campaign slogan, but adding the unheroic last lyric of the song from which it had come: "The whole town's talking about the Jones boy . . . *and he's only nine days old!*" On primary day the youthful challenger had lost by five to one.

"Yes," said Hawkins, "the hidden vote stayed hidden." Senator Gore's aide replied that the only thing Mainers now had to worry about was Nixon's plan to vacation in the state.

"It's *usually* good to keep things well hidden," said Tim to Hawkins. He realized that his level of inebriation had caught up to that of the reporters at the railing. And being out in the open with Hawk, in a setting so much more public than even the Charlottesville restaurant, was making him giddy. Maybe he shouldn't have said what he just did, but Hawk seemed to get his meaning and laughed over it: "There are all *kinds* of things hidden here."

Fuller pointed to the figure of G. David Schine, who had entered with an attractive girl Tim recognized as Iris Flores, one of the private's regular girlfriends; she had been interviewed in executive session but never called upon to testify in public. In the closed hearing she had described herself as an "inventor" trying to market her latest brainstorm, a new-and-improved nylon brassiere strap.

Joe and Jean McCarthy might be home tending their wounds, while Cohn burnt the midnight oil back in the office, but here, Tim thought, was Schine, smiling—in uniform, no less—and being *mobbed*, followed around by Dorothy Kilgallen, Hearst's gossip writer, who took down his every word.

"Mr. Fuller." Tommy McIntyre, full of vigor and vim, gleaming with a hard nonalcoholic brightness, approached Hawkins and shook his hand.

He displayed a certainty—apparent from the way he nodded at both of them—that the connection between Mr. Fuller and "Master Laughlin," as he sometimes called him, was hardly casual.

Hawkins did nothing to disabuse him of the idea. "So where's the ostensible boss?" he asked, meaning Potter. Tim wanted to sink from the hotel's rooftop to its basement.

"Home in Arlington with the missus," said Tommy, neither surprised nor displeased by the query.

Tim tried not to stammer. "It would've been awfully hard for him to come here. After all, he hired Mr. Jones."

"And he fired him, too," said Tommy. "We *like* Senator Potter having things both ways. It's this flexibility that gives him a certain *utility.* "

A secretary from Senator Kefauver's office came and pulled Hawkins away. "Someone I want you to meet," she said.

Tommy took the opportunity to tug Tim in the opposite direction. "Look at them lappin' it all up," he said, tracing the whole senatorial panorama with his glass of 7Up. "Some of the girls they've brought along could get 'em charged under the Mann Act. Of course, their aides have to settle for simpler pleasures, with smaller penalties. Jenkins over there will be heading off any time now to the men's room at the G Street Y."

Tim looked skeptically toward Lyndon Johnson's executive assistant, a family man by all accounts.

"Oh, yes," said Tommy. "He'll have time enough to make it back here after a bit of relief—even if there's got to be an arrest, a booking, and a fifty-dollar fine in between. He'll tell himself it was all the fault of the alcohol."

"I'm not doing so bad myself," said Tim, nervously setting down his highball.

"You look steady enough to me," said Tommy, whose eyes were now fixed on Private G. David Schine.

"I'm trying to remember which does what," said Tim. "The Mann Act and the Volstead Act, I mean."

Tommy laughed. "The first one strives mightily to protect underaged innocence. Oh, it's a terrible law to be caught violating." After a pause, he added: "But set a thief to catch a thief."

Tim pointed toward Iris Flores. "She certainly *looks* twenty-one."

"Oh, she is," said Tommy, baring yellow teeth as he laughed. "That's not *Schine's* problem."

Was it, Tim wondered, remembering Alsop's information, someone *else's* problem? Perhaps a problem Schine knew McCarthy had? Was Tommy on the verge of revelation? Tim had wondered for months why the older man kept plying him with riddles. It had to be more than Celtic fraternity or some sadistic impulse to harrow his naïveté. But still there was no answer, and as always Tommy—now making a clear-eyed beeline for Senator Flanders—was off even more quickly than he'd materialized.

From behind, Tim heard a woman's soft Southern voice beginning to sing "Hey There." He felt an ice-filled glass being pressed against the back of his neck and realized it must be Mary Johnson. He turned around and smiled. "Me with the stars in my eyes," he sang in return. "That ice felt good. Where's Paul?"

"At a phone, ordering us a car. He figures we'll never get a cab downstairs."

"You're leaving so soon?"

Mary laughed. "It's a miracle he lasted this long."

Tim noticed the way she said it, as if Hildebrand's prudential nature might be troubling her more than Hawkins' daredevil one.

"Would you let me make you dinner some night?" she asked.

"Really?"

"Really," she assured him. "Just the two of us."

"Of course," he replied, knowing there *would* be a third, incorporeal presence at her table. For the first time in his life he would be talking to somebody about Hawkins Fuller, saying his name, making judgments and speculations about him, offering amusing stories in which he himself figured. But were there any stories that Tim could actually tell? Ones that didn't have nakedness and the bedroom for their costume and setting? Banishing this reverie, he spoke again at last: "Hawk got dragged away to meet someone."

"I know," Mary said. "I was taken over there, too." She pointed toward a spot by the railing.

"Oh, my gosh," said Tim, "that's Mrs. Wilson!"

The widow of the twenty-eighth president remained plump and pretty, sitting in a white metal garden chair atop this hotel whose opening she had attended in 1917. He watched Hawk standing over the former first lady, charming her. She was playfully swatting him with a heavily ringed and braceleted hand, its adornments probably having come wholesale from her first husband, Mr. Galt, whose old jewelry store survived a few blocks away.

"No," said Mary. "Fuller was taken to meet the one standing next to her."

Tim noticed a well-tailored blond girl alternating her gaze between Hawk and Mrs. Wilson, smiling as if her life depended on it.

"She's pretty," said Tim.

"You think so?" asked Mary, who then seemed surprised by her own cattiness. "Some distant relative of Senator Saltonstall's," she explained. "Down from Massachusetts for a summer course at the National Gallery. Lucy something-or-other."

CHAPTER TWENTY-TWO

July 20, 1954

Dear Tim,

The christening will be at Church of the Holy Rosary on S.I. (Jerome Ave.)—Sunday, Aug. 1, just after the 11:00 Mass. There will be a little party afterwards, but we'll expect you and Mom and Dad for breakfast beforehand.

The baby is twice the size she was when you saw her, and Mom (who I must say was a big help) has finally decided she can go back to Stuy Town. All the middle-of-the-night crying does make Tom very cross, which peeves me (since he's not around to hear it all day), but I suppose we'll get through this patch. (They say even Marilyn M. and DiMaggio are having their troubles.)

What a strange Fourth of July! I was still woozy from the anesthetic when you all got here . . . not exactly the holiday picnic you'd been expecting when you came up from Washington. Being a week early was the last thing I'd expected, but I was so glad you were here to see Maria when she was brand-new.

We'd missed you at Easter, and at Mother's Day, and on Father's Day, too. (I miss you period, brother. Or should I say "godfather"!) Even on the Fourth, I could tell through the haze I was in that you were eager to get back to the ferry and Penn Station . . . eager to be far away. A week ago Mom told Dad there's a kind of veil between you and the world these days, which made me think of that flimsy old curtain (a "scrim"?) on the stage in the Holy Cross auditorium. Mom says she's sure you leave more out of your letters than you put in.

Grandma Gaffney heard all this between Mom and Dad and put a stop to their conversation by squawking: "If Timmy's got something to tell you, he'll tell you."

So tell us. I don't want to pressure and pester you, but you are my

baby brother, not to mention Maria's godfather, and I worry about you.
Think about clueing me in a little . . . even if you <u>are</u> a government
bigshot now.

With love from Frances, Tom, and Maria Loretta

XXX

P.S. Grandma G. says the baby's name "makes her sound like a dago."

The pages of Francy's letter now lay, limp with lunchtime humidity,
on Tim's office desk. Realizing he still wasn't ready to respond, Tim
folded the letter and put it into his left pants pocket, the right one already
being occupied by a postcard he'd received from Maine, where Hawkins
would be staying until August 1. As the baby's godfather, he could hardly
miss going up to Staten Island that day, but in truth, he'd give almost
anything to remain in Washington, on the chance he might be allowed
over to I Street for a first-night-back reunion.

The approaching click of Potter's canes, along with the high-pitched
voice of Tommy McIntyre, made Tim clear the remains of a sandwich and
its wax paper from his blotter. Returning from a closed lunchtime session
of the subcommittee, the senator and Tommy were pulling a small
entourage of reporters, including Kenneth Woodforde, into the office.

"A Pulitzer!" Tommy cried. "A Pulitzer to the first photographer who
gets a shot of Cohn saluting Zwicker!"

McCarthy had scheduled a subcommittee meeting to investigate
reports of subversion at a Boston defense contractor, but the Democrats
had wrested away the agenda, and Potter, by voting with them, had just
created a 4–3 majority forcing the resignation of Roy Cohn. The committee counsel was now expected to begin his own long-deferred military
service in the National Guard at Camp Kilmer—under the very general
that McCarthy, back in February, had pronounced "not fit to wear the
uniform."

For a second, Tim's mind went longingly back to General Airlie and
the rest of the spectating brass that Mr. Welch used to assemble in the
Caucus Room, but another burst of glee from Tommy put an end to any
daydreaming. "Dave and Royboy will be wearing the same shade of
khaki now!" he shouted. Senator Potter tried to project dignity against
Tommy's merriment, concluding whatever remarks he'd been making to
Woodforde by stressing "the importance of getting back to serious inves-

tigations, ones that will respect people's rights while uncovering the truth. You know, Mr. Woodforde, these Communists are real."

"Since you acknowledge their reality," Woodforde asked, "does that mean you're now ready to recognize Red China?"

Potter looked baffled.

"Wise guy," said Tommy.

"Can't blame me for trying," replied Woodforde, who closed his notebook and let the two other reporters proceed without him to Potter's inner office.

"There's more of them to recognize all the time," said Tim, once he realized he'd been left alone with Woodforde. "Communists, I mean."

"Thanks to magazines like *The Nation?*" asked Woodforde.

"Well, yeah, actually. It looks as if we've now got twelve *million* more to recognize in Indochina." A peace conference at Geneva, following the Communist victory at Dien Bien Phu, was about to divide Vietnam in two.

"You mean those twelve million people who'd be so much happier and freer being ruled by the French?"

"Yeah, those," answered Tim, trying to speak with a smile. "The ones who are having their new country designed by Molotov."

"*Two* new countries," Woodforde reminded him.

"Right. Korea, Germany, China, now Vietnam. All those big half loaves, and the Communists always stay hungry."

"The Communists will be evacuating South Vietnam within ten months," said Woodforde, reciting what had been pledged at Geneva.

"You don't believe that, do you?" asked Tim. "Or that they won't kill any more French priests in the meantime?"

"None that don't have it coming."

Tim shook his head and turned on the radio, not in any real display of anger, just to make plain that he couldn't continue a conversation in this vein.

Over the airwaves, the voice of Roy Cohn was explaining the toll that this past year had taken on his parents in the Bronx. Senator Potter, tape-recorded ten minutes earlier, was wishing him well. A statement from McCarthy's office, just released and now being read by the announcer, struck a less forgiving note: "The resignation of Roy Cohn must bring great satisfaction to the Communists and fellow travelers. The smears and pressures to which he has been subjected make it clear that an effective anticommunist cannot long survive on the Washington scene."

Woodforde was smiling—over this formulation that might soon become McCarthy's epitaph for himself—when a colleague from *U.S. News* stuck his head in the door: "Come on down. Flanders is starting his speech."

Woodforde waved for Tim to join them in the gallery. "Here's something we can all agree on, no?"

Still uncertain about the censure movement, Tim nonetheless felt glad of a truce and agreed to accompany the two reporters. He fell in step beside Woodforde, wondering as they double-timed it down the corridor why some part of him felt drawn to this left-wing provocateur.

The gallery was more crowded than the floor. Democrats—worried about appearing overeager—were thin on the carpeted ground below press and spectators. But rhetoric was soon off to the races. Flanders invited his colleagues to consider "the Senator as Führer," even if that role had come to McCarthy "without conscious intention on his part." A chance for Joe to change his ways was being offered, the Vermonter insisted, "in a spirit of Christian charity."

"See," Woodforde whispered to Tim. "Even the priests approve."

"Paul says it's over a hundred degrees in St. Louis."

"I guess we shouldn't complain," said Tim.

Mary Johnson, who'd had to persuade the boy to remove his seersucker jacket, fluffed the chicken hash on the burner and disagreed. "Oh, sure we should complain."

"Doesn't it get even more steamy than this in New Orleans?" Tim asked.

"They know how to build *shade* there. We used to spend half the day in the dark, behind the shutters."

She looked at him as he set out the plates and napkins, and had trouble believing he would spend half his life like that, hiding in shadows. He reminded her a little of Lon McCallister, that slight, sweet actor who'd had to kiss Katharine Cornell in *Stage Door Canteen* and had just walked away from the movies at thirty. Right now she herself felt a little like the grand Miss Cornell, or at least Our Miss Brooks, though she couldn't be more than a few years older than Tim.

"So, have you heard from him?" she was suddenly moved to ask.

He brightened up as if they'd decided to go straight to dessert.

"A postcard from Bar Harbor," he answered, reaching for it in his pocket. " 'Dear Skippy,'—that's a nickname he has for me—'Nothing up here but the Bucksport papers, and even they still echo with praise for Citizen Canes.' That's what he calls my boss. 'I won't return until the first, by which time an air conditioner is supposed to be installed in every front window of 2124 Eye Street. You can come over when you need to get that scapular unstuck from your overheated skin. Sheen's TV show, by the way, doesn't reach these parts, so Mother will have to remain in the clutches of the Reformation for a while. HF.' "

She saw his face contract with embarrassment as he finished—not because it was too much; because it was too little. Where were "love" and "wish you were here," or even a double entendre about the lighthouse pictured on the front of the card? The scapular might suggest intimacy, but of a small, controlled sort, a rationing prompted not by fear of the postman's prying eyes, but wariness of the boy's ravenous heart.

She had to give him the chance to display his feelings, had to force herself to say some words that would allow that: "You must miss him."

The gratitude on his face was immediate, though he stopped short of saying anything.

"We even miss him in the office," she declared, helpfully. "Though, of course, he *is* impossible."

"He is, isn't he?" said Tim, whose laughter was still more nervous than relieved. As if remembering his manners—and that he ought to share such pleasure—he asked: "Is Paul impossible, too?"

Mary thought for a moment. "Paul is, I'd say, very . . . possible."

Tim smiled. "Is that a compliment?"

"*Possibly.*" She doubled her Southern accent to keep him amused, while realizing that this was not a question she wanted to entertain. "Okay," she said, "the hash is finally hotter than the room." She poured a tumbler of ice water for herself, and a glass of milk for him. He reached for it quickly, as one would for a ringing telephone. "Did he tell you that? About the milk-drinking, I mean."

"Yes," said Mary, glad to give him this small, additional thrill, though in truth, while Fuller might be indiscreet about the boy's existence, he never said too much about Tim himself.

She had gone as far as she could in one night. She could *not* take conversation about Fuller, let alone Paul, any further. But what else could she ask this boy about? He had less ambition than any young man she'd ever met in Washington. He already *had* a career—a vocation, she supposed—in Hawkins Fuller.

"So," she said, resorting to a topic of the day, and a question that didn't come out as well as it might have. "Do you think the army will make a man out of Roy Cohn?"

The Sand Bar's piano player started in on "Some Enchanted Evening," and Tim ordered a bottle of Senators beer. He couldn't remember the one that Mary's fiancé brewed, but this would do fine. And *he'd* be fine here. He had heard Hawk mention this place once or twice, and he'd decided to walk all the way to it from Mary's apartment.

As exciting as it had been to talk with her about Hawk—and as grateful as he'd been for the permission—he had ended the evening feeling like a specimen, a sympathetic object of study. Mary seemed to recognize the same thing herself, and just as clearly to regret it, but her own attempts at being natural had somehow made things worse. In saying goodbye, she'd apologized for any awkwardness and expressed the hope that their dinner might be considered "a first try"—thereby heightening, once more, the atmosphere of scientific inquiry. However appealing she might be, he'd been relieved to get back out onto the streets of Georgetown, and now, a half hour later, to this bar in Thomas Circle. The place was bringing him a step closer to Hawk, the way smelling one of his shirts might do, were he only permitted entry into the I Street apartment while Hawk was away.

Two stools to his left, a slightly built man with dyed hair and plucked eyebrows nodded to him. He nodded back and, never having been by himself in a bar—let alone this kind of bar—worried that he might have just given a signal that was open to misinterpretation. As soon as his bottle of beer arrived, he got up, deciding to drink it against the wall at the other side of the room. But the man with plucked eyebrows shook his head and pointed to a sign behind the bar. NO DANCING. NO CARRYING DRINKS.

Tim mouthed the word "thanks" just as the man's friend returned from the bathroom.

"You're crazy," said the man, resuming the argument he and his friend had evidently been having.

"I am not—I repeat *not*," said the bulkier friend, "putting in for promotion."

"You work at the *Interior* Department, Donald, not the Atomic Energy Commission."

The bartender, to keep them from exploding at each other, began to sing "Don't Fence Me In."

"They still investigate," said the Butch One, as Hawk would have called him.

The fairy rolled his eyebrowless eyes and said nothing.

"There's a Master List," the bigger one insisted. "Of *us.*"

"No, there's *not*," said the fairy.

"Behave," the bartender instructed him. "He's the daddy."

The two of them walked off toward the jukebox, leaving their drinks where they were. The piano player was starting his break, so they put in a nickel for "How High the Moon."

The bartender, well-muscled and weatherbeaten, pointed to the Butch One and speculated to Tim: "I guess when you've managed to get out of Rich Square, North Carolina, you figure you don't need to be promoted on top of things. Where are *you* from?"

"New York City," said Tim.

"Ah," replied the bartender. "A hard case." Meaning, Tim guessed, that there was no place any bigger he could escape to, no anonymous haven where he could be himself and—as he so obviously needed to—relax.

Across the room a skinny Negro scolded his white boyfriend: "You do *so* know. My black taffeta with the pleats!"

With a tilt of his head, the bartender signaled a bouncer to eject the overexcited colored boy. Tim couldn't hide a certain relief and maybe even his feeling that justice was being done by the regulation of such effeminacy. The bartender, he knew, could see him pining for normality, for the chance to believe he still lived with the rest of the world.

"It was more fun in here ten years ago," the barman assured him. "Soldiers every night. Of every stripe and kind."

The cat still had Tim's tongue, and the bartender made one more attempt: "Let me guess. He's married. Or ambisextrous?" Tim laughed a little.

"Bingo," said the bartender, moving away to mix someone else's drink. "Relax, apple pie," he said by way of farewell. "But be careful who you talk to."

Tim wondered about the advice: Might someone actually hurt him? Maybe there *was* a Master List? Could the Negro's boyfriend, or even the guy with no eyebrows, actually be an informant?

He stayed only another minute. While riding the streetcar home, passing the *Star's* building on Pennsylvania, he reached over the open window to clean his hands in the raindrops that a thundershower had left upon the glass. Then he dried himself with his handkerchief, not wanting to smudge the ink when he took Hawkins' postcard, once more, from his pocket.

CHAPTER TWENTY-THREE

September 8, 1954

The defense of Joe McCarthy against censure had begun presenting itself this morning, but the senator's talented young lawyer, Edward Bennett Williams, still seemed to be spending the bulk of his effort on keeping his client quiet. As to the allegation that McCarthy had abused General Zwicker during the subcommittee's February hearings in New York, Williams had so far offered only the testimony of a salesman who'd taken a tourist's peek at that day's brief open session and could report that he had heard General Zwicker, under his breath, refer to the junior senator from Wisconsin as a son of a bitch. Which, it was now implied, had justified all that followed.

The censure hearing now stood in lunchtime recess, so Tim lowered the radio on his desk and ate his sandwich. He looked out the window at the Capitol lawn, still strewn with tree branches blown down the other day by Hurricane Carol. Mary Johnson's little kitchen window, which Tim was now used to sitting beside through long, difficult conversations about Hawkins Fuller and Paul Hildebrand, had lost a pane of glass during the storm, whereas at Hawk's apartment, where Tim spent the hurricane's worst hours, the loud hum and rattle of the new air conditioner had blunted one's awareness that anything unusual was happening outside.

The appliance, extravagantly extolled by Hawk, was never off. "Are we doing this just to keep warm?" Tim had laughingly asked while they had sex one unseasonably cool, but still air-conditioned, night. "That's *always* the reason for doing this," Hawk responded, leaving unclear whether he was referring to his own low emotional temperature or the futility of all human endeavor.

Over the past month, Tim had actually been allowed to spend the night a couple of times. On these occasions, for long stretches Hawk would hold him close, ostensibly against the air conditioner's cold. But even so, Mrs. Mesta's party remained the last time they'd been out in public together, and Tim still knew never to come over unannounced, or with groceries, or to answer the phone without being told to.

"Well," said Tommy McIntyre, now hurrying into the office, "old Joe's hand just shook when he swore the oath."

Tim put the radio back on; the recess was over, and there would be no muzzling the defendant now that, at his own insistence, he'd taken the witness stand.

"It's a shame the republic has any other business!" crowed Tommy, whose enjoyment of McCarthy's travails was undiminished. "But your friend Mr. Fuller will be here a little later, about something entirely different."

"My friend?" asked Tim, reflexively lying.

"He's coming over with his boss, Morton. The great solon"—Tommy pointed to Potter's office—"is on their docket once again. They're all supposed to fret about our majority leader's brilliant suggestion that we break off relations with Russia." Walking away, Tommy added, in regard to Fuller: "Just thought you'd like to know. Anticipation being the pleasure it is."

Hawkins and Mr. Morton arrived at the high point of McCarthy's testimony about General Zwicker. The director of Congressional Relations went in to see Potter on his own, while Fuller sat down on the edge of Tim's desk and began listening to the radio.

"Did you say 'not fit to wear the uniform'?" asked Edward Bennett Williams.

"No," McCarthy answered. "I said he was not fit to wear the uniform of a *general*."

Tim cracked up. "The Jesuits would love that, Hawk!"

Fuller smiled.

Looking at him, Tim tried to imagine Hawkins years from now, with a pipe, the two of them seated in front of the radio after dinner. It was, he knew, a fantasy more ridiculous than any plot ever featured on *Mr. Keen*, but the thought of it warmed him while debate continued over Zwicker's uniform. Tim thought of Hawk's old navy dress whites hanging in the closet on I Street; once or twice he'd felt the urge to put them on, not to partake of their owner's godlike aspect but to assume the mantle of simple masculine normality, the movie-and-magazine ideal he remembered from his own, presexual World War II.

It was more fun in here ten years ago. Soldiers and sailors every night. Of every stripe and kind.

A burst of whistling issued from Tommy McIntyre. Indifferent to the business between Potter and Morton, he'd returned to the outer office and cranked up the volume of the radio. "So, are the two of you having supper together?"

"No," Tim hastily answered.

"Good," said Tommy, turning his face to Hawkins. "I need Mr. Laughlin to dine with me."

"Be my guest," said Fuller.

The response, however casual, still implied that the permission was Hawk's to give, and the answer excited Tim all afternoon, long after Hawk had left. He was still feeling a nervous pride from the exchange when he and Tommy arrived at O'Donnell's, down on E Street.

They ordered the filet of sole, though Friday remained two days away, and Tommy began their conversation with the news that Howard Rushmore, an ex-Communist who for a little while had been the subcommittee's research director, had just become the editor of *Confidential* magazine. "He was always pushin' a story about Mrs. Roosevelt and her nigger chauffeur. Well, maybe that legend of love will finally see the light of print!"

Tim stared at the tines of his fork and figured Tommy would soon get to the point of their being here.

After a long pause, the older man asked: "You know how he perspires when he walks?"

Tim knew that he meant Potter. "Yes."

"He did even then. Years before the legs were gone. I saw him do it in '38."

Oh, I've known Mr. McIntyre for years.

"He was already trying to date Lorraine," Tommy continued. "Her old man was a fish dealer, a big wheel in town, and Charlie wasn't getting anywhere. Not as a potato farmer's son who'd been working in a cannery to put himself through State Normal College in Ypsilanti. He'd wanted to go to law school, but no dough, and he'd ended up a social worker in Cheboygan." Tommy finished off his 7Up. "I think he sweated from sheer strain, from the dull mighty *effort* he gave everything. I remember seeing him one afternoon from behind a big empty crate on Huron Street. His face was drenched."

"What were you doing there?"

"Sleeping. Living. It was my first stay on what's demotically known as Skid Row, though in Cheboygan I never skidded. I *stuck* to the fish paste on the sidewalk." With a look, he indicated that there was no need for Tim to ask questions. The story would come, unbidden.

"I'd been a reporter for three papers in Detroit, at least when I wasn't drinking. But at that point I'd been drinking since '36, when I'd done a little work for somebody's campaign for governor, can't remember whose. Can't remember any of that besides getting knocked around pretty badly by some boys from the other side."

He told the waiter to bring Tim a second old-fashioned. "And another 7Up for myself." Tim half understood that *he* was supposed to drink tonight, in some act of surrogacy. Tommy looked at the arriving old-fashioned in a way that suggested he was perilously close to falling off the wagon.

"Yes," he said, crunching a bread stick with his yellow teeth, "we were both fine citizens of Cheboygan, Michigan. He stayed stuck in the social-aid bureau and got to supervising it by the time he went off to the war. But that was later." Tommy crunched the bread stick. "In '38 he was my caseworker, though they called it something else back then."

"Was he unfair to you?" asked Tim, fearing the winds of what he now realized was an epic, ancient enmity.

"He was as just as Judge Hardy!" cried Tommy, with a laugh. "No, let me clarify that. He was just to *me*." His mottled face contracted with anger. "Not to *her*."

Tim knew he wasn't referring to the future Mrs. Potter.

"Annie Larchwood," said Tommy. "She's still alive, though she barely knows it. She's a drinker, too. Became one after her husband, Mike—an organizer, a Communist—got forced off his job on the line. Need I say, Master Timothy, that he drank as well? He walked out on her on his way to hell. Died from the stuff. I met Annie at his funeral. Amplification: I fell in love with her at his funeral."

Tommy's skull looked like a grenade. Tim tried to signal that he was paying close attention, as if that might keep the pin from being pulled.

"She went on relief, and soon enough got to the end of the money. To keep the checks coming, she pulled some kind of fast one, and straight-arrow Charlie, who ran *her* case, too, cut her off. But then, in a moment of weakness, when he was despairing over the fishmonger's daughter, he put her back on the rolls. After she agreed to sleep with him."

Tommy's contempt was total—it embraced Potter's rectitude as much as his lapse.

"She gave in and got knocked up with the son Mike had never managed to give her. The snot-nosed little issue turned fourteen last year."

Tim thought it an odd formulation. Last year?

"When I brought him to New York," Tommy added. "He's a filthy punk, though he has his uses. Drink up."

For the moment Tommy would go no further. In the brief silence, Tim swallowed more of the old-fashioned. Then he asked: "What makes you hate McCarthy so much?" It seemed the logical next question; with his loathing for Potter now explained, Tommy could move on to the next titanic grudge inside him.

The analysis that followed turned out to be patient, almost professorial. "All of Annie Larchwood's troubles began with the hounding of her red husband, a better man than McCarthy *or* Zwicker. All of Annie's troubles *continued* with Charlie, who's one of nature's blind little do-gooders. No," he said, noting the puzzlement on Tim's face, "I'm not some old aggrieved Commie with a pious beef. In fact, I'd make a pretty good anarchist; I told that to Woodforde the other day." He took a second and last forkful of fish. "What I am mostly is a drunk, whether or not I'm drinking. Same way you're a Catholic, whether or not you're taking Communion. Which these days, I suspect, you're not."

"I hate Communists," said Tim, trying to change the subject.

"Of course you do," said Tommy, sweetly mocking.

"Does Senator Potter know he has a son?"

"Senator Potter knows what I tell him," barked Tommy, before resuming the mode of earnest tutelage. "Yes, I did have the pleasure of imparting that news when I began helping the staff. Let's say that the possession of such knowledge has helped me to make our great solon somewhat useful where the junior senator from Wisconsin is concerned."

Tommy finished the last of his 7Up, and with a tap of his index finger commanded Tim to keep going on the old-fashioned. "Oh, it's not as if no one's got nothing over *me*. Joe and Royboy know I got imposed on Charlie by the automobile fellas, to keep him voting on the straight and narrow. Yes, I gave the auto men a prior decade of sober service, in the papers and in campaigns."

Everybody's money comes from someplace, Senator. Everybody's people come from someplace. Tim remembered the quick threat to Potter, the poisoned meat in the sandwich of bonhomie that McCarthy had served that afternoon last March. Tommy would have heard the remark from the outer office, where he'd decided to wait.

"But Joe and Roy don't know I got myself imposed on Charlie for my own particular motives. And they don't know I've got something far bigger on them than they've got on yours truly."

There would be no further explanation tonight. Tim reached for a peppermint and kept his eyes on the tablecloth. "Why did you tell me all this?" he asked at last.

"Because I've seen you looking at Mr. Fuller. And I know that your life will be given to his as surely as Annie Larchwood got mine. I told you because you'll *understand*."

Tommy pushed aside the just-brought coffee and leaned into the table. His eyes shone with a brutal sympathy, letting Tim know that, from this moment on, for the foreseeable future, he lived not just in Hawkins' clutches, but in Tommy McIntyre's, too.

"I should go," Tim said, weakly.

"Use it for a taxi," said Tommy, refusing Tim's dollar bills. "I know where you're headed."

When he got to I Street, his head off-kilter from the old-fashioneds, Tim looked up and saw that the apartment was dark. He wondered if he should sit on the steps and wait until Hawk returned with some week-night conquest. For a few minutes he stood on the sidewalk, trying to decide, until he felt an enormous, unexpected surge of anger. In his mind's eye, Hawk was bobbing atop the clean blue ocean in his pressed naval uniform, while he himself was being dragged to its weed-choked depths.

Drunk as he was, he could feel the hint of autumn in the air. A

"School's Open Drive Carefully" poster flapped against the streetlamp. NO DANCING. NO CARRYING DRINKS.

He walked up the building's steps and, once inside the vestibule, took down the super's posted instruction that tenants keep their new air conditioners pitched at a five-degree angle toward the street; drips were damaging rugs and seeping into floorboards. On the back of the paper, he wrote a note to leave in Hawkins' mail slot:

> You said knowledge is insurance. Against *what*? The chance that somebody might turn out to be what he *appears* to be? That somebody might not own somebody else? I'll *never* own you, no matter how many times I hum "You Belong to Me" in the shower. But *I* belong to *you*—whether you like it or not.

After the cab ride, he had no money for even the streetcar. And so he walked all the way home, miles, wishing he could sing in his chains like the sea.

CHAPTER TWENTY-FOUR

November 10, 1954

With crowds to be controlled at both the eastern and western approaches to the city, the District of Columbia police found themselves split in two on the morning before Veterans Day. Across the Potomac, on Arlington Boulevard, Nixon was dedicating the Iwo Jima Memorial, and at Union Station trains were disgorging hundreds of riders wearing "Make Mine McCarthy!" buttons. They also carried placards ("Twenty Years of Treason!" "Joe Knows!") that sprang to sudden, vertical life once they hit the platform and began marching to Capitol Hill. By eleven a.m. the corridors of the Senate Office Building looked more like the floor of a nominating convention. Debate on the censure resolution was at last under way, and though things appeared to be moving in Senator Flanders' direction, he elected to remain behind locked doors.

Over in the Capitol building, two brightly colored items sat on Tim's desktop: the emerald-covered report that was now driving the censure debate toward a vote, and an oversized birthday card for Senator Kennedy, still recovering from back surgery in New York. Festooned with greetings from the SOB, it now awaited Potter's signature here in the Capitol.

Miss Cook approached Tim's desk, sighing: "That colored corporal's family is here. In the conference room."

Tim looked at his watch. As they'd feared, Potter had failed to make it back in time from the Iwo Jima dedication.

"Plan B," said Tim, rushing off to the House cloakroom to press Congressman Rhodes into service.

Corporal James Borum, a young Washingtonian who had enlisted in the Marines in '48 and died three years later in a North Korean prison camp, had no connection with Rhodes's home state of Arizona, but once the congressman arrived in the conference room near Potter's office, there was at least an elected official who could present a flag and decoration to the boy's family.

Corporal Borum had no connection to Michigan, either, but from time to time Potter's interest in North Korean atrocities still broke through the McCarthy drama like a weak, overlapping signal on the radio dial. The senator's office had lately decided to honor this soldier, who had only this year been officially declared dead.

A grandmother, Mrs. Drumming, along with a brother and an aunt, stood mute and respectful while Rhodes read the citation, though it was apparent they would have preferred James Borum's corpse, never released by the North Koreans, to a medal. Tim also believed he could detect in the brother's face an awareness that the family, told Senator Potter had been caught in traffic, was somehow being honored and insulted all at once.

Tim wondered if he was supposed to say something about "a grateful nation," but when he shook Mrs. Drumming's hand, he wound up whispering, "I'm sorry for your trouble," the words he'd heard murmured at every Irish wake he'd ever been to.

And with that, embarrassed and relieved, he dashed off to the Senate gallery.

The chamber was in an uproar. Desks were being pounded, as refusals to yield reached the ceiling of the packed gallery, where all eyes stayed on Jean McCarthy, sitting very straight under a statue of John Tyler. Her smile, Pepsodent bright, was the same one she'd had for the cameras the day she came back from New York with her broken leg and Robert Jones announced his Senate candidacy.

As the debate moved toward a climax, her husband moved irretrievably beyond his lawyer's control. McCarthy's buzzing declamations stirred the reporters' pens and thrilled the nerves of his supporters: "It is not easy for a man to assert that he is the symbol of resistance to Communist subversion, that the nation's fate is in some respects tied to his own fate. It is much easier, I assure you, to be coy, to play down one's personal role in the struggle for freedom."

No, he would not let this cup pass. He would meet his end insisting that he and freedom were one and the same. Coyness was for others; it had been for Welch; it had been for Zwicker. *Don't be coy with me, General* . . . "I take it you would rather I be frank, that you would rather acknowledge and accept the fact that McCarthyism is a household word for describing a way of dealing with treason and the threat of treason."

"And so it is," muttered one antagonist next to Tim.

"And so I shall," declared McCarthy.

His citizen followers, their placards checked at the door to the gallery, remained hopeful, but his dwindling corps of legislative allies was already thinking of what-might-have-beens. After the army hearings, when Eddie Williams began constructing a legal strategy, Senator Dirksen had tried to start a rehabilitation campaign, but none of the town's best public-relations men smelled success in the client being proffered.

If the vote goes against him, Tim thought, his followers will act as if there's been a coup d'état, and they'll summon the whirlwind to fill the vacuum. He looked over at Jean McCarthy, whose expression had not changed, and he decided to get some air on the Capitol steps.

Outside, he sat down behind a woman reading about Dr. Sheppard's murder trial in a copy of the *Daily News* that had been discarded by one of the demonstrators from New York. Was there, Tim wondered, more eternal verity in that story—the philandering doctor who'd butchered his wife—than in this one? Weren't Tommy McIntyre's politics dictated and trumped by his romantic obsession?

Kenneth Woodforde, Tim suspected, was an actual Communist. But as such he would at least be a believer in *something*—as opposed to Hawk, who believed in nothing, or Senator Potter, who believed what he was told to. And as opposed to himself, a believer in contradictions: that McCarthy was the devil doing the Lord's work; that Christ was Lord and yet His laws could be disobeyed.

Maybe real belief required imprisonment, or at least regimentation. The POWs testifying before Potter had felt their bodies transformed into organisms of certainty and faith—*Out of that many men, nobody cracked*—by the very torture that had sought to break them. General Airlie, perhaps never beaten or shot, nonetheless seemed to have a creed that had been spit-polished into honest, unwavering sureness.

Which, Tim wondered, did he himself miss more? God's love or His authority? Where could he go—to what secular church—to turn himself in?

He looked up at the nearest flagpole on the Capitol roof. Unlike on the afternoon he'd been hired, nothing flew on it, not even momentarily; no banner for Mill Valley, none for Cheyenne. No reason to put his hand on his heart.

"Stormed at with shot and shell! Mildly they rode and—well? So much for the ten thousand six hundred."

Raising his glass, Fuller finished this brief Tennysonian tribute to the 10,600 State Department employees around the world who had by now, according to a quote from Scott McLeod in the *Evening Star,* all been through the new security procedures.

"Yes," said Mary, cutting into the last of her steak. "But only the most *elite* troops have been through the Miscellaneous M Unit."

"We happy few. We band of inverted brothers."

She winced.

"You started it," said Fuller.

"I know, I know," she said, returning his smile and wondering why she should be bothered by a direct admission of his being queer. She wondered, for that matter, why she was out having dinner with him here at Harvey's. And she wondered most of all why she continued to string out her engagement to Paul, as if they were Victorian cousins waiting on an inheritance.

No, she was *not,* "in spite of everything," in love with Fuller. She had searched her feelings, honestly, in that department. Then what was it?

"So, how are the capital's cutest couple?" asked Hawkins.

He meant Jerry Baumeister and Beverly, who now went everywhere together.

"Inseparable," Mary answered.

"Good for them."

"You mean it."

"I do. Safe, companionable, detached. An ideal situation."

"They're thinking of getting *married,*" she protested.

"What could be more detached than that?"

She pushed her plate away. "Speak for your own parents."

"Okay, change of subject: How did the brewer like the party?"

The Queen Mother had come to Washington, and the British embassy had the day before given her a massive afternoon reception, with room enough on the list for even Mary Johnson and an escort. She had pressed Paul into service after Fuller mentioned that he himself was taking Lucy Boardman, the hard little Saltonstall relative who'd stayed on in the District after her summer course at the National Gallery.

"He didn't enjoy it as much as *your* companion seemed to," said Mary. "Anyway, it wasn't a very hot ticket if the likes of me got to go. The crowd looked like something out of Cecil B. DeMille."

Both of them raised their heads at the sound of another voice. "Probably even *I* could have gotten in."

Two nights ago Mary had told Tim about her dinner plans with Fuller, but she'd never expected to see him here.

Fuller was startled, too, though he didn't let his expression change. He pulled out a third chair from the table and, as Tim settled himself, wondered about the gleam in his eye. Back in September, Tim's aggrieved note, left in the mail slot on I Street, could be ascribed to drunkenness and the upset caused by McIntyre's revelations. Fuller had never mentioned it to him, just urged him to find out the rest of McIntyre's story.

But *this?*

"He missed my birthday," said Tim, looking at Mary and pointing to Hawk. "Eight days ago." Then he turned to Hawk and pointed at Mary: "She remembered." Finally, he turned back to Mary and pointed to Hawk: "Like I said, *she* forgot."

"Maybe I'd better leave you two gentlemen alone," said Mary.

"I'm pretty much *always* alone," said Tim.

"Fuller, you should take him home."

"Home?" asked Tim. "Where would that be? Not 2124 I Street. That's not home."

"No," said Fuller, calmly getting up. "But it's where we're heading."

The two of them put Mary in a taxi and began walking west. Tim was unsure exactly what fate awaited him; he wanted only to say that he was sorry, that he shouldn't have done what he just had. And yet, after the hours he'd wound up roaming Capitol Hill this afternoon, triply confused about the trinity of Hawkins, God, and McCarthy, he couldn't help himself. How easy, almost gay, Charlottesville suddenly seemed. Right now he wanted not to be slapped, but to be thrown under the wheels of the DeSoto that was passing.

The silence, unbearable, continued as he and Hawkins turned the corner onto I Street. "I'll go home," Tim finally said.

Still Hawkins said nothing.

"I'll never do that again," Tim promised.

"No, you won't."

Panic seized him; he waited for the next clause to strike like an ice pick—*because you'll never be seeing me again.*

Hawkins tugged him into an alley and pushed him against a wall. "You're right," he said, his face inches from Tim's. "*You* belong to *me*, and as the advertisement says, I'm the man who has everything. And I always will."

He thought he could see Hawk having to struggle to get the words out, having to make an effort to say something this cruel, and he took a small, crazy comfort from that fact, like a man catching the scent of flowers as he plunges off a ledge.

"Take it or leave it, Skippy. You've got five seconds."

"I'll take it."

CHAPTER TWENTY-FIVE

November 29, 1954

"It's a great privilege to be with you tonight!"

At the distant podium, Jean McCarthy looked buxom but clerical, a pretty white collar showing above her plain black dress. "I only wish my husband could be here, too. I want you to know how deeply touched Joe is by the tremendous fight you are waging."

"Dear Christ," said Hawkins, handing his mother's opera glasses to Tim. "Looks like yours truly isn't the only State employee not supposed to be here tonight." With Hawk's finger guiding his gaze, Tim managed to see, a dozen rows down and over to the right, the figure of Miss Lightfoot, whose hat suggested a highly alert chicken. She was in full cry with the crowd of 13,000, chanting "WHO PROMOTED PERESS?" while applauding Jean McCarthy.

"I can't figure out the hat," said Tim, who had to resist admiring the zeal that had compelled this woman to flout the rules against political activity by federal workers and travel all the way from Washington for this rally in Madison Square Garden. "I think it's maybe supposed to be an eagle," he guessed, still staring at the headgear.

"No, it's the cuckoo on a broken clock," said Hawkins, who'd never told Tim about the interrogation its wearer had instigated, nearly a year ago, in Room M305.

Every courting couple that Tim knew had gone to at least one basketball game or boxing match at the Garden. In fact, Tom Hanrahan had popped the question to Frances right here during a welterweight bout. Tim supposed that tonight would be the closest he'd ever get to such an experience; he'd even joked to himself that the Garden would always be "our place" for him and Hawk, given their both having been here before, however unknown to each other, at the Draft Ike rally back in '52.

He had certainly not expected to be with him here tonight. Tommy McIntyre had called the apartment in Stuyvesant Town on Saturday, as the Thanksgiving weekend began drawing to a close. Tim and Frances and their mother had just come back from a matinee of *Teahouse of the August Moon* (he'd been more curious to see *Tea and Sympathy*), and Tommy had asked him to stay in New York a little longer to be his eyes and ears at the anti-censure rally planned for Monday at the Garden. Tim had thought it a strange request—what could he see from these mezzanine seats that the papers wouldn't report or the radio wouldn't air?—but he'd said yes. And before he could think too much about it, knowing that Hawk extended every holiday weekend as far as possible, he'd picked up the phone and called the Charles Fuller residence at Park and Seventy-fourth.

Mrs. Fuller had answered, her voice almost a whisper, not at all the throaty dowager he'd been expecting. He'd almost wanted to tell her it was "Skippy," the namesake of her Bishop Sheen's angel, but she'd quickly handed the phone to Hawk, who explained that he was on his way out to "a little party for the Saltonstall niece thrice-removed, or whatever she is." He'd laughed at Tim's own invitation as soon as he heard it: "Are you trying to get me fired?" he asked, going on to explain the provisions of the Hatch Act.

Tim hadn't really thought of that, but knew, once Hawk cited the prohibition, that he would say yes.

"I'm in," Hawk had answered. "What could be more fun than a chance to see the Hottentots drunk on political firewater?"

GOD BLESS MCCARTHY said a badge worn by the man on Tim's right. NO TO CENSURE, YES TO A MEDAL said his sign. The Pledge of Allegiance, which now contained the congressionally authorized words "under God," had already been recited twice tonight, and a roaming spotlight, on cue, had just fallen on the figure of Roy Cohn, whose illumination provoked a tremendous roar as the former committee counsel mounted the platform to give the last speech of the evening. He was played onto the stage by the Hortonville (Wisconsin) High School Band, whose members, living close by McCarthy's hometown of Appleton, had been flown to New York earlier in the day.

"If the Senate votes to censure," cried Cohn, maintaining the volume if not profanity of his private conversations, "it will be committing the blackest act in our whole history!"

"To hell with the Hatch Act," Hawk said into Tim's ear, over the crowd's screams of approval. "I should be putting this whole evening on an expense report. Look at all the useful data I can give to Morton. Names booed: Acheson, *The New York Times.* Names cheered: Knowland, MacArthur, McCarran."

"Yeah," Tim shouted back. "It would have taken a regular Walter Lippmann to figure out who'd make each list."

"Skippy the Bitch!" said Hawkins. They both laughed as the crowd thundered but, mindful of the need for protective coloring, they also took care to applaud.

How easy, Tim thought, the last three weeks had been. The rules were now plain, inviolable, the way it had been when God, not Hawkins, had been God; the way it must be behind the Iron Curtain. He told himself there was comfort in the end of aspiration, in knowing this was all one would ever be allowed. He would let this be the other Church that he was seeking, the only rules and authority he needed.

Everyone hurrahing for McCarthy knew, in fact, that his end was near. The debating Senate had already voted cloture and would vote on censure itself anytime now. One could picture the moment when Jean McCarthy, in a sort of dewy, defiant mourning, would remove her pretty white collar and make her dress completely black.

The Reverend Cuthbert O'Hara, once imprisoned in Red China—an older, more persecuted version of Father Beane—rose to give the benediction. Tim crossed himself, not for additional camouflage against the crowd, but with a moment's sincere shame over his doubts and apostasy. He could not deny what he still believed in his heart of hearts: that the censure of McCarthy *would,* despite everything, be a victory for the Communists.

As his head came up from prayer, he tapped Hawkins on the arm. "I've got to find a pay phone and make my call. You won't run off?"

He didn't know why he'd been asked to report in immediately—to call collect, no less—rather than just give Tommy a description of the rally when he got back to the office tomorrow afternoon. But as soon as the phone in Washington picked up and he heard the older man's voice, it was clear: Tommy wanted the peculiar thrill of hearing Tim reconstruct the futile rally *in situ*, amidst its actual dying roar. It was also clear that the herald's confusion and conflictedness were exciting him in some further, cruel way.

Tim realized that Tommy was off the wagon. Through the line he could hear the clink of a bottle and a glass, and no voice save Tommy's own, which gleefully interrupted his paraphrase of Jean McCarthy's remarks. "And to think it's all because of Charlie's little boy!" Tommy cackled.

For a moment he thought Tommy was referring to himself. But then he understood. "You mean Senator Potter's son?"

"Yup, Charlie's little bastard. The kid's got ten fewer IQ points than his father, which is saying something, but he's a handsome enough lad to speak to people's weaknesses. You know what Joe's weakness is, don't you?"

"Boys?" asked Tim, as flatly as he could.

Tommy laughed loudly. "Boys, girls, your old-maid auntie. When he's hammered he'll grope anything—slobber over it with tender, lustful kisses."

This is what had happened in New York. This is what Alsop had told Hawk about.

As the fading cries of the crowd continued to reach Tim from the Garden's exit ramps—*"THE MAN! THE 'ISM'! McCARTHY!"*—Tommy explained that the plan had been for the house detective to rescue the boy "at a point where Joe had been compromised, and photographed, yet nothing too serious had happened to the little angel." But there'd been "a bit of a backfire. After I'd paid him my own good money, the damned house dick decided to bring the picture to his boss's offspring, our good friend Dave Schine. Jesus Jumpin' Christ! I didn't realize I'd set up the little assignation on one of the Schine family properties!"

Tim could hear Tommy pouring himself another.

"Does the boy's mother," Tim asked, "know what happened?"

"She's too poor and too drunk to care," answered Tommy, who went on with his story. "Yes, that was my blunder. The house dick decided the picture would fetch a higher price from the soon-to-be Private Schine than the one it commanded from me. Dave could keep the photo to protect Joe or to do him in. Either way, however he inclined, it was worth something to him."

One last multitudinous demand to know who promoted Peress reached Tim's ears, while out of his left eye he noticed Hawk chatting up one of the red-white-and-blue-armbanded ushers, somebody handsome. He cupped the receiver's mouthpiece and nearly shouted to Tommy: "What am I supposed to say? That I'm sorry you failed?"

"*Failed?*" shouted Tommy. "I *succeeded*! I may have brought Joe down a little more *slowly*, a trifle less *spectacularly*, but coming down he is, because of those hearings. Which all derived, Master Laughlin, from what me and Charlie's boy managed to accomplish, however inadvertently, in that hotel room. Every bit of pressure to treat Schine special in the army derived from that picture—not the goddamned nothing of a picture they wrangled over in the Caucus Room! Dave let Joe know he had it, and from that moment on, if Royboy insisted Dave get an ice cream sundae every morning at reveille, Joe was ready to initial the request."

"*MAKE MINE McCARTHY!*" The audience had dispersed to the point where the chant, like an echo of something long past, barely made it up the ramp to the pay phone, which Tim, pretending the connection had been broken, now hung up.

He left with Hawk, walking east on Fiftieth. "I feel sick" was all he said as they reached Broadway.

"You can't be. You had exactly half a hot dog."

Tim shook his head.

"Are you off your milk? Haven't had any since noon?"

If he were drunk, the way he'd been that night at O'Donnell's, he really would be throwing up. As it was, he managed to keep in step, turning south with Hawk below the Winter Garden Theater, over which Mary Martin's hamstrung effigy flew as Peter Pan.

What Tommy had told him: Was it the fantasy of a revenge-crazed drunk or potentially the scoop of Kenneth Woodforde's—maybe even Joe Alsop's—life? If it was true, why did the thought of telling the details to Hawk now make him feel sicker than six old-fashioneds would? Because harboring someone else's filthy secret made his *own* secret, his love, feel filthy as well, as if it, too, were nothing more than appetite, compulsively gratified. Telling the story would make things even worse. Hawk would claim to be as amused by McCarthy's helplessness as he'd been by the crowd's fervor—or as he was this minute by the city's night crawlers, passing by with their own secrets.

The two of them entered Times Square, where all the neon in the world could not lift the fact of night. "Surely you're not going to walk me home?" Tim asked, as playfully as he could. "All the way down Broadway and over to Stuy Town?"

"Nope," said Hawkins, squeezing the back of his neck as they passed the statue of Father Duffy.

"And surely the night is too young for Hawkins Fuller to be going home by himself?" He smiled up at Hawk, showed him, as he'd been doing for weeks, what a sport he could be.

"Yep," said Hawkins. "Way too early."

They were soon at Forty-third Street. Hawk faced west, ready to cross, and Tim realized: *the clarinet player.*

Should he keep chattering and walk him there, be the ultimate good sport, as they'd imagined he'd have been if they'd encountered each other three years ago, at the Draft Ike rally?

No, he wouldn't, because he had just seen it, only feet away, sitting in this lurid forest of light like a cottage, its own weak, non-neon glow making it pure, *a clean well-lighted place,* the one he now knew he had to reach, the place where they would take him in. *This* was the secular Church he had been seeking.

"Okay, Hawk, I'll see you in the funny papers."

Already crossing the street, Fuller turned back for a second and snapped off a mischievous salute.

Tim returned it and then walked in the opposite direction, toward the little structure nestled so oddly in Times Square, like a single cotton stitch upon a sea of sequins.

He opened its door and entered the first of the three offices it contained. He filled out several forms, told a lie on one of them, and then, at 10:45 p.m., raised his right hand and enlisted in the Army of the United States.

PART THREE

DECEMBER 1954–NOVEMBER 1956

America I'm putting my queer shoulder to the wheel.

—ALLEN GINSBERG

CHAPTER TWENTY-SIX

December 25, 1954

The homily was coming from Washington's National Cathedral, but as Mary gave half her attention to its telecast by NBC's New Orleans affiliate, she could hear actual church bells, their sound arriving on a light wind from Jackson Square, half a mile away.

Her father called out from his study: "Mary, my darlin', your gentleman is on the telephone."

"I'll be right there."

She walked, hesitantly, toward the other room, feeling guilty over her father's use of "gentleman" rather than "fiancé." She had never told Daddy about the engagement to Paul; not when it was made, not when it was broken.

Mr. Johnson rose from his wooden swivel chair and tilted the shade of his brass desk lamp, as if to allow his daughter a softer light in which to conduct what the look on her face indicated would be a difficult conversation.

"Paul," she said, taking the receiver.

"Merry Christmas, Mary."

"I had the television on. I could hear Wilson's grandson—Dean Sayre—giving the sermon in D.C."

"Right," said Paul, uncomprehendingly. He had no more taste for historical trivia than for the immediate political kind.

"Are you with your family?" Mary asked.

"Yes, we're just back from church. Mount Olivet Lutheran, not the cathedral."

"Daddy and I didn't even make the effort. We've gotten to be very freethinking in the last couple of years." She tried laughing. "Actually, his knee is bothering him. He just didn't want to go out."

"Knee-thinking."

"I suppose." *Bless his heart.* She felt a surge of affection toward Paul's effortful wit.

"Look, Mary," he said, after a pause. "There's a girl called Marjorie Wheeler. She keeps books for my brother, and I'm wondering if it's okay for me to take her to a party next week, for New Year's Eve."

"Of course."

"Okay. It just felt funny. I wanted to check."

He was enough like other men to want her jealous over this—and she *was* jealous, a little bit—but he was also nice enough for the request to be genuine. She could picture him, a thousand miles away, looking at his shoes.

"Honest, Paul."

As she said it, she felt another small wave of affection. Maybe, if he hadn't always been so solicitous of her feelings, he might have drowned her reluctance, overwhelmed it, and floated the romance to an altar. But she'd been the same way with him; even now the two of them were left stumbling through a handful of courtesies before they could decently hang up the phone.

She had broken the engagement three weeks ago on the illogical grounds that Paul was the marrying kind. Her attraction to that solid type depended to some extent on a belief in herself as its opposite—a girl still cut out for unusual adventures and unusual personalities, like Fuller, or even Tim Laughlin. Yes, it was time to put an end to her girlhood, but she couldn't yet put an end to this sense of herself, or to the feeling that the man who could truly speak to it might still walk through the door of Congressional Relations or send a drink to her table at Harvey's. To marry Paul—with whom on some days, usually bad days at the office, she felt she was in love—would be to get married for the same reason Beverly and Jerry Baumeister now seemed likely to: to find shelter from one's particular storm.

She went back to the living room and saw her frail-looking father reading the *Times-Picayune.* They usually cooked on Christmas, but today they would settle for a restaurant in the Quarter, sitting down to dinner at about the time Beverly and Jerry would be exclaiming over their hearts of lettuce with Russian dressing, the first course of the special at the Hotel Harrington, to which Beverly had said they would go with her boys after seeing the tree on the White House lawn.

The NBC commentator, in an ecumenical spirit, was now reading Pius XII's Christmas message, apparently composed before the pope's collapse on December 2, the day of McCarthy's censure—a fact, Mary suspected, that Miss Lightfoot, had she been Catholic, would no doubt have found significant. "If only," spoke the stricken pontiff, "men knew how to live out their whole lives in that atmosphere of joy, with those feelings of goodness and peace, which Christmas pours forth on all sides, how different, how much happier the earth would be!"

Mary also wondered what Miss Lightfoot would think of a homosexual joining this man's army. Returning to Washington after the rally in New York, Tim at first had said nothing about his enlistment or anything else. He'd made himself scarce until she'd called his office, at which point he spoke only of how Lyndon Johnson, in preparation for the Democrats' takeover of the Senate, was managing to overwork even the Republicans.

Things had certainly not been busy in CR—it was easier selling Ike's foreign policy to the midterm-triumphant Democrats than it had been to some of the former Republican majority—and so Mary had at last insisted on Tim's joining her for a long weekday lunch at Reeves' cafeteria, where over ice cream sodas he admitted that he was due to report for basic training at Fort Dix on January 11.

She'd insisted on knowing why, and he'd responded with unconvincing declarations about anticommunism and doing his bit and putting his money where his mouth was, refusing all the while to admit that volunteering was his extreme means of breaking with Fuller. Mostly he'd concentrated on his ice cream soda, which he may have hoped would get his weight above the minimum required by the induction physical.

Even now she didn't know why he'd joined, though she imagined that he would have the self-discipline to get through it. He had been able at Reeves', after all, to resist asking her about Fuller, the cherished topic of their every previous conversation. She gathered that he'd not even seen him since the night he'd signed up in Times Square.

He didn't tell her the enlistment was a secret, but she'd kept it one until leaving Washington three nights ago, when she air-mailed a Christmas card to Fuller at his parents' apartment in New York: *Can't you do something about this? Or undo it?*

In fact, she'd been hoping, when the phone rang just before, that it might be Fuller instead of Paul.

Frances's baby reached for the celery stalks in the cut-glass centerpiece and shrieked when she was thwarted. Uncle Alan, his nerves even now a little raw from the war, winced at the sound. Apologizing with a glance, Frances tried to soothe her daughter with a tiny spoonful of mashed turnips.

Except for little Maria Loretta, the Christmas dinner table had fallen silent, Grandma Gaffney having made it clear she blamed her own daughter and son-in-law for her grandson Timothy's absence. Frances's attempt to explain it had only made things worse.

"What did you say was the name of that place?" asked Grandma Gaffney.

"Fides."

"Sounds like a dog."

"It's a Catholic settlement house in Washington," Frances noted once again. "On Eighth Street," she added, not that the address meant anything to anyone around the table. "Tim told me in his card that he'd spend Christmas Eve giving out food baskets to the poor, and that afterward he'd go to midnight Mass."

Grandma Gaffney, who had not been to church in forty years and who found pious Catholics more irritating than the Jews, once more frowned.

"I'll bet Tim's just trying to save his money," offered Paul Laughlin, knowing his mother-in-law would find this explanation more tolerable than any involving charity.

"You could have sent him a bus ticket," said Grandma Gaffney.

"He didn't seem all that happy to be here at Thanksgiving," Tim's mother pointed out. She'd been crumpling a paper napkin in her right hand. Uncle Alan wasn't the only one with nerves.

"I'll bet he's just too damned busy down there," suggested Uncle Frank. "That's a big job he's got, for a kid. Though I wish he was working for McCarthy and not this Potter guy. You watch," he added, wiping up some cranberry sauce with a slice of bread, "Joe'll bounce back."

Tom Hanrahan, while hardly a foe of McCarthy's, scoffed at the possibility. "I read that Joe commissioned a poll about running for president in '56. I think he got three percent."

"Tim is fine," said Paul Laughlin, changing back the subject. "*Our* card said he'll soon be taking a couple of trips to Michigan with the boss, but that even so he'll get up to New York before Easter. He promises."

No, thought Frances, he *hadn't* been happy here at Thanksgiving. She could remember when they'd gotten home from *Teahouse of the August Moon* and she'd found him in their parents' bedroom, his sleeves rolled up, talking on the phone with that Irishman he'd mentioned from his office. When the call ended, she'd asked about the cuff links he'd set down on a doily. "HF?"

"Hawkins Fuller," she remembered him saying without pleasure or defiance—without anything, really, except maybe a kind of exhaustion. "It's a man's name. He gave them to me."

She'd looked at her brother and left the room, saying a prayer for him, as she was doing now, while she let the baby lick a drop of gravy from her fingertip.

"My lung man is in the capital," said Fuller's uncle Ned, with some difficulty. "When I come down to see him, you and I should have lunch at the Sulgrave. We need to have a discussion."

Uncle Ned's poor health was the chief reason most of the Fuller family had gathered here in New York instead of Maine for Christmas dinner. Looking at Ned's skeletal frame, Hawkins couldn't understand how his uncle might weather a trip to the District, let alone why he continued to keep one of his specialists down there.

Fuller's father was even more quiet than his brother-in-law today, and as the first round of cocktails jingled into the room on an old cart, Mrs. Fuller appeared so relieved by the distraction that she didn't bother to check her wristwatch, as she usually did, to make sure it was at least past one.

Her sister, Hawkins' unmarried aunt Valerie, finally put a topic

upon the air, expressing agreement with the French parliament's decision to reject a NATO treaty that would allow the Germans to rearm.
Valerie's one great affair of the heart having occurred in Paris thirty
years ago, her approval of all things French was expected to last a
lifetime.

Mrs. Fuller, an internationalist who still regarded Wendell Willkie as
having been a most attractive candidate and man, wanly disagreed: "Ade-
nauer says he's prepared to be patient."

"So, in a way, was Hitler," said Aunt Valerie. "The last time."

From across the room, Hawkins looked at the small tableau presented
by his mother and aunt. Neither was exactly driving the holiday spirit at
full throttle. By way of contrast, a picture from yesterday's papers sprang
to his mind: Mrs. Perle Mesta, surrounded by gamboling orphans at the
Christmas party she'd given in her Washington apartment. The only
children here above Park and Seventy-fourth were in a room down the
hall with their mother, the sister Hawkins disliked only a little less than
the one at Uncle Ned's New Mexico place, over which they'd all be fighting, it now seemed, soon enough.

Hawkins' brother-in-law, Robert, an orthopedic surgeon whose unhappiness lay in knowing that he would never be department chief as his
father had been, began a long, almost footnotable denunciation of the
hospital that was allowing this situation. Robert's disappointment hung
ever more thickly on the living-room air until the girl at last called them
to the table, where the food might be easier to push around than the
conversation.

Mr. Fuller sliced the ham.

"Excellent work," said Hawkins. "Robert's father couldn't have done
better." When no one laughed, he added that it was "without *question* a
neater job than Dr. Sheppard would have managed."

"Hawkins, honestly," said his mother.

"You're right," he replied, retracting his reference to the Ohio surgeon
who'd finally been convicted of slaughtering his wife. "He was only an
osteopath, hardly fit for comparison."

He knew, even as she begged him to change the subject, that his
mother was thanking God for the life and mischief in him, for the vitality that she, somewhere inside, still had a measure of herself—even if,
except in the televised presence of Bishop Sheen, she retained no ability

to display it. Mrs. Fuller was now dutifully back on the subject of German rearmament, pointing out to her sister that even Churchill was for it.

"It will provoke the Russians," declared Valerie.

"And this time they'll overrun *both* the Germans *and* the French," said Mr. Fuller, verbal at last. "And probably our own boys over there to boot."

Hawkins found himself imagining the front lines of such a war, maybe a year or so from now. *They'll have to put rocks in his pockets*, he thought, *just to keep him from bouncing out of the jeep.*

When international affairs were exhausted, Robert got everyone to the mince pie with a renewed recitation of the hospital's underappreciation of orthopedists. Hawkins tried to remember: Didn't Mary's father need to get his knee fixed? Hadn't that also been in her Christmas card? He excused himself and went to his old room, across from the one inside which his sister's children were still stuffed. On the desk, beneath the St. Paul's pennant and the picture of Bill Tilden—who *couldn't* have guessed that one?—Mary's envelope still sat. It was next to a pair of whimsical mittens that the relentless Saltonstall girl had knitted. He supposed she wanted him to think of her as a spirited girl, Marie Antoinette playing the milkmaid.

He took a piece of stationery from the desk's middle drawer and wrote: "Dear Skippy, I didn't raise my boy to be a soldier. . . ."

CHAPTER TWENTY-SEVEN

January 10, 1955

"It's hard to know what to save," said Tim, looking at a Herblock cartoon of McCarthy as a baboon. He'd clipped it from the *Post* eight months ago.

"Save *yourself*," said Tommy McIntyre, who'd just approached the desk that Tim was cleaning out. "Let Uncle Sam feed you three squares a day. Put on a little flesh. Get away from all this."

"Oh, he'll be back," said Miss Cook, bustling in with Tim's separation form. "Look at Senator Barkley!" Harry Truman's vice president had in November been elected to his old Senate seat and the other day restored to his committee chairmanships.

"Perhaps even 'the Jones boy' will one day reappear among us," offered Tommy.

"Where *is* Bob Jones?" asked Miss Cook. Seven months after the Maine primary, no one seemed to know his location or what he might be doing. With no response to her question, Miss Cook proceeded to muse on the difficulty of keeping up with all the changes on the Hill—in particular, of trying to imagine the Democrats' Senator McClellan heading what everyone would almost certainly keep calling the McCarthy committee.

"As hard to believe as another Roosevelt in the Congress," said Tommy, reminding them that both branches of the family, Teddy's and FDR's, had for most of this century confined themselves to the other end of Pennsylvania Avenue. But last night, Jimmy Roosevelt, the second son of the late president to be elected to the House, had stolen the show at the Congressional Club reception.

"You take care of yourself," said Miss Cook. "And send us a postcard." She gave Tim a kiss, and left him alone with Mr. McIntyre.

"You going to wait around for Charlie? To say goodbye?" asked Tommy.

"I don't think so," said Tim, recalling the lie in his Christmas card home. *I'll be visiting Michigan with the boss.* He hadn't needed such embellishment, but he'd been determined, and still was, not to tell his mother and father and Frances about enlisting—not until he was irretrievably at Fort Dix. And he'd be there in less than twenty-four hours, if he could keep himself, for one last day, from tearing across town to the State Department or, even worse, the apartment on I Street.

"But I did like Senator Potter," he finally said. "He was nice to me." He paused, regretfully, and added: "I could have worked harder."

"You worked hard enough," Tommy assured him. "And when Charlie caught you looking out the window, he just figured you were in love."

"I *was* in love."

"You *are* in love. But don't worry, Timothy. Charlie thinks it's a girl, I guarantee you. You know the extent of his imagination."

Tim went back to filling the box. He had never admitted anything to Tommy, but never lied to him either, certainly never pretended there was a girl.

"You won't forget Mr. Fuller," said Tommy, in the low tones of a fortune-teller. "Not just because you've started toting a rifle. Any more than I forget *her* by hoisting a glass."

"Are you hoisting one these days?"

They were both surprised by his nerve in asking. Unlike Tommy's questions—asked only to make plain that the asker already had the compromising answer—Tim's was an actual inquiry, a way of learning whether there was anything he should be doing to help this cruel, loving man.

"Yes, I am, Timothy. I am indeed."

"I could tell from the phone call I made from the rally. When you told me all that awful stuff."

"Awful?" countered Tommy, already again combative. "You might consider all the good that 'awful stuff' did."

"What good has it done *you*?"

McCarthy had fallen but Potter was still on his prosthetic feet, and Tommy, his hunger as yet unappeased, looked to be on his way back to the Cheboygan gutter from which he'd been plucked. However sincerely Tim had asked his last question, he could feel the thrill of its aggression, a sensation similar to what he'd experienced one night a few months ago when to his astonishment Hawkins, with some wordless guidance from his hand, had insisted that Tim penetrate *him*. The act had ended up as another form of submission, during which he seemed to be gathered in, enfolded and protected in a different way from the usual, but for an instant, at its beginning, he had enjoyed a sense of himself as being brutally in charge.

Now, as then, he subsided quickly into a renewed willingness to serve. "There's a Father Hackett," he told Tommy, "over at St. Peter's on Second and C. He meets on Monday nights with people who—"

"People who are drunks?" asked Tommy.

"Yes."

"Why should you want me sober? After all these *terrible* things I've done and insisted on pouring into your ears, I should think, Timothy, you'd be glad to see me trampled by the pink elephants."

Tim wrote out the church's address and Father Hackett's name on one of Potter's business cards. He handed it to Tommy, whose bloodshot eyes he was now close enough to see. He could also smell a peppermint fighting the whiskey on Tommy's tongue.

"You said it yourself," declared Tim. "We're alike. But I don't have what you've got to fall back on."

"A taste for drink to prop you up?"

"No," said Tim. "I'm you without any anger. And I have a feeling I scare you."

I didn't raise my boy to be a soldier.

Here in the apartment it was even harder to decide what he should pack or throw away. He could put Hawkins' letter into the silky cloth flap inside the suitcase lid—but what was he to do with the empty milk bottle? Bring it to Fort Dix? Should he have shipped it to Frances and Tom's on Staten Island with the other stuff he'd sent this afternoon, which wouldn't arrive in New York until he himself had reached Jersey?

One suitcase was all he'd carry; he supposed its contents would fill about half the footlocker they'd give him in the barracks. Stuffing his missal in between some underwear and socks, he again resolved to make his confession before Easter. It would be too risky to let an army chaplain hear it; he would take a bus into town, or even wait till he had a pass for New York City.

Folded inside the missal was a prayer he had clipped from the *Star*, a newly approved English version of the words for extreme unction, murmurs to bring the dying back from the brink or escort them safely over it. *O Redeemer, we implore Thee, by the grace of the Holy Spirit cure the illness of this sick man and heal his wounds; forgive his sins; and drive away from him all pains of mind and body. In Thy Mercy, give him his health, inward and outward....* He had memorized the sentences, and he whispered them now.

Without a knock, the door opened. Hawkins, in his Harris overcoat, came toward him, stopping inches away, looking first into his eyes and then around the room. Picking the milk bottle up from the desk, he reached into his pants for two cents, the refund for an empty. He gave Tim the pennies and put the bottle into one of his overcoat's huge pockets.

"Do you want the cuff links back?" Tim asked.

Hawkins took hold of him, tightly, and pressed him against the overcoat, damp with drizzle. "You don't need to do this," he said.

"Yes, I do," said Tim. "Besides," he added, trying to sound cheerful, "the draft will get me eventually."

"I'm not going to wait for you, you know."

It was hardly a possibility that required denial. The two of them burst out laughing.

"Come on," said Hawkins, tilting his head toward the front door. "Finish up."

They were going out? Tim didn't think he could bear it, though it would be worse if Hawk started pushing him toward the bed, now stripped of its sheets.

"I have a five-thirty bus to catch," said Tim. "*A.M.*"

Hawk threw the last handful of things into the suitcase before picking it up and moving him out the door.

The night was warm and the drizzle had just stopped, and the Capitol, shiny as mercury, seemed like a spaceship ready to disgorge Michael Rennie in *The Day the Earth Stood Still*, which Tim now remembered seeing one Saturday night up at Fordham with Bobby Garahan. Hawk said they would pass up the streetcar and walk down Pennsylvania Avenue, whose shabbiness, he declared, was not a disgrace but rather a gesture of humility by the strongest republic on earth. "You think so?" Tim asked, trying to keep the air crowded with chatter, dreading the wordless moments when the swish of the rattan suitcase against Hawkins' coat was the only sound.

"Two more blocks," Hawk said, pointing to the Old Post Office, their destination, a gigantic Romanesque pile between Eleventh and Twelfth streets. Once there, Hawkins took them around the back to an unlocked door. "Tip from an FBI friend," he explained.

Hoover's Bureau now had a portion of its training academy in the building, which the Postmaster General had long ago ceded to a motley assortment of small federal agencies and government record collections. Fuller led Tim through the dim after-hours light to a bank of elevators. "Not that one," he said, instructing Tim to wait for another car. "Number one is solely for the use of Edgar and Clyde. Or so I hear."

They rode to the ninth floor, as high as any of the elevators went. Stashing the suitcase by a radiator, Hawkins then piloted them through a door and into the clock tower, which rose several stories and could be scaled only by ladders attached to its stone walls. Up they climbed, past the kind of narrow windows designed for medieval archers holding off a siege. Going first, looking like a tweed-costumed Errol Flynn, Hawkins made fast acrobatic progress toward the tower's bell-less belfry. His sudden arrival at the top, where no windows or screens enclosed the arches, startled a dozen pigeons from their nighttime roost; they clattered into flight, taking off in the direction of the White House.

He pulled Tim up the last steps and onto the belfry's floor, so that the two of them stood above the tower's northern clockface, looking down on Pennsylvania Avenue and the *Star*'s building across the street. The sight of it, and its streetcar stop, was so painful that Tim moved to another arch, one that faced more to the east. Through it he could see the Navy Yard and the smokestacks of St. Elizabeth's, the insane asylum still holding Ezra Pound.

"You think I'll wind up there?" he asked.

"Doubtful," Hawkins replied. "I have the higher actuarial risk. You know, the mad Mayflower type."

Softly, Tim said, "I have to get over you."

"Yes, you do."

"Then let's take desperate measures!" Tim brightly cried, turning around to face Fuller with a smile. "Hawk," he said, pointing to the overcoat's pocket, "hand me that."

Fuller gave him the empty milk bottle, which Tim took back to the Pennsylvania Avenue arch.

"Hold me over the ledge." The tower's stone shelf extended far enough out to block any view of the sidewalk below. "Just hold my ankles so I can lie on my stomach and see over."

Hawkins gave him a skeptical look but took hold of him above his loafers. "This may be the only part of you I've never touched."

"Don't make me laugh," said Tim, inching forward on his stomach until he could finally see the sidewalk. No one was coming. The milk bottle, still in his right hand, caught the moonlight. Empty of gold or frankincense, it was still the most precious casket he could offer up to God, the treasured thing that he could renounce along with its original giver. He loosened his hand and let it fall three hundred feet to the ground. The sound that came back up wasn't glassy at all, just a small pop, the kind made by a gun that had been fitted with a silencer.

Hawkins reeled him in and set him down. "You can keep the two cents," he said.

In one corner of the belfry there was a small pile of blankets, none too clean, left over from others' trysts. Fuller moved the stack to a different corner of the tower and sat down on it. Their faces, he explained, would be awakened by the light of the sun when it rose in the east. "Don't worry," he said, coaxing Tim toward him. "I'll get you to your bus."

As the wind rushed through the arches, Hawk held him, tenderly stroking the side of his face, trying to transfer from his own body what Tim realized, with fresh despair, was relief at his departure.

He clenched his teeth, summoning the resolve to say it: "Promise you won't write."

"I promise," Hawkins said.

CHAPTER TWENTY-EIGHT

March 11, 1955

69th Infantry Division
Fort Dix, N.J.
March 11, 1955

Dear Francy,

Well, I'm 5½ weeks into it, and maybe this time I'll get the whole way through. "Last time, you will recall"—as one of our old serials used to say—I made it to nineteen days before that chest cold put me in the camp hospital. That got me "recycled": everybody who drops out has to start over from the beginning, because it's too hard to find slots *in medias res*. (How much Latin do you remember?)

So, guess what? This round, for everything except knowledge of the Uniform Code of Military Justice, my first set of marks are even <u>lower</u> than the last. This is attributable, I guess, to natural incompetence and a tougher company commander, a second lieutenant who's very demanding but nice enough underneath. So far he's called me "shitbird" only twice, and he's allowed us to perform the rifle-reassembly test in simple lights-out darkness instead of with blindfolds. (Some commanders do that—I'm not kidding.)

So: two and a half weeks to go.

Coming in, back in January, I was told to gain ten pounds; I've managed to lose three. It's so cold here that the barracks furnace (coal! just like 9th Avenue) never stops puffing. But for real bone-rattling chill, nothing can beat last week's bivouac. We were doing "camouflage and concealment" maneuvers, and I couldn't puncture the can of evaporated milk with the opener: the stuff had frozen solid!

I've got the top bunk again. The other seven guys in the squad are mostly like the ones I used to give a wide berth to back at St. Agnes', but

I've made friends with a nice doctor (they draft them in droves) who's got a wife (pregnant) back home.

Strange to think of Dad being here in the CCC twenty years ago. (He once told me it was the only place he ever saw reefer!)

I'm sorry I haven't written. You scold me about it worse than Mom, who's sort of given up on the subject. You ask if I'm running away from something, or someone. Mostly the drill instructor! He'll actually pound you on the back if you're not marching fast enough with your rifle. (The M-1 is a lot easier to reassemble than it is to carry.)

I might have to welsh on my Easter promise. On Sunday, April 10th, I could be on my way to wherever it is I'll be doing Advanced Individual Training (not as customized as it sounds). I don't have my assignment yet, and God only knows what they'll decide I'm suited for, but that's the story.

Say hi to Tom and kiss Maria Loretta for me.

Love,

Beetle Bailey

P.S. Please don't worry. All shall be well.

Timmer xxx

Folding the letter, he wondered what it would be like to run away from something *with* somebody, the two of you fleeing the same thing together. In the papers, Princess Margaret's RAF boyfriend was now saying that they would be willing to accept exile if they were allowed to marry. It sounded like the grandest of fates: to be safely joined in some realm beyond the one that had refused to provide the two of you a place. Of course, all of this first assumed that both of you actually wanted each other.

He had trouble being ashamed of writing so few letters, not when he always had more to leave out than put in. Was he really supposed to tell Francy about the guy in the squad who was, he felt sure, like himself— this draftee clerk from a New York City government office who had pronounced the old olive-drab uniforms more "attractive" than the new Army Green ones and observed that camouflage-and-concealment sounded "a little like Max Factor's latest"?

Maybe that guy would be the one to bug out? To go sobbing to the headshrinker in the camp hospital? Actually not, thought Tim. More likely it would be the loudmouth from Bridgeport who loved to hold his M-1 in one hand and his crotch in the other, and say—

> This is my rifle
> This is my gun
> This is for killing
> This is for fun—

as if it weren't the two-hundredth time they'd all heard it.

The falling marks he'd just mentioned to Francy still had him slightly above average in "coordination" and "resourcefulness" (no one understood how they measured it), but below par in "aggressiveness." All this had probably been predictable from the Armed Forces Qualifying Test he'd taken at the examining station in D.C. before leaving for Fort Dix. He'd run into Kenneth Woodforde at a cafeteria right after sitting the exam, and the journalist had mocked his enlistment, revealing himself to be 4-F and expressing regret only about having gotten his classification on physical rather than moral grounds. "They discovered my bad shoulder before my voter registration," he said, the first concrete indication Tim had ever had that Woodforde might really be a Communist.

———

Department of State
Washington, D.C.
March 11, 1955

Dear Dog-Face,

I don't know how you can sign yourself that way, and it's the last time I'll ever use it as a salutation, but there you go.

Thanks for the snapshot. White sidewalls, no? Isn't that what they call the haircut? They make you look even younger.

Are you sure they can't detail you back to civilian life for a week or two? I could use some extra help here: Senator Knowland wants to start World War Three by having the 7th Fleet intercept a Finnish tanker that's heading to Red China to deliver jet fuel, and Beverly is spending more time over at the Congressional Secretaries Club than she is here. Someone in Senator Stennis' office bent the membership rules so she could take a small wisecracking part ("very Eve Arden," she says) in "Revisin' and Extendin'," the revue they'll be doing to benefit some clinic in Georgetown for retarded children. I think Mrs. Nixon was pictured with a couple of them in yesterday's *Star*. (The children, not the secretaries.) So if you see a mushroom cloud, it's the result of Beverly not being at her typewriter to send Senator Knowland and his colleagues those gentle policy pleadings from Mr. Morton.

Even so, it's hard to blame her. These days she appears to be the happiest person on the floor; maybe in the whole building.

When I told Paul—yes, we're still friendly, and yes, he's still dating the bookkeeper—that you hadn't been notified about your advanced individual training (have I got the name right?), he said to be sure and tell you not to let them turn you into a bean-burner, which I gather is a cook, and which I gather his bookkeeper is a much better one of than I. (I know you'll be able to straighten out the grammar of that sentence.)

Let me know what they *do* make you into. And where they're sending you next.

Love,
Mary

————

"Plucky wog!" exclaimed the Englishman at Couve de Murville's table.

With his own two hands, Prime Minister Nehru had the other day saved himself from a knife attack, knocking a would-be assassin off the running board of his limousine.

De Murville, the French foreign minister, nodded impassively to his lunch companion here at the Sulgrave, but the Englishman's loud compliment caught the attention of Ned Fuller and his nephew, Hawkins.

Still, Ned had no time for thinking about subcontinentals; the *Germans* were again crowding his mind, thanks to Hawkins' aunt Valerie, who the other night at dinner in New York had loudly voiced her distress over France's belated capitulation to German rearmament. "Fortunately, the Frogs are still carping about the Saar," Ned now told his nephew. "That gives her a little encouragement."

Hawkins sipped a spoonful of consommé.

"I'm afraid," said Uncle Ned, "that you and I have some important things to talk about. More important than whether you or your sisters are going to get my place in New Mexico." He coughed into his water glass; the lung man down here was not doing much good.

"You mean the world situation?" asked Hawkins. "The French and the Germans?"

"No, your father's financial situation."

Hawkins pushed away the soup bowl. "Tell me it's unexpectedly good. I'm all ears."

"It's terrible. Bad investments. And bad choice of a girlfriend. The latest one."

"Myrna."

"Maura," Ned corrected. "It's bad enough he pays her bills. But he seems to be paying her debts, too—all the freight her last boyfriend wouldn't pick up. And your mother is only making things worse."

"Mother doesn't make scenes."

Ned lit a cigarette. "No, she doesn't. And she doesn't make investments, good or bad. What she's *been* making are a lot of charitable donations— to *Catholic* charities, no less. She's spent down a lot of her own capital, and your father's besides."

"Each according to her means," said Hawkins.

"Meaning?"

"She can't quite bring herself to kneel at Sheen's altar rail. So she sacrifices at the teller's window."

Ned shrugged and blew a smoke ring.

"What are the implications?" asked Hawkins.

"For you?"

"Of course." Hawkins pierced the cracked crab with his fork and smiled.

"Rather dire," said Uncle Ned. "How do you feel about living off your salary? It may come to that. I hate to tell you, but you're not even getting that house in New Mexico."

Hawkins looked at the choice forkful of crab. "Should I send this back and get a hamburger?"

"Don't worry about me," said Ned, who was paying for lunch. "Cancer's already tightened my belt. And I never had that much in the first place. Maybe a fifth as much as your profligate parents."

Living off his salary: Hawkins judged the idea to be no more endurable than it would be to any of his Harvard trust-fund buddies who'd gone into publishing. One might as well tell Lucy Boardman's father to live off what Wellesley paid him to teach art history.

"Pull your chair back," said Uncle Ned.

Hawkins obliged.

"Just trying to get a look at you. See how expensive your tastes are." Ned paused, consideringly. "I can't see the shoes. I hope they aren't in a league with the suit."

Hawkins finished his crab and asked for a cigarette while they waited for coffee. His shoes and suits were good enough to last a long while, he thought. But at some point he'd need money for trouble. One day his luck would run out; he would slip up in a way that required more than the fifty dollars for a men's-room arrest at the Y. Money, put to bail or blackmail, would be what saved him.

"The nerve of Dad to be spending everything on his *own* indiscretions!"

Hawkins laughed as he said it, but Ned, unsmiling, coughed hard, rose from his chair, and waved off his nephew's assistance. "Let me head to the gents. I'll be fine."

As he waited for his uncle to return, Hawkins drank his coffee and regarded both de Murville and the Gilbert-and-Sullivan character at the other table. They were beginning to blur into a portrait on the wall when the waiter approached with a message.

"A phone call, Mr. Fuller. From a Mr. Sorrell at the Pentagon."

"Thanks." Hawkins headed for one of the telephone cabins, thinking how much easier it would be to focus for a moment or two on Skippy's future instead of his own.

He understood from a letter he'd seen on Mary's desk that there still might be time to affect a decision about Private Laughlin's AIT, even if his Fort Dix days with the Fighting Sixty-ninth—*there* was nomenclatural combination!—would be over in a couple of weeks.

He knew someone, of course. He'd left the message with Sorrell just an hour ago.

"Andy," he said, taking the receiver. "You always were quick."

"Got your own little Private Schine, do you?"

"What about the Monterey Language School?"

"That's hard to do. Actually, it's hard to do anything like this, but I'll accomplish what I can. Tell me his aptitudes." He chuckled at the word.

"Writes nicely. Clever. Terribly sincere right-winger. No particular drive. A tender disposition. Would be a wonderful boy Friday to some major general."

Sorrell's leering chuckle became a full laugh. "I see."

Fuller said nothing, just waited for an answer.

"Well," Sorrell at last replied, "maybe USAIS, the information school in upstate New York."

"I suppose that's better than having him learn to type all over again at Fort Benjamin Harrison."

Or, God forbid, putting him into a combat arm. He once more pictured Tim bouncing toward a European death in some jeep, the same mental image he'd had at Christmas, but filled in this time with the detail of the white sidewalls he'd seen in the picture on Mary's desk.

"Give me until tomorrow morning," said Sorrell. "I'll do what I can to get him back to you smooth and unscratched. The way you like them, right? At least sometimes." Getting no response, Sorrell added hopefully, "I'm still that way myself, you know."

Fuller laughed. "Thanks, Andy."

CHAPTER TWENTY-NINE

June 22–24, 1955

The bugle notes of reveille, tinny and recorded, reached the barracks at Fort Polk by means of a loudspeaker, but Tim had no need for them. He had already been up for an hour, on his knees in the nondenominational chapel. As on other mornings, he was finding that its pale brown walls, unadorned by any graven image, lent a sort of abstract severity to the devotions he was trying to perform.

If the First World War had seemed to hang over Fort Dix, thrown together in 1917, it was the Second that shadowed Fort Polk, onetime center of the Louisiana Maneuvers, whose millions of broiled and dehydrated participants had, more than a decade ago, included Tim's uncle Alan. Recently reopened to quarter the First Armored Division, Polk was still operating at only a fraction of its 1940s self.

The built-in shade that Mary Johnson had described as a constant of New Orleans architecture didn't seem to figure at this installation seven miles from the town of Leesville. He'd arrived after a confusing final week in Jersey. First he'd gotten orders for the U.S. Army Information School at Fort Slocum, but then an assignment officer overruled them on the grounds that he was already better than most USAIS graduates at the things they got taught. And so he'd been put in this on-the-job training slot instead: working on *The Kisatchian*, the camp newspaper here at Polk, where he'd shown up carrying the same suitcase he'd taken from D.C. to Fort Dix back in January. He'd also brought along a Davy Crockett cap rifle, a friendly present from several other shitbirds in basic, where he'd been widely conceded to be the single worst marksman in the company. So much, he thought, for above-average "coordination."

When he finished his prayers this morning, he'd be reporting to Major Brillam, *The Kisatchian*'s editor. Tim liked him and the work, which could involve almost anything: rewriting recipes submitted for publication by officers' wives; printing the official instructions for dealing with radiation skin burns; editing a local enlistee's original story on the remarkable intelligence of somebody's pet ostrich in Metairie.

This week he'd been laying out stories on the UN's tenth-anniversary celebrations in San Francisco. Ike had talked of "my country's unswerving loyalty" to the organization, and old pictures from its founding—some with Alger Hiss seated behind Secretary of State Stettinius, just as he'd sat behind FDR at Yalta—had been reappearing over the wire services. *I will not turn my back on Alger Hiss.* Forget what Acheson had said; was there anyone, Tim wondered, who had *watched* his back around Hiss?

Days at *The Kisatchian* were longer than they'd been at the *Star*, and Tim tended to find most of his off-duty entertainment in the paper's office. He almost always wound up back there after dinner in the mess or a late trip to the PX. There were so few books on the base that he'd yesterday bought an issue of *Good Housekeeping*, since it promised a whole novella by John P. Marquand. The barracks radio was always tuned to the fights or hillbilly music, and he realized that by the time his enlistment was over, most of the serials to which he'd remained so faithful would be gone from the dial. He'd once driven into Leesville with some guys in his squad to see *This Is Cinerama!* and on the base they'd all been made to watch *Face to Face with Communism*, an armed-forces feature about an air force sergeant spending a nightmare furlough in a U.S. town that appeared to have been taken over by American Communists. Happy ending: the sergeant learns it was just a role-playing exercise by the vigilant locals.

Major Brillam always called him "son," as Potter had, and the officer had been impressed to discover in his file that Tim had worked for a United States senator. He threw as much responsibility his way as possible. The other week he'd told him that "We're trying to avoid creating more Ronald Alleys," Alley being a thirty-four-year-old officer who'd betrayed his fellow POWs in Korea; since one of Brillam's buddies worked in Indoctrination, the two officers had decided that Tim should talk to a class on the base about his experience with Potter's atrocity hearings.

The recruits snickered when Tim wrote on the blackboard and his chalk line wandered uphill, but they all took notes and one or two wound up regarding him as a person of worldly experience. However fraudulent that had made him feel, the episode did encourage him to believe that he was doing something purposeful. The same went for his work on the paper. The other day he'd written a story on an operation by the "Winds of Freedom" campaign, which had launched a fusillade of hydrogen-filled balloons from a field in Bavaria. Designed to explode at thirty thousand feet over Czechoslovakia, the balloons had showered down pamphlets listing Free World radio frequencies for the captive citizens below. The Czech UN delegate had expressed annoyance at the provocation, prompting Tim to write that "the winds are blowing, literally and otherwise, from West to East." Major Brillam later told him that the "otherwise" was okay, but the average cracker wasn't going to know what the Sam Hill "literally" meant.

What was the motto his doctor pal at Fort Dix had taught him? First do no harm? Well, when he couldn't be doing something useful, that's what he now vowed to do in the world: no harm to others or himself. He would keep his head down, the way he had on the obstacle course while crawling on his stomach with live ammunition flying overhead, or even the way he'd kept it down during the roller-coaster scenes in *This Is Cinerama!*

Lingering in the chapel, he checked his watch and closed his eyes to say the last of his prayers, but all that came to mind, yet again, was his failed attempt at confession, at St. Francis Xavier in Manhattan, on the Saturday afternoon before he'd left Fort Dix.

Bless me, Father, for I have sinned. It has been eighteen months since my last confession.

He'd been able to hear Father Davett, identified by the nameplate on the confessional, shifting on his bench behind the sliding panel. The "eighteen months" had made the priest anticipate something exceptional, so he was moving closer for a better listen.

I missed my Easter duty, Tim had continued, hopelessly, aware of how much further he had to go.

Father Davett: *Yes?*

I was in love with a man. The memory of Tommy McIntyre's voice—
"You *are* in love"—had seemed to find him in yet some further abyss, a
pit of lying.

How old are you?

Twenty-three.

Did you have impure thoughts about this man?

No.

He'd said it with conviction, believing that to say yes would be bearing
false witness against the ecstatic, starlit thoughts he'd always had of
Hawk.

Somehow he'd tried to keep going, to see if he could reach a merciful
middle ground.

Father Davett (confused): *Did you have carnal awareness of this man?*

Yes.

Have you ceased to?

Yes.

Are you sincerely sorry?

No.

Father Davett (exasperated): *Then why are you here?*

I intend to stop. I have stopped.

That is not enough. You must be sincerely sorry.

I can't be sincerely sorry.

How could he explain? Without Hawk's love in return, his own love
had become unbearable. He had stopped because what they did together
could not be sprung from the world of shame and suppressed terror and
blackmail, from Tommy McIntyre's extortive market of secrets. He'd once
believed that he and Hawkins had lifted themselves above the wicked
Earth by doing what they did in bed, but that sense had been replaced by
a realization that joining their bodies only chained them to the electrified
cage of who had what on whom.

His love had been real—*literally* divine, if that meant inspired from
above. He would now renounce—as he'd refused to, the first morning
after, at St. Peter's—but he still would not regret. Maintaining this last
distinction might be the only courage he ever showed in the world.

You must, Father Davett had finally said, *be sincerely sorry. That is
demanded for every mortal sin.*

As if on a diving board, he had remained unable to leap. *I can't.* He'd realized that the priest thought all of this a quibble, that he would have preferred him to lie, to make a good confession by making a bad one.

Renunciation shows consciousness of guilt. Therefore you are sorry.

No. I can't give that to God.

Why not?

It's too much.

Nothing is too much to give God.

I've already returned to Him the best gift He ever gave me.

What is that?

The man I loved.

After that, Father Davett had slid shut the screen, driving him like a moneychanger from the temple.

Even so, even now at Fort Polk, he craved the forgiveness and release that the deep-voiced, by-the-book priest might have provided. And he knew that he would try again.

———

THE NATION

Washington, D.C., bureau

June 22, 1955

Dear Laughlin,

You're fondly remembered in Potter's office. About an hour ago McIntyre gave me an airmail stamp and suggested I write you. "A foine idea," as he might say.

You've just missed a great show here. McCARTHY: THE COMEBACK. The audience found it so unintentionally hilarious it closed two nights after opening. The plot is easily summarized:

A rare dry weekend had left the leading man well enough to come to the Hill on Monday morning, day before yesterday, carrying with him the text for a resolution. It insisted that President Dulles bring up the "satellite" nations when he talks to the Russians in Geneva next month.

But the Democrats had a handy high horse to ride in opposition: "Sir, do you not sufficiently *trust* the President, a man from your own party, to let him negotiate with a free hand?" Before long even Knowland and Co. had to hop on. The whole bunch of them voted the thing down, 77–4, a couple of minutes ago.

Nonetheless, for two days our Savonarola of the Dairylands must have felt alive again. He chewed up the Foreign Relations Committee calendar and had a dozen reporters following him around, as if it were the grand old days of '53 and he'd just hounded another Jewish bookworm to the poorhouse. Every flashbulb that popped threw a smile onto his face, like he'd thrown one more jigger of bourbon down his gullet.

Bob Stevens, Secretary Milquetoast, has resigned to go back to supervising the family fortune. (Do they allow you to include actual armed-forces news like this in that paper you're putting out?) More significantly, Ridgway has retired, because he realizes the army he gave his life to is now obsolete. The Air Force will conduct the next war, while his old branch of the service will be left to herd radioactive civilians through the bombed city streets. (Thanks, by the way, for that touching bit of meteorology you sent, the balloon story. But put your own finger into the wind and you'll begin to feel which way it's really blowing. Did you somehow miss seeing the real papers the day the Warsaw Pact was formed last month?)

McIntyre insists you're fleeing some great sorrow, but won't say which. Forgive me, Laughlin, but you don't look to me as if you're built for a life of passion.

See you when you're back here on a pass sometime. My new painter girlfriend will cook you a meal. She extends abstract expressionism right onto the dinner plate.

Regards,
Kenneth Woodforde, 4-F

P.S. About Potter's little burp of courage last year: can you tell me if there's more to the story than's been told? Strictly off the record, of course.

———

"You've heard of *Darkness at Noon*, Miss Johnson?"

"Yes, Fuller."

"Well, the summer solstice has given us brightness at dusk. Or at least what should be dusk. Too nice not to be out in. I'm leaving a little earlier than usual."

"Leaving earlier than early, you mean."

"Leaving now, to be precise."

McCarthy's Geneva resolution had sent the Bureau of Congressional

Relations into action on Monday morning, but victory had proved so easy that by Wednesday there wasn't much left to do. Now, on Friday, things were even slower, and once Fuller left, Mary decided she would answer Tim's latest letter before going home herself. In her reply she would take care—as Tim always did—never to mention Fuller. Unnatural as this seemed, she knew it was for the best. A more difficult task would be responding to the kind of political-religious tract that Tim's most recent letter, like the one or two before it, had started to resemble.

She at least had quiet enough in which to concentrate, Beverly having left early, too. Quite stagestruck now, Bev had a part in the Bethesda Players' production of *The Little Foxes*; Jerry was helping to make her hoop skirt with some wire he'd brought home from the hardware store he still worked at.

> Department of State
> Washington, D. C.
> June 24, 1955

Dear Tim,

Well, it's a silent Friday afternoon here, befitting a world on which peace has apparently descended. Why didn't anyone think of it before? I refer to this Molotov resolution out in San Francisco—a stroke of genius, I should say, simply to <u>proclaim</u> the arrival of "peace, cooperation and friendship."

I can imagine what you

Someone had entered the office. With no one at any other desk—Miss Lightfoot's replacement had left early, too—Mary got up to greet whoever it was.

The visitor, heavyset but attractive, perhaps a bit over forty, motioned for her to sit back down at her typewriter while he strode toward her.

"Miss Johnson, you don't remember me. The name's Fred Bell."

"I'm afraid I don't."

"The last time I saw you, a couple of years ago, I was bringing you a cracker with some fish on it. At the Estonian embassy. Actually the Lithuanian. We were borrowing the place."

"Oh," said Mary, bits of that sad little evening coming back to her. She recalled her skirt feeling too long, and Fuller taking off into the night.

"I own some shoe factories up in Massachusetts. I'm on the deportees' committee."

"Yes," said Mary. "I'm remembering something about a violinist."

"Pretty close," said Mr. Bell. "Oboe. My cousin. The one who gets to play music in Tallinn. The other cousin, the peasant, is still deported, still on a Soviet collective. You and me also talked about eggs. And then your handsome boss whisked you away."

"What are you doing here?"

"Losing. Like always." He laughed. "A bunch of us rushed down on Monday when we got word of the resolution being introduced. We were dumb enough to think we could help it pass. Real controversial, wasn't it? 'Please, maybe, could you just possibly, if it isn't too rude, bring up the satellites? Oh, too provocative? Too dangerous? Sorry! We apologize!' "

Mary nodded, deciding not to mention that she'd spent two days marshaling votes against the proposal, even though she'd known in her heart that its only objectionable aspect was its toxic sponsor.

"A couple of us have stayed in town making the rounds. Without much point, as usual. But I've seen everybody I could on the Hill and figured I'd come over here. I still have your handsome boss's card." He showed it to her. "I've learned that barging in has more chance of success than calling ahead."

"I'm afraid that both the handsome boss and *his* boss aren't in."

Mr. Bell shrugged. "More of my luck. Maybe I *should* have called ahead." He put Fuller's card back in his wallet. "You're pretty handsome yourself. You can use that word with women, can't you?"

He'd almost, Mary thought, said "dames."

"I'm not sure I'm old enough for 'handsome,' " she replied.

"Have dinner with me."

"You're married. A guess."

"I'm married. A *good* guess."

As if another voice were talking for her, she asked: "Where would you like to go?"

CHAPTER THIRTY

July 23–24, 1955

Tim had sweated through his first shirt on the five-hour bus ride from Fort Polk, but here in Mr. Johnson's remarkably cool library a second one was holding up fine. He had put in for his weekend pass nearly a month ago, and Mary had promised they would have some time alone after dining with her father. Tim and Mr. Johnson had been conversing for the past ten minutes, while they waited for her to finish getting ready. About a quarter of the books in the room appeared to be bound in leather, and about half of those were in French. Mr. Johnson had explained that on his mother's side he was a Claurin.

"Things are looking up," the older man now declared. "Never before have East and West wasted so little time reaching a deadlock."

Ike was coming home from the Geneva conference tomorrow, having proposed joint aerial reconnaissance and the sharing of military blueprints between America and Russia. It remained doubtful that the Soviets would say yes.

Tim laughed politely before replying. "Nixon thinks the summit 'cleared the air,' " he said, venturing toward a difference of opinion with his host. "But I think it made things worse."

"I can't claim the East-West bon mot as my own," Mr. Johnson responded. "It came out of some man's column in the *Times-Picayune*."

Mary had warned her father about the recent overheated expressions of faith and politics in Tim's letters, and Mr. Johnson was trying to keep the conversation light. His daughter decided that she would do the same. Entering the library, Mary declared, "I'm always happy to hear Nixon criticized. Even if it's from all the way over on *that* side."

More perfumed than Tim remembered, she leaned over and gave him a sisterly kiss.

"Very Audrey Hepburn, no?" she asked, touching her new shorter haircut. "That's the intention, anyway."

"I think I miss the style you had," Mr. Johnson said, wistfully. "Your mother's hair fell to her waist every night as she came into our bed."

The phrasing jarred them all with its intimacy, and Mary wound up returning the conversation to affairs of state, explaining that the president's cable from Geneva, describing the progress of the conference, had arrived at the State Department early Thursday afternoon, just before her departure for New Orleans on the ovenlike *Crescent*. "So I was very up-to-date. On that and other things besides. We even knew about poor Cordell Hull." The death of FDR's secretary of state had occurred only this afternoon, but on Thursday morning awareness of its imminence had sent some longtime employees scrambling for black crêpe to hang, once Mr. Hull was gone, from the department's Twenty-first Street windows.

Strong spicy smells were coming from the kitchen. Josephine, a Negro woman who took care of Mary's father during the week, had come to cook their meal. "It's a treat to have you here," Mr. Johnson insisted to Tim, "and it will be a treat to have Josephine's dinner. Most weekends I subsist on something frozen that she's left, or a plate of red beans and rice that I can manage to make myself." He looked skeptically at Tim's thin frame. "Are they feeding *you* well enough?"

"Oh, just fine, sir."

"Well," said Mary, "they're already getting Capitol Hill ready for your return. They've finished the foundations on that new Senate Office Building, the one going up where that little slum on First Street used to be? They'll have the whole thing done in a couple of years."

She realized, suddenly, that she needed to concoct a fib. "I got all of that from Beverly. I think I wrote you about how much time she was spending on the Hill this spring."

Tim, certain that she'd gotten this architectural update from Hawkins, who visited the Capitol twice a week, just nodded.

Mary now surmised what he was thinking, which was not at all what had made her worry. She had lied to protect a secret of her own, not Tim's feelings. She'd seen the construction herself, during the two weekends Fred Bell had come down to Washington to see her, weekends the two of them had spent in a little room at the top of the Carroll Arms. Each Sunday afternoon, when Fred would phone his wife in Massachusetts to report on all the preparation he was doing for the next day's lobbying, she would take a stroll around the Hill that took her past the construction site.

"I may not come back to Washington at all," said Tim, "but if I do I'll be your neighbor a couple of times a month. The Army Reserves in D.C. are so hard up they drill in a State Department lecture room! Right at Twenty-first and C."

His face flushed with nostalgia for the handful of visits he'd made to Hawkins' office. Mary saw his color rise and wondered how on earth she'd be able to tell him what she had to.

Mr. Johnson excused himself to check on Josephine.

"You're sure you won't stay here tonight instead?" Mary asked Tim. He'd checked into a guesthouse in the Quarter. "Dauphine Street is quieter than most, but still, it *is* a Saturday night, and—"

"You're forgetting I grew up a few blocks from Times Square," he said, laughing. "Trust me, this is nothing! And if you're worried about the money, remember: I'm making seventy-eight whole dollars a month on top of three meals a day and all the milk I can drink."

"I need to talk to you about something after dinner."

"Are you getting back together with Paul?"

"No, no. But it does concern an engagement."

"Beverly Phillips and Jerry Baumeister!"

Mr. Johnson was coming back into the library.

"No, not them," she whispered. "It's somebody else."

"Josephine's boy," Mr. Johnson announced with a certain wonder, "wants her to take him to Disneyland." The amusement park's opening had been all over television last week.

Mary looked at Tim from the corner of her eye. No, he hadn't guessed the news she had to tell him.

"Fantasyland?" he asked her father, trying to ascertain which precinct of Disneyland interested Josephine's boy particularly. "Frontierland?"

Mary excused herself to get a pack of cigarettes from her bedroom, and once there, standing still with her left hand on the dresser, she remembered the conversation that Fuller had drawn her into on Monday afternoon, just before close of business.

Getting married? she'd asked, incredulously.

Having children, too, no doubt, he'd answered.

Why, Fuller?

Why not?

Because you're—

Because I am, even so, good value for her money.

No, you're not.

He'd said nothing, just smiled.

Why now?

A hitch in time saves nine. He'd begun moving toward the door by that point.

Should I say anything to him? she'd asked. *I'll be seeing him this weekend, you know, when I'm back home.*

I know. I keep reading the letters you deliberately leave open on your desk.

What should I tell him, Fuller?

That it makes no difference. He'd already taken his hat from the clothes tree.

Of course it makes a difference, she'd protested.

Does Mrs. Bell make a difference, Miss Johnson?

You're a son of a bitch.

Yes, I am. He'd then put on the hat.

No, you're not.

No, I'm not, he'd said, without any archness, before asking, quietly, for a simple favor: *Make it easy on him.*

She now lit one of the cigarettes and returned to the library, where there seemed to be a lull in the conversation between her father and their guest.

"Tim has just finished explaining to me the difference between Frontierland and Fantasyland," Mr. Johnson told his daughter. "But we've concluded that Josephine's son wants to go to another land entirely."

"Which is that?" asked Mary.

"Tomorrowland," said her father.

Tim's brown eyes were wet and huge. She could see that, in the time she'd been out of the room, he had guessed the identity of the groom.

"Hello, darlin'! Why so sad?"

He thought the voice might be a prostitute's, like the one he'd heard on Bourbon Street a half hour ago, but here on Dauphine, a little before midnight, the words were coming not from a doorway but a low second-floor balcony, and the voice belonged to a man. There were two men, actually, near the railing. One of them had curly gray hair; the other, the one who had spoken, was somewhat younger, maybe in his thirties, but already balding.

"I'm okay," Tim called up to him.

"Heavens, *really*? We'd hate to see you when you were under the weather. You come on up here." He pointed to an entrance that led first to a back garden and then the apartment upstairs.

Still struggling, as he'd been for the last two hours, with the single faint image he had retained of the woman he now thought of as *her*, the way she'd appeared last year on the Hotel Washington's rooftop, Tim went into the garden. Passing flowers thick and fragrant, their stems stronger-looking than the white wrought iron of the bannister and balcony, he fought off another picture, recently assembled by his imagination, in which Mr. and Mrs. Hawkins Fuller and their children sat surrounded by bicycles and wrapping paper on a Christmas morning.

The younger man already had a drink for him. "I'm Wel, short for Jeffrey Wellison. And you are?"

"Timothy Laughlin."

The older man, introduced by Wel as Mr. Shaw, extended his hand while clicking a Tums between his teeth. Tim could see a roll of the tablets lying on the tray with the pitcher of drinks. Very tall and possessed of fine posture, Mr. Shaw was probably no more than forty-five. His hair—Tim could see this close up—was more than curly; it was like coiled wire. His features had a Negro aspect, and Tim wondered if he might be an octoroon or even a mulatto, terms he knew from the movies. Whatever he was, the man's whole manner marked him as an aristocrat.

"And tell us," he asked, "what brings you to New Orleans, Mr. Laughlin?"

"I'm in the army."

"You're not really!" shrieked Wel. "We would have welcomed you with *trumpets* if we'd known! As it is, you should sit down."

"Are you on a pass?" Mr. Shaw asked.

"Yes, I'm a private, a communications specialist at Fort Polk. I go back tomorrow."

"Now, Clay, you heard him. He's *on* a pass, so making one in his direction would be *redundant*."

Mr. Shaw laughed apologetically at his companion's remark, and peeled another Tums from the roll. Tim found himself surprised that anyone living in this city, awash in spices, might actually suffer from heartburn.

Wel poured a little sachet of powder into his own drink. "Atoms for peace!" he exclaimed, lifting the glass in what appeared to be a toast to himself.

"Forgive Mr. Wellison's flamboyance," said Mr. Shaw. "The granules are just a sweetener."

"Sure they are," said Wel, before stage-whispering the word "Benzedrine" in Tim's direction.

Mr. Shaw returned a bit helplessly to the notion of atoms for peace, making it the occasion for a general toast: "To the spirit of Geneva. And to Private Laughlin's arrival in our city."

Tim took a sip of what he guessed was a martini. He followed it with a shrimp whose strong sauce Mr. Shaw seemed to be avoiding.

"There *is* no spirit of Geneva," said Wel. "In fact the man on the radio was saying that China's going to attack Formosa before all the bigwigs have cleared out of Switzerland. While everybody's distracted, the Russians won't be able to restrain the Chinks. Not Chinks. He called them something else. Chiclets?"

"Chicoms, I suspect," said Mr. Shaw.

"Is he right, honey?"

"Yes," said Tim.

"Well," said Mr. Shaw, with the slight nervousness that seemed habitual to him in Mr. Wellison's presence, "if any world war does break out, we have Private Laughlin here to defend us."

"And plenty of vodka to offer the invaders!" cried Wel, suddenly agreeable.

"I thought it was the Chinese who were coming," said Mr. Shaw, gently.

With a volume that startled the two older men, Tim all at once declared: "Bulganin wants the Chinese to act as 'observers' in Europe! Peacekeepers!"

Mr. Shaw recovered from his surprise and shook his head, agreeing to the irony and injustice of the prospect. Wel, losing interest in the international situation, busied himself by emptying one half-full bowl of peanuts into another.

Embarrassed by his own volubility, Tim changed the subject, asking Mr. Shaw: "What line are you in, sir?"

"So sweet!" exclaimed Wel. "He makes you sound like a shoe salesman, Clay. And *he* sounds a little like Dorothy Kilgallen."

Mr. Shaw made a forbearing expression: "I'm in international trade," he explained to Tim. "Imports and exports. Mostly putting other importers and exporters together with one another."

"Clay's a *matchmaker*," said Wel, who was combing his hair in front of a heavily framed mirror. "When he travels the world, I feed the cat here and have his mail forwarded."

"How long have you been friends?" Tim asked.

"About ten years," Mr. Shaw explained. "Since just after the war."

"We're in the '*just* friends' stage now," Wel added. "Sisters. It comes to that with the seven-year itch. Well, seven months in our case." He laughed at Tim's evident perplexity. "I don't think he's seen the movie, Clay. He was probably at *The Seven Little Foys* instead. Anywho," Wel announced, picking up his cigarette lighter from the tray, "I'm going to leave you two and mosey back home to Chartres Street."

"You don't live here?" Tim asked. The apartment wasn't just fancy; it appeared to be enormous.

Wel shook his head. "More convenient all around." He gave Tim a peck on the cheek—"Say hello to all our fighting men!"—and made a fast exit.

"May I freshen your drink, Timothy?"

"Thank you, Mr. Shaw."

Without Wel, the room itself, however ornate, seemed to acquire a more masculine aspect. Mr. Shaw now appeared almost huge, more hand-some and less guarded. Tim had the sense that Wel's departure had occurred because he'd completed his work by bringing a guest here. Looking toward what seemed to be the largest bedroom, beyond a set of French doors, Tim noticed a silver crucifix attached to one of the walls. In a corner stood a black bullwhip, like something the Lone Ranger might have captured.

Mr. Shaw, topping off their drinks, saw him looking and laughed. "Don't be alarmed, Private Laughlin. That's left over from Mardi Gras."

The martini glass, with its high center of gravity, threatened to spill. Mr. Shaw took it from his hand and set it on the table, then placed an arm over his shoulders. The exotic-looking man sighed with what seemed a craving for something deeper than sex, some wildly imbalanced align-ment. Tim recognized it through an awareness of the same desire—its other, symmetrical half—within himself.

"I think you should stay here tonight," said Mr. Shaw. "You'll be per-fectly safe." He pointed to the whip. "We can put that between us, like Tristan's sword."

There was a brief silence, perhaps encouraging. And yet the gentle-manly Mr. Shaw soon sensed, whatever might be in the air, that his guest was too sad and nervous to go much further. So he made them both some coffee, told some army stories of his own (a Bronze Star rested not far from the crucifix), and listened to an anguished outpouring about Hawkins Fuller. After an hour or so passed, he was walking Tim to his rooming house across Dauphine Street, and telling him: "You'll hear again and again that he's 'not worth it.' And that will be true. It will also be the stupidest thing anyone ever says to you."

According to the Sunday-morning paper, two hundred and fifty thou-sand children were receiving Communion in Rio de Janeiro this week-end; Cardinal Spellman, in Brazil on a visit, had said a midnight Mass prior to the huge outdoor Eucharist.

Sitting in the back of the cathedral in Jackson Square, Tim envied the privileged innocence of these quarter million boys and girls he'd just read about, but mostly he wondered what Saturday-night stories might be told by the tired morning-after souls in his midst, right here in New

Orleans. He checked the bus ticket stuck in his missal—and then noticed a small green light go on, indicating the presence of a Father LeTour in the confessional just ten or twelve feet from the pew.

It didn't seem possible: all his life he had known only Saturday confessions. But perhaps this city's superabundance of temptation necessitated a few freewheeling shortcuts toward forgiveness. He noticed that three or four people had already lined up at the booth with their still-brand-new sins—lucky, shadowed souls who within a half hour would be kneeling at the altar rail, as newly innocent as any Brazilian boy or girl.

On impulse, he acted: put his bus ticket back into the missal, marked his seat in the pew with the book, and got up to join the line, which was moving quickly. Father LeTour appeared to be passing out absolution with the speed of a chaplain on the battlefield.

He would try not to think. He would try just to do it, to get back to and then somehow past the point at which he had been refused by Father Davett. He could not live forever without God's full presence; he could not—having last night understood that Hawkins was gone forever—accept the permanent loss of God's grace, too.

His mind raced with logic and analogy: McCarthy had called Geneva a "dismal failure," since there hadn't been any talk of the satellite countries, whose enslavement was the moral crux of the whole Cold War. That was the truth—and shouldn't the truth be accepted even from a sinner? Furthermore, shouldn't a sinner be accepted if he *told* the truth? Which was to say, couldn't he himself be accepted back into the Church with just renunciation of what he had done, unaccompanied by any admission of regret?

He had wanted to stay with Mr. Shaw last night. He had not been very drunk, just sad and shocked over Hawkins' engagement. Mr. Shaw's exotic allure, his potent combination of the hulking and effeminate, had attracted him. There had been, as they'd sipped coffee, one repelling moment—a gentle, last-ditch suggestion that he put on what appeared to be a child's set of pajamas—but more than anything else Mr. Shaw had seemed manly and cherishing, qualities that he himself, now denied both Hawk and God, desired intensely.

What had stopped him from getting into bed—he knew the whip would never stay in its legendary place—had been the thought of Hawk, who, he'd decided months ago, near the end, should be the only man he would ever know in this way.

So, he now reasoned, while the person just ahead of him in line entered the confessional: if Hawk had once been sin, he was now the giver of chastity. Why couldn't those two things cancel each other out and let Timothy Laughlin go back to being what he'd once been? Why couldn't he, safely reunited with God, retire the active memory of his earthly love, frame it like the picture of some dead loved soldier on a mantelpiece?

"Bless me, Father, for I have sinned; it has been twenty-one months since my last confession."

No shifting, no sense of surprise from Father LeTour. The priest replied in what Tim now recognized as a Cajun accent: "Yes, young man?" The "young" sounding like "yoang."

Tim had so often replayed his abortive confession to Father Davett that he could now recite his own part from memory. But Father LeTour seemed to be working from a different script, or none at all. To each admission that emerged from Tim's lips, the priest replied, merely, *Mmm-hmm.*

"I intend to stop. I *have* stopped."

"Mmm-hmm."

"But I can't say 'I'm sorry.' I can't give that to God. It's too much. I've already returned to Him the best gift He ever gave me."

Father LeTour at last came to soft-spoken life. "And what was that?"

"The man I loved."

"Did you give him back to God in the spirit of a gift?"

Tim had to admit that that hadn't been the case; his return of Hawkins to God had been grudging and desperate.

"No, Father."

"*Can* you give him back to God in that spirit?"

"Yes!" said Tim, well above the confessional's normal whisper. "I can."

"Then say three Hail Marys and do that. God loves you."

A little before eleven a.m., with his two hands clutching the missal and part of his mind unable to stop wondering why Father LeTour, unlike Bishop Sheen, did not use the subjunctive—*God love you*—Tim walked down the cathedral's center aisle and received the Body of Christ Our Lord.

CHAPTER THIRTY-ONE

September 25–28, 1955

"So, is it true?" asked Fred Bell. "Do they really stand him on a box before the cameras roll?"

He and Mary had just seen the decidedly short Alan Ladd in *The McConnell Story.*

"That's what they say," she answered. She hadn't paid much attention to the picture—neither the based-on-real-life heroics of the title figure, nor the scratchy little voice of June Allyson as the air ace's perfect wife. Truth to tell, she would have been content not to go to the movies at all, and to spend the evening as they'd spent the whole afternoon, upstairs in the Carroll Arms, in bed with just room service and each other—though minus the bottle of Hildebrand-family beer that had been standing up, accusingly, in the ice bucket.

It was now half past twelve on Saturday night. The Sunday papers had long since reached the streets, but here in a candy store a block from the Ambassador Theater, Fred was displaying more interest in the radio than in the already-obsolete *Star,* for which he'd just put down his fifteen cents. A Washington news announcer was reporting on a press conference still going on out in Denver, not far from where the president had gone for a fishing vacation.

So much for the "digestive upset" that had been reported this morning! The doctors were now admitting that Ike had had a heart attack and was in an oxygen tent, and that Vice President and Mrs. Nixon had "gone into seclusion, leaving their young daughters at home on Tilden Street in the care of a trusted secretary."

"Fred," said Mary. "There's a radio back in the hotel." Which she hoped he wouldn't listen to once they got there. Fred might be only the third lover she'd had, but of that small sample he was far and away the best, full of ardor and eye contact; she was eager to get back to doing just what June Allyson and Paul, staring at her through the Hildebrand label, would no doubt disapprove of.

At last she felt Fred's hand on the small of her back, urging her out of the store and onto Eighteenth Street.

"Taxi!" he called.

But once the Diamond cab arrived at the curb, she heard him ask not for the Carroll Arms but for Tilden Street.

"Where on Tilden?" the driver asked.

"Just drive down the three-thousand blocks. Past the embassies."

"What are we doing?" asked Mary.

Fred continued instructing the driver. "I don't know the exact number, but there'll be a little crowd on the lawn, newsmen and so forth."

"We're going to the Nixons'," said Mary, having just remembered Tilden Street from the radio.

"Yeah," said Fred. "To stand outside the house."

"Why?"

"Because if this is the moment, I want to be there."

"The moment when Ike dies?"

"The moment when we get a president who'll actually fight, who'll roll them back." He proceeded to review for her the vice president's steely anticommunist credentials. Sure, Nixon sometimes had to say things against McCarthy or in favor of Geneva, but everybody knew that the man who'd brought down Hiss and Helen Douglas would stand up to the Russians—if he were blessed with his own presidency.

"Blessed?" asked Mary, looking at Fred's excited profile while a string of Connecticut Avenue streetlamps flashed their glow onto and off his skin. He appeared even more aroused than he'd been behind the heavy curtains of their room in the Carroll Arms.

The car radio was explaining just how Nixon had learned the seriousness of Ike's condition, when the taxi caught up with the twenty or so reporters and gawkers on the vice president's front lawn. At an upstairs window, behind sheer curtains, the silhouettes of two small girls, delighted by the commotion, were jumping up and down on a bed.

Fred told the cab to wait, and once on the sidewalk with Mary he put some questions to a man with a microphone and a walkie-talkie. No, he learned, there really wasn't any news. The press conference in Denver had just ended, and a heart specialist had flown out to Colorado, but that was about it.

Mary took Fred's arm and drew him back to the curb. "I want to ask you something. Are you hoping that the president of the United States will die?"

Fred paused for a moment's thought before replying. "I'm hoping the president will fight."

"The *current* president," Mary insisted. "You want to see the hero of D-Day die for Estonia?"

He looked straight at her. "I landed on Utah Beach eleven years, three months, and nineteen days ago. I do the arithmetic every morning when I brush my teeth."

There wasn't much to say to that; she looked longingly at the cab.

"Maybe you should take it," said Fred. "I'm too keyed up. I've got to stay awhile more."

"All right."

"You're not mad?"

"No. Confused maybe."

He was already looking for a way to make it up to her. "How about I pick you up for church?"

"No, thanks," she said, laughing from sheer surprise. "I'm not going by myself, and I'm not going with you, either."

"Come on," he cajoled, smiling in the mischievous way he ought to be smiling back at the Carroll Arms, coaxing her over some new threshold of adventurousness. "There's a Polish church on Thirty-sixth Street," he explained. "Father Kaminsky does the eleven-o'clock Mass, and he's a spellbinder. I guarantee you he'll have something to say tomorrow morning."

She looked at him disbelievingly, but he persisted, as if she were only displaying a customer's last bit of resistance toward the product being offered: "I went to hear him once with a guy from the Polish group that sometimes makes the rounds with us down here."

"Fred, I am not going to Mass to pray for the ill health of Dwight D. Eisenhower."

"Well, I wouldn't do that, either."

"Let's say you wouldn't do that *exactly*." She looked back toward the cab, whose meter was still running. "Call me sometime before you go back home." She accepted a kiss, against her better judgment, and got into the taxi, still carrying the copy of the *Star* from the candy store.

Inside her place on P Street, she made herself a drink and climbed into bed with the paper, passing up its stale front page in favor of the book reviews and wedding announcements—"the ladies' sports pages," Paul used to joke, though in Washington you would sometimes find the groom's name, not the bride's, in the headline: MR. HERBERT ENGAGED TO WED. No matter how pretty the future Mrs. Herbert might be, her fiancé's father had been governor of Ohio, and that settled that.

There was the phenomenon again, in the upper-right-hand corner: MARRIAGE OF MR. FULLER ANNOUNCED. The news was being spread by his soon-to-be in-laws, Professor and Mrs. Chester Boardman of Wellesley, Massachusetts, parents of Lucy Catherine, the fiancée. "The bridegroom-elect, a deputy assistant secretary in the State Department's bureau of congressional relations, is the son of Mr. and Mrs. Charles Fuller of New York City." The little story had everything right: St. Paul's, the war record, Harvard, Paraguay, Oslo.

Mary put aside the paper and wondered if she'd even tease Fuller about it on Monday. No, she could no longer do that. Too many things had galloped beyond the pale, herself included maybe.

At least the item wouldn't run anywhere near Fort Polk. She had heard from Tim only once since New Orleans, a letter full of talk about the Eucharist and the Russians' persecution of Cardinal Mindszenty. His merry side had been there in one of the margins—an ink sketch of Major Brillam hurling an editorial thunderbolt against whatever laxness had permitted weevils to invade the mess hall—but mostly the letter shook with a febrile zeal that left her both upset and envious. Fred, too, had this electric susceptibility, this touch of true-believing that must be connected to male ardor in bed. *The little Irish tiger cub:* she now remembered Fuller dropping that offhand excuse when he arrived at the office even later than usual one morning.

All of them, from Hawkins Fuller to Beverly Phillips, were dangling from the world tonight, unaligned nations or shaky protectorates, struggling toward independence or falling into unwise alliance. She felt a pang for Paul and his simple marital urge. If she'd let things turn out differently, the two of them might be climbing into bed right now, turning off the television in some nice house in Alexandria.

She herself was caught between two banked fires. Her recent pursuit of passion, for all its illicit pleasures, seemed at the moment as obligatory as another person's quest for security and the norm. If she were truly carried away by love, and Fred, she might by now be turning the handle of some basement printing press, cranking out the latest stack of Free Estonia Now pamphlets, helping her man to turn the tide. As it was, come Monday she and Fuller, if Ike remained alive, would no doubt be spreading the message of continuity, steady as she goes, to the fire-breathers on the Hill, shoring up all the caution Fred wanted to blast away with liberty's blowtorch.

She let the *Star* fall to the floor, and she clicked off the light.

"You know," Senator Goldwater reflected, "I'd ten times rather play cards with Hubert. Dick Nixon is one of the shiftiest sons of bitches I've met since I got here in '52."

Fuller smiled, even tilted his head back to accentuate amusement, though he really didn't need to strive for effect. He liked this handsome half-Jew, half-Episcopalian from Arizona.

"May I tell that to Mr. Morton?" he asked.

"You can tell it to the goddamn *New York Times*, for all I care," said Goldwater. "Though I know you won't."

"No, sir."

Fuller stood up to leave, having gotten what he wanted—an assurance that Goldwater, like the other bellicose senators he had to visit, would throughout the tense coming days confine himself to supporting get-well-Ike resolutions, and not overcompensate for any appearance of governmental distraction by having America rattle its missiles in their hardened silos. So far only McCarthy was believed to be scenting opportunity within the crisis. Several reports since Saturday had him thirsting anew for politics, not just Jim Beam.

"Two more stops to make," said Fuller, shaking Goldwater's hand. But his progress toward Senator Hickenlooper's office was halted in Goldwater's reception area by the sight of Senator Charles Potter and Tommy McIntyre.

Citizen Canes was sturdily upright, his balding head under a cheap, snap-brim Stratoliner that the missus had probably picked up at Herzog's, thinking it would make him look snazzy. Which was not an adjective one would apply to McIntyre, with his rheumy eyes and gin-blossomed cheeks. He appeared to need a couple of canes more than Potter did.

"A pleasure, Senator," said Fuller, extending his hand. "Even if this accidental encounter doesn't save me any labor. There's no need, of course, to come see you in this uncertain time. We know your instincts will be superb."

Tommy coughed. "You're laying it on pretty thick today."

Fuller, tilting back his head in the same move he'd used on Goldwater, felt almost relieved that the broken-looking Irishman hadn't lost his nasty gab.

"I appreciate the compliment," said Potter, catching sight of the man he'd come to visit. He raised one of his canes and winked its little electric light. "Barry!"

Goldwater waved him forward.

"I'm here to pick up my model," Potter explained to Fuller. With the excitement of a boy, he headed toward the inner office, pointing as he went to one of several plastic miniatures of the RC-121, the "flying radar station," that were on display. Goldwater, a colonel in the Air Force Reserves, had piloted the plane over the Pacific last weekend.

Left alone with Tommy, Fuller was delayed in taking his leave by some compliments the ravaged little man had to offer. "Congratulations on your engagement. I saw mention made of it in the *Star*."

"Thank you, McIntyre."

"I'm sure she's a beautiful girl."

"Very."

"I lost *my* girl almost a month ago." Tommy shifted his gaze to the window. He had a look of sheer agony, and the dampness on his eyes had swollen into actual tears.

My girl? Was this, Fuller wondered, remembering Tim's piece of the story, the drunken woman in Michigan, the labor widow supposed to be at the heart of McCarthy's implosion?

"I'm sorry to hear that."

Tommy's face turned angry, and not so much toward the world as toward Hawkins Fuller in particular. "One can't count the number of women who have been betrayed by men, nor the number who will be. What's your girl's name again?"

"Boardman," said Fuller. "Lucy Boardman."

"That's right, that's right," McIntyre responded, as if to suggest he was updating the police files he kept in his head. "By the way, back at the office we don't hear nearly enough from your friend, Private Laughlin."

"What are you hearing from the constituents? Good wishes for the president's health, I imagine?"

"Actually," said Tommy, "most of the wires concern the acquittal of those apes who killed the Till boy down in Mississippi. It's nice to know more than a few people don't believe a colored fellow should necessarily be beaten to death for whistling at a white woman."

The remark vibrated with Tommy's shrill sympathy for the oppressed, but it also carried a threatening whiff, an intimation that Fuller, a sexual trangressor himself, must find stories like the Till boy's particularly unsettling.

Fuller confined himself to some cool, safe sarcasm: " 'No Negroes on the jury because none are registered to vote in the county.' That was the official local explanation. Which I suppose we'll report with a straight face over the Voice of America."

"A nice part of the country for your boy to be in."

"It's time for me to call my office," said Fuller. He tipped his hat to avoid shaking Tommy's hand, and when he got to a pay phone at the end of the corridor he rang the bureau.

Mary picked up.

"I was expecting to hear Beverly," said Fuller.

"She's down the hall collecting some telexes."

"Why isn't the new girl doing that? We do have a receptionist now, don't we?"

"She left early. She's gotten engaged, as a matter of fact. Just at lunchtime. Her mother came by to take her out for a celebration."

"There's a lot of that going around. And the mothers seem to like it."

"Well, my mother's dead, Fuller."

"So's mine, almost."

"Let me get your messages."

Cold as ice, thought Fuller. Things could not be going well with the married shoemaker.

"Congressmen Lovre and Dies returned your calls," said Mary. "And Senator Pastore's office phoned—nothing urgent. Also, the boss has talked to C. D. Jackson, who's come down to the White House from New York. Everything seems to be fine. Mr. Morton says there's no need for you to see Senator Bridges, or even Welker."

"Good," said Fuller. "The natives aren't restless. Ike can breathe easy in his oxygen tent."

"Last but not least," said Mary, "your fiancée phoned to say that she'll be coming by the office at five-thirty. She'd like for the two of you to go out for an early dinner and a movie."

"What's playing?" Fuller asked.

"I highly don't recommend *The McConnell Story*. June Allyson and Alan Ladd."

Have you ever frequented a Washington, D.C., establishment called the Jewel Box, at the corner of Sixteenth and L streets?

The tufted purple walls. The bartender who looks a little like Alan Ladd.

"Miss Johnson, you'll need to ring the future Mrs. Fuller and tell her that Monday is my night out with the boys."

A day after their surprise wedding at Grossinger's, Eddie Fisher and Debbie Reynolds were in D.C. The ceremony had been put off until Monday night, in deference to Yom Kippur. "Eddie is of the Jewish faith," reported the wire-service story in the *New Orleans Item*. It was with a similar sense of responsibility that the bridegroom had postponed the couple's honeymoon, so that he could keep a commitment to perform for the Coca-Cola bottlers holding their convention at Washington's Statler Hotel.

"So, does this go in?" asked Private John Nontone, holding the Eddie-and-Debbie clipping. Though a day old, the story might still find its way onto the "Lighter Side" page of *The Kisatchian*.

"Yep," said Tim, speaking from his experience at the *Evening Star* and almost six months here. "Eddie is a vet. He was even in Korea. I'll rewrite it to highlight that."

"You're the boss," said Nontone, a twenty-year-old from Delaware who'd arrived at the base three weeks ago.

"You want one of these?" asked Tim, offering Nontone a cookie from the package that had just arrived.

"God, they're awful," said Nontone, after a single bite.

"I know."

"I hope your mother or your girl didn't make them."

"A friend's girl," Tim explained, as he went to work on a page layout. "I guess it's the thought that counts."

Gloria Rostwald, Kenneth Woodforde's painter girlfriend, was the baker, and the cookies she'd produced resembled little cinderblocks. They were cookies trying hard to be something less frivolous than cookies; the gray squares wanted you to know that they would no more be caught wearing sprinkles or icing than one of their maker's paintings would sport a representational figure.

The box they'd come in had contained no note from the baker, only one from Woodforde, written on Saturday night and urging Tim to be careful with the enclosed edibles:

Unlike Eisenhower, you might have *real* digestive problems after eating these. That was a nice little smokescreen, don't you think? Here's hoping Nixon, now that he's in charge, doesn't add a year to your enlistment. As it is, the Italians are one election away from a Communist government (yes, people do *choose* such things), so NATO may not prove much in the way of a first line of defense for the good old USA. Which I've started to see more than enough of in my (old) Chevrolet. The magazine has me out in the hinterlands looking for hot progressive prospects for next year's elections. I'll let you know who they are as soon as I find any. —KW

Once he finished answering Francy's latest letter—ducking her exhortation that he come home for Christmas—Tim would have to send Woodforde's girlfriend a thank-you note, maybe with a p.s. telling Woodforde himself that, if leprosy could be pushed back, then communism could, too. The sermon during Sunday's radio Mass for shut-ins, which Tim had listened to before going to church on the post, had been all about advances being made against the disease in Dr. Schweitzer's lab and Father Damien's old colony. What, the radio celebrant had wondered, should Christians do when such a familiar symbol of dispossession and God's mysterious ways became extinct? Rejoice!

"Here's another one," said Nontone, coming back with a second clipping. "In?"

The item concerned the decision of Marie Dionne, one of the quintuplets, now past twenty, to return to the convent she'd left, homesick, the year before.

"Out," said Tim, leery of letting Major Brillam think he was riding his own hobbyhorses onto the pages of *The Kisatchian*. Around the base he was known, cheerfully enough, as a holy roller, even if when applied to him the term meant something different from what it did in the Louisiana hamlets just beyond Fort Polk's perimeter.

Actually, the Dionne story interested Tim quite a bit, because these days—in a way he hadn't allowed himself in years—he was thinking a lot about the seminary, and how he might apply once he'd finished up with the army. Now that he was past Hawk, had made his renunciation and been reconciled to the Church, he was beginning to believe he might be allowed to move beyond the whole issue of his "tendencies"—as he'd so far managed to do here in the army. He didn't know whether he had a real calling for the priesthood, but he cherished the idea that he might still receive one—a sudden, glorious annunciation that could happen anywhere, in the motor pool or even the PX.

Right now, waiting for his mail (with army logic, letters arrived more slowly than parcels), he went back to reading his biography of Cardinal Mindszenty. He had arrived at the prelate's "Statement of November 18, 1948," made just weeks before the Russians arrested him, forced him into a clown's costume, and beat him with truncheons:

> Such a systematic and purposeful net of propaganda lies—a hundred times disproved and yet a hundred times spread anew—has never been organized against the seventy-eight predecessors in my office. I stand for God, for the Church and for Hungary. This responsibility has been imposed upon me by the fate of my nation, which stands alone, an orphan in the whole world. Compared with the sufferings of my people, my own fate is of no importance.

Tim could feel in this pronouncement the peace and strength that certainty give, a serene immunity from persecution or even simple need. He had returned to the book a half-dozen times yesterday, and would get back to it as soon as he opened the two envelopes Nontone was now handing him.

One had been sent by his mother, who these days addressed him with the nervous politeness someone might employ in a first approach to a skittish Korean orphan. Today she was asking what he'd like to have for his birthday, still five weeks away.

The second envelope appeared to have no return address, just a Washington postmark, but there was, Tim now noticed on the back flap, a small handwritten name: *Miss Beatrice Lightfoot.* Inside, neatly cut from the Sunday *Star*, was the item MARRIAGE OF MR. FULLER ANNOUNCED. *The bridegroom-elect, deputy assistant chief . . . to be married on Saturday, December third.*

Tim's mind gave no thought to the sender, or to how she had known where to find him. The anger and despair that swept through him— worse now than that night in New Orleans—arose only from his dispos- session. He was seized by a sudden, dizzying lust for Hawkins, for the long-ago smell and taste of him. He felt hollow, literally, without the man he loved inside him.

This unexpected tumult would have been a furious temptation had its object been anywhere near or obtainable. As things were, the storm of sensation could only torment Tim like a punishment without a crime, a midnight visit from the secret police. But, unlike Mindszenty, he had no peace or strength or certainty. His reconciliation with God, he knew, was just a tar paper shack, ready to be blown to bits while his cries went unheard on the wind.

He closed his eyes and prayed for help.

"From the look on your face I'm guessing you don't like to travel."

Major Brillam was standing over him.

"Sir?"

"You haven't gotten your orders yet?"

"No."

"Your unit's headed to France. I'm going to miss you, son."

CHAPTER THIRTY-TWO

December 16, 1955

"I therefore announce my candidacy for the Democratic presidential nomination," declared Senator Estes Kefauver. "I intend to conduct a vigorous campaign. As in 1952, I will enter a number of state primaries. I am a firm believer . . ."

Here in the second row of a chilly ballroom at the Willard, the *Star's* Cecil Holland leaned over to pick up the trademark coonskin cap that had landed beside him when Senator Kefauver tossed it, for the photographers, into a nonexistent ring.

"If you're so cold," whispered Holland to Mary McGrory, "why don't you make use of this?"

"It's not even twenty degrees outside," she answered softly, while assessing the fur cap's possibilities as a muff. "It *would* be rather pretty without the tail."

"The tail is all Kefauver's going to be," declared Joe Alsop, to Holland's right. "They'll waste him as the VP candidate on another losing run by Stevenson."

"You think so?" whispered a man from the *Baltimore Sun*. "He just said he wouldn't take the second spot."

"He'll take it," said Alsop, perfectly certain. "From what I hear, Stevenson's heart is in worse shape than Ike's. If Adlai gets an electoral miracle, he won't get an actuarial one, too. He'll drop dead during his first year in office. That's the way Estes will be thinking come the convention. He'll take it."

A young woman from the Scripps-Howard papers, appalled by such ghoulishness, shot Alsop a glance. For good measure she paid Kefauver a compliment, telling the reporter on her left: "Pretty shrewd of him to get in on the Davy Crockett craze." She pointed to the coonskin on Miss McGrory's lap.

Alsop groaned. "Oh, God," he complained to Holland. "Poor little nitwit."

Holland laughed, knowing as well as Alsop that the cap derived not from Davy Crockett but one of Kefauver's early campaigns, during which an opposing political boss mocked him as a "pet coon."

At the lectern, the senator was now citing assurances he'd gotten from Harry Truman himself that the former president wouldn't block his nomination in favor of Stevenson's, as he'd done in '52.

Kenneth Woodforde turned around to the third row and whispered to Tommy McIntyre, one of the dozen or so Hill staffers mixed in with the press this morning: "Stevenson doesn't need Truman now that he's got God." The Illinois governor's recent move from the Unitarian to the Presbyterian Church did look calculated enough to make even the girl from Scripps-Howard roll her eyes once it was mentioned.

"He's come to understand," Woodforde explained to Tommy, "that the deity really *is* the insurance salesman down the street, not that cosmic To Whom It May Concern."

Miss McGrory, in a voice even softer than Woodforde's whisper, defended Stevenson. "He's *still* a Unitarian. There's no UU church near his farm in Libertyville, so he's making *do* with the Presbyterians."

"Careful, Mary," said Cecil Holland. "I'll have to take back Kefauver's coonskin if you're still so madly for Adlai."

"Kefauver himself is a little like God," announced Alsop, in his most mandarin way, not bothering to whisper at all. "He spends more time *hearing* the afflicted than in giving them relief." He referred to all the committee investigations the Tennesseean had held since coming to the Senate in '49—hearings on organized crime, steel prices, juvenile delinquency, boxing. Most of them had produced more television coverage than legislation.

Right now Kefauver was answering a question about which primaries he'd be entering; it was followed by another about what the polls were showing. He could not, of course, comment on the most important sounding of all, which would take place tomorrow at Eisenhower's Gettysburg farm, when Dr. Paul Dudley White put his stethoscope on the president's chest. If all was in order, the eminent cardiologist had promised, Ike could make his own decision about whether to run for a second term.

Bored with Kefauver's optimism, Tommy spit into a paper cup and wondered if there was a bar open anywhere in the Willard at ten-thirty a.m. He tapped Woodforde on the shoulder and asked, "Why are you wasting *your* time with this? You ought to go up to New York and find Welker. Write a few hundred words about the egg running off his face."

Woodforde laughed. The Idaho reactionary and his wife, about to embark on a Caribbean cruise out of New York, had the other night been sitting in their cabin when a surprise party of revelers burst in with platters of caviar, a giant floral wreath, jeroboams of champagne—and two flashing cameras. The bon voyage bounty had all come from the hard-left longshoremen's union, whose leaders thought they could embarrass the senator with all the gun-crazy McCarthyites who kept voting for him out there in the Wild West.

Tommy handed Woodforde a press release he'd gotten from Welker's office this morning decrying the "obvious attempt to get even with the Senator for his outspoken criticism of communism and his personal fight against the Commies."

Woodforde smothered some laughter over the last mimeographed word, too childishly crude for even McCarthy to use. He whispered to Tommy, "It's usually about now that Welker starts hinting he's up against the fags to boot. But I'm not sure that's going to work with Tough Tony Anastasia."

Cecil Holland leaned across Miss McGrory's coonskin muff to remind Woodforde that the stevedores' union *was* pretty full of Communists.

"Yeah," said Tommy, "ones with TVs and houses in Levittown." Not his kind of Communists, not the ones from twenty years ago, the ones like Annie Larchwood's husband.

Miss McGrory shooshed the males around her, and then declared: "At least Kefauver is more or less self-made." A stenciled biography reminded the reporters here that he'd worked his way through law school waiting tables.

Ignoring Miss McGrory—the sort of genteel liberal that wearied him—Woodforde turned back once more to the combustible McIntyre. "So this defector coming home: are Potter's constituents complaining they'll be contaminated by having him in their midst?"

After several years in China, Richard Tenneson, a Korea POW who'd gone over to the enemy, was today returning to his family's farm—but in Minnesota, not Michigan, Tommy corrected. "They can complain to Humphrey," he told Woodforde.

"This guy's not exactly one of the all-American stoics Potter had before his committee. Even now he's not fully contrite."

"No," said Tommy. "If this kid had testified, Charlie would have pitched such a fit his canes would've shorted out."

"And Potter's apoplectic moments are pretty few and far between. Wouldn't you say so?"

"Charlie doesn't have many moments one could even call conscious," said Tommy, spitting again into his cup. "And I don't have to tell you that that's off the fucking record."

Undeterred, Woodforde got to his real question: "Then what accounted for his apoplexy, or at least high dudgeon, a year and a half ago? At the end of the army nonsense."

The memory forced Tommy's yellow teeth into a big smile: "You mean his burst of moral fervor?"

"Yeah," said Woodforde, trying to make his insistence appear casual. When Tommy said nothing more, he tried another tack. "Who else knows anything about it? Besides you, that is."

Tommy's grin retracted itself into a wary pout. "Oh, it's a very small circle. Like the number of Kefauver's advisers with any sense."

"Would it include my old acquaintance Private Laughlin?"

Tommy wheezed, phlegmily, while rising from his chair. "I think I'm allergic to that goddamned coonskin."

"*Étaient-ils Résistants?*" Tim asked. He pointed to the knot of men cheering on the National Assembly candidate who'd just cited his wartime service from the steps of the Rheims city hall.

The man standing next to Tim answered in English, and with knowing laughter. "Oh, we were *all* resisters. Every one of us!"

With no translation for the meaning to get lost in, the remark's tone seemed to contain equal measures of sardonic pleasure and shame. Tim decided not to press the matter, settling for self-mockery about his bad French. "*Un américain évident, oui?*" he asked, pointing to himself.

"Yep," said the Frenchman, sounding the syllable like a movie cowboy. He stubbed out his Gitane, shook Tim's hand, and obeyed a summons from his wife, who had just emerged from the bakery. The pair walked away from the *mairie*, indifferent to the rest of the political speech.

They were an exception. Tim and two guys from the radio unit who had passes today had been told not to wear their uniforms, since all varieties of French political passion seemed to be rising with the approach of the January 2 elections. Coming into town, Tim had had no need to consult Jerry Baumeister's old pocket dictionary, which he'd been sent over with by Mary, to grasp the pro-Communist slogans and À BAS USA he'd seen festooning the walls and alleys. There were so many signs for so many candidates that you half expected the plaster baby in the city's Christmas crèche to be holding one, too.

The cathedral was Tim's destination this afternoon, but he found it hard not to get caught up in the auditory duel that was starting between the orating candidate—now blaming Prime Minister Faure for the loss at Dien Bien Phu—and an opposing claque that shouted, over and over, "*Salaud!*" Tim could hear Gallic echoes of "Who lost China?" in the exchange, and for a moment he imagined himself back in the Senate Caucus Room a year and a half ago. The dangerous memories surrounding that time at last propelled him toward the cathedral and onto his knees, beneath the haloed carving of an unknown saint.

Some nearby votive candles looked like the pipes of an organ in flames, and the church's chalk walls, wrested over centuries, block by block, from plains all over Champagne, bore not only the marks of the First World War's bombardments but also scars from the French Revolution. Tim reckoned that he had been repairing his own shelter for nearly a year, starting over whenever some gust, like the news of Hawk's engagement, knocked it down. There were times when he was beginning to believe he'd built himself a snug little chapel, but there were still those other nights when it would be blown away in an instant, and he would have to dig himself a foxhole with a few desperate prayers, hoping to stay hidden from harm until morning.

Earlier today, at the café near the *mairie*, he'd had a ham sandwich and some *pâté de grives*, a regional specialty that the waiter eventually confessed was made from the thrushes one saw fluttering in and out of the local bushes. Tim had eaten what he could of it while reading the *Herald-Tribune*'s article about a Budapest AP correspondent named Marton who with his wife had just been arrested and tried as a spy. Their fate?

Unknown. Tim imagined them in a cell down the hall from Cardinal Mindszenty.

These stories of freedom's instant and complete disappearance had an ever-tighter hold on his thoughts. He'd lately been making himself read a book called *Religion and the Modern State* by an Englishman named Dawson. He'd acquired it on his one trip to Paris, when he'd gone looking for mystery novels in an English-language bookshop, and he was carrying it with him even today. Its thesis—that all the kingdoms of state would disappear, become useless, "as soon as the light comes"—had made him understand more exactly the nature of his patriotism. The intense attachment he felt to his own country—the world's bulwark against totalitarianism—derived from America's permitting him to go about his real business in the world, which was the search for a revelation so great, for a peace so absolute and ecstatic, that he would in time be lifted away from the world entirely. His own country, his own state, allowed this quest; the opposing state didn't. And yet, if his life and everyone else's managed to fulfill itself, then even America would subside into irrelevance. Right now one had to protect it from its enemies, but finally it would drop away like the first stage of a rocket that took one to a thoroughly different universe.

He had tried, clumsily, to explain all this in a letter to Kenneth Woodforde, who had replied with a telegram that the mail-room officer handed over with raised eyebrows: CONGRATULATIONS, LAUGHLIN, ON BECOMING A MARXIST—STOP—YOURS UNTIL THE STATE WITHERS AWAY, KW.

He had taken to praying with a fervor beyond anything he'd previously achieved in his life, and to fasting as well, at least occasionally—not for any penitential credit the effort might provide, but for the lightheadedness it brought on, the physical floating he could feel after about thirty-six hours. Longer than that, he'd joked to Woodforde, and he couldn't do his job for the benevolent, temporary nation-state.

And yet maybe these moments of exultation were no more than spiritual dizziness, and he himself was just a "dizzy dame," what Hawkins used to call the nightclub-obsessed boyfriend of some older man he knew. He would never be a systematic thinker or half as quick as Woodforde. In fact, along with the Dawson book he had purchased a copy of T. S. Eliot's essays—partly to further his religious way through this dangerous, secular world, but also, he knew, because when he saw the spine he had been seared by a memory of Hawk standing naked in the dark, purring the lyrics of one of his Eartha Kitt records:

> T. S. Eliot writes books for me;
> Sherman Billingsley even cooks for me;
> Monotonous . . .

The bus back to Verdun left at three-forty, and when it pulled out from the center of Rheims, Tim found himself sitting amidst several men and women in their sixties, American husbands bringing their wives back to the war they had fought four decades before. Verdun itself was a kind of giant cenotaph to the month-after-month slaughter of 1916, though that battle held none of these men's particular memories. They had arrived with the rest of the Americans the following year, for the last of the blood and derangement, which still on occasion exploded from the region's landscape, when some farmer's tractor disturbed a mine that had been slumbering for forty summers.

This was the kind of story Tim wrote up for *The Com Z Cadence*, the official newspaper of the army's Second LOC, or Line of Communication, a significant stretch of the Americans' ever-burgeoning Cold War home away from home. Running from Verdun to Orléans to La Rochelle, the Second LOC had been established as a backstop, in the event the First LOC, strung through Germany, got overrun by the Russians. The Yanks may have come late to Verdun back in '17, but this time they'd come to town early, manning the 7,965th Area Command in advance of the next war.

The Com Z Cadence—the Last Voice You'll Hear, as the staff liked to joke—specialized in morale-building local color and human interest. In the last couple of weeks Tim had done stories on the flower sellers outside the U.S. cemetery at Varennes, and the never-idle two-thousand-foot runway at Saran. His biggest accomplishment had been a story he'd freelanced to *Stars and Stripes* itself about the engineering depot at Toul, where Caesar's legions had once camped and where their American successors, after spending a first winter in tents, had by now built a whole town of warehouses, barracks, and chapels. They'd even fielded a baseball team called the Toul-Nancy Dodgers.

The bus let the tourists off in town and continued to the base, whose horseshoe-shaped welcome arch reminded him of the neon sign greeting tourists to Reno, as he'd seen it years ago on a postcard sent by Uncle Frank. Inside the caserne, Tim shared a large room, down the hall from the First Signal Group's cryptographers, with seven other guys. The barracks dated from just after the Franco-Prussian War—a war he'd barely heard of—and some recruits said you could still smell the stables that had once been on the ground floor. Tim's own floor, the third, was served by a single shower, which provided a measure of hygiene hilarity for letters to Francy and Tom, communications that he kept immaculately free of the politics and religion he sent to Mary and to Woodforde.

"Un visiteur—pour vous!" said the local woman who manned the message desk.

Tim cocked his head in disbelief.

"Oui!" she insisted, pointing to the little excuse for a lounge down the hall and to the right. "He is here on, how do Americans say, his honey*moon*?"

For one moment, his heart pounding, he thought it might be Hawk: *to be married on Saturday, December third.* It *was* the sort of thing he would do, a show of the brazen insouciance he couldn't live without displaying. But then he realized it had to be Jerry Baumeister, who must have made his *mariage blanc* to Beverly Phillips and come here on a side trip from Paris to show her another portion of the culture behind his now useless master's degree.

Once inside the lounge, Tim saw that he was wrong in this guess, too. "Paul!" he exclaimed.

The "brewer"—he could hear Hawkins saying it—extended his hand. "Private Laughlin."

"Where's Mrs. Hildebrand? Congratulations. I just heard."

"Thanks," said Paul, who went on to explain that his wife, Marjorie, until recently his brother's bookkeeper, was resting in town at the Hôtel Bellevue on the Avenue de Douaumont, which neither of them could really pronounce. They'd been married last Saturday, the tenth, and had come over to Paris on TWA. Even though it was a honeymoon, Marjorie wanted to see the patch of ground in Ardennes where her brother had been killed late in '44, as well as the "Red Schoolhouse" over in Rheims, where the Germans had surrendered to the Allies. When they were through with this historical circuit, they would start making their way to London.

Tim told them he could get information from FAFLO, the French-American Fiscal Liaison Office—"we've got initials for everything"—about discounts for a Europabus they could take from Paris to Calais.

Paul nodded thanks.

"She never told me you were getting married," said Tim, lowering his voice and somehow unable to say "Mary," as if the new Marjorie Hildebrand might actually be here instead of at the hotel.

"She asked me to check up on you," explained Paul. "Make sure you were okay."

"I write to her more than to my sister!" Tim said, with an overhearty laugh. "She *knows* I'm fine."

"She says you don't talk about much except God and the Communists."

Tim hoped his hand was covering the title of Dawson's book. He continued speaking through simulated laughter: "She doesn't tell *me* much, either. Like about your getting married, for instance!"

Hildebrand wondered what she did and didn't tell this kid, whom he liked well enough despite his condition, which he probably couldn't help and might still be young enough to grow out of. Had she confided her sputtering affair with the Estonian—as she'd confided it to him? He doubted it, since in his own case Mary had almost made a present of the story, an intimate parting gift on the eve of his marriage.

"Did she tell you," asked Paul, "that her friend Beverly has left the office?"

"Really?"

"Yeah, just a couple of weeks ago. She's joined the staff of some Illinois congressman. She made a connection with his office when she did that charity show on the Hill. Mary says she never liked working for State after they fired her friend Jerry."

"I came over here with some of his French books."

Paul nodded. "Are you allowed to show me around?"

"Sure," said Tim, pointing the way forward. They walked back toward the message center, but after several steps, more to test himself than anything else, he stopped and asked: "Did Mary go to Fuller's wedding? On the third?"

"Yes," said Paul, reluctantly. "In fact, I was her date." A part of him wanted to rest his hand on the kid's shoulder, but too much else in him was repelled by the possbility as soon as it came to his mind. "That crazy woman, the one who used to be in her office, showed up at the back of the church."

"Oh, *her*," said Tim, laughing.

Nine hours earlier Fuller had been traveling from Union Station to the I Street apartment in a cab that got trapped in traffic around Dupont Circle. A colored man had just leapt to his death from the top of the Connecticut Avenue underpass.

"They want to kill me! They want to kill me!" the man had shouted to the policemen urging him toward safety. The remark had been passed down two long lines of idling vehicles by a morbid pedestrian walking the sliver of space between them.

"And I suspects he's right," Fuller's driver, also colored, had whispered, sadly and to no one, while his passenger thrummed his fingers on a beribboned package containing a silver bowl.

Married thirteen days ago, Fuller and Lucy had gone for their honeymoon to Acapulco, a destination that made his aunt Valerie sniff with surprise that her nephew's old-money bride should be aping the flashy Catholic Kennedys. As it turned out, the wedding trip had been cut short several days ago by the death of Uncle Ned, whose funeral in New York Fuller was returning from today. Lucy would stay on there for one more night, then go up to Massachusetts for a few items she wished to bring with her to their new home.

He, in the meantime, would take possession of the little brick house, attached on one side, over in the Parkfairfax section of Alexandria. The development had sprung up quickly during the war, but was leafy and handsome by now, a half-time home to many younger congressmen, and, these days, if Fuller wasn't mistaken, to Citizen Canes himself. His own possessions from I Street would go over tomorrow in a truck driven by the built Italian boy who sometimes did yard work for Andy Sorrell, and who, Andy assured him, could be had.

Lucy had been highly presentable at the funeral, never overdoing a gesture. She'd had a veil on her hat, but a small one, and it had been pulled back, off her face. She'd looked appropriately grave without shedding tears. And yet, while the money on both sides of her family was older and ampler than what had ever been on either side of Fuller's—and although the art-historian father had put a thick patina of culture onto the Boardmans—there *was* something of the arriviste about her. She betrayed a strong, potentially useful insecurity that made her seem almost a shopgirl who felt she had to keep earning her splendid new husband. With the actual shopgirls of the world, her manners and aspect of entitlement carried the full birthright of arrogance, but in all that concerned Fuller she displayed an undisguisable nervousness. Unchecked, this might grow toward panic and make her demanding, but properly managed, it should keep her nicely off balance, Fuller reasoned, just the way she'd been in the three days between his application for the marriage license (easily revocable) and the actual wedding, which had been carried out down here, quite modestly, at St. Margaret's Episcopal.

The phone had been ringing when he came into the apartment this afternoon: Lucy, half-teasing and half-nagging about his having neglected to get it turned off. He made a note to do so as she went on to explain how she wanted them to go hear the Yale Glee Club in Lisner Auditorium on Monday night. Her father had been a member "eons ago," and the concert could be her and Fuller's first trip into town together from Parkfairfax, assuming he didn't himself want to arrive at the auditorium directly from the office.

To all of which he had responded, without audible irony, "Yes, dear."

His reasons for marrying had proved stronger than ever at Ned's funeral, held inside St. James' Episcopal on Madison Avenue, a hell of a lot fancier than St. Margaret's on Connecticut. Fuller's least favorite sister had been wearing a big turquoise amulet, as if it were the latchkey to Ned's New Mexico house. His father, now judged to have lost much of his sense ahead of his money, was mostly shunned by his own partners. And his mother, looking neither particularly resentful nor present, had worn a gold Catholic crucifix with a chunky graven image of Christ's cadaver attached to it, the whole thing more vulgar and a lot more expensive than his sister's necklace. Both his parents were under sixty and already doddering. Aunt Valerie, buzzing with vitality and animus, could be seen turning into some baleful family retainer out of Balzac, wondering what she was to do with these *ancien régime* characters she'd been saddled with.

A good thing old man Boardman had paid for the little wedding down here in D.C. In fact, at the subsequent funeral Fuller had found himself guessing that the new in-law might quietly be kicking in to help out with Uncle Ned's departure, Ned having been pretty badly depleted at the close. As Fuller had listened to the tiny boys' choir, which he'd sung in himself twenty years before, he'd wondered if either of his parents had even remembered to make the customary donation for the little angels' high-pitched services. Probably Mother had, unless she'd recently spent that pittance, too, on Irish priests bringing the Word to South American Indians.

Now, as he poured himself a drink, the late news was murmuring out of the television, which Lucy, on her one inspection of his "bachelor apartment" had suggested might not be large enough for the place in Alexandria. Maybe he'd just give it away to the Italian boy tomorrow morning. In any case, its swan song here, now coming through the mesh, would be these dronings by Kefauver about the important work he'd done investigating juvenile delinquency.

That's me. I'm your hoodlum, your little j.d.

Fuller looked at the kitchen chair, surprised to remember the ardent kisses of a particular morning, and the way Skippy hadn't been able to unzip either of their pants fast enough. All in all, a much more bravura display than what he could expect from the one in the bedroom now, this sweatered college kid he'd met ice-skating on the C&O canal a couple of hours ago. He already couldn't remember the name, only that he'd been calling him Dicky, for Dick Button, under the small bit of available moonlight. His own name would remain a convenient secret, since he'd removed the strip of paper from the doorbell down on the first floor—the one bit of packing he'd accomplished so far.

"Be right in," Fuller called out to Dicky, who was lying on the bed, still in his sweater, as patient for his unwrapping as Lucy had been on the wedding night at the Hay-Adams.

He looked again at the kitchen chair, remembering the morning he'd been strapped to McLeod's magic, inquisitorial machine; remembering, again, the hour before that, here.

Have you ever considered yourself to be in love with another male?

CHAPTER THIRTY-THREE

May 24, 1956

"Welcome to the 7,965th, sir."

Major Conroy, the public-affairs officer, shook Senator Potter's hand and escorted him to the small dais that had been set up at the front of the enlisted-men's club. "I know you're already acquainted with this fellow."

"Hello, son," said Potter, shaking Tim's hand. "Good to see you in uniform."

Tim thought Potter didn't look entirely certain about whom he was greeting. More than a year had passed, after all, since his departure from the office. But there was no time for more than a handshake. He'd been assigned to write about this quick visit from several members of the Armed Services Committee, who were over here inspecting several American installations and were soon to leave for the LOC's headquarters in Orléans. Potter did not have a seat on Armed Services, but as a war hero who'd escaped with his life from this region, he had been invited to junket along by Scoop Jackson, his old Democratic colleague on the McCarthy committee.

The other Democrat here was Mississippi's John Stennis; Mrs. Smith of Maine and Styles Bridges of New Hampshire made up the Republican side of the delegation. "Stylish" Bridges, Hawk had always called the latter, who looked a little like the actor Lyle Talbot. Moving quickly to his seat, Tim didn't shake hands with any senator besides Potter, though he felt a slightly ridiculous desire to ask Mrs. Smith if she knew what had become of Robert Jones since she'd beaten him in the primary two years ago.

"We haven't had this much excitement here," announced Major Conroy, "since Billy Graham dropped in last summer!" Amidst general laughter he turned the proceedings over to Senator Stennis, the senior majority member, who explained through his bad teeth and impenetrable Southern accent that the group would be winding up its fact-finding travels at the new NATO air-forces headquarters in northern Italy.

"Unfortunately," Mrs. Smith added, "Ambassador Clare Boothe Luce won't be there to greet us. She's home in the States for a bit, recovering nicely from a bout of illness. I was hoping for a bit of female company, but it appears I'll have to keep putting up with these gentlemen instead."

"Ah, Mrs. Luce," whispered Kenneth Woodforde. "Mother Superior as imagined by Harry Winston."

Besides a man from the AP, who wore a button saying FREE THE MAR-TONS, Woodforde appeared to be the only American covering the delegation. Weeks ago he had sent a letter with the news that he'd be traveling with the senators, and he had laughed when Tim replied by asking if *The Nation* would be paying his way over. He was here on some money advanced to him by Harper & Row, for whom he was producing a book called *Armed and Dangerous: America's Permanent War Footing*, an exposé of defense-contractor gluttons and their legislative ladles in both houses of Congress. It would be as strident, he promised, as the publisher would permit.

Picking up on Major Conroy's Billy Graham remark, Senator Jackson told the recruits who'd been mustered to attend the event: "We hope that during your period of service over here you have absolutely *no* excitement whatsoever. We just want you to do your jobs in peace and then to come home in *one* piece."

Amidst the applause and whooping, Woodforde asked Tim: "So what were you doing when they dragged you over to this show? Peeling potatoes?"

"Wrapping up a Princess Grace souvenir wedding plate to send to my mother."

"I hear the heir she produces will look a lot like William Holden."

"Do you have a *question*?" Senator Jackson inquired, testily, pointing to Woodforde.

"Yes, I do. Why, when the United States professes to support the United Nations as a freewheeling arena for the airing of differences, have your senatorial colleagues on the Internal Security Committee been calling for the expulsion of the Soviet delegate, Arkady Sobolev?"

Jackson replied with the kind of scorn Tim remembered him displaying once or twice in the Caucus Room. "Mr. Sobolev understands a little
about expulsion himself. As you know perfectly well, five young Soviet
sailors recently defected and were given asylum while they were in New
York City. And not long after that some of Sobolev's muscle men managed to hustle them onto a plane out of New York and back to Moscow.
Anyone want to take bets on whether they're still alive? You're confusing a diplomat with a thug, Mr. Woodforde."

Woodforde maintained a smirk as he wrote down Jackson's response.

Senator Bridges, a natural grandstander, decided to lighten the moment
with a little pandering. He pointed to the sign at the back of the enlisted-
men's club and began reciting its injunction: " 'In the eyes of foreign
people, you are a mirror reflecting everything the United States looks
like and stands for. By your appearance and actions, so is your country
judged.' Good advice. But I've got only one question for the men: How
are they feeding you?"

During the derisive roar that followed, Woodforde spoke loudly into
Tim's ear: "Christ, he might as well be Bob Hope with the golf club. I'm
half expecting Virginia Mayo to come out."

When the ruckus died down, the AP man asked the senators where
Estes Kefauver, a member of the committee, was today.

Mrs. Smith replied that she "shouldn't speak for the majority" but
"could only imagine he's campaigning in Florida." Stennis, who wished
no success for Kefauver, a desegregationist from the neighboring state of
Tennessee, pursed his lips. While this went on, Tim regarded Potter, the
only one who'd said nothing so far—as mute as he'd typically been on
the McCarthy committee. He looked absent, even lost. Perhaps his mind
was back in '45 now that he'd returned to France, but still, unless a roar-
ing automotive economy carried him over the finish line in Michigan, he
looked like a bad prospect for reelection two years from now.

"You have a pass at twenty-one hundred hours," Woodforde told Tim.

"I do?"

"Yes, the public-affairs officer seems to believe that even *The Nation*'s
man can be brought around by a full display of cooperation. Everything's
supposed to be at my disposal until tomorrow morning. Including the
correspondent of *The Com Z Cadence.*"

"You're not following them to Orléans this afternoon?"

"I'll catch up with the marionettes in Italy."

"Okay," said Tim, tentatively. "I'm just a little worried about time." He was on deadline, he explained, with another story—about the Spiritualaires, a singing quintet of Negro servicemen.

"You've got time," Woodforde assured him. "And I'll bring you up to date on things back home. Your old boss, McIntyre, has all kinds of interesting matters to impart. About some of your old friends." He looked at Tim, waiting for the last remark to register. "So where do I come by for you?"

Sure enough, when nine p.m. arrived, it became clear that Major Conroy had permitted Woodforde into even the caserne. Arriving punctually to take Tim out for a beer, the writer rolled his eyes while pointing to copies of *National Review* and *Encounter* that lay atop Tim's footlocker.

Tim explained that the first was part of a subscription his father had gotten him, and the second a single issue he'd picked up at the English-language bookshop in Paris.

"We know," Woodforde explained, "that *National Review* is made possible by the family money of a crazy individual. It'll be a while before we learn where *Encounter*'s money comes from, but when we do you'll realize it's as much an organ of the United States government as *The Com Z Cadence*."

"Are you ready for a drink?" Tim asked, giving him a serene smile.

The two of them walked back to the enlisted-men's club where the Senate delegation had been presented this morning. The makeshift dais was gone, and a handful of GIs were hoisting Cokes and beers. "I'll bet most of them spend a year in France without ever drinking a glass of wine," Woodforde observed.

"Why didn't you bring your girlfriend over? What painter could resist Paris?"

"No American with the least bit of talent has gone to Paris to paint in twenty years. They go to your hometown, New York City, Corporal Laughlin."

To someone whose idea of the artist's life remained easels and berets near the Moulin Rouge, this was a revelation like one of Hawk's old life lessons, those ex cathedra pronouncements meant to complete what the two of them jokingly used to call his "education."

"So," said Woodforde, sitting down at one of the oilcloth-covered tables, "how are the Negroes?"

"You mean the Spiritualaires?" asked Tim, brightening.

"Yes. God's Mills Brothers."

"They're terrific. They may even make a record." He started to sing "Swing Low, Sweet Chariot" in the lowest register he could manage.

"I'm sure you'll write them up as proud Americans happy to be serving in our color-blind army."

Tim downed half his beer and felt merrily combative. "You know, they get an English translation of *Pravda* at the HQ in Orléans, and it sometimes makes its way up here. The last copy I saw had a story on some Young Communist League members who *want* to be sent to Siberia. To help 'build the nation.' "

Woodforde pointed to the sign Senator Bridges had hammily quoted this morning: *You are a mirror reflecting everything the United States looks like and stands for. By your appearance and actions, so is your country judged.* "You think what your clean-living minstrels are experiencing is really so different from a little forced labor?"

"They're not minstrels, and of course it is."

Woodforde smiled with indulgent superiority.

"Are you a Communist?" Tim asked, sincerely. "Or just an anti-anticommunist? I've always wanted to know."

"Communism hasn't arrived," Woodforde explained, as if it were a genre of painting that hadn't yet made it to New York. "When it gets here, it'll be something quite different from Stalin, though its opponents will keep waving *that* bloody shirt forever."

Tim could see that Woodforde had been rattled, if not quite toppled over, by press reports of Khrushchev's big "secret speech," in which the current dictator had apparently laid out the crimes of the former one to their full, breathtaking extent. Even so, the chasm between the writer and himself was still too wide to keep shouting across, so Tim narrowed the divide to the spectator sport of domestic politics, mentioning a wire-service story he'd seen about a televised debate between Stevenson and Kefauver.

"Two wet firecrackers," declared Woodforde. "Amusing, though, to see the great liberal Stevenson allowing the voters of Florida to believe that, race-wise, Kefauver might as well be Paul Robeson. Wait until Kefauver's people start spreading the story of the 'pansy party' Adlai's supposed to have attended over here in Paris not long ago."

"Is that true?"

"Does it matter? Besides, when it's all over, Joe Alsop will have been proved right. Kefauver will take the number-two spot. And then they'll both lose together."

Tim got a mental picture of the columnist ogling Hawk at the Sulgrave Club's coat check—*I could tell you what I've got on Joe Alsop*—a picture first imparted on the awful night, a month or so before the hearings began, when Hawk had come to the Capitol Hill apartment. *Maybe the two of us can become the three of us.*

"I have a friend," said Tim, "who calls Alsop Walter Liplock." He knew he was quoting this only for the chance to hear Hawk's voice in his head.

"Would this friend be your friend Fuller?"

"You know Fuller?" asked Tim, trying to sound casual.

"I've met him once or twice. Most of what I know about him comes from your other friend, McIntyre."

Tim rolled a peanut between his fingers.

"Which reminds me," said Woodforde, reaching into his pocket for a note penciled in what Tim recognized as Tommy McIntyre's hand: *You should write to your friend. 3423 Mt. Eagle Place, Alexandria. He misses you.*

Tim's eyes welled with longing and rage. He knew that Tommy was sending this not because of the extreme romantic nature they supposedly shared—*I told you because you'll understand*—but for the cruel pleasure of control, even more satisfying when exercised across a vast distance.

"He's special to you, isn't he?" asked Woodforde.

Did the soothing manner of this leading question approximate a defense attorney's direct examination of his client? Or, Tim wondered, did it mirror the sympathy of the police detective putting queries to a distraught victim? No, he decided: it was the tone of a reporter trying to get a story.

"Why are you spending all this time with McIntyre?" he at last responded. "Have you developed a sudden interest in Potter's position on overfishing the sea lamprey? Maybe you're writing the senator's biography? *Legless and Dangerous: The Citizen Canes Story.*"

"Easy, Laughlin," cautioned Woodforde, still soothing, but hardly in retreat. "I go to Potter's office to see McIntyre himself. He *knows* a lot, shall we say, though he does like to tantalize as much as to tell." He looked straight at Tim. "I don't care about you and Fuller. That's your business."

"What's *your* business?"

"I want to know why Potter did what he did a year and a half ago, at the end of the hearings."

"Oh, please," said Tim, tossing the peanut to the floor. "No one cares anymore about those procedural votes."

Woodforde replied in a good imitation of Tommy's Irish voice: "You boys all think you're so clever. *So* worldly wise, believin' Cohn had somethin' on McCarthy. You never ask yourselves if *Schine* had somethin' on Joe."

At this remove Tim had to ask himself if he could even remember who had had what on whom. He had tried for a year and a half to wipe from his mind the sordid revelations Tommy McIntyre had cackled into the phone line between D.C. and Madison Square Garden: how the drunk McCarthy had been tempted with Potter's bastard son. *Boys, girls, your old-maid auntie. When he's hammered he'll grope anything.* How the photo of McCarthy succumbing had wound up in the hands of David Schine instead of Tommy. And how it had brought McCarthy low nonetheless. *Dave let Joe know he had it, and from that moment on, if Royboy insisted Dave get an ice cream sundae every morning at reveille, Joe was ready to initial the request.*

Tim finished his beer as Woodforde opened a second one for him, which he began drinking fast, remembering how Hawk used to say that "by the third one you could get Skippy to vote for Norman Thomas." And that was without thirty-plus hours of fasting, which, except for a glass of milk, he'd undergone since yesterday afternoon. He'd go until midnight tonight, when he'd take a vision-seeking walk around the base perimeter.

Lightheaded, he looked at Tommy's note—a whisper from Iago. He hated him, he decided, just as he hated being here in the army as the only way to escape his love for Hawk. He decided he would hate Woodforde, too.

"So that's all you know?" he finally asked the writer.

"Does any of it involve Fuller?" Woodforde persisted.

Relishing a sense of power, the feeling that at last *he* had something to give or withhold, Tim answered: "See if you can find an eighteen-year-old punk named Michael Larchwood in Cheboygan, Michigan."

Woodforde wrote down the name.

"See if you're smart enough to find out what his real last name is, or ought to be."

"Why don't you tell it to me?"

"I've got to go," said Tim, getting up, none too steadily, and starting for the door. "I'm craving the opium of the people."

"So," asked Fuller, "was this de Staël a White Russian with a Blue Period or a Blue Russian with a White Period?"

Mary pulled from her purse a Phillips Collection brochure about Nicolas de Staël, the exiled Russian painter who had last year committed suicide in Paris. She offered the gallery's booklet as proof, answering the real question on Fuller's mind, which was whether she'd in fact had a lunchtime tryst with "the Estonian."

"I'm disappointed," said Fuller.

"Are *you* living vicariously through *me* these days?"

He laughed and disappeared into his office, but both of them knew there was an element of truth in what she was suggesting. Since his wedding, his hours at the department had become more regular, and his phone rang far less often with calls from young men not doing government business.

A new boss had also affected his routine and behavior. Mr. Morton had left at the end of February to run for the Senate from Kentucky, and he'd been replaced by Robert C. Hill, a serious New Englander, not yet forty, who probably wouldn't be around for long. Mr. Hill had already had the ambassadorships to Costa Rica and El Salvador and was said to be after the big prize in his region of expertise, the embassy in Mexico City. In the meantime, he was proving a tougher nut than his predecessor. Apropos of Sobolev and the sailors who'd defected, he was asking hard, almost Nixonian questions of the department's UN liaisons, but he had also been pushing back against the department's Senate critics, telling them they were ill-informed whenever that was the case, as it frequently was.

Hill and Fuller were not each other's cup of tea, but the acquisition of a wife had made the latter even more socially deployable than he'd been before. On Sunday afternoon, Fuller had glamorously represented the bureau at the Afghans' independence-week party over on Wyoming Avenue, where the top-drawer little crowd had included Justice Douglas and Senator Saltonstall, whom everyone at State was aware of as a distant relative of Fuller's bride.

Putting away the museum brochure, Mary opened an envelope sent over by Congressman Yates's office: from Beverly, it turned out, a sketch of the wedding dress—a sly, knee-length knockoff of Grace Kelly's—in which she would be married next month.

Mary had begun to think of herself—without much regret, she tried to believe—as an old maid, even if her affair continued with intermittent ardor. Fred would never offer to leave his wife, and she would never ask him to. She would never have his undivided attention, and he could no longer have hers when he talked of the latest atrocity or opportunity for Estonia, as he did on the phone several times a week.

Indeed, here he was now:

"Hello, baby."

"Hello, Fred."

"I'd love to see you Monday, but I'll be picketing you instead."

She had heard about the anti-Sobolev demonstration being planned for the sidewalks outside the department. "Maybe we could manage a quick kiss behind the police van?" she offered.

"Maybe."

"Fred, I was joking."

"Oh," he said. "You know, there *is* a way we can combine the two activities, baby."

"Really? Tell me."

"Late September, outside the General Assembly in New York. All the exile groups are getting together for something pretty gigantic. On a weekend. I can book us into the San Carlos Hotel; it'll feel like a honeymoon."

Or a farewell, she thought.

"That didn't come out right," he apologized. "I just meant we'd be in a different place altogether, not your city, not mine."

She tried to imagine herself shopping for shoes on Madison Avenue while Fred carried a placard through Turtle Bay. Maybe she would feel like a wife who'd accompanied her husband to a convention of druggists or petroleum engineers.

"I'll take you to *My Fair Lady*," he added.

"Estonia will be free before you can get tickets. But I accept the invitation to New York."

She could not shake the feeling that this proposed weekend, still months away, would be the end of it. But she would rather they had their goodbye scene there than here, so she wouldn't keep running into the memory.

A moment after the two of them hung up, a delivery boy from the cleaners on Virginia Avenue entered the office. Through the cellophane bag she could see it was a tuxedo he was carrying.

"Mr. Fuller?" he asked, looking at the ticket.

Mary pointed to the right doorway, but having heard his name, Fuller was already emerging. He paid for the garment and asked the boy to hang it in his office.

"And where are you off to *tonight?*" asked Mary.

"White House Correspondents' dinner. At the table of a UPI man, whom I'll no doubt convince we've handled Sobolev and the sailors *exactly* right. Let me show you what you'll be missing." He opened Mary's *Washington Post* to a photo of Patti Page and Jimmy Cagney, the evening's entertainment, rehearsing at the Sheraton Park.

"Well, aren't you a Yankee Doodle Dandy."

Fuller pointed to Patti Page. "That doggie in the window was her reflection."

Mary laughed hard, even while wondering whether this wasn't a line he'd heard from the comic piano player at the Chicken Hut, one of the bars Jerry Baumeister unblushingly mentioned from time to time, the way a regular man about to forsake bachelorhood might bring up bygone nights with his buddies at the corner gin mill.

As Fuller read her the story about the evening's dinner, she realized why she detested Lucy. It was because she herself believed in nature, in Fuller's fulfilling what she now accepted as his own. She also had begun to feel, perhaps contradictorily, that Jerry and Beverly were fulfilling some aspect of *their* natures; marriage for them would be the cementing of something childlike and fraternal and curiously authentic. But Fuller's union with Lucy was no civilized companionship, or even some piece of sophisticated realism; it was a corrupt bargain that the two of them had struck. Fuller thought he was on top of it, but Lucy's needle was in him deeper than McLeod's had ever been.

"Is Lucy coming here before the dinner?"

"No."

"What about the tuxedo?"

"That's for Monday night. Something with the Joint Chiefs. Tonight is business suits, but I *will* be heading back to home and hearth between here and the Sheraton Park."

"Well, the sight of you and Lucy getting ready for a party must look like a 'Diamond Is Forever' ad." She was being *very* polite.

"Actually, we'll be *un*dressing. I've committed to making a baby, and the calendar has been calibrated like an atomic clock. The fertility gods are supposed to be in full cry between now and seven." He checked his watch. "I'll be leaving early."

"Would you like a boy or a girl?"

"I'd like a reprieve."

He could see a look on her face that said *tell me*: tell me that you know it's a mistake; tell me why you really did this; and tell me whether you aren't really going off to meet a boy instead. But Fuller was thinking that the only mistake he'd made had been with the Italian boy. As Andy Sorrell had predicted, Tony Bianco could be had—but, as it turned out, only inconveniently. The kid had been back to Alexandria twice, without an invitation, the first time parking a block away, waiting for Fuller to pass by so that he could ask him for the price of a new set of tires. The second time he'd reappeared by mail, requesting help for his mother's operation—for which Mrs. Hawkins Fuller charitably let her husband write a check on the joint account while she suppressed her common sense and they both silently hoped this would be the last such communication.

No, this was not the big feared slip-up that had motivated him into marriage, but it was a slip-up nonetheless, and from it Lucy had tacitly extracted the agreement to make a baby, another tie that would bind, and earlier than he'd expected.

CHAPTER THIRTY-FOUR

October 31–November 7, 1956

"Major Conroy's looking for you."

"Let him look," said Tim, shooting Private Meyers a joyful look. He was hunched over one of the radios, picking up English-language transmissions out of Hungary. For the past week, these broadcasts had been more thrilling than any long-ago episode of *Inner Sanctum*. His mind and spirit had been sparking and overloading, as if the radio console were the source of his own electricity. It was now 9:30 a.m., and he'd been helping the operators with transcription since five o'clock.

Beginning Sunday, after fruitlessly gunning down hundreds of Hungarians who'd risen up in revolt, the Russians had been slowly withdrawing to their bases all over the country. Soviet tanks still sat in front of the parliament building in Budapest, but according to Radio Free Kossuth, a new Hungarian flag—red and white and green—was flying from the dome. The country's Olympic team, on its way to Melbourne, had already redesigned their uniforms.

Major Conroy entered the radio room. "You're still at it," he told Tim, his tone somewhere between indulgence and exasperation.

"Who could leave?" was Tim's exuberant reply.

In spite of himself, Conroy came closer to the radio and listened, while Private Meyers handed Tim a piece of transcript someone had made off a station transmitting in French from one of the southern provinces: during the night Soviet troops had sent a confusing signal by making some circular movements between Záhony and Nyíregyháza. But the new premier, Imre Nagy, whom the Soviets had been forced to accept last week, was declaring that everything remained on track. In fact, Hungary would even be leaving the Warsaw Pact!

Major Conroy begged to remind everyone that at this very minute the British and French were bombing Egypt in order to maintain control of the Suez Canal. "Don't lose your heads." No one had even mentioned the presidential election, six days away.

"O ye of little faith!" declared Tim, reaching for a piece of transcript he'd made while the sun was still coming up: " 'After two years of enforced silence, in the last few revolutionary days, we have formed the first Christian organization, the Christian Youth League. We have to contend with indescribable difficulties and therefore we ask you, our sister organizations abroad, to come to our assistance morally and materially.' Major, you can send a check, or a parcel, to number 6, V. Nagy Sandor Street in Budapest."

"Laughlin, you have an assignment today for the *Cadence*."

"Yes, covering trick-or-treating by dependents under twelve at the Toul base. Major, come on!"

"We drive down there in half an hour. Not one minute beyond that."

Tim shrugged with a kind of joyful hopelessness. He was not going to let anything put a crimp in the moment of deliverance.

"Half an hour," repeated Major Conroy, as he exited.

About twenty minutes later, Private Meyers came over and tapped Tim on the shoulder: "I think you'll want to see this."

It was something copied off Radio Free Kossuth: "Cardinal József Mindszenty, Prince Primate, was liberated on Tuesday by our victorious revolution and arrived at his residence in Buda at 0755 this morning. Because the road seemed unsafe, the Primate was brought to Budapest in an armored car guarded by four tanks. In all the villages they passed, the people threw flowers to the Primate and the soldiers. The cardinal told the correspondent of *Magyar Honvéd:* 'I want to be better informed of the situation before I do or say more.' "

Meyers caught Tim murmuring, prayerfully.

"I guess this is a big deal for you, huh?" He shrugged. "What do I know? I'm just a Jew from Secaucus."

Tim felt a moment's shame: How did one put a single man's suffering against the extermination of the Jews? But the thought, he reasoned, was an absurdity. One put Mindszenty's persecution *with* the Jews' sufferings, just as one day the as-yet-untallied dead within the Soviet Union would be added to the century's mass grave. Nazism and communism were the same thing; every man in the street knew it. The difference between them was a semantical matter for the fancier poli-sci professors at Fordham.

"Corporal Laughlin," called Major Conroy. "*Now.*"

"Yes, sir," said Tim, double-timing it to the jeep. He carried the Mindszenty transcript like a relic.

Half a mile into their trip to Toul, he tried speaking his mind to the major: "Eisenhower's offering ten million dollars in aid to the new government. That's pretty paltry, don't you think?"

"No politics, corporal."

"Okay. I promise to concentrate on finding vivid descriptive terms for all the Davy Crockett and Princess Summerfallwinterspring costumes I'll be seeing."

He closed his eyes as the jeep drove over the chalk plains still soaked with blood and salted with the bone fragments of two world wars. They continued on past the living, the wars' survivors who were now oxidizing toward normal deaths and perhaps salvation. He believed that he was being carried at last toward transcendence and freedom, toward a solution.

"You're muttering, Laughlin. Speak up."

"Sir. *Gloria Patri et Filio et Spiritui Sancto, sicut erat in principio—*"

Major Conroy shook his head. "At ease, Corporal."

"Amen, sir."

"Tranquillity is just around the corner."

Fuller waited for her to respond and after a moment gave up. "You're not laughing."

"I get it, I get it," said Mary. The reference was to Undersecretary of State Herbert Hoover, Jr., now acting chief of the department while the aging John Foster Dulles underwent an emergency appendectomy at Walter Reed. Dulles had collapsed at home early this morning, a day after returning from New York, where he'd convinced the United Nations to adopt a resolution calling for the end of hostilities in the Middle East. With Hungary still unsettled and the election now only three days away, Mr. Hoover wanted all hands on deck, with no excuses made about its being a Saturday.

The president's own calming statement about Suez—conceding that the British, French, and Israelis had made an "error" in attacking Egypt—seemed to be helping him at home, if not abroad. The Democratic ticket appeared to be sinking fast, swamped not only by the electorate's instinctive rallying toward the incumbent during a crisis, but also by the Soviet premier's kiss-of-death endorsement of Stevenson's desire to stop testing the hydrogen bomb. By now Ike had not only Hoover's son in his corner but one of FDR's, too: the youngest Roosevelt, John, had come out for him. And Joe McCarthy, rising from alcoholic slumber, had announced that he would seek his old committee chairmanship if the Republicans took Congress next week along with the White House.

In truth, there wasn't much to be done here in the bureau this afternoon. Most congressmen were out of town campaigning for their seats, and the amalgam of tension and idleness was working on Mary's nerves. As soon as she heard Fuller getting off the phone with the secretary's people upstairs, she went into his office.

"Any more news from the doctors?"

"Yes," he replied. "They told us yesterday afternoon that 'we're' pregnant. What started them using *that* pronoun? Dr. Spock?"

Mary looked at his blotter for a moment—it held the latest poll numbers on whether the U.S. should get out of the UN—before leaning down to kiss him on the cheek.

"Congratulations. To you and Lucy. How far along is she?"

"Two months. Maybe two and a half. And a nervous wreck. The doctor recommends she take up smoking."

"What are *you* going to do for nerves, Papa?"

Fuller sighed. "Maybe I'll give it up." He looked through the doorway. "Is Hill still around?"

"Yes. You're going to have to hang on a little longer." She made herself smile as she walked off.

They'd not had much to say to each other these past few months, though the silence between them had itself been like a conversation, an ongoing mutual acknowledgment that she knew—up to a point—what things were like for him now, even if he was still determined to see them through. In public, he and Lucy remained on their shiny trajectory, attending the shah's birthday bash at the Mayflower on the same day last week that Mary had been added to a group of wholesome-looking State employees chosen to accompany a Soviet delegation on a tour of Ike's and Stevenson's respective campaign headquarters. The Russian from the Academy of Sciences had complained about the Washington humidity and explained that having only one name on the ballot in Soviet elections was not a problem: "You can strike it out and write in another." He allowed that this didn't happen often.

Mary looked up at the sweeping second hand on the clock and felt nearly as exasperated as Fuller to be here. Suez did, after all, appear to be in the hands of the UN, and the Soviets did appear to be continuing their withdrawal from Hungary, despite a few confusing signs: troops and tanks were staying close to the airfields, but only, it was said, to shield the Soviet dependents being evacuated from Budapest.

The phone rang, promising a bit of relief from the tedium. She wouldn't care if it were only some eager-beaver young GOP congressman, out on the hustings, asking for the exact answer to give about the Middle East.

"Baby."

It was the first she'd heard from him since they'd broken things off up in New York—so amicably that, several minutes afterward, they weren't sure they'd really done it.

"Hi, Fred."

"I *knew* you'd be in."

She could hear the excitement. He sounded like a college student who'd been up on No-Doz for a week.

"I hate to disappoint you, Fred, but from what I heard a half hour ago, Mr. Dulles is likely to be fine. And even if he doesn't make it, Herbert Hoover, Jr., is not exactly Nixon."

Fred didn't seem to remember their small adventure on the night of Ike's heart attack.

"Are you voting for him?" Mary continued. "For Ike, I mean."

"Yes, while respectfully holding my nose."

"Beverly's taking me to the Statler on Tuesday, with the Bethesda Stevenson Club."

"You're going to have an early night."

"I could use one."

"How come?"

"No particular reason," she replied.

"So are we still good-enough friends that you'll call me with the least little thing you hear about the Baltics?"

"It amazes me that you believe somebody is going to come down the hall to tell me anything other than that the new file boxes I've ordered have come in."

Fred scoffed at her modesty. "There's a lot to be said for being near the action. Keep listening: your Mr. Hill might come down with a case of loose lips."

"Fred, what exactly do you expect to happen in Estonia?"

"*Wildfire*, Mary. Think about the way it spreads. Why did the Hungarians rise up? Because five days before they did they heard about some Poles in Wroclaw dragging the Soviet flag through the gutter. Eisenhower should stop trying to calm things down. He should be fanning the flames."

"I'll tell that to the next Young Republican who calls."

"Get ready for a new birth of freedom," said Fred, more sonorously than usual.

"Fred, I need to go. Fuller wants something," she fibbed.

She hung up the phone and put some lotion on her hands. *Two months. Maybe two and a half.* Counting on her moistened fingers, she calculated that Lucy's baby would probably come in late May, only a bit earlier than her own.

———

IKE IN LANDSLIDE; DEMS HOLD CONGRESS

At the LOC's Orléans headquarters, Tim worked at fleshing out the *Cadence*'s election edition. Even bannered as such, it would maintain the paper's resolutely light touch and confine the political story to the front page's left side. The three right-hand columns were being held for "7,965th Chefs Get Tips from Paris' Best." News from Hungary would go on page two.

"Can you stand some more?" asked Lieutenant Dillenberger, who had noticed Tim's grief-stricken demeanor when he'd arrived here yesterday afternoon from Verdun.

"Sure. I like pain."

Everything in the stack of dispatches and transcript was awful, as it had been for the last three days, ever since the Soviets began using bombers and tanks to crush the uprising. The rebels were now mere resisters, trying to hold on with Molotov cocktails and paving stones. Refugees were crossing the border into Austria, some of them carrying pots of Hungarian soil. A Soviet puppet named Kadar had replaced Nagy, and Sobolev, the Russians' UN delegate, was saying that the U.S.S.R. would just ignore any resolutions on Hungary the General Assembly might finally decide to pass. Meanwhile, Premier Bulganin had made the novel suggestion that the U.S. and Soviet Union intervene *together* in the Middle East—against the British and the French.

And here was the latest from Radio Budapest, which had resumed toe-ing the Soviet line: "*In these difficult hours let us remember the great Socialist revolution of October 1917. Now, in the light of the open excesses of the counterrevolutionaries, the tremendous significance of October 1917 becomes even clearer to us. The Soviet peoples have set the world an example.*"

"Anything from Radio Free Rakoczi?" asked Tim, without much hope.

Lieutenant Dillenberger sifted the most recent pile of transcript and handed Tim an appeal from the holdout station: "*We are fighting against overwhelming odds! This is our message for President Eisenhower: if during his new presidency, he stands by the oppressed and those who are fighting for freedom, he shall be blessed. . . .*"

"At least *we* know where we *are*," said Dillenberger. "A couple of reports say some of the Russian recruits think they're in Berlin and World War Two's still going on. Christ, they must be dumber than the guys we get from Oklahoma."

Tim continued reading transcript and wire-service copy, which now included the news that Mindszenty had gone to seek shelter at the American embassy in Budapest. At three p.m. Major Conroy came in to get him. The two of them were due to ride back to Verdun together. With a small movement of his head, the officer ordered Dillenberger out of the room.

"Get a grip, Corporal Laughlin."

"Yes, sir," said Tim, who only now realized he had tears on his face.

Major Conroy put a hand on his shoulder. "I am not General Patton. I am not about to smack you and say 'Snap out of it.' But snap out of it."

Tim saluted, went off to wash his face, and five minutes later rejoined Conroy near the line of jeeps outside. It turned out—a small mercy—that they would be returning to the base in an American sedan, with the major allowing him to ride alone in the backseat. All the way to Verdun, Conroy kept up with conversation offered by the driver, a Pfc and rabid Red Sox fan; it was almost suppertime when they arrived back on the grounds of the 7,965th.

As Tim started for the office, the major had one last message for him: "You'd better eat your damn dinner, too. I don't know what *that's* about, but if I see you settling for a glass of milk again, I'll report you."

"Yes, sir."

He went straight to his desk, piled with the *Herald-Tribune* and the London papers, all of them full of Ike's victory. Beneath them lay a letter from Kenneth Woodforde, who must have used one of his congressional connections to get it into the air pouch. It was dated Monday afternoon, when the Soviet attack had been in full force:

Dear Laughlin,

I found Michael Larchwood (in jail for grand theft auto, by the way), and I now have a pretty good idea of what went on back in '53 and '54. But given what's *now* going on, I've lost interest in my little historical exposé.

I never answered your question about what I was, Communist or anti-anti-Communist. Maybe I'm going to be the first anti-anti-anti-Communist. After the last two days I realize that the C's in power are about as likely to change as your One True Church. I've lost my appetite in more ways than one.

So I thought I'd let you know that your indiscretion about young Larchwood is safe with me. Fact is, I couldn't prove anything without the photo Schine's supposed to have, but (see above) another fact is I don't have the stomach now to pursue it.

One other thing: Fuller and his wife are expecting a child next year. I tell you this only so that you don't hear it from McIntyre, who I suspect would derive some odd pleasure in imparting the news. I apologize for playing that card when I saw you back in May.

Woodforde

P.S. Do remember that this failed uprising was meant to be, in its own way, a *socialist* revolution. They wanted to be neutral, not "just like us."

Tim got up and headed to the mail room, where the Frenchwoman was getting ready to go off duty. He asked if he could still send a telegram, to 3423 Mt. Eagle Place, Alexandria, Virginia, U.S.A.

7965TH AREA COMMAND—07 NOV 56

HAWK—

RUSZKIK HAZA!

WHEN YOU GO TO THE DEPARTMENT TOMORROW—PLEASE—IN WHATEVER WAY YOU CAN—DO SOMETHING.

T.

The Frenchwoman asked if she correctly understood the spelling of the exclamation. "And it means what?"

"Russians go home. My two words of Hungarian."

She nodded, and made a last quick scan of the yellow piece of paper on which he'd composed the message.

"*C'est tout?*" she asked. "Nothing to add?"

His stomach dropped; he felt himself struggle to keep from inserting the three words he'd nearly written with the pencil: *I love you.*

"*Non,*" he said. "Nothing to add."

PART FOUR

DECEMBER 1956–MAY 1957

How should we like it were stars to burn
With a passion for us we could not return?
If equal affection cannot be,
Let the more loving one be me.

—W. H. AUDEN,
"THE MORE LOVING ONE" (1957)

CHAPTER THIRTY-FIVE

December 1–3, 1956

Leaves were burning along three stretches of curb on Martha Custis Drive. Raking his front yard, Fuller glanced down the adjacent street, somehow half expecting to see Tony Bianco in his parked car. But months had passed with no sign of the part-time moving man. Fuller was free to concentrate on the smoky aroma riding the breeze. It might be December, but the crisp air and sky belonged to the October Saturdays he remembered from St. Paul's. This was New England weather, held up at the Mason-Dixon Line for a month and a half.

The Army–Navy Game, near the end of its second quarter in Philadelphia, was playing on his new English portable radio, an anniversary present from Lucy. Knowing he'd be working outdoors this afternoon, she had decided that her husband should have the expensive gift, smart and snug in its leather case, two days early. It sat on the front steps of the house, and its reception was excellent.

Lucy now waved to Fuller from the open upstairs window. Still in her quilted yellow peignoir with its little bow at the neck, she had her sketch pad balanced on the sill. She was drawing with the expensive pens Fuller had gotten her from Fahrney's and handed over this morning after she made her own premature gift. To show that she was indeed using them to create her tight, folksy drawings—what Grandma Moses might have produced with ink instead of oils—she raised one of the pens for her husband to see. Her other hand held a filter-tipped Salem, the brand that was helping to soothe her through a fourth month of pregnancy. She had still hardly begun to show, not even when she wore something besides this billowing nightgown.

Fuller had begun sweating through his flannel shirt. He waved back to his wife and then walked around to the side of the house to get at whatever leaves might be resting under the carriage of their new Plymouth. The car reminded him that he could, if he felt the inclination, make a quick run before dinner to the keypunch operator (dumb as a post, and with that little mustache) in the rented room off Chinatown. Or even a quick stop at Andy Sorrell's place just over the bridge.

The radio announcer, vamping through halftime, genially mentioned that Ike had violated the customary presidential neutrality toward today's game by telegraphing his good wishes to the Army coach. The station then cut to a Red Cross appeal for donations to ease the plight of those Hungarian refugees now reaching freedom's shores.

PLEASE—IN WHATEVER WAY YOU CAN—DO SOMETHING.

He had done nothing about Hungary, unless you counted pocketing a phone number from the good-looking Budapest university student who'd recently been paraded through the bureau like some kind of war trophy. Everyone *else* was doing something about Hungary; the department had been consumed by the refugee operation. An eleventh planeload of exiles had arrived the other day at Camp Kilmer up in Jersey, and before the cloyingly named Operation Mercy was finished at least twenty thousand more would be allowed in, thanks to some fancy interpretive footwork with the immigration laws.

But a hundred thousand were still in camps along the Austrian border. Nixon would be heading over to visit them in a week, and after that, Congress would start hearings on the conduct of U.S. policy (had there been one?) during the uprising. Fuller imagined that at least one of his CIA buddies would have hell to pay for the general failure to anticipate rebellion along the Danube.

RUSZKIK HAZA!

He was glad he had been the one—not Lucy—to open the door when the telegram arrived. What exactly, he'd wondered, did Skippy want done? Air strikes? Maybe just an air*lift* for all the priests the embassy in Budapest couldn't hold? He'd also wondered why this frantic little cry—he could almost feel it being whispered into his ear, between ardent kisses of his neck—was coming only now. It could hardly have to do with just Hungary. Whatever it meant, it felt helpless, like the furtive leafleting said to be going on even now in the streets of Budapest.

Fuller lit a match and watched the leaves catch fire. He had no compelling desire this afternoon for the keypunch operator, let alone Andy Sorrell. He felt himself, unexpectedly, wanting someone and something else. The radio, filling up the rest of halftime, had begun to play some old Tommy Dorsey songs, Dorsey having choked to death on a forkful of food earlier in the week.

> *I'm getting sentimental over you.*
> *Things you say and do . . .*

He looked over his shoulder and back toward the house. On the breeze, smoke from Lucy's cigarette joined the smoke from the leaves.

It would be Monday before he actually wrote the letter, and only after he got Mary to answer an important question.

"So," Fuller asked, tapping her on the shoulder, "how much longer?"

Irritated, she swiveled around in her typist's chair: "How much longer until *what*?"

She didn't look well. Her face was puffy, and while it might be *le dernier cri*, the sack dress she was wearing did nothing for her but hide her figure.

"How much longer until Skippy gets home?"

She had long since stopped leaving Tim's letters on her desk. In fact, the last time Fuller had spoken of him was nearly a year and a half ago, at the time of the engagement. *Make it easy on him.*

"He's due back after the first of the year," she answered. "With plenty of reserve duty left to perform, since it was only a two-year enlistment."

"Will he be performing in New York or down here?"

"Down here."

She saw pleasure in his expression. Was it a surge of sentiment? Or appreciation of his power in having created this geographic anomaly— causing Tim to enlist in New York, but as a Washingtonian who even now would be returning to the District?

"I'm guessing," Fuller said, "that you know what he wants to do once he's back. Rejoin Citizen Canes' listing ship?"

"He doesn't write me that often, Fuller. Not as much as he used to."

Fuller kept looking at her, no matter how unnerved and jumpy she appeared, no matter how preoccupied—the way she so often was these days. He knew that she knew.

"He wants to do something with the refugees," she explained. "He doesn't know exactly what. He takes the whole Hungarian business personally somehow. I don't understand why."

Why is what she wanted to know from Fuller: Why *now*? Why the rekindling of interest in him? But she didn't ask; she just broke away, relieved to greet the girl bringing Mr. Dulles's autopen downstairs to the bureau.

It was the secretary's first day back in the office after a long recuperation in Key West: last month's emergency surgery had revealed a cancerous growth on his intestine. Today Mr. Hill had prepared a letter that would go out to every congressman and all ninety-six senators, in which Mr. Dulles cheerfully announced his own return, thanked the lawmakers for their good wishes, and said how pleased he was once more to be standing with them, shoulder to shoulder, on the brink, against the Soviets.

Fuller helped Mary to set the writing machine on a countertop near her desk.

"I hate that dress," he said.

"So do I." She'd copied the Dior pattern from one of the French magazines Jerry bought for his new wife. "It's an 'H-line.' "

"It looks like an oil drum."

"Thanks."

"I'm trying to compliment you. Don't hide your light under a bushel. Or inside a sack."

She tested the autopen on a blank sheet of paper and felt glad to see Fuller disappear into his office. She was furious with herself for having let the weekend come and go without deciding what she would do. There was still not much to hide under the Dior, but in another month that wouldn't be the case.

There was a place way down on F Street where she could be rid of the baby for a hundred and twenty-five dollars and be back here the next day. She'd gotten the address and the price, just like the magazine with the Dior, from Beverly, who had heard of it from a girl in Senator Douglas's office who'd been knocked up by the man who each year wrote most of the air force budget.

Or she could go back to Louisiana and become the oldest resident of the Ursuline Sisters' home for unwed mothers. True, she already had a high school diploma, but maybe she could at last master algebra from one of the visiting tutors. More plausibly, she'd been considering a small, discreet establishment in the Garden District, run by a wealthy Catholic woman, where older young ladies tucked themselves away during their last few months and then swiftly surrendered their babies to an orphanage—had them whisked away in a warming pan like the bastards and pretenders of historical legend. All this would shield her father's eyes from the embarrassment, but she couldn't shield Daddy from the whole truth. She was determined to tell it to him, unless it finally involved F Street.

And if she chose adoption? What afterward? Perhaps she'd go teach English at Beauregard Junior High, disappearing in plain sight for the rest of her days.

She fed the letters into the machine—*Mr. Hubert B. Scudder, 1st district, California; Mr. Clair Engle, 2nd district, California; Mr. John E. Moss, Jr., 3rd district*—and all at once knew that she had to get out of the office, immediately, without even telling Fuller. She put a note on the receptionist's desk, saying she felt sick.

"Good!" Fuller told the girl several minutes later, once she conveyed the news. "Maybe Miss Johnson will come back in one of her old New Look skirts."

He returned to the two documents he'd been composing—a half-finished thank-you letter to Congressman Fulton of Pennsylvania, who had taken it upon himself to defend Eisenhower's Hungarian actions as the only prudent course, and a letter to what Fuller guessed was the administration's leading critic among corporals of the 7,965th Area Command:

They'll be processing them at Camp Kilmer (I think that I shall never see . . .) *until May. The Austrian desk, which really was just a desk until a month ago, is now two large rooms more tightly stuffed than Fibber McGee's closet. . . .*

Letting Skippy know that he remembered his chatter about the radio: a more shameless seduction than the one he'd carried out some weeks ago on a Catholic University junior.

There's all sorts of interviewing, plus clerical and "liaison" work going on in half a dozen buildings around town. If you want to do something like that, it should be easy enough for me to set it up.

You said please do something. Well, I am—I'm passing the buck to you.

He sealed the letter, still surprised at the ripple of unease he'd experienced writing it—an unstable mixture of desire and hesitation, with even a sense of personal fault blended in. He couldn't quite credit the last, since the exact nature of his desire was once more to grant the protectiveness that came with ravishment, something he'd not done, or felt himself doing, since the departure of *Cpl. Timothy P. Laughlin,* to whom he now addressed the envelope, the ink of his fountain pen bleeding through to the onionskin inside.

Protection: what Skippy craved; what one paid and loved the gangster for.

Fuller put this last thought to the side of his mind, like a department memo stamped FFA, For Future Analysis. He rose from his desk and breezed past the receptionist. "Going to mail a letter," he explained, as if there weren't two Outgoing trays less than three feet away.

He exited on Twenty-first Street, thinking of how the building would before long extend itself all the way to Twenty-third. Next month, if their aging hearts and bowels held out, Ike and Dulles would stand here in their homburgs slathering mortar onto the cornerstone of the addition. Fuller was pleased to anticipate the building as a labyrinth twice its already huge size. It was even now, he decided, big enough for Timothy to stay discreetly lost in, though it still might be preferable to have him beavering away in one of the department's satellite offices somewhere else in the city.

Fuller walked down H Street toward the Potomac, past the university's buildings and the boys in their letter jackets. Maybe he'd keep going all the way to the river, or drop into the Foggy Bottom Wax Museum and stand with the handful of visitors fitting themselves into the goofball tableau of the St. Valentine's Day Massacre.

Valentine's Day: Lucy, he now recalled, wanted to go to Bermuda for it. He slid this thought, too, to the edge of his mental blotter, as the university's terrain gave way to Foggy Bottom's crumbling little brick houses, toy cottages attached to one another for dear life. The Negroes had made this shaky spot their own for decades, until the whites started coming back when the department relocated itself to the neighborhood after the war. What the bulldozers hadn't gotten was now falling into the hands of renovators. Eleanor Dulles, the secretary's sister, had herself bought and fixed up one little row of the miniature dwellings; she'd made them what the real estate ads called "darling," and sold one or two to the sort of boys in the department who had something to fear from Scott McLeod.

Yes, the mephitic old neighborhood, having sagged for a century with its poor drainage, ammonia factory, and tinderbox warehouses, was slowly recuperating toward a placid modernity. Where the gasworks had stood when Fuller first arrived at State, foundations were now being laid for the kind of white-brick apartment building that back home was turning stretches of Park Avenue into sets of high-rise dentures.

He reached the corner of Twenty-fifth and H, still not having put the letter into a mailbox, when he spotted, lo and behold, the brewer, poking around the weeds and tin cans in a yard belonging to a red-brick house, just as narrow as the others, but a little taller, with a comical turret at the top.

Paul Hildebrand caught his eye and they waved to each other. Mary's old suitor stepped out of the yard and onto the broken sidewalk, leaving his survey of the premises to the two employees he had with him.

"Well," said Fuller, looking up at the turret while he shook Hildebrand's hand, "this one is pretty baronial for the Bottom."

"A regular Taj Mahal. I'm not sure what we're going to do with it." Hildebrand pointed in the direction of his nearby small brewery, visible from this corner, though dwarfed by the much larger Heurich's plant beside it. "We still own two or three of these little dumps," he explained, pointing to the row of houses running up Twenty-fifth. "Heurich used to have most of them. They got built in the nineties, mostly for the Germans and the Irish, who all took off once the streetcar came in. No reason to actually *live* here when for a couple of pennies a day they could get in and out to make their living making beer. The colored have been in the houses ever since. This one's so far gone it's been abandoned for a year. Our accountant only realized the other day that the pittance of rent had stopped coming in. We're here trying to decide whether to fix it up or knock it down." He paused to take a look at some missing cornices. "I'm a little taken aback. I didn't realize I was a slumlord."

Fuller watched one of the other men pulling at some branches to see whether the window behind them was whole or broken.

"It's a haunted house inside," Hildebrand continued. "Cobwebs. A couple of old couches, some busted cupboards with jelly-jar glasses. Christ, a colored woman who passed by five minutes ago told me there were still privies in the alley during the war. Mrs. Roosevelt came poking around one day, shaking her head. How's Mary?"

He seemed to hope the fast elision would keep Fuller from realizing he'd mentioned her name.

"Not herself, I'd say," Fuller answered. "This afternoon she lacked the energy to stay on my back about something annoying I'd said."

Hildebrand tested a piece of wrought-iron fence that looked as if it might give way in his hand. "I wish she'd get out of there. Find something that made her happier. How's married life?" he asked, hoping for a cordial, dishonest answer. He knew more than enough of Fuller's story from Mary.

"The berries. In fact, today's my anniversary."

"Already?"

"There's a baby coming in May."

"Congratulations." Hildebrand smiled and extended his hand.

"And yourself?" asked Fuller. He couldn't remember the name of the girl the brewer had married.

"Things are fine. I wish business were a little better. No heir yet."

"Well," said Fuller, laughing gently, "I've been truant long enough. I'd best be getting back to the office."

Hildebrand shook his hand for a third time and prepared to resume inspecting the house.

"So what do you think you'll decide?" asked Fuller. "About this place."

"I think we'll probably knock it down. But not until summertime at the earliest. In this town it takes more permits to demolish something than it does to build."

"So you'll just leave her locked up until then?"

Hildebrand laughed at the place's worthlessness. "What lock?"

CHAPTER THIRTY-SIX

January 22, 1957

Tim thought Woodforde's foot must have crunched another peanut flashbulb—there were loads of them amidst the detritus of yesterday's inaugural parade—but a backward glance through the fog on F Street left him uncertain.

"A Nixon poster," Tim's companion at last explained.

The winds were picking up, sharpening the contrast between this morning's weather and the sunny calm of yesterday afternoon, when Tim had watched the parade from the corner of Thirteenth and Pennsylvania. His vantage point, the pedestal of Pulaski's statue, had been so good he was able to pick out even the types of flowers in the Nixon girls' corsages.

Now, less than twenty-four hours later, as he and Woodforde plodded eastward, it was hard to concentrate on anything but the thick gray mist.

"Think of all those poor private planes," said the writer, in mock horror. "Unable to get back to Greenwich or River Oaks before dinner."

"I thought you'd converted," said Tim. "At least sort of."

"I am a man without an ideology. Which in our century is worse than being a man without a country." Woodforde had sat out the inaugural parade at a one-o'clock showing of *The Girl Can't Help It*.

"You need a church," said Tim.

"You need an exorcism."

In the aftermath of the Hungarian catastrophe, the two young men had conducted a prolific and forgiving correspondence. A peculiar understanding and sexless affection had grown up between them all through November and December as their airmail envelopes traveled back and forth over the Atlantic. Before Christmas came, Woodforde was suggesting that Tim, once he got back stateside, move into a portion of the big, shabby commercial loft where the writer and his girlfriend were residing.

He'd been living there for two weeks. His drywalled-off room took up only a small fraction of what felt like a spacious version of the 7,965th's barracks. Five other painters besides Gloria Rostwald had their own pieces of the vast premises one block from Woodward & Lothrop's. Not only was his landlord living in sin, Tim had written Francy; he himself and all the rest were residing illegally, against the District's zoning regulations.

Each of the artists, Gloria had explained, worked with acrylic paints on canvases that hadn't been primed. They were trying to constitute an innovative "color school," acting as if Washington were a creative destination on the order of New York or Paris (as that city had *once* been, Tim was careful to remember). The group's paintings were pretty, but also gauzy and faint, he thought. Whenever he looked at them, he wished they'd come into clearer focus, the way he wished the city now would, as he and Woodforde continued marching east.

The writer was on his way to the Hill, and Tim would accompany him as far at Fifth Street, where he'd veer off to St. Mary of God, the Hungarian church. He'd been working there on behalf of the refugees now streaming into town, taking his meals in the rectory basement and coming home with pin money for his efforts. He paid his rent to Woodforde and Gloria with what he'd saved from his army pay, which was most of it.

"Those poor Hungarian souls," said Woodforde, looking down Fifth Street toward Tim's destination.

"You wouldn't believe what some of them have been through."

"Exactly. Ten days of Kate Smith records and apple pie at Camp Kilmer. Makes you shudder."

"See you later," said Tim, clapping Woodforde's shoulder and dashing off into the fog, his heart almost light with purpose.

Since arriving back in the U.S., he had still not seen his family. Francy and Tom were threatening to come down from Staten Island if he didn't get up to them soon, but the lack so far of any reunion didn't seem strange—not when he hadn't seen Hawkins, either.

Why, he'd asked himself a hundred times, had he ever sent the telegram? Had he succumbed to a simple moment of weakness while he was angry at God over Hungary? Had a loss of faith in Him prompted a return to that other object of worship, Hawk?

The letter of reply from Alexandria had arrived when he was packing up his things inside the barracks. He had not responded to it in turn, since, strictly speaking, he didn't have to. *I'm passing the buck*, Hawk had admitted, allowing any suggestion of a job to remain nonspecific. Even so, Tim could now feel Hawk's presence across town, like the golden chalice behind the tabernacle's curtain.

He had told himself—was telling himself even now—that he could not go through all that again, not after having made himself right with God, who was allowing him to feel useful in a small way with the refugees. The country had already turned its attention away from the exiles, but there had been no slackening of zeal inside the rectory at St. Mary, Mother of God, where a few minutes after leaving Woodforde Tim was busy with money orders, cans of cling peaches, and pediatrican referrals.

It was the middle of the afternoon before Father Molnar's secretary came to tell him he had a visitor.

In a wrinkled suit and stained tie, Tommy McIntyre looked as if he'd barely managed to pull himself together for someone's funeral. Tim wondered for a moment how he kept himself from being fired, but of course there was no mystery to that: Tommy could still, at any time, use his knowledge of Potter's son against the senator. With the approach of next year's election, the boy's existence would be an even more potent fact than it had been in '53. Michael Larchwood's being in jail was a bonus cartridge in Tommy's ammunition belt.

"Sir," said Tim.

"Sir," replied Tommy, with the comic courtliness each had sometimes displayed toward the other in better days.

Tim abruptly stumbled into sympathy: "I heard that Mrs. Larchwood died. I should have written you."

"Ah, yes," said Tommy. "I suppose you heard all about it from the left-wing scribe. He doesn't come by much anymore."

Tommy looked around at all the sorting and packing, seeming to admire its efficiency, before he added: "I suppose he told you about the scion."

"He mentioned that he stole a car and went to jail."

"Yes," said Tommy, affecting a sentimental sigh. "Impetuous youth. I had a visit from the lad shortly before his little scrape."

"Woodforde didn't tell me."

"Woodforde didn't know. Master Larchwood's a somewhat rougher character than the one we saw in '53. A faintly *threatening* presence this time 'round. It seems he labors under the delusion that those of us in the employ of America's lawmakers are rather wealthier than we are. I disappointed him with the news that I had no more cash to give him than I did three years ago, back at that excellent Schine-family hotel."

Tim knew that Tommy would any minute be bringing up Hawk, seeking the peculiar pleasure of watching Timothy Laughlin squirm at the suggestion that he and Tommy McIntyre had hopeless love in common. To forestall this, he made a nervous joke: "Have you come to offer a donation?"

"No," said Tommy, straight-faced. "I've come on a mission of mercy."

He asked Tim to accompany him to the house of an old friend on the Hill—a worse drunk than himself, he swore. "I've been encouraging the fellow to quit. Friendly advice from the pot to the kettle." He paused for a second or two while Tim scrutinized his face. "I did go myself, a couple of times, to the father confessor you recommended at St. Pete's, but it didn't quite take. So I'm wondering if *you'd* give the pitch to my pal. My own skepticism would be a little too evident, I'm afraid, but he might be susceptible to an angel of charity like yourself." Tommy gestured toward the wooden crate that Tim was packing with boxes of powdered milk and Nestlé's Quik. "Or at least to a more sober voice than my own," the Irishman added.

Tim guessed that Tommy had found him through Miss Cook. He'd called the old office last week in connection with paperwork that his reserve unit required about his last salaried civilian employment. Wary of both Tommy and the clock, he now looked up and saw that it was only three, too soon to leave.

"They're hardly in a position to dock you," Tommy argued. "Why don't you take a stroll with me? The weather's improved considerably."

Out on the street, walking toward the Hill, Tim felt his thoughts turning to the possibility of reconciliation. Was what he'd accomplished with Woodforde unthinkable with Tommy? Or even Hawk? Of course he and Hawk had never really quarreled, but maybe there was some subtle formula, like Father LeTour's in New Orleans, that would bring them back into a sort of relationship, some platonic fealty he could practice without violating the worship of God. Perhaps he could exist as a neutral state, like India, between two great powers.

At number 335 on C Street, a vaguely familiar young man, on his way out, opened the door. None of it added up. The house was not the least disordered inside, and a female voice, in quiet conversation with a man's, could be heard coming from the second story.

"Heading back to the office," the young man said to Tommy. "Go in and sit down."

"I don't understand," Tim said.

Tommy showed him a seat in the living room as if this were his own house, and then nodded toward the staircase. A male figure was descending, each step making several more inches of him visible. A belly protruded, and the gait was less than steady. Finally, the emerging head above its shoulders proved to be covered with the mottled face of Joe McCarthy. The senator was combed and freshly shaven, but for all that, like Tommy, barely pasted together. The female upstairs, presumably Jeannie, could probably claim credit for whatever physical cohesion he managed to display.

McCarthy came forward to shake Tommy's hand. "McIntyre."

"Senator, let me introduce you to another son of Ireland."

"We met in your office, early in '54," said Tim.

McCarthy responded with a cry of comic agony: "Fifty-four! Ohhhhh!"

Tommy and the senator warily entered into conversation about the new Congress, whose alignments Tommy was demonstrably better informed of than McCarthy. There was, Tim thought, an odd cordiality between the two men, each of whom, he had to remind himself, had something on the other and took him for an enemy. Together here they seemed comrades: each of them pained and defeated, both of them Irish and drunk.

McCarthy made a crack about Mrs. Luce's final departure from the embassy in Rome: "Now the only ring she'll have to kiss is Harry's."

"If not the one he's bought for his girlfriend" came Tommy's fast reply. Both men laughed and McCarthy got up to make drinks. Tim said he'd have a Coca-Cola.

"So Alcorn's now heading up the National Committee," observed Tommy.

"Fuck Massachusetts," McCarthy replied. "Goddamned 'Eisenhower Republicans.' "

Even Tim knew that Alcorn was from Connecticut, not Massachusetts.

"Right you are, sir," said Tommy. "One day a man will come from out of the west and put an end to all this. Maybe Goldwater, maybe somebody we don't even know yet."

McCarthy nodded at his own sagacity and finished pouring drinks. Once they were distributed and he'd settled himself in a club chair, he let Tommy take the conversation to its next topic: "Looks like my man's going to have a tough race next year. Against this fellow Hart."

Unaware of Potter's likely opponent, McCarthy asked: "Is he a Jew? 'Hart' and 'Harris' and 'Cooper' always are."

Tommy left McCarthy uninformed that Hart was a Catholic and the lieutenant governor of Michigan, adding only: "At the very least he's going to scare the hell out of Charlie."

"Good!" shouted McCarthy. "But that doesn't take much, does it?" He gulped his drink and warmed to the subject: "God, I'd love to see him get his legless ass kicked out of Congress. At least he's off the committee." He referred to the latter body as if it still belonged to him.

Tim could see where this was going: Tommy had decided it was at last time to bring down Senator Potter. His simmering rage over Annie Larchwood's death had blazed up into something like his old fury toward McCarthy himself. This time he would reverse field and make McCarthy the instrument of Potter's undoing. Tommy would alert the senator to the existence of the illegitimate son; then, rather than tip the press himself, he would keep his part anonymous by letting Joe spoon them the news. With a friendly wink he'd tell McCarthy it was best to make reporters believe the story had come from some loyal old gumshoe on the committee staff.

Tim also knew why Tommy wanted him here while McCarthy learned the secret. His presence would provide the senator with a kind of confirmation, since Timothy Laughlin's face, never able to mask anything, would testify to the story's truth. And of course his being here would also give Tommy the pleasure of seeing "young Timothy" harrowed yet again.

Tommy watched in silence as McCarthy took a further few sips of his drink. There was no danger the senator would ask why Tommy wanted his boss undone. There was always a reason in the world of who had what on whom, and it would be more convenient for McCarthy not to know, for him just to marinate and savor the suddenly fulfillable fantasy of seeing Potter get his comeuppance.

When Tommy spoke again, it was to tell McCarthy, casually, that with a little help this fellow Hart might pull things off. But before McCarthy could respond to the suggestion, the sharp cry of an infant came from the second floor. "My baby!" yelled the senator, grinning broadly before bounding upstairs to the child he and Jeannie had just adopted from the New York Foundling Hospital. Cardinal Spellman, who'd seen no need to ask too many questions about the acquisition, had helped things along.

Tim decided that this was the moment to escape the house. But McCarthy was almost immediately back in the living room, somehow managing to keep a firm, tender grip on the blanketed baby. "Jeannie says Princess Grace just had a girl of her own! The palace in Monte Carlo put it out over the radio. Ain't that swell? Well, *that* little girl can't be any prettier than *this* one!"

They might all be at some post-christening shindig inside McConnell's beer hall on Ninth Avenue. Tim wouldn't be surprised if he were asked to favor everyone with a song.

"Ain't she *grand?*" asked McCarthy, looking more like the baby's uncle or grandfather as he thrust it into Tommy's arms for closer inspection. Overtaken by his own sentiments, Tommy appeared unable to resume the mission that had brought him here, and in the commotion of the baby's transfer Tim at last managed to slip away.

He got as far as the vestibule before he felt McCarthy's hand on his shoulder.

It should have been frightening, but it wasn't. McCarthy himself looked innocently wounded, wanting to know what the hurry was. "You *do* look familiar," he said.

"We met just before the hearings, the day after Senator Potter got a copy of 'the Adams chronology.' "

"When Charlie was trying to get me to fire Roy!" McCarthy laughed, as if remembering some comically bad season with the company baseball team.

"Yes," replied Tim, at a loss for more to say as he looked for another escape route from Tommy's vengeful world. He could feel himself being lashed to it by the telephone line that had once reached into Madison Square Garden. *Boys, girls, your old-maid auntie. When he's hammered he'll grope anything* ...

He moved for the door, but McCarthy kept coming toward him, with an enormous, devouring smile. Reaching for the handle, Tim heard himself saying, inanely, to keep the man calm: "I was also at your wedding. Helping out Miss Beale for the *Star.*"

"No kidding!"

McCarthy proceeded to smother him with a hug, to give his neck a boozy kiss and his crotch a hard locker-room squeeze.

"We're going to christen her Tierney!" he called out as Tim raced toward the street. "Come to the church!"

CHAPTER THIRTY-SEVEN

February 21, 1957

Two days ago, Lyndon Johnson had complained on the Senate floor about Secretary Dulles's lack of response to his letter protesting the administration's apparent willingness to impose sanctions on Israel over the continued presence of her troops in Egypt.

So now the CR Bureau had a sizable fire to put out. How odd to find all these congressional crackers and cornpones suddenly so enamored of the Jews, thought Mr. Hill, the bureau's director, who didn't know whether Dulles's delay in replying reflected a deliberate stall, or a desire to insult the majority leader, or just the secretary's protracted convalescence. The old boy was still looking awfully frail.

Several feet from Hill's office, Hawkins Fuller sat in his own, having just finished up with Mr. Jerome Duggan, chairman of the American Legion's legislative commission. The Legion was ending a three-day conference that had included a big dinner at the Statler last night. Speaker Rayburn and Nixon had both shown, and Fuller had been there with Lucy.

The evening's other big affair had been staged by the International Rescue Commission for Hungarian Relief, at the Mayflower, and the Fullers had stopped off there, too. After introducing Lucy to the Goldwaters, Fuller had listened to an ex–Budapest State Opera singer perform the Hungarians' national anthem in a moment that seemed designed to evoke the "Marseillaise" scene from *Casablanca*. The crowd had contained the usual charity-ball locksteppers, most of the women looking like Margaret Dumont, but there had also been many fervent, unfamiliar faces, so eager to help that they would have settled for bread and water for their twenty-five dollars.

Fuller had listened gravely while József Kövágó—six and a half years a prisoner of the Russians, six and a half days the mayor of free Budapest—told his stirring tale to the audience, among whose nonhabitués, Fuller had suddenly noticed, sat Skippy, an honest-to-God guest at an event Betty Beale was chronicling for "Exclusively Yours."

Catching his eye, Fuller had nodded, as if the two of them had last seen each other five minutes before at the coat check instead of two years ago inside the New York Avenue bus depot.

Tim had just stared back, as startled as Kovajo must have been when the door to his cell was flung open—or slammed shut.

"Mr. Fuller, I have a Mr. Laughlin out front."

Yes, here he was, a day later, at four o'clock in the afternoon. Fuller had known it would happen since last night; no, since he'd gotten the telegram three months ago. Actually, he'd known it all along, since the empty milk bottle had dropped from the tower.

He waited a minute, looking in his middle drawer for the blank job application he'd put there three weeks ago, certain even then that Skippy would come along to claim it. He set the manila envelope on the blotter and walked to the receptionist's desk.

Tim was reading the front page of today's *Star*.

"Hawk."

"*Mister* Laughlin?" asked Fuller, quoting the receptionist. "Not Corporal?"

"Only on weekends." He was flashing his fast, nervous smile.

Fuller tousled his hair. The receptionist, new, looked at them quizzically. They walked back to Fuller's office, Tim on noticeably unsteady legs.

"Well," said Fuller, pointing to one of the New York papers piled on a chair. "Roy Cohn is thirty years old. He gave himself a big birthday party the other night."

"Was Private Schine there?"

"Home with his fiancée, according to Miss Kilgallen. She doesn't note Roy's feelings about the girl—only that he seems to be unhappy over Zwicker's being promoted to major general. You can't say he forgives and forgets."

The cat still had a part of Tim's tongue.

"Imagine," Fuller continued, "if Zwicker were still commanding Camp Kilmer. All those poor Hungarian refugees having to get their teeth drilled by a Communist dentist." He cleared the papers from the chair. "Here, sit down."

Tim had never been inside Fuller's actual office, and he was reminded of its owner's old apartment by the negligence of the arrangements—the tennis racket lying atop some out-of-order encyclopedia volumes, the cardboard coffee cup next to the broken thermometer on the windowsill. He felt the old desire to hoard and decode the objects in evidence. He was relieved to see no photograph of Lucy Fuller, and his heart leapt at the sight of the Lodge biography.

"Here," he said, handing Fuller the book he'd brought with him today, a copy of *The Last Hurrah*. "A birthday present. Belated." Three weeks ago, on the first of the month, Fuller had turned thirty-two.

> *For Hawk—*
> *This time you get the book in advance.*
> *I want the job.*
> *It would be wonderful.*
>
> S.

"You missed thirty and thirty-one," said Fuller.

I have to get over you.

Tim tried to ask himself why he was actually here. Because Tommy had dipped him back into the world of who had what on whom? Forced his head beneath its compromising sewage and tried to hold him there? But if *that* was the reason, had he come here seeking the poison's anti- dote or its best dispenser, the beautiful Lucifer who had, after all, given him his first trip through the underworld?

"You're going to be a father," he said.

"A careless one. In May, I've heard."

Are you my brave boy?

Tim stared at the familiar tweed overcoat lying on a table strewn with file folders, and he thought he was starting to cry. "Is there really some- thing for me to do?" he asked, as briskly as he could.

Fuller picked the manila envelope up from the blotter. "Come with me," he said.

Outside, in the aisle leading through the rest of the bureau, Tim asked: "Where is she?"

"Miss Johnson? She took early retirement." Fuller noted Tim's look of surprise. "You honestly haven't seen her?"

"No."

"Or Grandma Gaffney, either, I'll bet."

"No, not her, either."

Fuller understood how completely he governed Skippy's world, even now, two years after the self-imposed exile. But he discarded the thought, telling himself that if *he* weren't in command, then someone else would be.

"Where *is* she?" asked Tim. "What happened?"

"You'll have to call her and find out." And when you know, Fuller thought, maybe you can tell me; she walked out—more than two months ago—and never came back.

Moving along the corridor outside the bureau, they passed photoportraits of Eisenhower, Nixon, and Dulles. Tim pointed to the latter. "His son is a priest, you know. Avery. A convert."

"Maybe the Reformation can ransom him back with an offer of my mother, who's still straddling the fence between Rome and Geneva. With a bank balance that these days could fulfill a vow of poverty."

An elevator took them down two flights and past the Miscellaneous M Unit.

"I'm pretty sure I can get a good recommendation from Senator Potter's office," Tim said hopefully. "I'm not sure he'd have much to say himself, but Miss Cook will write something nice, and he'll sign it."

"No florid encomium from McIntyre?"

"I don't ever want to speak to him again."

"You once said as much about me."

He started to stammer out a reply, but Fuller relieved him of the need for one by picking up the pace and administering a cheerful poke in the ribs. The gesture depressed Tim; it lacked the intimacy of the hairtousling a few moments before and seemed to suggest that they were just joshing old friends. He suddenly feared that's all they might in fact become, a fate more disrespectful to their former romance than impassioned estrangement would be.

Entering the office that seemed to be their destination, Tim heard Fuller ask the receptionist if they could see Mr. Osborne. The girl buzzed him while Tim regarded a recently framed *Time* cover on the wall behind her desk. The magazine's Man of the Year was the Hungarian Freedom

Fighter, an artist's handsome conception of those who'd made the doomed revolution.

Once Mr. Osborne emerged, Tim judged him to be about thirty-five. He looked athletic and a bit severe, but he greeted Fuller with a hearty clap on the shoulder. It turned out the two of them were handball partners at GWU.

"Osborne, this is Timothy Laughlin, a veteran of the United States Army, a staunch defender of the Second Line of Communication in France, and a proud member of our underfunded reserves. You're going to schedule an appointment with him to discuss one of those positions being set up to administer the Refugee Relief Act. He has excellent writing skills, passable French, congressional staff experience, a charming disposition, and a terrifying grandmother."

Apparently used to Fuller's palaver, Leonard Osborne said only, "Sure." Turning to Tim, he added, "If you like, you can come back right now and fill out the first of the forms."

"Nope," said Fuller. "No time."

"Okay, then. Tommorow morning at ten o'clock. Bring a résumé," Osborne instructed Tim. "When you get here I'll take you three doors down the hall to the man who's really in charge. You'll find, I'm afraid, that nothing happens very fast around here, even when it's an emergency." He explained that the Refugee Relief Act, once it actually passed, would entitle anyone fleeing a Communist state to asylum.

"Thank you, sir."

Tim's ingratiating smile gave way to perplexity as Fuller nudged him back into the corridor.

"Hawk, this is great, but I could have seen him now." He waved the manila envelope with the application he'd gotten from Fuller himself. "It's not as if I can't take the rest of the day off from St. Mary's."

"You'll be better off having your résumé with you."

They'd reached the end of the corridor. Fuller guided Tim down two flights of stairs and then opened the door to Twenty-first Street. "Put on your gloves. It's cold out."

"You don't even have a coat."

"We're not going far. Only a few blocks up and over."

They walked fast to H Street and then turned west. In just his blue suit, Fuller attracted even more stares than usual.

Brightening, Tim asked: "We're not going to see Mary, are we? You can't walk all the way to Georgetown like that!"

"No, you can see Mary on your own. Christ, it *is* cold."

Tim removed his scarf and looped it over Hawkins' neck, as if garlanding a Christmas tree. Fuller responded by putting an arm around his shoulder, in such a way that would have left anyone thinking this was his kid brother.

They reached a red-brick house that was in total disrepair at the corner of Twenty-fifth Street.

"There's no lock," said Fuller. "Go inside and wait for me. I'll be back in five minutes."

Tim had found army life easy because all his life he had more or less done what he was told. And it was of course the same now; in a moment he was inside the house and trying the nearest light switch. It didn't work; nor did any of the others. The only available illumination, a fading late-afternoon azure, came through gaps between the mostly broken window sashes and the brown paper covering the panes of glass. There was dust everywhere, but also evidence of recent visitation: pillows plumped and straightened on the couch; a newspaper from last week beside a jelly-jar glass on the counter by the sink.

The house was so narrow that Tim had the sensation of being inside a locker at school. But it was tall, too, dominated by a staircase running up the eastern wall. Everything suggested verticality and ascent. Even a little cut-glass chandelier, unlit, drew one's eyes to the ceiling above a bay-windowed alcove that might once have held a small dining room table. The space's bare little octagonal floor looked like the abandoned ballroom in a doll's house.

Tim climbed to the second floor, past a bedroom with some rags on the floor and a small WC that, however filthy, seemed newer than the rest of the house's interior. Seeking the turret he'd glimpsed outside, he continued up to the third story—a half-finished attic, really—where he found it, a little cone whose walls leaned in above a pile of clean blankets that had been spread upon the floor. Next to them stood a space heater that, in the absence of any other electricity, had been hooked up to two fat dry cells. The darkness outside was growing, and soon the only possible light would have to be coaxed from the glow of this contraption's coils.

Where had Hawk gone? And what could he accomplish in a matter of five minutes? Would he be bringing someone back with him? Maybe Mary, after all? Or some other third party? *Maybe the two of us can become the three of us.*

Or maybe Hawk had left him for a few minutes in this dark space above the littered street to reacclimate himself to the fact that he would always have to wait for Hawkins Fuller, for each brief chance to be alone with him, separate from the rest of the world.

He removed the brown paper from one of the turret's two tiny windows and let in the last now-inky light of day. He looked out across the street to the empty space where the neighborhood's gasworks had once been, before he sat down on the blankets and tried to be patient. He told himself that later tonight he would borrow Gloria's typewriter and construct a new résumé. He would get to bed early—it was easy with no more radio of his own—and tomorrow, once the interview was through, he'd get back to St. Mary's in time for lunch. If he got the job, he would offer up the work to God, confident he was helping those who'd arrived from Hungary to worship Him once again.

He prayed for Hawk to hurry, to get here while he could still pretend these were really the thoughts in the front of his mind.

Last night, when he'd seen Hawk's face, he'd thought his heart would collapse into itself. He'd forced himself to keep talking to Father Molnar, pouring forth chatter about how much the work at St. Mary's meant to him, and Father Molnar, who'd depleted his life savings by half in order to come up with the twenty-five dollars for his own dinner ticket, had expressed delight.

He'd lain awake most of the night thinking what a delusion it had been to believe that two years away could do anything, that he could be strong enough to come back to D.C., or that he had come back for any other reason than Hawk. This morning he'd gotten up for early Mass at St. Mary's, dragging himself from the artists' loft as if God were a boyfriend he was seeing on the rebound; and then this afternoon, only an hour ago, he'd raced from the church to the streetcar to the glass doors of State as if it were October of '53 and his heart had not yet been flooded and battered in all the ways it had been since then.

The last man whose breath he'd smelled was Joseph McCarthy. Now, as his surviving heart pounded louder and louder, mimicking the volume of the footsteps coming up the stairs, he wanted only to feel and taste the air coming from Hawkins Fuller's mouth.

And there he was at last, in the room, Hawk, the silhouette of his figure visible in the dark.

Fuller lit a match and held it under his face, which blazed up like one of the La Tour paintings Tim had seen in Paris. He walked forward. "Take your scarf."

Tim rose from the blanket and slid the muffler, knitted by his mother, from Hawkins' neck, while with the hand not holding the match, Fuller reached into his pocket for a candle. Lighting it, he looked for a place to prop it up and, unable to find one, he let it drip a wax base onto one of the turret's windowsills.

Tim's spirit leapt with a deduction: *He hasn't been up here with anyone else; he would already have figured out the problem with the candle if he had. He made this place for us.*

Fuller reached into the other pocket of his suit, which in the candle's new light, Tim could see, bulged with a paper bag. From it Fuller extracted a pint bottle of milk. He pulled off its small cap and tossed the little circle of cardboard onto the blanket, like a poker chip.

"Drink."

Tim took two swallows and then Hawkins tilted the bottle further back, until more milk was coming out than Tim could swallow. It ran down his cheek and chin, and Hawk began to lick it off, and twice, once gently and once not, to bite him. He took off Tim's shirt and then he removed his own.

In the rush to speed both of them toward nakedness, Tim spilled the rest of the small bottle onto the bare, warped floor near the blanket.

"Don't cry over—you know," said Hawk.

But he was crying anyway. "I love you, Hawk." He pressed himself against Fuller's body, which was still tanned from the trip to Bermuda with his wife.

Holding Tim's shoulders from behind, bringing his lips to the boy's ear, Fuller felt how much he had missed him—the smoothness, the frailty, the chatter and the tender heart. And so, to reclaim the protective thrill that would come with ravishment, he felt himself starting to say the words he knew he shouldn't, words that were actually a bit more true than he would have expected them to be, but sufficiently porous and no doubt strategic that, if he believed in Skippy's loving god, or even in his own austere one, he would be asking for forgiveness as soon as he said them.

But he said them anyway: "I love you, too."

CHAPTER THIRTY-EIGHT

March 11–25, 1957

"How do you stand it? This is *awful,*" said Mary, sipping the glass of milk. "But Dr. Sullivan insists it's a good idea."

Tim smiled at her from the same chair he'd occupied when she first had him to dinner here three years ago.

"So," she said, pointing to the pregnancy that was now quite visible, even under her navy-blue maternity blouse. "*You* were embarrassed to come see *me?*"

He laughed. As soon as he arrived, he had confessed—in the high-pitched tones of wild happiness—the resumption of his romance with Fuller.

"I hesitated to call you when I first got back," he now explained, "because I knew that if I came here we'd talk about him."

"And you didn't want to tempt yourself with even the sound of his name."

"Something like that. And then, once things *did* happen, I felt I shouldn't come around because of, you know, her." It was the one part that shamed and frightened him. As if things hadn't been bad enough before, Hawkins Fuller now had a wife.

"I actually read up on it," he continued. "I wasn't sure whether *I* was committing adultery by being with someone married. It turns out that I am, whereas I'd hoped my guilt in that department might be limited to leading Fuller astray."

They both laughed.

"Thanks again for these," said Mary, pointing to the handkerchiefs brocaded with shamrocks that Tim had bought at Garfinckel's. "They're pretty."

In fact he'd gone shopping for a St. Patrick's Day present for Hawk, but realized that there was now a problem of detection—what if Lucy found it?

"Still," he said. "It's awful. I've had to shut her out of my mind. And despite everything I'm still taking Communion. Just making up my own rules! It's all different from the last time. With him, I mean."

What he wanted to tell her and couldn't was the *reason* the whole cosmos and catechism had rewritten themselves. Everything was different because Hawk had said "I love you, too," a showering of grace more powerful than any papal dispensation. He couldn't tell Mary because he believed that unless he guarded this secret, Hawk's words and their meaning might evaporate. It didn't matter that Hawk had said them only once. He had *said* them—and unlike, it seemed, the catechism, they would remain in effect forever.

"What I can't understand," he did say, "is why you don't disapprove. I know you always liked me, but you never liked the idea of *it*, and now it's worse because of her." He couldn't bring himself to say Lucy's name.

"Maybe my own experience has *broadened* me," she said, patting her stomach. "In more ways than one."

And yet, some part of her was absurdly distressed to think that she— if Tim's reading was correct—had committed adultery, too. She had described to him the pregnancy and her plans: to leave next month for the pious lady's establishment in the Garden District, as if she were awaiting a virgin birth.

For all his own revelations, Tim had been too much a gentleman to ask who the father was.

"You think it's Paul's," she said, all at once unable to have him go on believing "the brewer" had been guilty of some sentimental slip-up a year after marrying Marjorie. "It's not."

She proceeded to tell the whole story of Fred Bell, who just the other day had testified as one of several "free world volunteers" before Representative Kelly's committee investigating the government's hobbled response to Hungary. "He got the Estonia spot on the witness list," she explained.

"That would be a pretty name for a girl," Tim suggested.

"Estonia?"

They considered it for a moment and started to laugh. Tim came over to sit on her side of the table. With his arm around her, he found Mary to be unfamiliarly plump. Still, in most respects she was herself. He knew there would be no crying; the shamrock handkerchiefs remained dry and unreached for. He drew her head to his shoulder.

"Does he know?" asked Tim. "The father, I mean."

"No, though he will if I stay in Washington much longer."

"Does Fuller know?"

"Same answer. The fiction I supplied to the department was 'complications from appendicitis,' necessitating a brief hospitalization, immediate resignation, and a long convalescence out of town. I've been lying low. And just lying. I had somebody tell the bureau that the real attack and surgery happened in New Orleans a few days after I left the office feeling poorly. I imagine Fuller suspects more strongly than Fred does. A couple of times the phone has rung and I've felt strangely sure that's who it was: Fuller. It's hard to be certain, but Beverly knows, which means Jerry knows, and Jerry has a big mouth, I'm afraid."

Tim thought of how, in his own position here tonight, Jerry or one of the "femme" friends Hawk sometimes spoke of would be making jokes about having become, just like Mary, the Other Woman. But it wasn't the sort of joke he could crack himself. He apologized instead: "I'm sorry I came over here so jazzed up and joyful, and then went on talking and talking about myself—even after I could see!" He placed a hand on the pleated rayon covering her belly.

"It's all right," she said, taking her head off his shoulder and putting his on hers. "You're *happy*, baby." She sounded very Southern, as if she were already halfway home. "Try to stay that way."

Two weeks later, as Fuller lit a cigarette, Tim said: "You haven't noticed. I've given those up for Lent."

"If you really loved God, you'd give up milk."

Or you, Tim thought.

"The American Communist Party has given up violence and spying," he replied instead.

"For forty days?"

"Forever, they say. There are 'various roads to socialism,' and democracy now seems to be one of them. Maybe all this will be encouraging to Woodforde."

Fuller thought of the conversations the two of them had had about the *Nation* writer, whose new inner conflict was so different from Skippy's enduring fervor. Timothy's blazing political belief matched, of course, the religious zeal, but to Fuller's mind neither had ever seemed to go with the simple freckled rest of him. He was like that Iowa schoolgirl Preminger had just picked to play Joan of Arc: no matter how hard she tried, once they released the picture you'd still be seeing a cornstalk instead of a burning stake.

"Hawk, one or two of the Hungarians I've met are hearing rumors the government's going to shut down the refugee program—that the U.S. is going to return to normal quotas or let in only the applicants whose relatives are already here. A couple of people waiting to get out of the camps in Austria may have committed *suicide*. I mean, we won't do this, will we? We'd be betraying them *twice*."

"Your elected officials just haven't gotten around to passing the bill that will keep the spigot open. I get to make phone calls on its behalf every day."

"Okay," said Tim, not fully reassured. "I had another note from Mr. Osborne, very nice. They have to do all these checks and so forth. That's what's slowing things down. You guys are worse than the army! Speaking of which: Major Conroy sent Mr. Osborne a 'superb recommendation.' So at least says Mr. Osborne. If it's true, it was awfully nice of Conroy: I'm pretty sure he thought I was a pain in the neck, especially at the end. Anyway, I just wish they'd speed things up and hire me."

He leaned in and kissed Fuller's bare chest. They had climaxed once already, but as they lay on the blankets together Tim was once more hard against Hawk's stomach, experiencing, he thought, a kind of unified happiness: God and politics and love were for once aligned in peaceful coexistence.

The other day he'd bought a portable radio and brought it here. Set to *Twilight Tunes* on WRC, it was now playing "These Foolish Things." Hawk, who had greeted the radio's arrival with a questioning look, casually reached over and moved the dial until he landed on *Bob and Ray*. Wally Ballou was running for mayor, and after a moment or two Tim was enjoying the comic routine even more than the romantic music. "They used to do 'Mr. Trace, Keener Than Most Persons,' " he explained to Fuller.

But at the first commercial he clicked off the little box, the better to concentrate on kissing Hawk, who soon flipped him over and entered him. Their rhythms and avidity matched; familiarity—their own history— now allowed them to merge with a completeness they hadn't been able to manage, even during the good moments, three years before. Hawk pulled on his hair a precise moment before they both came.

The days had grown a bit longer, but even so, by the time the two of them were finished the streetlamps had come on. Realizing it was time to go find his Plymouth and drive home to Alexandria for dinner, Fuller retrieved his car keys from under one of the blankets.

"Are you eating much these days?" he asked, brushing his hand over Tim's rib cage.

"I'll buy myself a sandwich on the way home," Tim explained through a dreamy yawn. "On nights when Woodforde's girlfriend tries to cook, everybody flees. You know, Mr. Osborne says the job *will* be in the main State Department building, so if it comes through I thought I'd try to get a little place not far from where you used to be on I Street. I can cook for myself then."

Fuller found himself suddenly wary. Inside Skippy a future little life was rising, as surely as the white-brick apartment house beginning to grow from the ruins of the gasworks across the street.

"Where exactly are my jockey shorts, Timothy?"

"I was hoping to steal them." He laughed. "Try under the plaid blanket, near the radio."

Fuller dressed in the gathering darkness, but with only a sandwich awaiting him, Tim lingered in the makeshift bed. Fuller glimpsed his face in the orange glow of the space heater; it looked like some small ornament lit by a Christmas bulb. Its cheer and serenity prompted him to remember the expression's opposite, a face Tim had shown during an especially tormented moment back in the early days, while he'd been explaining yet another spiritual infraction he was afraid of committing.

"Tell me, Skippy. Why give up *anything* for Lent when you're not even taking Communion?"

"I *am* taking Communion." Tim's eyes remained closed and he was smiling. He seemed to be falling asleep, pleasantly exhausted.

It was becoming clear to Fuller that Skippy now believed everything between them to have been somehow miraculously sanctified; he seemed to have reached the conclusion that he, too, could live as a bigamist. Just as Hawkins Fuller could go home to Lucy, Timothy Laughlin could go home to God—until it was again time to meet here, which the two of them would keep doing until the house was torn down, at which point they would presumably start going to the "place not far from where you used to be on I Street."

From the moment he had allowed things to resume, Fuller had feared that Tim would end up making trouble, would become a hysterical version of Tony Bianco, threatening a scene—not for money but assurance, for some further allotment of affection. One morning he would show up on the Fullers' suburban doorstep, wracked with anger and some fresh twist of biblical shame.

But here he was: happy, calm, wanting not so much as a second "I love you." He had taken, it seemed, some vow of emotional poverty that he was willing to keep six days a week, if only on the seventh, or close enough, he could be released from it here. He would grow old in this city, become like all the other skinny, obedient clerks and bookshelvers keeping their heads down at the Library of Congress, the ones who'd come to town years before to escape the fists and cruelties of their fathers and the village hearties. He'd learn to cook, to go to Sunday-afternoon concerts at the Coolidge Auditorium with his chums. He'd save his money to go see the occasional musical in tryouts on its way to New York. He'd lose the political zealotry, once he finally realized politics to be no more than the widgets turned out by this particular company town. The religious quaverings would subside, too, displaced into solemn, furtive acknowledgment of "Mr. Fuller" when they passed in the corridor, and into more flamboyant weekly worship of the same in the little place off I Street, where a picture of the beloved would be kept out in a frame near the record player, except when Fuller himself or anyone other than Skippy's fellow nelly clerks came to visit.

Timothy Laughlin would not be the big trouble that Hawkins Fuller feared, the trouble against which Lucy's money would shield him. No, Skippy would be a grim safe harbor, one that would trap him in a domesticity even danker than the one across the river in Alexandria. The thrill of protectiveness and ravishment would be long gone, replaced with a cup of coffee and a slice of cake and an ongoing obligation to fuck the good little aging boy who had "given up everything"—the nelly clerks would start to tell him—for Hawkins Fuller.

Dressed now, Fuller lay back down on the blankets and took Tim in his arms. The two of them wriggled around until they were spooning, with Tim holding Hawk from behind, momentarily falling asleep against his back, while Fuller faced the turret's circular wall. Unheard by Tim, he whispered: "I'm sorry."

And he was, he thought; maybe even more than he knew.

As he started down H Street toward the office and his Plymouth, Fuller passed the worst of the neighborhood's gingerbread shanties and wondered just how impressed the Negroes of Foggy Bottom were by the knowledge that one of their own, the State Department's Dr. Ralph Bunche, had been dispatched to sort things out in the Middle East. Fuller imagined that the feds would eventually name a park for Bunche somewhere along here, probably once the last of the Negroes had been priced out of the area.

He entered State on Twenty-first Street and found a couple of people still in the bureau. He half hoped that Mr. Hill might be there to see him returning to his desk at such a late hour. Inside his office he hung up his tweed overcoat and then his suit jacket, both of them smelling faintly of the brewer's condemned love nest.

The news clippings that filled his In box showed Dulles and Ike talking to Macmillan in Bermuda, where last month, lying on a chaise longue in her swimsuit, Lucy had at last begun to look pregnant. Someone had also dropped on his desk a memo announcing that Llewellyn Thompson would now move from the Austrian embassy to the Russian. No cookie pusher he, everyone agreed, though Fuller and Mr. Hill would still have to make a few mollifying visits to the SOB before he could be confirmed. Styles Bridges, for one, would almost certainly be among those claiming that Thompson had been a little too sympathetic to "our so-called Soviet allies" back when he'd been the second secretary in Moscow during the war. Someone might also note that the nominee hadn't married until he was forty-four.

Fuller made his shirtsleeved way back out of the office and into the corridor; he then took the stairs down to Osborne's office in Eastern European Affairs. Alas, his handball partner and everyone else in EEA had gone for the day, just as Hungary had gone from being an emergency to an ordinary geopolitical given.

Starting back for his own office, Fuller decided—all at once and instead—to travel the most direct route toward accomplishing the task he had in mind.

The door to the Miscellaneous M Unit stood open, surely a first and no doubt because of an ambassadorial appointment that would be even more widely discussed than Thompson's: Scott McLeod's rumored, imminent dispatch to the Dublin embassy, a reward for the years of scrubbing he'd done here and a quiet way of saying that that job might at last be done. Even so, McLeod would have his Senate enemies as surely as Thompson had his. Hence the open door: no harm showing off the friendly informality with which his operation had done its business at State.

Fred Traband was putting on his coat. "May I help you?" he asked.

"Fuller. Congressional Relations."

"Oh, right." Traband's look of friendly recognition was replaced by disdain. He tried to recall any word he'd had about Fuller's being summoned once again. Perhaps this time the Harvard man had done something so flagrant he wouldn't be able to fool the machine.

"It's about a fellow who's getting close to a refugee-relief job."

"What about him?" Traband asked.

"He's got a few problems in the area you once questioned me about. For his sake and the department's I think the appointment ought to be blocked right now, before some Hungarian begins blackmailing him to get asylum."

Make it easy on him.

Traband's expression softened. Maybe he'd been wrong about Fuller all along. Or maybe the guy had experienced the sort of behavioral conversion that the Miscellaneous M Unit always insisted was possible. He looked at his watch. "I'm running late," he said. "But the boss is still here. Why don't you go in and give him a word to the wise?"

How to Be a Man, thought Fuller, in the last seconds before he shook hands with Scott McLeod.

CHAPTER THIRTY-NINE

April 21–22, 1957

The Laughlins' Easter dinner was taking place in Stuyvesant Town, Grandma Gaffney having at last ceded her holiday territory with the proviso that this was her absolute limit: she would never get on a ferry to Staten Island.

"Those damned priests take advantage of you every whichaway," she was now telling her grandson. She did not like the idea that Tim was working for sandwiches and pocket money.

"It's *charity*," Francy explained for her brother. "It's something *good*." In fact she did think it strange that Tim had been doing unpaid church work for three solid months.

"*Don't* think of it as charity, Grandma," said Tim in his own defense. "Think of it as a good investment, like those two shares of AT&T stock that Grandpa used to have, the ones that kept splitting."

He was the only one allowed to tease her, but while the others all laughed, she just stared at him, a vision of the prodigal, and wished through her tight-set lips that Francy's horrible little daughter would stop romping around the room.

For everyone at the table, Tim's return had been more the focus of the day than their new outfits from Gimbel's or even the turkey. Finally moist, now that its preparation had shifted to Mrs. Laughlin, it still owed its presence on the table to Grandma Gaffney, who insisted that ham was something the Protestants served on Easter. "Does she know she's aligning herself with the Jews?" Francy had whispered to her brother when the porkless platter emerged from the kitchen.

"I wish you were still working for Joe!" declared Uncle Frank, who'd never fully conceded the fact that his nephew had actually worked for

Senator Potter. "He'll be back yet, you wait and see! They say he's going to be leading the charge for this fellow McLeod. The English papers are supposed to be up in arms because we're sending the Irish a 'cop' for an ambassador. They seem to think his methods are a little too *tough*—that he's been spreadin' all that fear through the precious State Department. For *them* to complain about anyone being unworthy of Ireland! Let's talk about the methods *they've* used over there for three hundred years. You don't, by the way, hear the Irish themselves complaining about McLeod, now do you?"

Rosemary Laughlin touched Tim's hand and remarked, feelingly, upon the "perfect weather for a perfect Easter." Still shy with her son after such a long separation, she asked him about the Egg Roll on the White House lawn. "*You'd* like to be there, *wouldn't* you?" she said to little Maria Loretta.

Tim explained that the Eisenhowers were actually spending the weekend in Georgia.

"Speaking of eggs," declared Uncle Frank. "*He* needs to be a little more hard-boiled."

The men at the table, even Uncle Alan, had grown more and more impatient with the chief executive. They seemed to be waiting for Nixon the way Fred Bell was, according to Mary; the prospect of an Irish alternative held no interest for them. "For Christ's sake," Uncle Frank had said a little earlier of John Kennedy, "his *father* went to Harvard." Nixon, Protestant though he might be, suggested the solid strivers who'd sat beside Paul Laughlin on all those nights and Saturdays he'd studied for his accounting certificate from LaSalle.

Tim scooped up Maria Loretta on one of her passes through the room. "You don't need the White House lawn," he said, "but I'll bet you *would* like all the cherry and dogwood blossoms that are out." He stroked the girl's shiny brown hair and agreed with her that dogwood was a funny name for a tree.

And as he looked at her he thought of Hawkins Fuller's daughter.

On Tuesday, he and Hawk had had plans to meet in the Foggy Bottom house at four-thirty, after Hawk got through on the Hill trying to shame a House committee into giving the Voice of America the full hundred and forty million dollars Ike had requested for it. But when Tim got to the turret, he found a note that Hawk had left atop the blankets only minutes before: "Catching cab to Georgetown U Hospital following premature birth of Susan Lydia Boardman Fuller. Barely five pounds. Say your beads for her."

Tim had spent part of this morning's Mass praying for the baby, whose sudden existence fascinated and repelled him. He felt glad that this extension of Hawkins Fuller into the world was a girl: a boy would have somehow made for a dilution of Hawk himself. Susan's being female allowed Tim to think that the baby belonged really to *her*, to Lucy, in the way a child's Jewishness was said to be passed to it through the mother. And yet, truth required him to admit that Hawk had helped to put this life into the world; its creation was something the two of them, *he* and Hawk, could never achieve together.

As he worried his way through all this once more, Francy tried to keep her eyes off her brother. But she thought she saw his mood taking one of the several dips it had in the hours since her arrival here this morning. She got up to clear the dishes.

Tim meanwhile tried to cheer himself with the thought that Hawk had also brought life back to *him*. The adultery they were committing was *their* creation, a sin the two of them were building together, and from which Lucy was forever excluded. This morning in church he'd prayed not just that Hawk's daughter be healthy, but that the lurid new light burning within himself not be scuppered like the last candle after the last Mass.

They had met only once since the afternoon when "These Foolish Things" had played on the radio. It had been a rushed encounter, Hawk acting the way Tim could remember from some mornings three years before—studiously brisk; lustful and withdrawn all at once. He had ascribed the behavior to worry over Lucy's increasingly difficult pregnancy. The premature birth had convinced him of it. The remoteness was inevitable, and nothing much to worry about. Think, too, of the note Hawk had left in the turret: for him to have been mindful of their afternoon rendezvous even at a time like that!

As he retold himself all this, his spirits came back up. "I'm going to do the dishes with Francy," he announced. "See, Grandma? Everything's exactly the same. Even here in Stuyvesant Town."

It was Tim's father who replied to this observation. Though he was the family striver, the agent of its transformative ascent, Paul Laughlin now declared, with a sudden wistfulness, "*Nothing* stays the same. Did you hear the pope this morning? Talking about atomic energy?"

He had been relieved to see his son, though he suspected that Tim was traveling on thin ice, carrying secrets that looked even now, while the boy walked to the kitchen, as if they might make the floor give way beneath him.

At the sink Tim washed and Francy dried, and the ventilating fan blew the last of the kitchen's cooking smells into the Stuyvesant Oval.

"You wouldn't let me do this a few Christmases back," Francy recalled. "I was pregnant with Maria. You may even have mentioned my 'condition.' "

"Did I?" Tim asked, laughing. "Well, it was a productive worry. See how healthy she turned out?"

"I hope the next one will, too." She rapped the wooden board beneath the dish drainer.

"*Are* you?"

"Yes, and believe me, in our neighborhood, you go three years without dropping another, people think something's *very* wrong."

"Do you want to sit down?" He pointed to a stool by the broom closet.

"Don't be ridiculous. But let's sit down together." She turned the faucets off.

"Lent's over," she said, handing him a cigarette as they settled themselves at the small table. "Talk to me."

"Bless me, Sister, for I have . . ."

"That's not a bad beginning. Keep going."

"I'm fine."

"You've been telling me that for three years now."

She reached back to the counter and picked up the cuff links he'd removed from his shirt when he started on the dishes. She pressed them into his hand. "I still don't know who 'Hawkins Fuller' is, but one of these Christmases or Easters that old lady will finally be dead"—she pointed back to the living room and Grandma Gaffney—"and while she's down there complaining about too few Jews being in Hell—"

Tim began to laugh, evasively. Francy pressed the cuff links harder against the palm of his hand.

"—I'll finally be cooking the dinner on Staten Island, where there'll be two children, no more, and my sullen son of a bitch of a husband." Over her brother's nervous, lighthearted protest, she continued: "And I want you to know that whoever this person is"—she pressed the cuff links even harder into Tim's hand—"he's always welcome in my house."

Tim spent the next morning in the city, shopping with his mother at Gristede's and then having an early lunch in midtown with his father. He talked to each of them about the job he still expected to come through before long. They asked him no questions that could be deemed personal, though he suspected Francy had urged them to. As it was, he took their reticence to be a manifestation of love, not self-protection.

He had, God forgive him, deflected Francy's own proffering of love. Forcing the cuff links into his palm had been a kind of secret handshake, and it had spooked him. Ending their conversation with a joke about the stigmata, he'd given her a peck on the cheek and turned the faucets back on.

His money had started running low, but after lunch with his father he went into Brentano's and bought James Michener's *The Bridge at Andau.* Amazed that a book about Hungary could be brought out so fast, like a magazine, he carried it aboard his bus at the Port Authority, where he looked north toward Forty-third Street and wondered whether Hawk's clarinet player could still be living there five years after Ike's rally at the Garden.

He was halfway through Michener's book by the time the Greyhound pulled into the District. Inside the doorway beneath Ken and Gloria's loft, he collected his mail and took it upstairs, his heart hammering at the sight of the State Department envelope, and pounding even harder once he tore it open and, above the signature "Leonard F. Osborne," saw the words "regret" and "due to security considerations" and "unable to offer you."

He stuffed the letter into his pocket and raced back downstairs, not knowing where he was going. He wanted to call Hawk at the office, but he couldn't bother him while the baby might still be in jeopardy. Besides, it was now past six; Hawk had probably left for home, and even for something as bad as this, Tim would not break his vow never to dial the number in Alexandria.

At the door to the street he found Woodforde, lighting a cigarette on his way out. A queasy, dyspeptic look played across the writer's face. "If I marry this girl," he said, "I'm going to wind up skinnier than you."

They started down F Street together.

"I didn't get the job," said Tim, thunderstruck all over again by verbalizing the news.

He couldn't tell Woodforde about the "security considerations," which, after all, had to be about *that*. True, Woodforde had expressed his own belief in the inconsequence of such things—*I don't care about you and Fuller, that's your own business*—but it was still too shaming to admit to himself, let alone anyone else, that he might *be* a security risk. He realized that he felt *guilty*, not angry, and he wondered helplessly how Osborne's people could have known.

"Sorry, kid," said Woodforde, sincerely. "You know, there are a hundred ways for you to help out the Hungarians and get paid for it without having to be inside Dulles's closed shop."

Tim counterfeited some cheer. "You're right. And I'd better find at least one of them if I'm going to make my—I should say *your*—rent."

"Don't worry about that. Listen, you want to copyedit *Armed and Dangerous*? The girl doing it in New York stinks, and I've got a little bit left of the advance that I can pay you with. McIntyre once told me your grammar is 'cleaner than a nun's shaved scalp.' "

"Thanks," Tim replied, abstractedly. "I'll think about it. But right now I've got to go in the other direction. I'll see you tomorrow."

"Okay, take it easy, Laughlin. Everything's going to be all right." Woodforde watched him walk away and then called out after him: "Come Cohn or come Schine!"

Tim tramped across the city for nearly an hour, all the way up to Georgetown. Passing two little French restaurants on M Street, he proceeded farther north, making himself believe that he was headed toward Mary's, though in fact he had another destination, a dangerous one, in mind. He wanted to see Hawkins' daughter.

He would just glimpse her behind the incubator's glass; no one ever had to know he'd come and gone. Since visiting hours would already be over when he arrived, this wouldn't really be a visit; he'd find some nurse who would let him take a peek, and while he stood in front of the window, a little like Stella Dallas, he'd be able to figure out what he'd been feeling about the child's presence in the world. The prayer he'd say for her would be made more potent by familiarity with its object.

A receptionist scolded him for showing up so late, past eight o'clock, and looked at him suspiciously before imparting the good news that Mrs. Fuller, after six nights here, had been discharged this afternoon. Moreover, the baby was thriving sufficiently to have gone home with her.

He thanked the woman and asked for directions to the chapel. She reminded him that it was late but allowed as how he could make a quick stop.

He prayed not for Susan Fuller but for himself; for steadiness. He told himself that he was just tired from the bus ride and weak from missing supper. He'd been rattled by the kind of bad news everybody has to put up with once in a while. Not getting the job might be a disappointment, but Woodforde was right: there were other ways to be useful. And while the mention of "security considerations" left him fearful, all of that might still be a mistake, or part of some generalized tightening-up that had nothing to do with him in particular.

Hawk loved him, and Hawk's child was healthy.

He prayed that Mary's would be healthy, too, and he promised, if he could think of a way, that he would help it, even after it had been adopted. He'd already told Mary he would take her to the airport on Wednesday, but he should ask if she wanted him to go to New Orleans, as company for the weeks ahead. He could stay at the rooming house on Dauphine Street, or even with Mr. Shaw, Tristan's sword lying between them.

For now he would find his way to a streetcar. He would go back to the loft, and tomorrow he would pack boxes at St. Mary's.

He would ask for no more than he already had, and things would yet be well.

CHAPTER FORTY

April 24, 1957

Mary dialed Eastern Airlines to confirm her late-afternoon nonstop to New Orleans. Seven months and two weeks was awfully late to be flying, but no one would notice anything under her boxy spring coat. Beverly and Jerry Baumeister were in the other room. They'd come to say good-bye and pick up a set of keys for the wealthy girl in Senator Douglas's office whom Beverly had found to sublet the furnished apartment for six months. The outside date meant nothing; Mary knew that she'd never be back.

"I'll be right out," she called.

"Take your time, we're fighting," answered Beverly.

Beverly and Jerry had treated Mary to a big late breakfast and, having both taken the day off, were now deciding whether to see a lunchtime showing of *Funny Face* or *Moulin Rouge*.

Jerry had been arguing for the latter, but Beverly conceded nothing to her spouse: "It's five years old and it's got Zsa Zsa Gabor. Why are they bringing it back to the MacArthur *now*?"

"To show solidarity with the Hungarians?"

Husband and wife laughed.

"Maybe to catch the overflow of Francophiles who can't get into *Funny Face*," said Mary, entering the room.

"Come with us," Jerry and Beverly urged in unison.

"I can't. Really."

Beverly saw that she meant it, and she nudged Jerry to get moving. "Okay," she said, tapping her purse. "I'll give Kay the keys tomorrow morning. I tell you, she's right out of *The Philadelphia Story*. God, Mary,

I thought *you* were sort of blue-blooded when we first met. And *so beautiful*. You, not her. I remember the first time you walked into the bureau." She burst into tears.

Mary put her arm around Beverly. Jerry looked on, as hopelessly as any other male would have.

"Your *baby's* going to be beautiful, too," Beverly predicted.

"Probably fatter than Fred," guessed Mary.

"Don't *stay* down there," Beverly insisted. "Don't disappear as if you're doing penance. Promise you'll come back."

"Back to *what*?"

"Back to *us*. And back to whoever else is just around the corner."

"You mean Mr. Right?"

"Yes. Or Mr. Second Right." She pointed to Jerry.

"Second right!" he cried. "I'm not just *around* the corner. I *am* the corner. Come on," he said to his wife. "Time for Zsa Zsa, dahlink."

He embraced Mary, and when he pulled away he, too, had tears in his eyes. They were both remembering that night at the Occidental. *Do you know what they do with guys like me in Russia?*

He took Beverly's arm—all three of them were crying now—while she handed Mary a small box. "It's a bon voyage gift, *not* a farewell present. And it's for *you*, not for—you know." She meant the baby, but that suddenly seemed too painful to say; the infant wouldn't be in Mary's possession long enough to prompt anyone's gift-giving.

Mary nodded. "I'll write," she promised, kissing Beverly.

When the Baumeisters were gone, she sat down on one of the freshly vacuumed couch cushions. She was wondering whether to open the little box when the phone rang.

Fuller's voice came through the receiver. "I never remembered to disconnect mine, either. The missus had to remind me to."

She supposed he knew everything after all. And why should she be surprised by that? Or surprised by his having waited until the last minute to be in touch?

"I've switched the service over to the Vassar girl who's moving in tomorrow," she explained, as matter-of-factly as possible.

"Go downstairs in five minutes. A cab will be waiting to take you to me."

"Fuller, I'm not going to the department."

"You're going to Quigley's drugstore. Near GWU. I'll be at the soda fountain."

"Why don't you just drive here in your Plymouth? My plane doesn't leave for hours."

"I know. It leaves at five-forty-five. But there *is* no Plymouth this week. It's out in Alexandria at the disposal of the nurse taking care of my little girl."

"How is she?"

"Remarkable. Very small but very calm. Quite discriminating. Stand-offish, I'd say. We call her Garbo."

I want to be alone. She almost said it, but it wasn't true. She was all at once nervous and again wanting company, even his. "If there's no Plymouth, why don't *you* take a cab here?"

"I don't want to be around if you have a surprise visitor, which is to say, if Skippy gets there early. Come on, head downstairs. The cabbie will be honking his horn any minute."

She was soon at Quigley's, on a stool, drinking the malted Fuller had already ordered for her.

He sipped a glass of seltzer, and for a minute or two they said nothing.

"So, he told you," she finally said.

"He told me."

"As of Friday, when I last talked to him, I'd have believed he hadn't."

"And you'd have been right. He never said a word until yesterday afternoon. When he called the office."

She said nothing, just wondered why Tim had told him then and not before.

"He called to ask after the baby," Fuller explained. "And about another matter. Also, of course, to set up a rendezvous."

"In the turret."

"His little castle in Spain."

She pushed away the malted and swiveled the stool, as if it were her typist's chair, so that she could face him. "You condescending, buck-passing bastard," she declared, as evenly as she could. "It's your romance, too. You *found* the castle for it."

"You're right. It was my romance, too."

Her hand went, involuntarily, to her stomach. It rested there, protectively, for a moment. " 'Was'? Does he know that?"

"No. He's dealing with a vocational setback right now."

The answer's coolness was, she realized, too much even for Fuller. The display of *sang-froid* suggested the opposite, an agitation that had prompted him to summon her here.

"Did he not get the job?" was all she asked.

"He did not get the job."

"That was the 'other matter' he called you about."

"Yes, but he wound up chattering mostly of you. In those little grammatical torrents that issue from him when he's nervous, as if he's reciting the Apostles' Creed. He was sentimental. For some reason he couldn't bear the idea of your leaving without *our* saying goodbye, you and me."

"Tell me what happened with the job."

"Osborne sent him a letter."

"I thought it was more or less settled, a sure thing."

" 'Security considerations' arose."

"About *him*?"

"Yes. I mean, they're obvious enough, aren't they?"

"How exactly were they obvious to Osborne? Or let's say more obvious than they would have been in February."

Fuller didn't answer. But when she looked at him, she knew. More than that, she knew that he *wanted* her to know—just as surely as Tim had once wanted to make a sincere confession to his priest, or some of Jerry's terrified friends had tried to tell McLeod's lie detector even more than they'd been asked to.

"You did this," she at last whispered.

Fuller took a sip of seltzer and regarded the countertop.

"Did you decide, after all, that he was *inconvenient*?" she asked in a furious whisper. "*This* is inconvenient, Fuller." She placed his hand on her stomach. "But it's mine—mine at least to ease into the world. Too bad there's no one down on F Street that you could pay a hundred and twenty-five dollars to to have Tim killed."

For all her disgust, her sense that he had done the most despicable thing possible, another part of her felt grateful to him, because what made the act despicable also made it definitive, the surest means of ending what had to end, now or later, with Tim's broken heart. And she knew, looking at Fuller, that his reasoning matched her own.

"You think you did this for *his* sake, don't you?" she asked. "You've convinced yourself of that, haven't you?"

"No, I did it for me. You'll do the other part, the part that's for his sake."

"And how will I do that, Fuller?"

"By putting me beyond the pale."

"You want me to tell him the truth."

"Make it hard on him."

She got down from the stool and closed her coat. A coed who was with her boyfriend smiled, enviously, in her direction. She wondered, absurdly, whether she could get a cab outside Quigley's or would have to walk to the main entrance of the department to find one.

"What about you?" asked Fuller.

"Me?"

"Were *you* ever in love with me?"

He asked it with an absence of ego, just a kind of sympathetic curiosity, taking the opportunity to tie up a loose end.

"No," she answered.

"Well, that's one small blessing."

"I wish it had been otherwise," she said.

"Why?"

"Because then I'd be able to forgive you."

She brushed past the coed, and he called out to her, with surprising gentleness: "You already have."

The ticket agent handed Mary a complimentary flight bag for her incidentals. Reaching for it with her left arm, she thought she saw the agent noting the absence of a wedding ring on the hand of this pregnant passenger. But maybe she was imagining things. She put her small purse and Beverly's gift inside the bag, which she left unzipped, before heading back to the departures lounge. Tim was still getting her luggage weighed—four suitcases full of separates and shirtwaists and books—and preparing to pay the overcharges.

He looked comically gallant, and sitting here, sipping her glass of sherry, she thought it ridiculous that she should need his help. She had recently decided that the essential cause of her plight, what had brought her here, was a fatal self-sufficiency, an inner chilliness that had left her unable to settle for Paul or fight for Fred. She was an engine that couldn't turn over; the only state of mind she could fully embrace was hesitation, a conviction that to accept one man or life was to forfeit another. She couldn't welcome or destroy even the baby that was quickening within her.

Maybe she didn't love Fuller because he was her emotional kinsman; maybe a small part of him did love Tim, just not a large or brave enough part to rout the others standing guard over the inviolable self.

Tim returned with a glass of milk and piece of pie.

"You should be having this," he said, offering the milk. "For Estonia's sake."

They tried to grin.

"Here," said Mary, giving him twenty dollars. "For the cabs and the overcharges. You'll need it to get home."

"Not on your life. I'll be working soon. Though not as soon as I'd hoped, it seems."

She said nothing.

"The job at State fell through," he explained. "Osborne's office sent me a letter saying I couldn't satisfy their 'security considerations.' Fuller says it's just somebody's bureaucratic reflex kicking in. That it's unfair but actually means nothing. He says the whole operation will change before long, and it's just my bad luck to be coming through before McLeod can get over to Ireland."

"No," Mary said firmly. "That won't change it."

"Honest, Mary, I don't understand it. I lived a perfectly clean life in the army, and there isn't a soul here besides you who knows about the way things are now between me and Hawk. Not even Woodforde. Not even Tommy McIntyre." This last name, his own unexpected utterance of it, made him go pale for a moment. "You don't suppose that, based just on the old days, '53 and '54, he could have—"

"It wasn't McIntyre."

"Well, it wasn't you. There's nobody else."

"It was Fuller."

"That's not so."

Make it hard on him.

"I saw Fuller this morning," she declared.

"No, you didn't. You would have told me before now."

"They call the baby 'Garbo.' I'll bet he told you the same thing."

He clenched his fist on top of the table. She pushed aside the milk and the pie and put her hand over his.

"No" was all he said—not a denial, just a refusal of her attention. He freed his hand but made no other protest. He looked at her like a technician reading a faulty instrument, one that had reported a flat scan when everybody knew there had to be a pulse. Once more he said "No," before getting up. He nodded at her, as if she were a stranger he'd sat down with by mistake, and he turned to go.

A strong impulse made her reach inside the flight bag and extract Beverly's present. She handed it to him, quickly, as if it were an illegal payoff she'd been assigned to pass along.

As she pressed it on him, she could feel a mutation of the gift's meaning. The box—she had looked inside before leaving the apartment—contained a glass paperweight, a sprig of cherry blossom suspended in colorless amber. It had been Beverly's way of telling her to come back to Washington. Now it was her way of saying to Tim that he would never come back here, but that what had happened between him and Fuller, however finished, remained alive somewhere, as sad and frozen and perfect as the blossoms on the branch.

So would her baby, forever ungrasped and unvisited by its mother, remain somewhere alive, still remembered and still real.

CHAPTER FORTY-ONE

May 6, 1957

The doors of St. Matthew's stood open, so Monsignor Cartwright's microphoned words about the dearly departed were able to travel not only to the seated congregants but all the way to those on the steps outside.

The deceased, everyone was assured, "had played a role which will be more and more honored as history unfolds its record." After all, Monsignor Cartwright reminded those assembled, the "watchman of the citadel" had had "the fortitude to stand alone."

"Never 'alone,' " whispered Cecil Holland, out on the steps, to Mary McGrory. "Not as long as Roy was around."

Miss McGrory flipped her pad back two or three pages. Its Gregg-shorthand squiggles had caught all the monsignor's comfortings and regrets, including his observation that "few public figures in our time have done so much for the United States and received so many heartaches for it" as the man now on his way to eternal rest.

Joe McCarthy had died Thursday night from a "liver ailment." Some said he'd gone peacefully, with Jean at his side, while others had him tearing at the IV tubes and bedsheets in a fit of delirium tremens. Whatever the truth, there would be three ceremonies to bid him farewell: the Mass here this morning; an afternoon service in the Senate chamber; a grave-side rite in Wisconsin tomorrow.

When the first of these ended and the mourners were ready to leave St. Matthew's, the vice president was at the front of them, descending the steps with his wife and Alice Roosevelt Longworth. Spectators were hard pressed to see anyone else from the administration emerge, and Nixon took care to speak to a wire-service reporter more in the manner of a political scientist than a politician: "Years will pass before Senator McCarthy's work can be objectively evaluated."

On Friday night at Gawler's funeral home, Tim had stood in a long line of the mournful, the curious, and the silently triumphant, waiting to file past the open casket in which McCarthy reposed. Despite the mortician's art, the corpse had looked nearly as gray as his tie. Two and a half hours ago, Tim had arrived at St. Matthew's early enough to have gotten a seat, but he had his suitcase with him, and it had seemed somehow disrespectful, not just awkward, to take it inside. So he'd stayed on the steps, watching the eight Marines bring McCarthy's closed coffin into the church.

Senator Kennedy was now exiting, his left hand in his suit pocket, his right hand brushing back his hair. He moved fast, almost furtively, as if departing from some questionable assignation. He breezed past his colleague, Senator Saltonstall, who, a few feet from Tim, was talking with Senator Martin about how the GOP was now down to forty-six seats. Miss McGrory and Mr. Holland began moving down the steps, the better to overhear this conversation, prompting Tim to sidle into a nearby clutch of observers, lest he be spotted by his former colleagues from the *Star*.

Even so, he was still able to hear them.

"Jack didn't look as banged up about all this as his papa," observed Holland. Joseph P. Kennedy had released a statement to the press that outdid even Monsignor Cartwright in paying tribute to the deceased. But Miss McGrory and Holland agreed that for cryptic brevity nothing could top Harry Truman's reaction to news of the senator's death: "Too bad."

Fred Bell, looking like a plump, boutonniered floorwalker at Hecht's, passed in front of Tim, who recognized him from an armband with the colors of the Estonian flag, as well as from the description, half comical and half longing, that he'd been given by Mary. According to her, Fred still didn't know he was the father of a child ready to be born in New Orleans.

Joe Alsop now marched down the steps, nodding hello to Betty Beale and looking satisfied that the unpleasant business of McCarthy's life, however abbreviated, was over at last. Close behind him came Scott McLeod, obliging the reporter at his side with a comment: "As I said in my Senate testimony on Friday, those criticisms of my appointment that are coming from abroad represent extreme minority elements."

"Is your work at State really done?" the reporter asked.

"To my knowledge no subversive personnel remain in the department."

Tim had fervently wished to avoid Tommy McIntyre, yet here he came, without Senator Potter, as happy as if he'd been to a christening.

"Mr. Laughlin!" he cried. "Christ, what a send-off from all the boys in their long skirts! I counted nineteen monsignors and seventy-three priests. I am not kidding." He showed Tim a small notebook in which he'd written down the figures.

"A page back from that—go on, flip it—you'll find the eulogy I'm trying to put into Charlie's mouth."

Those who had the opportunity to be with the late senator on social occasions or when chatting with him in his office knew that, regardless of differences which might have existed on political issues, Joe was never vindictive. He was a warm, human, and exceptionally charming person.

"Didn't you find that yourself, Timothy? Didn't he strike you as such? He'll be the first solon since Borah to be laid out in the chamber. A lovely touch—to follow the great Prohibitionist with a drunkard. The final seal of repeal!"

Tommy's failure to get a rise out of Tim, whose face remained weary and blank, inspired the Irishman to more strenuous rhetorical effort. Looking like the kind of gargoyle this plain American cathedral lacked, he hardly moved his rictus as the words came forth in a cackling spray: "Of course Charlie may be too much in *demand* to render this paean just yet. You should have seen him Friday night at the Mayflower! Receivin' he was the annual award of the Goodwill Industries people. 'Outstanding Champion' of the nation's handicapped. I must say, even the blinking canes couldn't compete with the other honoree, a crippled telephone operator from Florida who dials with her feet and types with her mouth." Ready to demonstrate the latter action, Tommy stuck a pencil between his yellow teeth. Revulsion at last gave Tim the energy to move, even if the only escape route would take him past Miss McGrory.

But she was occupied fending off a fierce scolding from a woman with a big red-white-and-blue cockade stuck to her hat. "Your paper writes malicious nonsense!" the woman insisted. "There is *no* possibility Mrs. McCarthy's baby will be taken from her. One-year 'probationary period' or not."

Miss McGrory nodded forbearingly and explained that she harbored no desire to see Tierney McCarthy returned to the New York Foundling Hospital.

The woman wheeled around to resume her march down the cathedral's steps, and Tim realized it was Miss Lightfoot, showing the distress of a radiation victim. He tried to move away, not because he expected to be recognized, but from pity at the garish sight of her, unglimpsed since the anticensure rally at the Garden. But her own baleful eye took him in and made the identification.

"You!" she cried, before lowering her voice to a sickening baby-talk imitation of the inscription he'd once made in the Lodge biography. " 'You're wonderful.' Well, your Mr. Wonderful was sitting right up near the front of the church, did you know that? With his boss, Mr. Hill. Offering their politic homage to Senator McCarthy, whom they thwarted during every single minute he was alive. And how is it Mr. Fuller even now *has* a boss and a job in that cesspool over there?" She pointed toward Foggy Bottom. "Because there are *still* people who protect his kind, McLeod or no McLeod."

Attracted by Miss Lightfoot's again-increasing volume, people began to stare. Tim struggled to get past her, needing to flee before Hawk, who he'd never imagined would be here, came down the steps and saw him. Tightening his grip on his suitcase, he thought he was managing to get to the other side of Miss Lightfoot when her hand was able to reach out and detain him long enough so that she could whisper, straight into his face: "*Cocksucker.*"

Finally at the bottom of the steps, he looked back up them like the tourist who never again expects to see the Acropolis. It was at this moment that he caught sight of Woodforde near the cathedral's doors.

The writer noticed him, too. Concerned by the suitcase, he made a gesture that asked: "What gives?"

Tim responded with a reassuring wave, but Woodforde knew better. He cupped his hands near his mouth and forcefully called out: "Don't." He'd sensed that something had gone very wrong between Laughlin and Fuller—and the single suitcase could hold just about everything Tim had in his part of the loft.

"You look awful!" Woodforde called down the steps.

"Thanks!" answered Tim, hoping to sound humorous, before making a getaway down Rhode Island Avenue. He had most of the day ahead of him before his bus was scheduled to leave: he'd gotten the cheapest fare, on a coach that wouldn't get its passengers to New York until after midnight. Even with Woodforde's copyediting money, four months at St. Mary, Mother of God had finished off his savings; for the first time in his life he wasn't sure where he'd be sleeping tonight. He'd not told his parents or Francy he was coming, and he couldn't picture himself arriving on either doorstep in the middle of the night. What he would do tomorrow, once he woke up, seemed even harder to imagine.

He wished, God forgive him, that he *wouldn't* wake up. Two weeks had done nothing to lessen his black realization that this time he had not renounced Hawk—oh, the noble ridiculousness of his two-year enlistment!—but that Hawk had renounced him.

He went into the Peoples drugstore to get a half pint of milk before taking his seat on the bench in Dupont Circle, where he knew he'd been heading all along.

He understood that Mary had revealed what she had at the airport—*It was Fuller*—to shock and toughen him, as if a bucket of the coldest water might effect his Lazarene rise from the stupor of unwise love. But he'd walked all the way home that afternoon feeling strangely certain he'd become invisible.

Yesterday he'd sat on another bench, on the Mall, watching smoke rise a thousand feet into the air: the Johnson & Wimsatt lumber yard, down on Maine Avenue above the docks where Mary used to buy fish, had burned to the ground, requiring every fire company in the city. Remembering, as the catechism had long ago told him, that despair is a particular affront to God—the rejection of every good He might still have in store for one—he had wished he were rising on the columns of smoke, incinerated but released, upward and gone.

He had decided to leave last night, while the radio was broadcasting the arrangements for McCarthy's funeral. He would go to St. Matthew's on the same commemorative impulse that had taken him to Gawler's and that had now brought him here. Before going to the church, he had made up his mind that he would stand where he'd stood after the wedding; he'd blend into the crowd and then he would go, would begin to get lost—so thoroughly he'd be untraceable even to Mr. Keen.

At the cathedral he had found half the cast of the old lights-camera-action Caucus Room. There had even been some discussion on the steps about whether a glinting head in one of the pews, visible only from the back, might belong to G. David Schine. Tommy; Miss McGrory; the lunatic Miss Lightfoot; and, as he now knew, Hawk. The two of them had been there together, each as unaware of the other as they'd been at the Draft Ike rally back in '52.

He put a straw into the milk and looked over toward the Washington Club. Today was turning out to be as warm as the wedding day had been. It was so lovely one could imagine Jean McCarthy tossing a funeral wreath as if it were her bridal bouquet.

Closing his eyes, he realized that he'd not said so much as a single Hail Mary for the repose of McCarthy's soul. Silently, he recited one now, and followed it with one for himself. He prayed not for forgiveness or happiness or even strength, but only to make the merest murmuring demonstration to himself that he was still alive. He went on to say a third and fourth Hail Mary and decided he would recite a whole decade, even though he lacked his beads.

As he prayed, he could see the orange light of the sun on the backs of his eyelids, and then, just beyond this interior glow, he could feel the tortoiseshell frames of his glasses being lifted from his face.

"How many fingers?"

He opened his eyes and answered: "Three."

The Father, the Son, and the Holy Ghost.

"There. You're healed."

Hawkins sat down and pointed to the receding figure of his boss, Mr. Hill, from whom he'd peeled away at the edge of Dupont Circle.

"Nice day for a funeral," he continued. "McCarthy's. We were there together, Hill and I, and decided we'd walk to our next milestone in legislative diplomacy."

"Where's that?"

"The Irish embassy, up near Twenty-third. I told him I'd catch up. We're early as it is."

"And why would you be calling on *my* people?"

Even now—shocked by Hawk's sudden presence, and still smothered in despondency—he had fallen right into the old bright febrile chatter, as if he were inside the turret or back on I Street, trying to please his beloved.

"We're going up to answer a few last questions that some Hibernian-

American legislators, Democrats all, have raised about Mr. McLeod's nomination. A small meeting at which the actual Irish will be assuring the senators they have no real objections."

"Ah."

Fuller pointed to the suitcase. "Do the Hungarians no longer require their cans of Reddi-Wip? Can St. Mary really afford to give you a day off from dispatching them?"

"I thought I'd go to New York."

"For how long?"

"I don't know. Awhile."

"Two visits to your sister in the space of three weeks? After no more than three in two years? She'll be a happy woman."

They were talking as if he'd be back, when they both knew he never would; talking as if he were unaware of what Hawk had done, when they both knew that Mary had been made the instrument through which he knew everything.

Make it hard on him.

It was Fuller.

"Here," said Tim. "Take this."

He withdrew a small object, covered in a handkerchief, from the pocket of his suit jacket. Putting the thing into his own coat without unwrapping it, Fuller was aware only that it had the shape of a baseball sliced in half and was surprisingly heavy.

"I hear it was a short funeral for such a high Mass," said Tim.

"There wasn't much to eulogize. And the corpse had to get to the Senate chamber. It'll be getting there more punctually than it had been showing up of late, from what I hear."

Tim stared beyond Dupont Circle toward Massachusetts Avenue and said nothing. After a moment, Fuller rose to his feet and then pulled Tim up onto his. The taller man put his arms around the shorter one and whispered, audibly this time, "I'm sorry."

"For what?" asked Tim.

Everything, thought Fuller. But he couldn't bring himself to say it.

CHAPTER FORTY-TWO

May 7, 1957

Tim bought the *New York Mirror's* early-morning edition at the only newsstand still open inside the Port Authority and discovered that, a few hours after making his quick getaway from McCarthy's funeral, Senator Kennedy had been awarded the Pulitzer Prize for his book, *Profiles in Courage.*

Just a few buses were still coming in at one a.m., and none were going out. Tim sat on a bench near the terminal's Eighth Avenue exit and read the *Mirror's* coverage of the funeral services. By the time McCarthy's body had reached the Senate chamber, Nixon was sitting in the front row and the galleries were jammed, but only one member of the president's cabinet had shown up. Father Awalt, who had married Joe and Jean in '53, had today said the prayers from the rostrum, while Senator Flanders bowed his head and Mrs. McCarthy watched from the cloakroom doorway. A Senate page had fainted from the drama and the heat. "You never get over your first," Tim could imagine Hawk or Woodforde whispering.

And then it was over. The body had been flown back to Wisconsin, with Johnson and Knowland leading a delegation of twenty-nine senators, by no means all of them true believers on the order of Styles Bridges, who had declared that "Joe literally gave his life to preserve freedom for all Americans." One columnist was urging Jean—now past thirty, after all—to run for Joe's seat and return to Washington as the colleague of all those liberal hypocrites who'd taken up half the seats on the funeral plane.

Tim was bone tired and uncertain of where he'd be spending the night, but his suitcase, fortunately, was much lighter than any Mary had taken to the airport. He'd thrown away half his things and left behind most of the rest in Ken and Gloria's loft. So he was now still able to get out and walk, first to Ninth Avenue and then a dozen blocks north, past the Laughlins' old apartment, as well as Grandma Gaffney's, where the lights had been out, he calculated, for at least four hours. A glow from the building's basement window revealed Mr. Mancuso, the super, to be up late, probably reading the sports pages beside the coal furnace there was no need to tend on a warm night like this.

Reversing direction and walking south, he reached the corner of Eighth and Fiftieth, where he spotted a fortune-teller, a crazy, gypsy-looking woman who had placed an old television tube—apparently her crystal ball—atop an upside-down wooden vegetable crate. He wondered at his own inability to stop and consult with her, as if, after all his transgressions, that one might still be too great a sacrilege.

Back on Forty-second Street, he climbed the steps of Holy Cross Church, just as he'd climbed them on the day of his First Communion and on every other day for morning Mass before classes at the school next door. The church was unlocked, and he took a seat in a pew at the back. Close to the altar sat two derelicts whose snores seemed to issue from the empty pulpit that had once vibrated with the homilies of Father Duffy himself.

He recalled being here on V-E day, at thirteen years old, a few months before transferring across town to St. Agnes' Boys' High. He'd sat in his blue-and-gold school tie, listening to a priest describe the new world that was surely aborning—while somewhere far across it, in the Pacific, Hawkins Fuller must have been asleep on his boat, wondering when he'd be asked to help invade Japan. The distance that had lain between them then seemed no greater than the two hundred miles of tonight's bus ride. If Hawk were this minute in the pew across the aisle, the distance would still measure out to the same vastness, any separation of their flesh being the distance in life that was now, forever, unbridgeable.

Tim decided that he would not pray tonight, not so much as a single "Gloria Patri"—not because he was angry at God, or too guilty to face Him, or too exhausted; only because he felt himself floating, like a dust mote in the vacuum of space, where there was no airwave to carry his cry. He looked up to the cross and the well-muscled figure of Jesus—a body that looked too strong to perish from even the suffocation that was the real cause of death by crucifixion. He remembered the Lenten seasons he'd spent in this church, all the long weeks when purple cloth wrappings turned the statues into mummies, denying their plaster beauty to the faithful. At those times he would crave the sight of Christ's bloodied face and, even more, His arched and gleaming torso. *This is my body.* Every Sunday, even during Lent, he would take the Communion wafer onto his tongue and into his mouth, Christ's actual flesh, not the mere symbolic commemoration of the Protestants. It was Christ's body that kept him alive, kept him from Hell and darkness. Only Hawk's flesh, which he could taste even now, could have made him abjure Christ's during that first year together. And even then he had hungered for both. Now, with the collapse of the convenient folly he'd lived these last few months—*I'm still taking Communion. Just making up my own rules!*—he would be without either.

He had no idea whether the ferry sailed for Staten Island at this late hour. Francy would be sure to take him in with less alarm than his parents might display, but it might be dawn by the time he reached her. At this hour he doubted that his grandmother would open her door, not even if she recognized his voice, though maybe Mr. Mancuso would let him sleep on the cot by the furnace.

Or he could just keep himself awake in an all-night diner, until it was light.

He took his suitcase and left the church, walking west to Ninth Avenue, where he once more rounded the corner and went north, just for a block, before aimlessly starting down Forty-third Street, back in the direction of Times Square. Halfway toward Eighth, he heard the notes of a clarinet, quite soft, coming from the top floor of an old brownstone across the street. The man playing had the instrument sticking out the open window, as if the neighbors would have no grounds for complaint so long as the sound didn't travel from his apartment to theirs through the interior walls.

Tim recognized the tune being played as "No Love, No Nothin'," a funny song from the war about self-imposed chastity on the home-front. But the man was playing it in such a slow and bluesy and beautiful way that it had become another song entirely. Tim put his suitcase down on the sidewalk and stood to listen, realizing now who the clarinet player was.

I had an assignation that night with a musician. Who does things you haven't even dreamed of.

He wasn't especially good-looking. Crew-cut and stringy, maybe somewhere between Tim's own age and Hawk's, he wore thick glasses and a T-shirt and probably nothing else below the line made by the windowsill.

And that's a promise I'll keep.
No fun with no one,
I'm gettin' plenty of sleep.

Sleep was what Tim wanted now, to sleep beside this man, to feel inside himself the body of someone Hawk himself had been inside; to connect with his beloved, his lost, by way of a conductor, if only until morning.

Maybe the two of us can become the three of us.

He waited until the song was done before he nodded upward, appreciatively, as if to indicate that he'd be applauding if it weren't so late and he weren't standing so close to someone else's curtained window. The musician nodded back and signaled with his fingers, making first a "five" and then the letter "A."

He crossed the street, pressed the buzzer, and as he climbed the stairs he crossed himself.

EPILOGUE

OCTOBER 16, 1991

U. S. Embassy, Tallinn, Estonia

So what will happen with the black man with the problems with the sex?

The polymath minister-filmmaker had asked Fuller, when he returned to the party from his walk, about Clarence Thomas's chances of being confirmed for the Supreme Court. And here, just past midnight, was the answer, left on Fuller's desk by Ms. Boyle. She'd figured he might come back up to the office, late, by himself; it had become something of a habit.

The piece of teletype said that Thomas had gotten through the Senate, 52–48, about an hour ago in Washington.

"Let's celebrate," he might have said had Ms. Boyle still been here. "Shall we break out a can of Coke?"

No, he would not have said that. Even he didn't make such jokes anymore.

He eyed the telephone and Mary Russell's letter. Its stationery listed her number.

He hesitated, beginning instead to write a letter of his own, to Mrs. Susan Fuller Simonson, his daughter, telling her he bet no man had ever received Halloween cards from his grandchildren so early, surely a sign of her organizational capacities as a mother. Puzzling over what to say next, he tapped his pen on the desktop—what ever had happened to blotters?—and allowed his gaze to travel back to Mary's letter.

He knew he was going to do it, so he might as well do it now.

He buzzed the security officer on duty and asked him to make the call; if he tried it himself, he would bollix up the long string of access and country and area codes.

"Yes, Mr. Fuller." Like the rest of the small staff, the security man was getting accustomed to the odd hours of the number two. A moment later he was buzzing him back: "Mrs. Russell is on the line."

"Fuller?"

The connection was astonishing. Ms. Boyle had not been exaggerating about the phones.

"Yes. Mrs. Russell?"

"Yes."

"Russell. Where did *that* come from?"

The telephone transmitted her laughter from Scottsdale after a moment's delay that, he understood, had less to do with fiber optics than the fact that even now, thirty-five years later, she was only laughing against her better judgment.

"Before you tell me," he added, "let me give you the number on this end. It's past midnight here, and if I lose you after the security man at the desk goes home, whoever comes on will never be able to patch me back through."

He read off a long string of numbers from his business card, and she repeated them. "Wait," he said. "That's the fax. Sorry." He then read the proper string, the one for the telephone, and she copied that down, too.

"There," said Fuller. "So what time is it where you are?"

"Two-thirty in the afternoon. Ten hours earlier."

"Not fourteen hours later?"

"No."

"Well, at least you're giving me the time of day."

No laughter.

"You got my letter," she said.

"Yes. So who is Russell?"

"My husband, Harry. I married him a year ago. I'm talking from his office in the house. He's out playing golf."

"Why did you wait so long to marry? Someone tell you the first forty years are the hardest?"

"I was married for twenty-five years, from '64 to '89, to Paul Hildebrand."

"The name's familiar."

"The brewer."

"Ah, yes! The lovesick brewer. How did that finally happen?"

"He came to New Orleans and found me, two years after he divorced his very nice wife and was still covered with guilt."

"Guilt. Is that going to be the theme of this conversation?"

"I don't know. You made the call."

"You wrote the letter."

During the pause that followed, he fingered the envelope it had come in. "What ever happened to the baby?"

"She grew up to be a wonderful young woman. This morning I'm designing the leaflets for her campaign for the school board in Amarillo. Desktop publishing. I'm a whiz at computers. She was raised by fine people in Miami and five years ago, just as Paul was getting sick, she managed to find me."

"What's her name?"

"Barbara. But I call her Toni. Long story. How is your own daughter?"

"Raising three children back in Maryland. Making Halloween cards three weeks early. I've never known a girl of her generation with less ambition."

"She got it from you."

"I'm taking that as a compliment. There's too much hard charging all around. *Especially* from the girls."

"Is *that* going to be the theme of this conversation? The social decline of the world we knew when we were young?"

The brief pause Fuller took was extended, for less than a second, by the satellite carrying his words to Mary. "I assume that he died of AIDS."

"He died of bone cancer. With considerable pain and a great deal of cheer. When he was diagnosed he sent me a note saying 'So much for all the milk!' I can't imagine that he was ever infected with AIDS, Fuller."

He lit a cigarette. Amidst all the multivitamins and bran, Lucy had never gotten him to stop smoking altogether.

"Providence, Rhode Island?"

"He never really lived anywhere else. For a little while, just after Washington, he went home to New York—in a bad way. Never finished his reserve duty. He admitted what he was and got dishonorably discharged. He more or less fell apart at his sister's house until her parish priest found him a spot with some order in Rhode Island. He only described it to me years later—half retreat, half sanitarium. He was enough glued back together to leave in six months."

Fuller had spent most of his life parrying questions, not asking them. The neediness of now having to do the latter bothered him, and he was certain, even without her face before him, that Mary knew it did. The dynamics of their old friendship, across eight thousand miles and thirty-five years, had flung themselves together in an instant, like the film of a building's demolition running on fast rewind.

"Why did he stay in Rhode Island?"

"There was no reason to be anywhere else. For fifteen or twenty years he worked in the books department of the Outlet Company, the last of the Providence department stores. When it went out of business he took a job with an antique books dealer in an old arcade just down the street. I visited him there about a dozen years ago."

"I'm doing the math. I'm guessing he took you to a Reagan rally. Unless it was bingo at St. Aloysius'."

She wouldn't answer.

"What was he like?"

"He bought me a nice Italian dinner. After drinks at his small, tidy apartment. He was very nervous—not about seeing me; he was just a fragile, nervous person. And yet curiously peaceful. He would have been nearing fifty then, but for all his gray hair he looked much younger. Thin. It was easy enough to still see the boy who first walked into the bureau."

I got the job. You're wonderful.

" 'Peaceful'?"

"Yes, you get off easy." She paused, letting it sink in, hoping it would wound him even as it brought relief. "I don't think he'd given a thought to politics in twenty years, and he wasn't the least bit religious in any ordinary way. He told me he went to Mass once in a while and never bothered with confession. But the peacefulness had come from God, I'm certain."

"And how are you certain of that?"

"Because he told me. He told me that one day twenty years before, he'd realized, all of a sudden, while walking down a street in the city some Saturday afternoon, that he'd spent his whole life trying to make God love him—and that this didn't matter in the slightest. All that mattered was that he loved God. He told me that once he knew this he was home free."

"Well, then, besides the milk, so much for Bishop Sheen, too. 'God love you'—the words that threw open my mother's checkbook."

"He said it was the same with you."

"What was the same with me?"

"That all that mattered was his loving you. That was enough, once he realized it."

"And you think *that* was true?"

"I think there was more to it than that. I think he was too nervous to try loving anyone else. But it was true enough. And I think it's more than you deserved."

She could hear him putting out a cigarette, the tiny hammering on an ashtray bouncing up through space and down again.

"The fellow who's your daughter's father," Fuller said. "Was he Estonian or Lithuanian? I can't recall."

"Estonian. They'd borrowed the Lithuanians' embassy the night we met him."

"I met him? I don't remember." He thought back to the morning's mental calisthenics and wondered if he'd done as well as he thought.

"Fred died in '79," explained Mary. "He would not have believed anything that's happened over there in the past two years, though he always claimed he could see it coming."

"I'm going home for good in a few months."

"Are you still with your wife?"

"Yes."

"Right," she said, having expected as much.

She could feel—he could feel it himself—that whatever emotions had prompted him to make the call had already subsided, that he was about to succeed one last time at doing what he had always done where Timothy Laughlin and that whole portion of his life were concerned. He had come back from it, dispensed with it; he'd closed and locked the cellar door and was climbing back up to the living room of his existence.

"He was buried wearing your cuff links," Mary told him. "His sister found them on his night table, back at his apartment, the afternoon he died in the hospital."

After a longer pause than the others he had taken, Fuller said: "He was a very nice boy."

I'm pleased to meet you, Timothy Laughlin.

"Goodbye, Fuller." She said it tenderly and hung up the phone.

He sat there for several minutes, attempting to think about the young man he'd eyed on his walk near the walled Old City tonight. He tried once more to figure out the best route to the Carnegie Endowment from this house in Chevy Chase that Lucy was still determined to buy. And he wondered if he might yet persuade her to have one couple, no more, over for the White Nights.

All at once he heard a whistling sound, like an electronic teakettle. The fax machine, he realized; it disgorged things only infrequently and usually when Ms. Boyle was here. But a paper was now coming out of it, insidiously, as if from an intruder who'd scurried away before he could be detected slipping it under the door.

Fuller got up to take it from the machine's tray. The small type at the top rim of the page said HARRY RUSSELL and showed the area code 602. Beneath that, he saw Mary's handwriting: "He sent me this sketch two weeks before he died. The house is still there. Paul never tore it down. It survived the brewery and is all fixed up."

The drawing was in Skippy's style, as recognizable as Mary's penmanship. He had done it, it seemed, from memory: the narrow, three-story brick house topped by its turret with two windows. Inside one of them a candle burned; behind the other, on the sill, stood a milk bottle. Below the sketch was a note from Tim to Mary:

Let him know that I was happy enough. Make it easy on him.
    T.

Fuller returned to his desk with the paper, which he brushed once with his hand, before putting it on a small stack of State Department forms held down by a glass paperweight, inside of which a sprig of cherry blossom floated. It had traveled with him for many years, from one country to another, throughout a world grown unexpectedly, and increasingly, free.

ACKNOWLEDGMENTS

Having more than once described the writing of historical fiction as being a relief from the self, I was aware as I worked on *Fellow Travelers* of venturing further than usual into my own life's preoccupations and fundamentals, however refracted they might be here by time and geography. I have, while writing this book, felt continually grateful to my parents, Arthur and Carol Mallon, and to my teachers, especially George Doolittle, Fran Walker, Elmer Blistein, and Robert Kiely.

Down the street from me in present-day Foggy Bottom, I must thank Steve Trachtenberg, Bill Frawley, and Faye Moskowitz of George Washington University, who contrived to keep the doors of Gelman Library open to me when I left teaching at GWU for a stint in the government. Most of this book was written in Gelman's sixth-floor reading room, after many hours with the microfilmed Washington *Evening Star* a few stories below.

In obtaining and understanding transcripts of both the executive sessions of the Senate Permanent Subcommittee on Investigations and the open sessions of the Army–McCarthy hearings, I had the help of Dick Baker and Don Ritchie, longtime historians of the U. S. Senate, as well as Brian McLaughlin of the U.S. Senate Library. Sara Schoo, reference librarian at the Department of State, was also generous with her time. And thanks to Joe Mohr for a superbly informative tour of the Old Post Office tower on Pennsylvania Avenue.

Of the many dozens of histories and biographies I've consulted, I would single out the special importance of David K. Johnson's *The Lavender Scare: The Cold War Persecution of Gays and Lesbians in the Federal Government* (University of Chicago, 2004). Professor Rick Ewig's article on the life and death of Senator Lester Hunt was helpful, as was the Web site of the History Office of the United States Army in Europe (USAREUR). Also on the Web: Richard A. Johnson's recollections of basic training at Fort Dix.

I would like to thank Mel Levine, formerly of the U.S. State Department, for advice about Hawkins Fuller's career path, and my friend Priscilla McMillan, whose writings and conversation have illuminated my knowledge of the 1950s and much else. And I'm grateful to Jim Steen for local Washington lore.

I hasten to point out—to those mentioned above and to the reader— that I have taken my usual small liberties with historical fact, and more than my usual license with historical figures.

My editor, Dan Frank, has again bolstered and challenged me in all the ways I've tried not to take for granted in our long association. He has my deepest gratitude. The enthusiasm shown toward this project by Sloan Harris, my agent, has been both sustaining and delightful.

Chris Bull has been my own proof of the axiom—and showtune lyric—that if you become a teacher by your pupils you'll be taught. In two decades of argument about politics, sex, and culture, he has usually outshone me in logic, and always in bravery.

I cannot imagine life in Washington without John McConnell, the gold standard for public service and devoted friendship.

And I cannot imagine life anywhere without Bill Bodenschatz.

THOMAS MALLON
Washington, D.C.
November 13, 2006

Thomas Mallon is the author of seven novels, including *Bandbox, Henry and Clara,* and *Dewey Defeats Truman.* Among his nonfiction books are studies of diaries (*A Book of One's Own*), plagiarism (*Stolen Words*), and the Kennedy assassination (*Mrs. Paine's Garage*). A frequent contributor to *The New Yorker, The Atlantic Monthly,* and other magazines, he lives in Washington, D.C.

A NOTE ON THE TYPE

The text of this book was set in a typeface called Aldus, designed by the celebrated typographer Hermann Zapf in 1952–53. Based on the classical proportion of the popular Palatino type family, Aldus was originally adapted for Linotype composition as a slightly lighter version that would read better in smaller sizes.

Composed by Creative Graphics, Allentown, Pennsylvania

Printed and bound by Berryville Graphics, Berryville, Virginia

Designed by M. Kristen Bearse